Praise for Rebecca Chance:

Praise for *Divas*:

'A classic tale of bitchy women fighting their way to the top' *Daily Mirror*

'A bright new star in blockbusters, Rebecca Chance's *Divas* sizzles with glamour, romance and revenge. Unputdownable. A glittering page-turner, this debut had me hooked from the first page' LOUISE BAGSHAWE

'I laughed, I cried, I very nearly choked. Just brilliant! This has to be the holiday read of the year. Rebecca Chance's debut will bring colour to your cheeks even if the credit crunch means you're reading it in Bognor rather than the Balearics' OLIVIA DARLING

Praise for *Bad Girls*:

'Glitzy, hedonistic and scandalous, this compelling read is a real page-turner' *Closer*

'A fun, frivolous read' *Sun*

Praise for *Bad Sisters*:

'I'd definitely recommend this book if you're looking for a sexy beach read this summer, or you just want to escape into another world for a while – Chance certainly delivers on all counts!' ChickLitReviews.com

'Blistering new bonkbuster' *Sun*

'A gripping and exciting novel' *Closer*

'An explosive read' *Star Magazine*

Also by Rebecca Chance

BAD ANGELS

Rebecca CHANCE

**SIMON &
SCHUSTER**

London · New York · Sydney · Toronto · New Delhi

A CBS COMPANY

First published in Great Britain by Simon and Schuster, 2012
A CBS Company

1 3 5 7 9 10 8 6 4 2

Simon & Schuster UK Ltd
1st Floor
222 Gray's Inn Road
London
WC1X 8HB

www.simonandschuster.co.uk

Simon & Schuster Australia
Sydney
Simon & Schuster India
New Delhi

A CIP catalogue record for this book is available from the British Library

Trade Paperback ISBN 978-1-47110-165-6
Paperback ISBN 978-1-47110-166-3
eBook ISBN 978-1-47110-167-0

Typeset by Hewer Text UK Ltd, Edinburgh

Printed and bound in Great Britain by CPI Group (UK) Ltd, Croydon, CR0 4YY

For everyone who supported me through writing this book – it was a really tough deadline. Greg, you put up with more than anyone, and I know it was bloody horrible for you! Thank you so much, my love. And Randon, thanks for the fantastic brainstorming. For someone who doesn't like to read bonkbusters, you're damn good at plotting them.

Acknowledgements:

Huge thanks to:

At Simon and Schuster: Maxine Hitchcock, who came up with the brilliant title and equally brilliant cover before I'd even written a line! And to Georgina Bouzova, Clare Hey and Emma Lowth on the editorial side, plus Sara-Jade Virtue and the amazing Marketing team – Malinda Zerefos, Dawn Burnett, Ally Glynn and Alice Murphy - who have done an extraordinarily creative job of promoting and marketing my books. Lizzie Gardiner continues to turn out covers that make everyone gasp in appreciation and admiration. Plus, in London, the sales team of James Horobin, Gill Richardson, Dominic Brendon and Rumana Haider and in Sydney in Sales, Kate Cubitt and Melanie Barton who have all been absolutely amazing.

At David Higham: Anthony Goff, my wonderful agent. Marigold Atkey has been hugely helpful and Ania Corless, Tine Nielsen, Chiara Natalucci and Stella Giatrakou in foreign rights do a fantastic job of selling Rebecca Chance overseas.

My lovely webmistress, Beth Tindall, for whom nothing is ever too much trouble.

Matt Bates, who is the dashing young Tommy Beresford to my Salome Otterbourne.

The dapper Mr Kandee for letting us use his amazing shoes for the covers and giveaways – aren't they gorgeous?

Laura Lippman, the best exercise/gossip/private whinge buddy that any woman could ever want. And Ruth Jordan, who started us on our workout and health support group. How I wish we all lived closer and could work out together, rather than virtually . . .

Dr Philippe Chout, who already makes some of the most beautiful women in London just that shade more perfect, and would be my absolute first choice if I ever got any work done. He very kindly bought me cocktails at a private members bar in Mayfair (sometimes my job is almost unbearably demanding) and not only answered all the questions I had about plastic surgery, but volunteered whole reams more of fascinating information.

Hayleigh O'Farrell at Pan Panorama who very sweetly took the time to guide me round one of the most amazing and luxurious skyscraper apartment blocks imaginable.

Randy Nebel, top gymnastic coach, who once actually had to sweep me off my feet and into his arms like Rhett Butler with a particularly inept Scarlett O'Hara when a roundoff back handspring I was trying went even worse than usual. Thank you, Randy, for stopping me from breaking my neck on multiple occasions - and for not laughing at me too much . . .

The real Jon Jordan, plus of course Ruth, Diane, Jennifer and Paul, my - and the whole world of mystery writers' - Milwaukee family.

I honestly don't think I could have written this book in a very short amount of time without the Rebecca Chance fanfriends on Facebook to cheer me up, distract me and give me lightning-fast advice on whether Brazilian men are circumcised/sex toys called Man Rammers. (The latter was John Holt, who is also entirely responsible for "Putin's Surprise".) Truly, without you lot to laugh and joke with as I tore through writing BAD ANGELS, I'd have gone absolutely mad instead of only slightly barking round the edges. Angela Collings, Dawn Hamblett, Tim Hughes, Jason Ellis, Tony Wood, Melanie Hearse, Jen Sheehan, Helen Smith, Ilana Bergsagel, Katherine Everett, Julian Corkle, Robin Greene, Diane Jolly, Adam Pietrowski, John Soper, Gary Jordan, Louise Bell, Travis Pagel, Lisa Respers France, Stella Duffy, Shelley Silas, Serena Mackesy, John Holt, Tim Daly, Lev Raphael, Joy T Chance, Lori Smith Jennaway, Alex Marwood, Sallie Dorsett, Alice Taylor, Marjorie Tucker, Teresa Wilson, Jason Ellis, Margery Flax, Clinton Reed, Valerie Laws, Simon-Peter Trimarco, and Bryan Quertermous, my lone straight male reader (bless). Plus Paul Burston, the Brandon Flowers of Polari, and his loyal crew – Alex Hopkins, Ange Chan, Sian Pepper, Enda Guinan, Belinda Davies, John Southgate, Paul Brown, James Watts, Ian Sinclair Romanis and Jon Clarke. Plus the ineffable sisters Dolores Feletia von Flap, Phyliss du Boire and Ida May Stroke. If I've left anyone out, please, please, send me a furious message and I will correct it in the next book!

Nicola Atkinson, Zarina de Ruiter, Georgina Scott, Laura Ford, Vikkie Cowey and Rose McClelland for their lovely reviews.

All the fans who volunteered their names for the escorts in the book!

McKenna Jordan and John Kwiatkowski for bringing my smut to Texas.

And as always – thanks to the Board. They are always there, watching. Like good angels.

December 22nd

Melody

I should have known better. Why on earth did I ever let someone take a scalpel to my face?

Melody Dale stared at her reflection, experiencing a brutally bitter comedown.

Only last year, she had been voted not only the most beautiful woman in Britain, but the sexiest one too. Her agent had been over the moon with joy: this simply never happened. It was an almost-impossible balancing act, but Melody had pulled it off. She had been pretty and approachable enough to appeal to women, avoiding being so overtly sexy that she alienated them, while still projecting enough sex appeal to have the readers of GQ casting their votes for her in droves as the girl they'd most like to spend the night with.

It wasn't a surprise that Melody had been voted Most Beautiful: her ethereal face, with its almond-shaped blue eyes and white skin, framed by a cloud of naturally jet-black hair, was hauntingly angelic, and her lithe body was elegantly slim, the figure of a twenty-four-year-old lucky enough to be able to eat anything she wanted, as long as she went to the gym on a regular basis. Winning GQ's Sexiest Woman of 2010 had been more of a feat, as Melody had resolutely refused to do any of the men's magazine covers or photoshoots that were usually the road to winning that particular accolade.

'I'm not taking my clothes off and letting my naked body be projected onto the House of Commons,' she'd said firmly to her very disappointed agent. 'I'm not putting on a bikini and Perspex heels and squatting down with my finger in my mouth. I'm not lying on a bed in lingerie sucking a lollipop, not even for Agent Provocateur. I went to RADA, I'm a serious actress – if I do *one* shoot like that, it'll haunt me for the rest of my life. I want to play Juliet at the RSC, not the hot-pants-wearing heroine in *Transformers*.'

'But you were a Bond girl!' Anthony, Melody's agent, had complained.

'*Exactly*,' Melody had said passionately.

She'd been picked straight out of drama school for the Bond girl part: she'd been cast as Angel Malone, a gorgeous burlesque dancer who made her entrance onstage in a tiny sparkling costume and huge feathered silver wings. After her night of passion with Bond, Angel was thrown off the turret of a French chateau by the villain's henchman. It had been a dramatic death, the white silk dressing gown she had worn photo-graphed to billow out behind her like the wings she'd worn for her costume, her black hair blowing in the wind. Bond, in the courtyard of the chateau, had helplessly watched her fall and vowed vengeance as the villain commented sarcastically: 'Not all angels can fly.'

'It's *because* I was a Bond girl that I have to be extra-careful,' Melody had insisted. 'People will expect me to sell sex. I'm not taking my clothes off for anyone.'

God, and look at me now, Melody thought miserably, staring at her reflection in the floor-to-ceiling window of the luxuri-ous apartment in which she was holed up. It looked directly over the Thames, whose grey-brown waters were murky and dismal in this cold London winter, dappled by big, heavy drops of December rain that was gradually turning to sleet. Just down the curve of the river were the skyscrapers of Canary Wharf, their glass and steel gleaming through the falling water, a cluster of the tallest buildings in the country, the Citigroup red umbrella shining through the mist. At night, lit up, the towers dominated the panorama, glittering with ruby, diamond, emerald lights; Melody would sit in front of the window and gaze out, down to South Quay, looking at the halogen strips that picked out the whole length of the Pan Peninsula building, wrapping around its sides like ribbon, turning it into the most expensive present in the world.

But by day, with the mist blurring the view, the glass became a kind of translucent mirror, and what it mainly showed Melody was her own splinted and bruised face.

The doorbell rang. Melody turned to look at the clock; in keeping with the five-star designer luxury with which all the apartments in Limehouse Reach were decorated, it was projected onto the high pale living-room wall, an elegant shadow tracery between the twin Damien Hirst dotted lithographs that hung over the Ligne Roset white leather sofas. It read 11 a.m. precisely: the new nurse was clearly very punctual. The last one had wandered by whenever it suited her, well aware that Melody was – as it were – a captive patient.

Wincing as she went, constricted by the bandages round her chest, Melody crossed the living room and made her way down the hallway, which was lined by sleek striped wenge-wood cupboards. She didn't even bother to look through the peephole: she only ever had one visitor, apart from the room service brought by the Four Seasons hotel next door, whose waiters could access the apartment building through a custom-built tunnel that connected the hotel's kitchens to the Limehouse Reach service elevators. She'd already had her breakfast – egg white omelette and berries – and wasn't due for her smoked salmon, beetroot and pea shoot salad till one.

The nurse had a surprisingly impressive presence. Melody's instincts as an actress acknowledged that immediately. It was like walking into a rehearsal room and instantly becoming aware that there was another actor present who would give you a real run for your money. Calm and centred, the nurse stood stolidly in the hallway, her white uniform perfectly ironed and starched, her dishwater blonde hair slicked back smoothly, not a hair out of place. She wasn't good-looking: her figure was square and solid, her features blunt. But her eyes, light blue and very clear, were full of intelligence and focus.

'I am Aniela,' she said simply, her accent Eastern European but her English careful and precise. 'I will be on duty over the holiday period. Siobhan should have told you yesterday that I was taking over the shift.'

'Yes, she did,' Melody said, moving her sore and swollen lips with care.

'Hello, Melody,' Aniela said, bobbing her head in a formal greeting. 'May I come in? I need to check how your surgery is doing.'

'Of course.'

Melody turned away, letting Aniela follow her into the apartment. In the gleaming glass window, she saw Aniela's figure shutting the front door, coming down the corridor, the white nurse's uniform widening her hips, the clumpy white orthopaedic shoes making her feet look even bigger.

'I need to check to see if I must put more gel dressing on your chest area,' Aniela said. Melody couldn't help mentally filing away Aniela's accent in case she needed to use it for a part in the future: *that is*, Melody thought miserably, *if I ever get a decent part again . . .*

Melody obediently sat down on the only dining chair that she ever used, one of a set of six around the glass table. Aniela placed her nurse's bag on the table and, very carefully, helped Melody slip off her pewter cashmere and silk cardigan wrap, and then the button-front T-shirt which allowed Melody to get undressed without having to reach her arms over her head to pull off clothing. When the wrap and T-shirt were removed, it was clear why lifting her arms should be avoided wherever possible. Melody's breasts were mottled with bruising at each side, small curved scars outlining the lower quadrant.

'Oh, very good,' Aniela said, nodding, her expression very concentrated as she knelt down to check out Melody's scars from below. Melody looked down at Aniela's head, at her blonde hair sleeked back into an almost painful-looking bun at the nape of her neck; everything about Aniela was impressively professional.

'These are healing very well,' she continued. 'You should be happy. It has been only a week since your surgery, correct? This is good progress.'

'Will the scars show?' Melody asked, her voice faint.

'You will have to ask Dr Nassri,' Aniela said. 'He will be back after Christmas. It is hard for scars to disappear, but I can tell you that you are healing very well – the wounds are completely closed, you don't need any more of the gel dressing. Soon we will give you Vitamin E oil and rosehip oil, to help the scars go.'

She drew a small packet from her bag, ripped it open and produced a sterilised wipe; cleaning her fingers with it, she then blew on their tips to make sure they were warm enough, and, with great gentleness, ran them over each scar in turn, something the previous nurse had never bothered to do. Melody felt her body respond, not sexually, but with desperate gratitude at having this moment of human contact.

How pathetic am I? Melody thought bitterly. *I was a movie star – I played Cathy in* Wuthering Heights, *Ophelia for the Royal Shakespeare Company. I was half of the hottest young power couple in Britain, I had a boyfriend I loved with all my heart, I was surrounded by people doing my hair, my make-up, costume fittings, glossy fashion magazine shoots. And now I've got tears in my eyes because some agency nurse comes to visit and actually touches my skin, gives me the warmth of another body against mine for thirty seconds . . .*

'You had implants removed. It's much harder to take them out than to put them in,' Aniela said, her gaze concentrated on Melody's wounds. 'But these scars are already a little flatter. You are lucky, your skin heals well. I cannot promise that they will not show a little. But I think they will be smooth.'

'Which means they can be covered up with make-up,' Melody said with huge relief.

'It is a shame you had the implants,' Aniela said with brutal frankness, smoothing a little cream onto the scars. 'Like this it is better. You are in proportion.'

Melody looked down at her tiny breasts on her slim frame.

'I know,' she said wistfully. 'But I can't help missing my D cups a bit. They weren't even that big, really.'

Melody was the size 8 that leading actresses were now required to be, and D cups on a barely 30-inch back weren't the enormous melons of a curvier glamour model.

'I didn't even want to get them, but after the operation, I used to hold them a lot,' she confessed to Aniela, surprised that she was telling her something so personal. 'You know, just put my hands there and feel them. They were so nice. I never had boobs before.'

'Then why did you take out the implants?' Aniela asked with paralysing directness. 'If you were so happy? You had no marks from the surgery. They put them in through your belly-button, very clever. Let me look at your face now.'

She pulled out another chair and sat facing Melody, very close now. The nurse smelt of soap and water. Her white skin was devoid of make-up, not even lip gloss; she didn't tint her blonde eyebrows and lashes.

She doesn't have a scrap of vanity, Melody thought sadly. *If I'd only been a little more like her, I wouldn't be in this mess now.*

Aniela leant in, squinting closely at Melody's face.

'The bruising is also good,' she said, surveying the twin black eyes that were now fading. 'I looked at the photographs Siobhan took three days ago before I came this morning. There was a lot of purple then, but now it is all gone, and almost all the green is gone too. When it is just yellow, you only have a few more days before it stops to show.'

'It's still really swollen,' Melody said in a small, frightened voice, reaching up her hand to touch her cheeks. Aniela promptly removed Melody's hand, placing it back in her lap. It was a swift, efficient gesture, detached and professional, and it made Melody feel surprisingly relaxed: this nurse knew what was best for her, would have no problems at all telling her exactly what to do.

And that means she's not lying to me about my recovery going well. I can trust her not to sugar-coat things.

'Pff! You have had major surgery, of course it is swollen!' Aniela said, shrugging dismissively. 'Remember what Dr Nassri says? Eight to ten days for the bruising to fade, but twenty-one for the swelling to go completely. You were in surgery for nearly five hours. He had to file down your nose, take out the cartilage implant, put cannulas in your cheeks to suck out the fat the doctor in Los Angeles injected into them.' The nurse raised her near-invisible eyebrows. 'You were *very* lucky that doctor didn't use fillers,' she observed. 'Once they go in, you cannot take them out because of the risk of nerve damage. If they move, there is nothing you can do. They are very bad.'

'I *know*,' Melody said devoutly, thinking of some of the A-list actresses she'd met in LA, whose faces had been irretrievably damaged by fillers. Injected high on the cheeks, to plump up a face and give it the youthful, rounded contours that savage dieting had removed, the fillers inevitably sank from where they had been placed, dragged down by gravity. And then more fillers were needed to compensate, balance out the shape of the face . . . Once you started, you couldn't stop.

She shivered, thinking about it.

'That's why the doctor used my own fat,' she said. 'He said it was the only kind of filler he'd use.'

Aniela nodded.

'The work done on you was good,' she agreed. 'But so much! I was surprised to read your notes.'

She touched Melody's chin, also bruised and swollen, and then started to untape and lift off Melody's nose split. Despite herself, Melody flinched a little; the nose was the most sensitive of all, even more than her breasts.

'Chin implant, nose implant, face fillers, your breast enlargement,' Aniela listed, looking at Melody's nose and nodding in approval at how it was healing before replacing the splint with great care and smoothing down the tape again to hold it in place. 'And now Dr Nassri has taken it all out for you. This is much harder, you know. Much harder to give you back what you had before, and to make it look natural, than to just make you prettier or younger. Natural is the hardest thing of all, the doctor says.'

'I know,' Melody said, tears pricking at her eyes. 'That's why I came to him. He's supposed to be the best.'

And he was certainly expensive enough, she thought ruefully. *Hollywood may pay you a ton of money, but after the agent, the lawyer, the publicist, the stylist, the plastic surgeon and the make-up and hair people have all taken their cut, it doesn't leave you rolling in it.*

The nurse stood up and crossed to the open-plan kitchen, all white and gleaming chrome, from its DuPont Zodiaq glass worktops and splashbacks to its porcelain-tiled floor. From one of the custom-built cupboards she extracted a mug – Vera Wang for Wedgwood, white bone china with a wide gold rim. The Limehouse Reach rental apartments were furnished impeccably: only the very best. Aniela dropped a camomile tea bag into it and held it under the Quooker tap that gave instant boiling water.

She put the mug in front of Melody.

'Drink,' she said firmly. 'You must relax for the healing to be most effective.'

Melody looked up at Aniela over the steam rising from the mug of tea, inhaling the delicate scent of infusing camomile and knowing that Aniela was right: she needed to stay as calm as possible. But how could Aniela understand how she was feeling? The stolid, capable expression on the nurse's square, farm-girl face, her wide shoulders and air of extreme competence all made Melody feel hopelessly fragile and pathetically weak by comparison.

I should show her, she thought suddenly. *She can't realise why I've had the surgery – she can't have seen the film. Well, why would she? It was just a piece of trash, it bombed in the cinemas. And Aniela looks much too sensible to go to see that kind of exploitative nonsense.*

Melody hesitated for a moment.

Is it too soon? Can I bear to see it, or will it tip me over the edge?

And then she looked at Aniela's calm, composed demeanour, took a deep breath, and stood, carefully, so she didn't strain her chest.

I do need to look at it sooner or later. And who better to hold my hand while I'm watching it than a hospital nurse?

'I've got something I'd like to show you,' she said, picking up her mug and walking over to the flatscreen TV, which was set in a black glass panel hanging from the ceiling, dividing the living room from the dining area. Below the panel was a matching black glass unit into which were set the music system and the various consoles, topped with a black marble shelf stacked high with a pile of DVDs: Melody was catching up on everything she'd missed while working flat-out for the last few years. Right at the bottom of the pile was the one she was looking for, though she couldn't even glance at its cover without wincing in as much pain as if Aniela were removing her nose splint.

Swiftly, Melody clicked open the jewel case and dropped the disc into the built-in player.

'Brace yourself,' she said dryly, indicating that Aniela should sit down on one of the sofas. Aniela might have drawn up a dining-room chair so she could examine Melody's surgery, but

Melody sensed that the nurse's training would not permit her to sit on a sofa without being invited to do so.

Melody fiddled with the remote controls. The TV sprang to bright, multicoloured life: a few seconds later, even Aniela's professional poise was momentarily shattered as she drew in her breath on a soft, short inhale of surprise at what she was seeing on the 52-inch screen.

It was the short loop of film that played in the background while you decided what to choose from the main menu. Quite naturally, the editor had picked a clip of Melody in action. But it wasn't the Melody sitting beside Aniela on the sofa. It was a pumped-up, lurid version, devoid of all the delicate beauty she had possessed before she took the part. Her cheeks were artificially high and plump, squinching up her deep blue eyes, so she had to open them wider than was natural to compensate. Her nose was unnaturally ruler-straight, her chin protractor-round; her lips were swollen like pillows, as were the round white breasts squashed up almost to her collarbones by the tight red corset she was wearing. On her bottom was a pair of bright blue pants, which, like the corset, were covered in gold stars and trimmed heavily with gold edging. And as she threw her arms wide and spun around and around, around and around, her lips parted into an O, and her implants bounced up and down, up and down, the sight of those plumped-up white breasts almost hypnotic—

'You look like a porno doll,' Aniela observed with crushing Eastern European bluntness.

Melody huffed a short, bitter laugh and clicked off the DVD again.

'*Exactly*,' she said. 'That's why the film tanked. I was supposed to be playing Wonder Woman. She's a goddess. Strong, independent, sexy on her own terms. Not a porno doll.'

'Well, men must have liked that,' Aniela commented, nodding at the now-blank screen. 'Many of them like the porno dolls.'

Melody laughed again. And even though the sound was still bitter, she couldn't help thinking: *This is the first time I've been able to look at that piece of rubbish since leaving LA – and I'm laughing. How weird that it's a complete stranger who helped me do it.*

'I don't think a single woman went to see it in the cinemas,' she said ruefully, turning to look directly at Aniela. 'Or bought the DVD. They rushed that out after the film tanked. With lots of extras of me doing stunts.'

Melody raised her hands, only to waist-height because of the breast surgery, and made little quotation marks as she said the last two words.

'Stunts?' Aniela said, her mouth relaxing into the hint of a smile. 'You mean, more of this?'

She put her hands under her own smallish breasts and wobbled them up and down with the nonchalance of a nurse who's seen so many naked bodies that she has no embarrassment left about her own.

Melody burst out laughing.

'*Exactly!*' she said. 'Ow, that hurts . . .' She pressed her hands gingerly to her chest. 'There was a whole bikini sequence – I had to wear the tiniest bikini you ever saw in your life, it was awful – they did all these shots of me diving into a lake, again and again, and that's literally all you see in one of the clips. Just my bum in a tiny string bikini.'

She started to pull a face, and stopped immediately.

'You see now why I had all the surgery?' she said passionately. All her emphasis was channelled into her trained actress's voice, since she was unable to use her features. 'I wanted to go back to who I was before. Pretend the whole thing never happened.'

'But why did you do it?' Aniela asked, curious. 'I have seen photographs, of course, for the surgery, of what you looked like, so that Dr Nassri could copy it. You were very beautiful. You had no need to do that to yourself.'

Melody heaved a long sigh, and sipped at her tea.

'My agent was so keen for me to go to Hollywood,' she said. 'I had loads of offers after *Wuthering Heights*. But my boyfriend wanted us to stay here. We'd made a pact – we met in drama school, and we got together almost straight away. We said we'd be serious actors, we wouldn't go to Hollywood till we'd done some years of stage in the UK first. I meant it, I really did. And James – that was my boyfriend, James Delancey—'

'I know him!' Aniela said, smiling. 'He is Doctor Who! He is very handsome, I think.'

'Yes,' Melody said softly, thinking of James, his floppy fringe, his sweet smile, his long, lean body. He was a real posh boy, a public-school, cricket-playing posh boy, but a lovely one, with a gentle nature, always ready to see the funny side of things, to lighten tension with a joke. She'd fallen for him the moment she saw him; she'd always fancied that type of boy, the kind that looked great in cricket whites or an officer's uniform, who'd be cast as the young hero in any TV adaptation of a historical novel; James had already played Pip in *Great Expectations*, Larry in *The Alexandra Quartet*, and Charles Ryder in a stage version of *Brideshead Revisited*. He'd been over the moon to be cast as Doctor Who, not just because he loved the show, but also because it was a pleasant change to be acting opposite aliens and wearing modern dress.

'And he is your boyfriend? Why does he not come to visit you? Siobhan says that you have no visitors. You are always by yourself,' Aniela commented.

Melody recoiled a little. It was all very well having a nurse who was completely unshockable to confide in, but the downside, clearly, was that Aniela had absolutely no British reserve whatsoever.

She looked at Aniela over the rim of her mug. There was nothing gossipy about the nurse, Melody could tell. Her years in the celebrity spotlight had made her very familiar with the tell-tale indications: the gleaming, beady eyes, the head cocked forward, eager for a snippet of juicy information that could be instantly tweeted as soon as they left you. Siobhan had been like that, always trying to pump Melody as she changed her dressings, casually dropping the names of James or Melody's other co-stars into her stream of chatter, hoping to prompt an unguarded response from her. Melody hadn't trusted Siobhan as far as she could throw her – which, in her current bruised, post-operative state, was no distance at all.

Aniela, Melody could already tell, was the polar opposite.

'We broke up,' she said. 'I haven't seen him in over a year. I went to LA, and the distance made things just too difficult.'

Well, that's the official line, anyway.

'But he could still visit you,' Aniela said. 'Or your family. It's good for the healing, to have people around. Not to be all alone, especially with Christmas coming.' She cleared her throat. 'You do not need to be here, you know,' she informed her patient frankly. 'You could go back to your home, and maybe have a nurse come every day if you wanted to. Though even that is not really necessary. Dr Nassri told you that, correct? There is really nothing for me to do any more, now that your wounds have closed and you are healing well.'

'I don't want anyone to see me like this!' Melody said, her voice rising. '*Look* at me! I want to hide out here and not see *anyone*, not until my face is recovered. I want to just hole up and hibernate till I don't look like—' she glanced at herself in the black glass border to the TV – 'like I got the worst of it in a street fight.' She looked down again. 'Besides, I don't have anywhere to go. I was sharing a house in Shoreditch with my boyfriend, and I moved out when we broke up. I don't have a place in London, and if I go to my family the paparazzi are bound to find out. There's nothing they'd love more than to get photographs of me looking like this.'

She shuddered.

'I understand. You want to be a bear,' Aniela said, a glimmer of amusement in her voice.

'A *what?*' Melody, asked, completely taken aback.

'You want to be a bear,' Aniela repeated, standing up. 'To hibernate, like you said. To hide in your cave all winter, until spring comes.'

And again, despite herself, Melody couldn't help giggling.

'Ow!' she said. 'Don't make me laugh!'

'I am sorry,' Aniela said, smiling down at her. She walked over to the DVD player, pressed the Eject button and popped out the *Wonder Woman* disc. 'I don't think you should watch this any more,' she said. 'No more porno doll.'

Snapping the disc into its case, she dropped it into one of the storage drawers and slid the drawer shut with a decisive click.

'I will come back tomorrow at the same time,' she said. 'You have my pager number? It is the same as the one for Siobhan.'

Aniela patted the little black gadget clipped to her belt.

'You may ring me when you need,' she said. 'It will not be a problem. There is only you and one more patient staying here over Christmas and New Year. I have plenty of time for both of you.'

'Are you here over the whole holidays?' Melody asked.

Aniela nodded.

'I look after only two patients here at Limehouse Reach,' she said, 'I sleep in the Clinic next door, and there are no operations until the first week in January, no one there to look after. So you may ring me without any worry. I am here twenty-four seven.'

'Won't *you* be lonely?' Melody said unguardedly, her dark blue eyes looking up at Aniela, full of concern. 'Sleeping in the Clinic with no one around? And not seeing your family?'

Aniela shook her head briskly.

'No,' she said, a brief smile flitting over her face. 'Not at all. I will be very quiet and peaceful. Now—' she looked at the shadow clock on the wall over Melody's head – 'I must go to meet my other patient. It was very nice to meet you, Melody.'

'You too,' Melody said, biting her lip to stop tears coming to her eyes; *you're being pathetic!* she told herself savagely. *Remember at ComicCon last July, you had to have a whole phalanx of security guys around you because the geeks would have torn you to pieces? You could barely breathe for all the crowds and reporters shoving mikes in your face and fans screaming questions at you! You couldn't wait to get back to your hotel suite and be by yourself! And now you're feeling sorry for yourself because the duty nurse is going and leaving you on your own . . .*

Pull yourself together, Melody. You made this bed and now you've got to lie in it.

The door of the apartment shut behind Aniela. Melody closed her eyes, determined not to cry. Over the past few months, she had cried enough for years to come, at the loss of everything that had fallen so easily into her lap: a wonderful boyfriend, a brilliant career. Now it was all in ruins at her feet.

I should never have done that bloody film.

'I know you said no blockbusters, no action films,' her LA agent had said eagerly over the phone. 'But, Melody, you gotta read this! They're mad for you – you've got the perfect colouring for Wonder Woman, and you can handle comedy. You gotta at least have a *look* at it . . .'

It was everything a comic adaptation should be. Funny, sexy, witty, packed with breathtaking action sequences. Wonder Woman herself was tough, wise-cracking, with the dry sense of humour of Robert Downey Jr's character in the first *Iron Man* film, a woman entirely in control of her own destiny, flicking her golden lasso, ensnaring the baddies. The showdown between her and the Nazi villainess, Baroness von Gunther, was both hilarious and genuinely dramatic. Melody couldn't put the script down; she spent the day wandering round the house she shared with James, reading out juicy lines to him, and when she finally finished it she drew a deep breath, dragged him down onto the sofa with her and begged him to read it, to understand why she was going to break the pact that they had made and audition for the part.

'We said we'd stay here for the next two years!' James had said passionately, pushing back the lock of hair that always fell over his forehead. 'We *promised* each other! You know what happens – people go off to LA before they've done enough stage here and you can never get that experience back!' His hazel eyes widened as another thought occurred to him. 'And when are they shooting? What about *Romeo and Juliet*? Rehearsals start in three months, Mel!'

It had been their dream at RADA to play Romeo and Juliet together, while they were still young enough to be convincing as teenage lovers. After James was cast as Dr Who, and Melody as Cathy in a film adaptation of *Wuthering Heights*, they were both well-known enough for producers to be eager to cast them in a stage production, and the idea of real-life boyfriend and girlfriend playing the star-crossed lovers had been irresist-ible. Sir Trevor Nunn was lined up to direct them at the Theatre Royal. They had talked of nothing else for months.

'Oh, of course this won't interfere with the play!' Melody had assured him, taking his hands. 'I'd *never* mess with that, I promise! I'll tell them that I'm committed to the play and that I couldn't possibly start shooting on this till the run's over – that's if I even *get* the part, which is very unlikely . . .'

But she *had* got it. Almost immediately. Millennial, the production company, had sent her a first-class ticket to LA as soon as they'd heard she was interested; the day after she arrived, she'd read for the executive producers, who had loved her reading as much as her looks – which, as her agent had already pointed out, were a huge point in her favour. Of course, you could take a blonde, brown-eyed actress, dye her hair black, give her blue contact lenses; but it was always preferable to cast a girl as Wonder Woman who naturally had her specific colouring, and Melody's Irish blood had also given her Wonder Woman's smooth white skin.

Melody was Millennial's top pick. She had everything: youth, beauty, classical training, and the freshness that came from being a new face. And thanks to a good ear, as well as her RADA training, she could do a pitch-perfect generic American accent. Delighted, they sent her to meet Brad Baker, who was already contracted to direct the film.

And that was where everything went so wrong.

Brad Baker was the most successful director of action films Hollywood had ever had. Stocky, aggressive, with the Napoleon complex of a very short man, there was nothing Brad liked more than to orchestrate vastly expensive movie shoots, full of explosions, special effects and CGI wizardry. He was a perfect fit for the breathtakingly original action scenes that the *Wonder Woman* scriptwriters had imagined. Unfortunately, Brad was a much worse fit for a film with a strong female lead.

Because Brad, famously, was a very unpleasant misogynist.

Melody had heard some of the stories about Brad: the most notorious one was how he had made a roster of Victoria's Secret models audition for the part of the female love interest in his most recent movie by coming to his house and washing his car, clad only in skimpy bikinis and a bucketful of soapy suds. The producers, however, very keen to cast a classically trained English actress, were now absolutely set on Melody playing Wonder Woman, and had instructed Brad in the strongest terms not to fuck this up by pulling any car-washing nonsense.

Brad had duly behaved himself. The drawer full of bikinis had remained closed, the Aston Martin in the driveway of his Malibu beach house had been buffed by the Mexican gardener rather than Melody. He had given her iced acai berry tea on the glass terrace with its commanding view of Carbon Beach, a wide golden crescent-shaped stretch of sand that led to some of the most expensive real estate in the world. It was popularly known as Billionaire Beach: Brad had taken great pleasure in pointing out the houses of David Geffen, Larry Ellison of Oracle, Jeffrey Katzenberg of DreamWorks.

'Jen's farther down,' he'd said nonchalantly, and Melody had realised he meant Jennifer Aniston. 'Nice girl. But she's kinda the exception. Actors just don't make enough money to live here, honey. They're in Malibu Colony, or on Broad Beach. It's the guys behind the scenes that make the real money. You know what this house cost me, five years ago? Thirty-three mill. And I paid *cash*. You tell me an actor who could come up with that kind of green!'

Brad had gone on to list the salaries he'd paid actors in his recent films. A dizzying array of famous names and eight-figure sums danced before Melody's eyes, dazzling her even more than the California sun. It was her first visit to LA, but she was quickly learning that this was how people in LA made conversation: they dropped more names than a kid did their toys, scattering them all over the place, not letting you get a word in edgeways as they streamed out Leos and Brads and Angelinas and Gerards with compulsive abandon.

Her LA agent had done exactly the same thing, told her a story about Roger Federer – a 'close personal friend' – and an umpire at Wimbledon, assuming that because she lived in London she'd be interested in a story that was set there. At first, Melody had panicked, thinking that she was supposed to have met all the people who were being named, contribute something to the conversation, but soon she'd realised that this was simply how they operated, their currency being proximity to the stars, and they were laying out their riches in front of her to impress her before they got down to business.

And Brad had certainly impressed her. The extraordinary, architect-designed house, nestling on the pristine coastline, the films he had directed, the people he knew – and the attention he was paying her – were all designed to sweep a twenty-four-year-old actress off her feet. He told her she was extraordinarily beautiful, perfect to play the twin parts of Diana Prince and Wonder Woman. He'd claimed the entire credit for bringing her over to LA, saying that as soon as he had seen photos of her he'd screened *Wuthering Heights* in his private cinema, known that she was the one, and had pushed the producers to view it too. Melody had asked, feeling idiotic, if he actually wanted her to read for him; she'd stuffed the script, now battered and crumpled from being thumbed over so much, into her bag, and brought it to the meeting.

Brad had burst out laughing and waved it away.

'Oh, baby, no,' he'd said airily. 'Script, schmipt. I love you Brits! Always thinking about the words! I guess it's all that Shakespeare – you read that, like, from birth, right? Well, you're in LA now, baby. Movie Town. And guess what's *way* more important over here?' He raised his hands in front of his face, framing a shot. '*Images.* I could give a shit about the words, to be honest with you.'

'But—' Melody had started nervously. The script was what had seduced her into doing this project, leaving a furious and resentful James behind in London; without its wonderful, sparkling wit, she'd never even have agreed to meet the producers and Brad . . .

Brad leant forward intently, staring at her with utter concentration.

'Right now,' he said, 'you know what's the most important thing in the world for me? The *only* thing I'm focusing on right now? You gotta know, right?'

Melody had shaken her head, baffled.

'*You*, baby. *You*. My leading lady. Because, you know why I wanna do this project? You know my work, right? Cars, bombs, explosions, guys driving trucks off cliffs to hit helicopters? *Bow! Biff! Bang!*'

Brad jumped up, pacing the flagstones of the terrace. Melody was sitting under the bronzed-steel pergola, protecting her white skin from the sun; she raised a hand to shade her eyes as she turned to watch Brad, who had reached the far side of the patio, where a floating flight of steps led down to the saltwater pool. He strode back, his short legs stumping to a strategic point where the terrace had been built out over the beach to accommodate a teak-and-steel lava-rock fire pit. Pausing dramatically, the sun directly at his back, he pointed at Melody, who was squinting now at his silhouette.

'*You!*' he repeated. '*You're* why I wanna do this movie! Here's how it went down: Millennial came to me and said, Brad, we wanna do a Wonder Woman movie and we want you to helm it, and I said, "Shit, guys, that's a chick flick!" You know? For girls! I could give a shit about what girls wanna watch!' He fixed her with a basilisk gaze. 'I'm being totally frank with you – I hope you get it, that I'm being totally honest about this, because I want you to know *exactly* how passionate I feel about this, *exactly* the journey I went on to realise why Wonder Woman was such a passion project for me.'

Both his fists pounded his chest, like a gorilla demonstrating his strength. And that was exactly what Brad was doing, Melody realised. A film director, especially one who worked on Hollywood blockbusters, had to have a core of arrogance, of certainty that their vision was the best, and the ability to impose that on cast and crew. Sammy Cox, the director of *Wuthering Heights*, had been as gentle as Brad was aggressive; she worked by coaxing, convincing, moving you along a path of her choosing, so that you thought you were making your own decisions about the character you were playing, but in the end, watching the finished cut, you realised that Sammy had been pulling your puppet strings, getting you to give the performance that she wanted from you all along.

Brad was a loud, boastful silverback to Sammy's clever, persuasive fox, but that didn't make him any less convincing. As he kept speaking, Melody felt herself being swept away on his sea of words, further and further away from land, and no matter how much she tried to put down an anchor, to withstand the waves of rhetoric, she couldn't hold out.

'Who *is* Wonder Woman?' Brad was demanding. 'That's the question I asked myself! And you know what I answered?'

He was approaching the table now, and he grabbed the back of the chair he'd been sitting in, rattling it on the flagstones with considerable force: Melody shrank back a little as she said, nervously:

'Diana Prince? I mean, that's her alias . . .'

'*No!*' Brad bellowed. 'Wonder Woman is an *Amazon*! She's a *goddess*! A *goddess* come to Earth! And you know what I thought of as soon as I realised that?'

Melody shook her head as Brad rolled on:

'*One Touch of Venus!* Fuck, I *love* that film! Have you seen it? Ava Gardner as Venus, the goddess of beauty! Most beautiful woman I've ever seen in my life – shit, I'm obsessed with her! And I thought: Hey, this is my chance to make an homage to one of my favourite movies of all time! With *you*!'

He pointed a stubby finger at Melody again.

'You're going to be a *goddess*,' he said, his voice throbbing with conviction. 'A modern *goddess*, a new Ava. Everyone is going to fucking *worship* you. I wanna put in way more Amazons – warrior princesses – a whole *tribe* of goddesses, and you'll be, like, the *queen*. The *empress*.'

Melody's lips were parted now: she was gazing at Brad with awe and wonder.

Ava Gardner? He's comparing me to *her?* Ava Gardner was one of the greatest Hollywood beauties of all time: screen legend, the great love of Frank Sinatra's life. She had been a star, rather than an actress, but it was a comparison that would have utterly dazzled any ingénue who had just been offered a huge breakout role.

'I played Venus in a school play,' she heard herself say. 'I had to give a big speech coming down a flight of stairs wrapped in a sheet – we couldn't afford proper costumes, it was supposed to be a toga. I was terrified it'd catch on something.'

'You see!' Brad narrowed in triumphantly on the only part of this that was relevant to him. 'You already *played* Venus! You're a goddess already!' He pulled away the chair whose back he had been holding, sending it flying away across the terrace, reached across the table and grabbed Melody's hands.

'You're a *goddess*! My Ava! I'm going to make you what she was – the Ava of your generation – the most beautiful woman in the world!'

Only Ava Gardner was famous in the 1940s and '50s, Melody thought now.

Before plastic surgery became so common that people in LA are surprised when you haven't *had it.*

It had started very gradually. Brad had known exactly what he was doing, how to manipulate her. Melody had been put up in a suite in the Hotel Bel-Air, with her own private infinity pool with views over the Hollywood canyons. Every night, Brad had taken her out to one exclusive party after another, dazzling her with his access to the most A-list celebrities, actors, directors, producers, all of whom were flatteringly keen to meet her. Since the runaway success of *Downton Abbey* in the States, the interest in British actors had intensified even more than usual, and Melody had found herself the toast of Los Angeles, invited everywhere, feted and garlanded as the new British breakout star, the new Wonder Woman.

Because, by that point, she had signed the contracts. It was official. Her UK agent had baulked initially, concerned that the filming schedule might clash with the *Romeo and Juliet* dates, and about Brad Baker's reputation as a sexist vulgarian; her US agent had naturally been over the moon. However, the sheer amount of money they had managed to extract from Millennial had swept away even the objections of the British agency. It was only James, in the end, who held firm, pleaded with Melody not to do the film, told her that they didn't need the money, that their pact to stay in London and concentrate on theatre work should be the deciding factor.

But Melody couldn't resist the lure that Brad was dangling before her eyes. She was going to be a goddess, the new Ava Gardner. She was going to incarnate an Amazon warrior, a feminist icon. And she was still committed to playing Juliet . . . she might have to skip a couple of weeks of the scheduled rehearsal period, but she'd work like a dog as soon as she got back to London, be word-perfect on her lines the moment she stepped off the plane ...

Only Melody never went back to London. She was plunged straight into the deep end in LA, utterly immersed in preparing for her role. Millennial sent her to boot camp to work on her muscle tone, and to a professional cowboy to learn how to spin a rope and throw a lariat, so that she could convincingly use Wonder Woman's magic golden lasso. She wanted to do as many of her own stunts as possible, and they flew in Randy Nebel, a gymnastics coach who had trained many Hollywood stars, from New York, where he was based, to teach her back flips and somersaults. Brad called her in for test shots and expressed some concern; her nose had a slight flaw, was fractionally imperfect from the left profile, did she know that? No, she didn't. He showed her the evidence, frowning: goddesses didn't have slightly imperfect left profiles.

Before she knew it, she was booked in for surgery. Very minor, the tiniest of corrections: they would take just a sliver of cartilage from behind her ear, whence its absence would never be noticed, and implant it onto the bridge of her nose, to make it perfectly straight. And they might put an equally tiny drop of Juvéderm into her lower lip, to make it just a little bit fuller, balance out her upper lip perfectly ...

Hmm. The surgeon had noticed that Melody's chin wasn't *completely* round; they could just tidy that up during the nose surgery, even her out. Not to worry, it was all ridiculously minor-league stuff; it wouldn't even be visible to anyone after the bruising had faded. She would simply look like herself, but now she would be perfectly symmetrical, that was all. Melody baulked, and the surgeon showed her before-and-after pictures of some of his famous patients, women who she would never have dreamed had had plastic surgery. Gazing in amazement at the photographs, Melody couldn't think of a celebrity name that didn't seem to have had work done. Men as well as women, though the latter outnumbered the former three to one.

But she still wasn't sure. She'd been voted Most Beautiful and Most Sexy in the UK, her looks – though obviously, as had been extensively pointed out to her by now, they weren't completely symmetrical – had been valued highly enough to have her cast as Cathy, as Juliet, and have her summoned from London to audition for Wonder Woman. Surely she didn't really need to have a plastic surgeon take a scalpel to her?

And then Brad came down hard. He was going to make her a star, catapult her onto the A-list in one go, put her on the cover of every single magazine in the world – and all he was asking in return was a minimal amount of cosmetic surgery! To tidy up some very small imperfections! Did she realise how ungrateful she was being, how much effort he had put into burnishing her image already, how lucky she was to have been handpicked by him to be a *goddess* . . .?

The producers took Brad's side. Even her LA agent said that she couldn't see why Melody was making such a fuss about such a small procedure; her agent was so Botoxed that she could barely move her face, had the tell-tale overarched eyebrows and nose wrinkles, so she wasn't in the position to make the strongest case. Still, Melody felt overwhelmed. Everyone back home in London was either deeply impressed at her huge career opportunity – apart from her fellow actors, who were insanely jealous. Henry Cavill had been picked from *The Tudors* TV series to play Superman, and there wasn't a male actor of his age in the UK who didn't envy him, just as there wasn't an actress who didn't envy Melody.

The only dissenting voice was James. And Melody didn't dare to tell him, because she knew that he would be on the first plane over to insist that she come home at once and not let anyone touch her face with a knife.

So she didn't tell him. She had the surgeries, just as Brad wanted. And they finalised the *Romeo and Juliet* decision for her; she was much more sore than the doctor had promised. Much too sore and bruised to contemplate flying back to London and throwing herself straight into rehearsals.

I knew earlier than I admitted that I wouldn't do the play, she acknowledged to herself. *I was so committed to the film by then – the training, the schedules.* She had Skyped James to tell him, and the sight of her face, post-surgery, had upset him as much as the news that she wouldn't be playing Juliet opposite his Romeo had infuriated him. She had let him down utterly, broken their pact. He had told her it was over, and though she had begged him to reconsider, she had known that he wouldn't. Sir Trevor Nunn had promptly cast Priya Radia, another up-and-coming actress with a youthful face and body, as Juliet.

Melody had put all her eggs in one basket. So, when Brad told her that the costume designers were very concerned that Melody wouldn't be able to carry off the costume, that her boot camp regime and gymnastics work had slimmed her down so much that her breasts had shrunk, and that he thought she should have implants – just to take her from an A to a B cup, nothing vulgar or huge – she had agreed to it without too much protest.

By then, I wasn't even myself any more, she thought now, looking down at her newly shrunk chest.

The surgeon had favoured Brad's wishes over hers. Melody had woken up with a D cup, not a B: breasts that bounced, as Aniela put it, like a porno doll over the top of the corset.

I was so upset I was hysterical. But I still knew the film would be good. The script was amazing, the lines were brilliant. I knew I'd be able to make all the one-liners sing, I was counting on that to keep me going . . .

It hadn't been until principal photography had started that Melody had realised that Brad had done a major rewrite of the script. Every single witty touch and flourish had been pruned away by his red pen, leaving a sexploitative, corny shell. Melody had cried, screamed, pleaded, tried to enlist her agent and the producers, but by then Brad had the reins firmly in his hands and no one could, or would, interfere with what he called his artistic vision. Melody had been in no way powerful enough to insist on final script approval in her contract; she was forced to stagger through months of a shoot for a film she had come to despise.

She and Brad fought constantly on set. Things got so bad that a video, made by a key grip on his mobile phone, of Brad screaming at Melody that she was damn lucky he hadn't made her blow him to get the part, and that she should keep her fake lips tightly shut so he didn't change his mind, was posted on YouTube and had racked up millions of hits. Brad had got what he wanted, made Melody into a pornographic image, and now that he didn't need to charm her any longer, he had had no hesitation in bullying her instead.

Wonder Woman tanked in its opening week. Rotten Tomatoes gave it an 8% and described it as the worst comic-book adaptation ever made. 'By comparison, *The Green Lantern* looks like *Iron Man*,' it commented. Melody's plastic-surgery-enhanced face, her bouncing bosoms, were mercilessly mocked on the internet and in the press, and two film parts for which she'd auditioned before shooting *Wonder Woman*, and which she'd thought were locked down, went to other actresses with more natural faces. Her LA agent dropped her. Melody's big break had left her broken.

Licking her wounds, her career in tatters, she'd fled back home to the UK. Nobody knew where she was; she'd told her family and friends she'd gone to be alone in Mexico for a while. The decision to have her surgery pre-Christmas had been absolutely deliberate; *this way, I can hole up in total privacy and try to fix the damage I've done.*

And now she found herself thinking of the nurse who had just left her, who was neither pretty nor slim, but who clearly was completely comfortable in her body. Aniela didn't have Melody's beauty, her fame, or the money that would allow her to pay for Dr Nassri and the Canary Clinic, to hole up in five-star luxury while she recovered, and yet Melody found herself envying Aniela with every fibre of her being.

Aniela has a job she knows she's good at, a proper profession which isn't based on how she looks or how much she weighs. Aniela would never be stupid enough to get plastic surgery done, to mess up her face and body so she barely looked like herself any more . . .

Melody heaved a deep sigh. She'd taken a very wrong turn; she'd been too stubborn and headstrong to listen to the man she loved, and now she was paying for it, literally and physically.

Please God, I end up with my imperfect face and my small boobs – and my old career, and James back with me. Please God, I get the chance to start all over again.

Aniela

Rich people and their problems, Aniela couldn't help thinking as she left Melody's apartment. The front door shut behind her with a quiet little click, perfectly calibrated, as everything was in Limehouse Reach. *Well, it should be perfect*, she thought dryly; *the rich people pay enough for it.*

Before this appointment, from a careful reading of Melody's notes, Aniela had been expecting Melody to be unsympathetic, and had braced herself accordingly. She had anticipated a spoilt, whiny rich girl, unable to make her mind up about how she wanted to look, using plastic surgery as a toy, the surgeon's scalpel something to be played with as she adjusted her appearance on a whim.

And yes, her problems are ones only people with too much money have. Too much money and too much time. But actually, she's very sweet. Very nice. It was generous of her to think about me, wonder if I would mind being by myself over the holidays.

Aniela felt her mouth crease into an ironic smile: Melody could have no idea how grateful she was to be alone, how much she enjoyed her daily visits to this insulated, utterly silent building. The dark veneered walls of the corridor, its slate-tiled floors, seemed to absorb any noise; the lighting was subtle and discreet, filtering out from recesses, bathing the interior of the apartment block in a gentle amber glow. If Aniela had been at all sensitive, of a nervous disposition, the absolute quiet of the nearly uninhabited building could have been positively eerie. A more feeble-minded woman, one who watched horror films where no sooner did a blonde in a nurse's uniform step into a lift than she'd be attacked by a serial killer, a vengeful ghost – or possibly even the vengeful ghost of a serial killer – would have loathed moving around the hushed, unoccupied floors of the sixty-storey building.

The apartments, which were built to the highest specifications, with a spa, ozone swimming pool, squash courts and gym, a library, private cinema, temperature-controlled wine cellars, a car elevator to take vehicles down to the garage, and an underground tunnel linking the skyscraper to the Four Seasons, next door, for twenty-four-hour room service, had some of the highest purchase prices in London. Apartments started at three million pounds; the penthouse that topped the building, three floors with wraparound terraces, had cost the oligarch who bought it a cool hundred and twenty million pounds.

But Limehouse Reach was one of the most expensive ghost towns in London. Not a single apartment was the sole residence of its owners; most had not only multiple homes, but luxury yachts as well. They summered aboard in Cannes and Sardinia, wintered in ski chalets in Verbier or Aspen, and divided the rest of their time between their palaces in the Middle East, dachas in Russia, Manhattan town houses and the European tax havens of Monaco and San Marino. There were over twenty nationalities who owned property at Limehouse Reach, and barely any of the proprietors were British. They dropped into London for meetings and to shop at Harrods and Harvey Nichols, or they bought the apartments to put up their children, who were studying at the LSE or SOAS. The university students gave some life and movement to the building in term time, but over the holidays they inevitably went to visit their families, deserting Limehouse Reach.

At the moment there was barely anyone staying in the entire building, according to the very bored doormen and security guards with whom Aniela had checked in that morning. Two patients from the Canary Clinic, and the oligarch, Grigor Khalovsky, who, of all the owners, was in residence most often: he was an exile from Russia due to an ongoing feud with President Putin which meant that if he set foot in his homeland, he would be unceremoniously thrown into prison. A Japanese family, here to show the Christmas sales no mercy, and a Middle Eastern one, ditto. Apart from that, the building was empty: there was practically nobody to enjoy the gigantic Christmas tree that Andy, the concierge, had painstakingly decorated in the atrium.

Aniela couldn't have been happier. The silence, the peace, the emptiness. The cocooned luxury. It was the opposite of the grind and hustle of her normal life, the crammed Tube and buses on which she travelled to the dirty, disorganised, understaffed and over-crowded NHS hospital in which she worked, perpetually frustrated by not having enough time for her patients and by the bad humour of her equally stressed colleagues. She had been working non-stop for five years now, ever since she came to London; a full-time NHS day job, plus any private hospital shifts she could pick up to supplement her income.

She sighed as she stepped into the lift, grateful that there was a slab of Carrara marble, white-veined with peach and grey, framed on the back wall, instead of the expected mirror panel. The last thing she wanted to see was the expression on her face, her mouth dragged down bitterly at the corners, as she thought about what had happened to the fruits of those five years of constant hard work. Every spare penny had been sent back home to her family in Poland, to help them build the house they had always wanted, tearing down a tumbledown old ruin on a plot of land belonging to her father's family, outside the city, and putting a modern farmhouse in its place.

It would be somewhere her parents could retire to, somewhere Aniela dreamt of living one day. She hated towns, had only come to London because the money was so much better here; her plan was to live in the countryside, to have her own farm. Most farms in Poland were small and privately owned, just eight hectares or so, enough to feed a family, but not to sell commercially; young people were drifting inexorably towards the cities, and older farmers were eager to sell land they could no longer work on their own. Aniela wanted to buy up the land adjoining her parents', to build up a beet and potato farm. Her two brothers weren't interested in joining her, but that didn't bother her: she wasn't afraid of hard work, and she would infinitely prefer to work her fingers to the bone in the comparative solitude of the countryside, with just some animals for company, than on a crowded ward in a London hospital, with ten people trying to talk to her at once.

She'd gone home every Christmas, every summer, eager to see the house take shape; plans were drawn up and discussed over much vodka, the foundations had even been laid. This year she hadn't been able to get back at all. She'd been so determined to slave away in London, salting away money, that she'd forgone a summer holiday.

And then, doubts had begun to creep in. The house was due to be built this year, but despite increasingly frequent emails from her asking for photographs of the construction as it took shape, none had been sent. Her emails had been either ignored, or replied to with short, cryptic sentences. On the phone her mother was always too busy to talk for any length of time. Aniela had had her ticket to go home for Christmas booked months ahead, to take advantage of low advance fares: but, on a sudden impulse, in mid-November she'd found herself clicking onto the Ryanair website and booking a last-minute weekend offer, getting a crack-of-dawn flight to Łódź, the closest airport, taking a train, another train, and then a long, slow bus ride, deliberately turning up on her parents' doorstep without giving them any notice whatsoever . . .

Aniela had wanted to take them by surprise, but it was she who received the worst shock of her life. Her doubts had only been nebulous, a sense that something wasn't quite right: what she found was confirmation that everything was completely and utterly wrong. Her parents, her brothers, must have organised major clean-ups of their flat whenever she was due to come back, because, with them unaware that she was due to arrive, it was a pigsty. Rubbish bags on the floor, cigarette ash everywhere, and, littering the narrow hallway, crates and crates of empty bottles of beer, dirt-cheap vodka, and the two-litre bottles of Sprite that so many Poles used to mix with their spirit of choice. Her parents and brothers should have been at work; it was Friday afternoon. Instead, they were in the middle of a bender that had clearly been going on for days, with most of the worst slackers from the neighbourhood in residence too.

The only positive aspect to the situation was that they were all too drunk to beat around the bush. In half an hour, the entire sordid, miserable truth came out. None of them had had jobs since Aniela left for London: they had been living on the money she sent back. Rather than being spent on the proposed new farmhouse, her hard-earned cash had been keeping her parents, her brothers and assorted friends in vodka. There wasn't a penny left. They had concocted some cover story to explain the lack of building work – various disasters, an architect and builder disappearing with their deposits – but had assumed they had a month more to work out the details before Aniela returned for Christmas; their feeble, inebriated attempts to lie to her were completely transparent.

Aniela hadn't even taken her coat off. She'd turned on her heel without another word, slung her overnight bag over her shoulder and walked out the door, knowing it would be for the very last time. To add insult to injury, her exit was followed by hysterical laughter; her family was at the advanced stage of drunkenness when everything seemed absolutely hilarious.

They aren't laughing now, Aniela thought bitterly. She'd had to change her phone number and her email address when the realisation that no more funds would be forthcoming sank into her family's collective brain. Panic set in. They'd apologised, promised to start building the house straight away, sent all sorts of assurances . . . *and begged me to start PayPal-ing them money again.* But Aniela held firm. She wasn't going to be fooled twice; from now on, she didn't believe a word any of them said. They'd left her with nothing, and now she'd left them for good.

Stop it! she told herself firmly, stepping out of the lift. *Don't dwell on the past, it just makes you bitter. You're earning so much money for working over Christmas and New Year, think of how much you'll be able to put aside when you get paid for this . . .*

Technically, the Canary Clinic should have had two nurses to cover its recuperating patients at Limehouse Reach. But there were only a couple of patients, and neither of them really needed a nurse at all; when Aniela had approached Dr Nassri and asked if she could take the whole Christmas and New Year period on time and a half, the Clinic, keen as any business to economise, had jumped at the offer.

Aniela rang the bell of the second Clinic-owned apartment, and stood a little back from the door, so its inhabitant could check who she was through the peephole. Mentally, she ran over the notes of the patient she was about to meet. Neither he nor Melody had had the usual, run-of-the-mill surgery – facelifts, liposuction, breast enlargements. Both of them were, in their way, unique, and Aniela had been very interested by the completely elective surgery this one had undergone; it had definitely piqued her professional interest.

However, as the door swung open, her mouth dropped open. Her first reaction to the man standing in front of her was completely unprofessional. His face was exactly as she had expected: as if he had gone twenty rounds with Mike Tyson. But it wasn't his face Aniela was staring at, hypnotised. It was his body.

My God, she thought, trying to catch her breath. *I've never seen a more perfect physical specimen in my life.*

A light sheen of sweat coated his body, and his muscles had the swell and distinct veining that indicated they had just been worked out hard, pushed to their limits. He was wearing only a pair of grey sweatpants, hanging low on his lean hips, well below his narrow waist, revealing the whole of his torso. His muscle definition, lean and ripped, was extraordinary; he might have been a professional athlete, a gymnast, strength and balance and flexibility all combined. Nothing had been over-worked for effect; everything was in Greek-god proportion, from the split caps of his deltoids, each of the three shoulder muscles so defined that Aniela longed to run her fingers over them, down to the curves of his pectorals, smoothly moulded breastplates, and the even ripples of his abdominal muscles.

It's like his body is wearing its own armour, Aniela thought. *And that's not even a six-pack: it's an eight-pack*. The V directly below his abdominals was sharply defined, arrowing down the jut of his hipbones, pointing to a destination below the waistband of the sweatpants. His skin was white and lightly freckled, pale and Celtic, and smooth, with only a light dusting of reddish-gold hair; but below his belly button, a tight little recess in his washboard stomach, a trail of slightly darker hair ran down to the knotted cord that was the only thing holding up his sweatpants. It was briefly interrupted by a long, irregular scar that cut across his lower abdomen, but soon straightened out again, disappearing down behind the ribbed grey welt of the waistband, down to the bulge of . . .

Aniela! Pull yourself together!

How much time had gone by? How long had she been

standing there, gawking at him? She cleared her throat and started to speak, but he said simultaneously, in a soft American accent:

'Aniela, right? I'm Jon. Sorry if I'm a shock – Siobhan can't have warned you about the face. It's not as bad as it looks.'

He turned, leading the way inside the apartment. His back rippled as he walked; it was like watching a leopard or a panther in motion. His bottom, tight under the loose tracksuit pants, could have belonged to a dancer or a speed skater – firm, high glutes with the minimal bounce of perfectly toned muscle. His arms—

Aniela, stop it!

'You have been doing exercise,' she observed, and was glad that her voice sounded severe; *better that than cooing with appreciation.*

'Yeah. Press-ups and pull-ups, mostly. Some side planks for the obliques. The doctor said no cardio.'

He picked up a towel that had been lying on the white glass kitchen counter and started to rub it over his chest, completely unselfconscious. Praying to high heaven that she wasn't blushing, Aniela said sternly:

'You should not be working out. The doctor said no exercise, not no cardio. You must only do gentle stretches for a few more weeks.'

His face was so bruised, so battered, so swollen, that it was impossible to read any expression at all; but she thought he briefly raised his eyebrows.

'Aniela, trust me,' he said, chucking the towel onto the counter. 'I've had plenty of surgery in my time. I'm not going to strain anything.'

'I will be the judge of that,' she said firmly. 'You must sit down now and I will see how your wounds are healing.'

Jon pulled out a chair from the dining table, and sat. His feet were bare, she saw, and even they were attractive; strong, well-kept, only a little reddish-gold hair on their backs, the toenails cut short, the veins as strongly defined as the ones running along his biceps and forearms . . .

'I will just quickly get a glass of water,' she said briskly, going over to the sink. Her back safely turned, she pulled the biggest grimace that she could, stretching every muscle in her face in a brief, crazy moment of release. It was a nurse's trick, when you needed to let off steam, a pantomiming that had always, before, been about something horrific.

Never before had she done it because a patient's body was so amazing that it had sent her spinning into near-insanity.

Over her shoulder she said curtly:

'Would you like one?'

'Sure,' he said.

She found coasters, and put the glasses down on the dining table, watching as he lifted his to his lips; everything on his face was swollen, purpled with the bruising. He drank slowly, carefully, not flinching in pain, even though the effort of swallowing must hurt him considerably.

'Are you eating okay?' she asked, looking around: there was no sign of a room service cart.

'Protein shakes,' he said efficiently. 'And I have a bunch of vegetables and fruit in the freezer, for juicing.'

Aniela nodded, drinking some water to steady her nerves. She couldn't put it off any longer; she set the glass down again and stepped close to him, close enough to smell the light, fresh scent of his sweat and, below that, soap. *He must have showered before his workout*, she realised, *and he'll wash again after. Americans are always very clean.*

Standing over him, she looked down at his scar. It sliced through the thick, strawberry blond hair, which had been shaved in a long strip before the surgery. Dr Nassri had cut Jon's scalp open from ear to ear, a huge incision, peeling the skin down from his face so that he could work on the entire bone structure. Whatever Jon would end up looking like, it would be completely dissimilar from the face that he had had before this surgery. His cheekbones had been filed down, his jaw restructured, his nose widened. It was a brutally invasive operation.

Siobhan had told her Jon had been in a car accident and had had a series of procedures in America with which he'd been dissatisfied, before coming to Dr Nassri to fix him: *but Siobhan's an idiot*, Aniela thought. *She just believes what she's told. She has no professional curiosity.*

Unlike me.

Aniela knew better than to ask any questions of this man. Some patients were dying to talk, and some wanted extreme discretion: Jon was polite and friendly, but nothing in his manner indicated that she should do anything but examine how his surgery was healing.

She bent over, so close to him now that her breath was on his skin, and began to peel away the bandages that held the gel dressing over his scar. As soon as the wounds were fully closed, the dressings would come off so that the scar that was forming could dry and heal, exposed to the air; but until then, it needed to be kept moist, and Aniela needed to check that it was all healthy pink tissue with no hint of necrosis.

Jon didn't move as she gradually examined his entire scalp. He might have been carved from stone. Nor did he ask any questions: he waited patiently for her to finish and pronounce her verdict.

'Two more days,' she said finally. 'Just to be safe. I will replace the dressings today and tomorrow, and after that I think there will be no more.'

'Because there'll be enough scar tissue,' he said, a simple statement.

'Exactly. You will be able to wash your hair then,' she said, trying for a light, easy comment. 'That will be nice for you.'

'Can't wait,' he said dryly. 'I've been doing the best I can with a little soap, but it's not the same as standing under a shower.'

Oh, no. I'm imagining him under the shower, water pouring down on his naked body – lifting up his arms, the biceps flexing . . .

Christ, Aniela, enough! Get hold of yourself!

She began to cut strips of the gel dressing and lay them, one after another, along his scalp.

'I don't need to tell you not to move at all as I do this,' she observed. 'I can see you know. You are keeping very still.'

'I'm isolating,' he said. 'That's why I can work out and know I'll be okay.'

'I'm sorry?' She didn't understand him.

'Isolating my muscles,' he said. 'Look.'

Without his head shifting a millimetre, he held up his right arm, straight out from his side. As Aniela watched, a ripple of muscle started just below the cap of his shoulder muscle, running down the firm, taut bicep, past the crook of his elbow, along his lean, flexed forearm. It was like a little ball rolling under the skin, a flexing pulse that ran right down to his wrist, completely under his control. Aniela drew in her breath sharply: she had never seen anything like it.

'Are you a magician?' she blurted out.

'I'm sorry?' Jon sounded genuinely surprised as he lowered his arm.

'Like one who does escapes,' she said, not knowing the right word. 'You know, like Houdini? He also trained his muscles to be very controlled.'

'An escapologist?' There was more than a flicker of amusement in Jon's voice. 'That's pretty astute of you. Yeah. I guess I'm something along those lines.'

Aniela had all the strips of dressing on his skull now: she reached for the bandages, aware that her hands were trembling. She hoped desperately that he wouldn't notice.

Just a few minutes more, she told herself. The view from above was just as distracting as the one from the front or behind: she was looking directly down on his strong, flexed shoulders, could see the even swell of his pectorals, the hairs glinting golden-red on his lightly freckled skin. Tiny beads of sweat that he hadn't completely dried with the towel were still visible on his trapezius muscles, and, with horror, Aniela realised that she wanted, more than anything, to lean down and lick them off, one by one, to taste each salty bead bursting on her tongue, to move further and further down the curve of his back, to the point where, just visible at the low-slung waist of the grey sweatpants, she could see the twin swell of his buttocks parting, pulling the marled fabric fractionally away from the skin to reveal a tiny V-shaped dark shadow—

'All done!' she exclaimed with huge relief. Her hands, thank goodness, were so well-trained by now that they had carried out the entire process of fixing the dressings in place without her even realising; neat and tidy, completely regular and efficient, with no sign of the turmoil she had been feeling. She jumped up, stuffing everything into her bag without her usual precision, and took two steps back, slinging the bag over her shoulder, ending up against the wall of built-in Gaggenau ovens that no Canary Clinic patient, in her experience, had ever turned on.

'I will be here at noon tomorrow,' she said swiftly. 'And I am at the Clinic the rest of the time, twenty-four seven. You can page me if there is anything you need, to ask a question. Anything at all.'

Jon nodded, the horribly damaged face on the perfect body the strangest of contrasts; seated, his lean body creased at the waist, his belly was still flat. In the split-second before she turned away, Aniela couldn't help noticing how there wasn't an ounce of fat on him.

She fled from the apartment as if she were being chased by the hounds of hell. The dark décor, the dim lighting of the corridors and lift had never been so welcome. It took the entire ride back down to the atrium for her to regain her composure: she was grateful all over again for the lack of mirrors.

'Everything go all right?' Andy, the concierge, asked from his desk at the far side of the huge lobby. The desk was custom-made to blend into the walls, which were heavily textured, a rippling effect created by thousands of long strips of highly polished wood set at slight angles to each other, rising a hundred feet to the high glass pyramid at the top of the atrium. Light played entrancingly over the entire expanse; an Italian expert in lighting design had been paid a six-figure sum to conceive and coordinate the way the underwater lights of the huge central fountain and the carp pond echoed perfectly the gently pulsing stream of light that ran around the rim of the glass pyramid. High above, through the big glass panels, the December sky was cold and grey, but here, inside the warmly lit atrium, with the rippling sound of water flowing over the huge polished steel balls of the fountain and feeding invisibly into the koi pond, there was nothing but calm and serenity.

'All good,' she answered. 'Patients doing fine.'

'Do they want anything? Anything at all?' Andy asked with the wistfulness of someone who knew there was no hope of a positive answer. He was, Aniela knew, a highly trained concierge, who had been poached from the W Hotel in Leicester Square specifically to look after the needs of some of the richest, most demanding clients in London. Though it would have been some people's dream to be paid to do barely anything at all in the most luxurious surroundings imaginable, it was clear to Aniela that Andy was champing at the bit to be given a series of highly complicated and near-impossible tasks to perform.

'Sorry,' she said, shrugging. 'You know what the Clinic patients are like. They watch TV, they order food, that's it.'

'All I've done this week is organise shopping trips,' Andy said gloomily. He was a very good-looking young man in his late twenties, with skin the colour of gleaming, red-brown chestnuts and a hundred-watt smile; it wasn't in evidence now as he slumped back on his ergonomic leather chair, running his hands over his smooth, shaved scalp. 'And they never want anything but the same old stuff, you know? I could put together a really fun tour – Borough Market, all these trendy little boutiques in Shoreditch, visits to designers' ateliers . . . ' He heaved a sigh. 'But all they want is sodding Burberry, Aquascutum, and Harrods. And lunch at Harvey Nichols Fifth Floor. Thank God Mr Khalovsky's due in today. I might actually get something to do.'

Aniela grimaced at him sympathetically; she could identify with the frustration of someone eager to do a great job and blocked from doing so at every turn. Andy didn't even get to perform the duties of a doorman, taking in packets, running the day-to-day life of the building; across the atrium was a much larger desk, at which a uniformed doorman was installed, and behind him was the office in which two security guards sat, monitoring the computer screens that showed every public area of Limehouse Reach.

Nodding at the doorman, who was playing a game on his Nintendo below the level of the desk, as happy to be unoccupied as Andy was aggravated by it, Aniela walked over to the discreet, unmarked door on the left of the desk, and held the key card that hung from her neck on a lanyard up to the electronic entry panel. It beeped green and the door unlocked; she passed through, down an anonymous, carpeted corridor, and through a fire door at the far end.

It led into the reception area of the Canary Clinic, which had been purpose-built to link into Limehouse Reach. Decorated in calming shades of sage green and off-whites, the reception desk a ripple of pale grey mosaic tiles, it spoke perfectly of affluence, discretion and the highest medical standards of hygiene and clinical excellence.

The main door was locked, the Clinic empty of staff; there were no appointments scheduled now until the New Year. Aniela put her bag down on the reception desk and went through into the office behind it, where all the files were kept in the same pristine order with which the entire Clinic was run. Jon and Melody's files were laid out on the white Formica table, where Aniela had gone through them that morning before her patient visits. Now she filled the kettle, dropped a bag of mint tea into a mug, added a dollop of honey, and prepared to settle down for an even more thorough reading of Jon's extensive patient notes.

There's some mystery about this man. I'm sure of it. And maybe, if I look carefully enough, the answers will be in here.

Jon

What the hell just happened?

W If he hadn't just had extensive reconstructive plastic surgery, Jon would have shaken his head in absolute disbelief at the encounter that had just taken place between him and the nurse.

Jesus, did I take a whole bunch of painkillers by accident? Where the hell was my impulse control?

He'd shown her his ability to isolate and move one particular tiny muscle after the other in series, something that he couldn't remember having ever let anyone else see. He'd agreed with her when she commented that he must be an escapologist – *no, even worse. She didn't come up with that word. I did.*

I must have gone temporarily insane.

Other people would have stood up, paced back and forth, their body restless as their mind worked out a complicated problem. But Jon didn't move, not an inch. He sat there in complete stillness, feet planted on the ground, hands resting on his lap, as his brain raced, playing back the last thirty minutes, trying to figure out what had just gone on.

There was something about her that made me let down my guard. I better figure out what the hell it was, because it damn well can't happen again.

It took a real feat of memory for Jon to think of the last time he'd let down his guard like that. *Probably when I was nine or ten, showing Mac the squirrels I'd shot for dinner. Hella proud of myself, cause the deer jerky was all gone, and this meant we wouldn't go hungry, Ma could do us a nice stew. And then he backhanded me right across the kitchen, because I'd taken the Winchester without telling him first, even though he was too damn drunk to tell him. Passed out on moonshine and Crystal Light.*

He hadn't remembered that moment in a long time. He'd had a real smile on his face as he strutted into the kitchen, squirrels dangling from his belt, setting the Winchester down carefully in the corner of the kitchen, in the gun rack. *Probably the last real smile I ever flashed,* he thought grimly. *Teeth all gappy and messed up.* He'd been teased about his teeth mercilessly by the other recruits at Marine Corps basic training; no kid in the States had teeth that bad unless they'd grown up where Jon had, the backwoods of Appalachia, with no medical insurance, so no access to doctors, let alone dentists. Occasionally a charity would fly volunteer dentists into one of the most deprived areas, set up an emergency clinic, and backwoodsmen would come from all over, queuing for days, pitching tents to camp out in line. Mostly all the dentists could do was pull the diseased teeth with a bit of Novocaine for pain relief, but that was better than getting a relative to do it with pliers and no anaesthetic at all.

The first thing Jon had done when he got some money was to get his teeth fixed. That was after they'd read his psych report and pulled him out of the Marines for much more specialised training than even they could provide, yanked him away from the San Diego boot camp before he graduated – *before his name could be officially recorded as having passed out,* he thought. *Put me down as one of thousands of dropouts who couldn't hack training, and flew me up to DC instead. Where they taught me all sorts of real useful and interesting skills. Evading capture, covert action. And how to kill people in about a thousand different ways.*

Evading capture.

And I just told that nurse I was an escapologist.

Not a muscle on his swollen, bruised face moved as he thought this over.

Siobhan, the previous nurse, had been a cheerful, giggly Irish girl, her looks similar to the Appalachian Celts of whom Jon was one; the mountains of Kentucky and West Virginia were almost entirely populated by Scots-Irish who had come over after the potato famine in Ireland, and ended up hard-scrabble farming or working in the mines, suffering from black lung, poverty causing malnutrition, inbreeding congenital defects and diseases. But Aniela, he could tell by her accent, was Polish. Jon had travelled all over the world in his long career, and he'd turned out to have a good ear, could recognise most accents after hearing a few words. And he'd picked up a fair amount of vocabulary too. Aniela, he knew, meant 'angel'.

Impatiently, he pushed himself to his feet. *This is a complete waste of time. Just keep your mouth shut tomorrow. Don't volunteer any information at all. Let her do her job and get the hell out.*

And after I don't need the dressings any more, she won't need to come in at all. I can just lie low here, waiting for the bruising to go down.

Jon had no intention of leaving Limehouse Reach until his new face had healed, until he could walk down a street without everyone turning to gawk at his injuries and speculating how he'd received them. His whole intention was to be as anonymous as possible, to fade into the background. That was how he had spent his entire adult life: fading into the background.

No, even before that, he thought, walking over to the corner window, staring down at the river below. *From when I was real small. Learning to curl into a ball when Mac was on a rampage, to stay out of his way. Slipping out into the woods when his back was turned, setting traps for groundhogs, taking the rifle as soon as I was strong enough to aim and fire, teaching myself to shoot. Knowing I'd have to provide for me and Ma, and Davey when he*

came along, 'cause all Mac'd do with the money he made from
brewing moonshine was spend it on meth.

The training Jon had given himself in his childhood, the
rigorous discipline he had imposed on his young body and
brain, holing up for hours on end in improvised shelters he had
constructed, squirming through bracken and mud, moving
into the perfect position and then waiting, soundlessly, for
squirrels or – infinitely more precious prey – deer, had turned
him into that most valuable of things to the Army: a born
sniper. He had nailed the target shooting at the Recruit Training Depot at San Diego, racking up hundred-per-cent scores,
making him of immediate interest to the brass, who had pulled
him out of basic and put him through a series of psychological
tests. He'd been interviewed by an Army doctor with the rank
of major, a staff sergeant and a quiet woman in civilian clothes
who didn't say much, just tossed out the occasional random
question that he didn't see the point of, but answered anyway.

He told them the absolute truth about almost everything:
his one big secret he held back, as he always would. But whatever he had said had got him on a plane to DC that very
evening, and then upstate to a secret CIA facility that specialised in black ops. Jon was on the fast track: he'd been
headhunted, and gradually he realised why. The Army wanted
to make him into an assassin.

And he let them. The team surrounding him, his CIA
handlers and the ex-Army men and women who trained him
and the couple of others who'd come in with him, handpicked
from the latest batch of recruits, were the only people ever to
take an interest in him, ever to think that he might be talented.
Interesting. Unique, even. And Jon, deprived of any affection
since birth, barely educated, malnourished, responded to that
interest like a parched flower finally given water: he drank up
eagerly everything they had to teach him. He was the fastest
learner the programme had ever had. For ten years, he trusted
his handlers implicitly, did whatever they said: went where

they sent him, killed whoever they told him to kill, asked no questions.

Until they pushed me too far. Asked me to take out a whole damn family.

And when that had happened, he'd used all the skills he'd learned from them to drop permanently off their radar. You didn't leave the Unit, ever. There was no resignation process; there couldn't be. Its members simply knew too much to be allowed to quit.

Jon had faked his own death, and found a plastic surgeon willing to give him a new facial identity. *But I didn't know what to do next,* he thought, watching the boats pass on the Thames below, the regular river clipper, whose schedule he knew perfectly by now. It was part of his training to be able to register every little detail of his surroundings, file them away in his subconscious, so that any break in a pattern would make him instantly alert.

So I just went on using the only skill I had. The one Uncle Sam spent a whole hell of a lot of time and money teaching me.

Drew Mackenzie, as he'd been then, had enlisted at seventeen. At twenty-seven, Drew Mackenzie died in a car crash and Gregory Cunningham was born. Gregory Cunningham set himself up as a hired gun, a hitman. *And he was a damn sight more careful about choosing his targets than the CIA ever was,* Jon thought with a rare flash of a savagery he did his best to suppress. But even with careful selection of targets, even making sure the only people he took out from now on were bad guys – drug dealers, kidnappers, rapists, killers – after seven busy and very lucrative years of hard work, Gregory Cunningham had found himself increasingly reluctant to take a life, even if his own were under threat.

So Gregory Cunningham had got in touch with a plastic surgeon whose son he had rescued a few years ago from a particularly vicious bunch of kidnappers. He'd refused any payment at the time, telling the surgeon that he'd take his wages in trade when he was ready. Dr Nassri had been eager to pay off his debt years later, when Jon had contacted him for his second – *and Jesus, hopefully last-ever* – reconstructive facial surgery. He'd chosen the name Jon for no reason at all, which was the best way: no old associations, nothing whatsoever to link him to his past and make it possible for anyone to track him down. But the surname he planned to take, when he settled into his new life – Jordan – was hugely significant to him.

I've crossed a big river, he thought, still staring down at the Thames. *Like the River Jordan. From now on* – and his gaze dropped to his hands – *these are never going to take another life. Like the Bible says, I'm turning my sword into a ploughshare.*

Those psychological tests the Army had given the seventeen-year-old Drew Mackenzie had been more acute than even the administrators had realised. They had spotted what they thought was the potential to kill, a lack of conventional moral values or inhibitions against acts of extreme violence, an ability to act instantly and instinctively, to prioritise his own survival above anything else, and they had thought that they could mould him into the perfect killer.

What they hadn't realised, and what no one but the small, tight clans of Mackenzies and Hendersons back in Jackson County, Kentucky, would ever know, was that Drew Mackenzie had enlisted in the Army still a minor, but already a killer. Because the day before he walked down to town and caught two buses to get himself to the Marine Corps Recruiting Station in Louisville, Drew had killed a man.

Grigor

'*H*o ho ho, everyone!'

Grigor Khalovsky bounced into the Limehouse Reach atrium with a huge smile on his face, his round stomach bobbling up and down under his bright red cashmere sweater.

'Andy!' he bellowed, waving at the concierge. 'Ho ho ho! Remember Christ our saviour was born on Christmas Day!'

'Yes indeed, Mr Khalovsky!' Andy said, springing eagerly to his feet. 'Welcome—'

But Grigor hadn't finished.

'To save us all from Satan's power, when we were gone astray!' he continued gleefully. 'O tidings of comfort and joy!'

He looked enthusiastically up to the gigantic Norwegian spruce tree behind the fountain. Andy had spent a very happy few days up stepladders, decorating it extremely tastefully with silver and red baubles from Harrods and a few discreet strings of fairy lights; the building's management had specified no tinsel, nothing too shiny that would distract from the light installation on which they had spent vast sums of money.

But staring up at the tree, Grigor's face fell.

'But there are not very many lights!' he complained sadly. 'And there is no theme! A Christmas tree *must* have a theme!'

'I was told to keep it subtle and discreet,' Andy said nervously, coming round his desk to stand a respectful pace behind the oligarch who owned the entire top two floors of Limehouse Reach.

'Subtle? *Discreet?*' Grigor rounded on him, throwing his arms wide in a pantomime of amazement. 'What do they have to do with *Christmas?* This is nonsense, Andy!'

'It's as tall as the tree at the Houses of Parliament,' Andy said, hoping that this would distract Grigor. 'And it's eco-friendly. I—'

'We need more *lights!*' Grigor roared, like the friendliest of bulls. 'More lights, more tinsel! More comfort and joy! And a theme! We must have a theme! What theme shall we have?'

He was a compact butterball of a man, grey-haired and jolly in his casual sweater and jeans; Andy was several inches taller than the oligarch, and dressed in a very smart burgundy uniform to boot. And yet it was Grigor who exuded authority from every pore, Grigor who effortlessly dominated the entire space. The doorman had sprung to attention behind his desk, the security guards had shot out of their office and were flanking him, pulling down their uniform jackets, trying to look as hard and macho as Grigor's own bodyguards.

It was a contest in which they would always come a poor second. Limehouse Reach boasted some of the highest levels of security features of any new building in London, including bulletproof windows, an air purifier to frustrate poison gas attacks and, in the most expensive apartments, panic rooms where the owners could take refuge if kidnappers or robbers should make it past the SAS-trained security guards. But alert as the guards were, they were basically patrolmen: two of them at the monitors, one on a regular circuit inside the building, two more outside watching the entrances to the main doors and the parking garage, on constant standby for an attack that they assumed would never come, because their presence guaranteed that no one would be idiot enough to try a home invasion or a kidnap on the premises.

Grigor's bodyguards, by contrast, were very well aware that an attack on their boss might come at any time. And they were more than ready. Two of them had commandeered a luggage cart and were wheeling it in, piled high with Grigor's Vuitton suitcases; another one was outside, checking the perimeter, while the other two had taken up position on either side of the atrium, covering all the exits, their hands clasped in front of them, their eyes flickering constantly between their boss and the areas from which danger might conceivably appear. They were dressed all in black, their heads shaved close, their muscles bulging under the unbuttoned jackets which gave them access to the weapons holstered beneath. They were all ex-Russian Special Forces, the *Spetsnaz*, experienced in counter-terrorism activities in Chechnya and Ingushetia, and there was no love lost between them and Limehouse Reach's security guards, at whom they sneered openly as they passed the desk.

'A theme, Mr Khalovsky?' Andy echoed weakly. 'Um, I—'

'Grigor! Please, I insist! Call me Grigor! We are friends, you and me!' Grigor reached out and clapped Andy hard on the back, causing the young concierge to stagger a little. 'We will be working closely together over the holidays, I can see! You, like me, are very happy that it is Christmas!'

'You know, I *am*,' Andy admitted eagerly, forgetting the professional reserve he was supposed to show when speaking to an owner. 'I *love* Christmas.'

There was a very good reason for this: Andy's childhood had been almost entirely devoid of happy Christmases. Separated from his teenage mother, who hadn't even known she was pregnant till she gave birth and couldn't remotely cope with a baby, he'd been taken into care; his mother's white suburban family had been shocked by her black baby and had wanted to get rid of the shaming evidence of her sexual preference as quickly as possible. For ideological reasons, the social workers had refused to place him with a white family, and their area had been thin on the ground for black adoptive parents.

So Andy had grown up in a series of foster homes, where money was always tight and Christmas barely in evidence: a child lucky enough to be endowed with a positive nature, however, he had pressed his nose against brightly decorated shop windows, traced his finger in artificial snow stencils, saved bits of glittery tinsel garlands, and dreamed of a time when he'd have the money to celebrate the holiday himself. His craving for luxury after a childhood of deprivation had led him to become a high-end concierge, a job he adored: secretly, he'd wanted to go overboard with Christmas decorations at Limehouse Reach, and had been very frustrated by the management's insistence on restraint rather than full-on sparkle and fake snow.

'I know you love Christmas, just like me!' Grigor bellowed happily. 'I can tell you are a comrade in arms! So, Andy—' he stepped to Andy's side and slung an arm around the concierge's shoulders – 'what shall we do to make this lobby special? To show my guests that here at Limehouse Reach, we are very merry and happy that Christmas is coming? Si-i-lent *night*, ho-oh-ly *night*,' he sang in a deep rumbling bass, which startled every Limehouse Reach employee, but not his bodyguards, who were clearly very accustomed to hearing Grigor burst into Christmas song. 'All is *calm*, all is *bright*—'

To his own amazement, Andy heard his own tenor pipe up, joining in with Grigor:

'Round yon *vir-ir-gin*, mother and child,' he warbled. 'Holy *infant* so tender and mild—'

Grigor, over the moon at having found a fellow caroller, beamed hugely, patting Andy avuncularly on the shoulder as they continued the song, even leaning against him, head on his shoulder, as they finished the last two lines:

'Sleep in heavenly *peee-eeece*, slee-ep in heavenly *peee-eeece*!'

Derek the doorman broke into applause, carried away by their enthusiastic harmonising.

'What about *The Nutcracker?*' Grigor suggested, his eyes lighting up at the idea.

'You mean—' Andy began, but it was hard to get out a complete sentence when talking to Grigor.

'Yes! The ballet! I love the ballet!' Grigor said happily. 'There are dancing mice, and pretty fairies, and nice smart soldiers! All things that children love! Go and buy many, many ornaments to decorate the tree. With the theme of *The Nutcracker*. And more lights, more shiny balls – more *everything*!'

'I'd *love* to,' Andy said devoutly. 'It's just that—'

'Sergei will ring the management,' Grigor interrupted, 'and tell them that I, Grigor Khalovsky, instruct you to do this! To make the lobby happy and cheerful. Not *discreet*! *Radi Boga!*' he added in disgust in his native language. 'For God's sake – Christmas is not discreet!'

Sergei, Grigor's secretary, who was scuttling along behind the luggage cart, nodded swiftly and pulled out his BlackBerry.

'Because on Boxing Day, I have a *very* big party,' Grigor announced excitedly, swinging round to include Derek and Limehouse Reach's security guards in the information. 'All the players from my team will come, after the big game, and all their wives and girlfriends and the children! So much fun! Christmas is really for children. I like to see all their happy little faces. There will be many, *many* presents arriving, and *I* will be dressing as Santa Claus to hand them out!'

'Oh, fantastic!' Andy said happily. 'I *love* to pick out and wrap presents! Do you need any help, Mr – Mr K?' He was unable to bring himself to call Grigor by his first name; no matter that Grigor himself had told him to do so, if a building manager heard it, Andy would be formally reprimanded.

'Sergei?' Grigor swivelled. The secretary, who was by the express penthouse lift, nodded again.

'Great!' Grigor boomed. 'Sergei will liaise with you, Andy,

for the presents that we need and for the decorations. He will give you credit cards. Whatever you need. It must be the best, you understand. Only the best. No expense spared, as you say in England. Oh!' A sudden thought struck him, and he clapped his hands in glee. 'Sugar plums! There are sugar plums in *The Nutcracker*. We must have lots of sugar plums for the party, to give to the children.'

'Ooh, lovely! I can definitely sort that out for you. And do you have presents for the ladies already?' Andy asked, his eyes widening with excitement at the prospect of going mad in Knightsbridge with Grigor's credit cards. 'I could *definitely* help with that too – and some gifts for the gents, of course—'

'Speak to Sergei,' Grigor said, flapping his hands between Andy and the secretary. 'You will organise everything perfectly, I am sure! I am very happy!'

He slapped Andy once more between the shoulder blades; Andy's cheeks puffed out with the effort of repressing a coughing fit.

'Now I will go upstairs and settle in, and soon I will have some guests. Very pretty guests.' He leered at Andy and Derek. 'We will have to talk more about these special guests, but that can wait. I have just been to America, and there I learned a very good expression. My dogs are barking. You have heard this expression?' he asked, his hopeful face clearly signalling that he was keen for them to answer in the negative.

Both Andy and Derek shook their heads.

'*Are* there dogs?' Andy asked excitedly, looking towards the entrance. But Grigor's two SUVs had been fully unloaded; one had been driven into the vehicle lift that descended to the secure parking garage, and the other was waiting to follow suit.

'No! It means that my feet are hurting!' Grigor lifted one leg a few inches off the floor and wiggled his suede Tod's loafer. 'I must bathe them now in salt. Woof, woof!' he chortled as he went towards the lift, his bodyguards forming an instant phalanx behind him. 'Woof, woof!'

'He's quite a character, Mr K,' Derek observed as the lift doors closed behind the oligarch.

'*You* call him Mr Khalovsky, Derek,' Andy said firmly. 'Show some respect.'

Having put the doorman firmly in his place, Andy turned to Sergei.

'All right there, Sergei?'

He shook the little secretary's hand with fervour. Sergei, who was devoted to Grigor and violently jealous of his position at his master's side, glared viciously at Andy, but the latter didn't even notice Sergei's animosity: he was much too busy imagining his whole themed tree, visions of sugar plums dancing through his head just as excitedly as Clara pictured them in *The Nutcracker*.

'This is going to be the best Christmas *ever*!' he sighed in happiness. 'Let's you and me sit down and plan out everything that needs to be done to make Mr K as happy as Larry, shall we? Oh!' A thought struck him. 'There'll be nannies, too! Those ladies don't come to a party with their kids without someone to look after 'em – we should get in some presents for the nannies, too, shouldn't we? I'm sure Mr K won't want anyone to be left out . . .'

By the time Grigor's special guests arrived, a couple of hours later, Andy was already in the Jimmy Choo boutique on Sloane Street, piling up the shiniest, flashiest handbags he could find. 'WAGs want bling,' he'd said efficiently to the shop assistant. 'Let's have a look at the showiest stuff you have. Leopard skin's ideal – and have you got anything with a lot of Swarovski on it?'

The WAGs for whom Andy was buying gifts chose to dress, as much as possible, to resemble expensive Russian prostitutes. So it was pleasantly ironic that the bevy of expensive British and Asian prostitutes who emerged from a pair of black cabs, to be met in the lobby by a waiting Sergei and ushered up to Grigor's penthouse, looked much more like elegant, sophisticated trophy wives, in their black jersey dresses, high, but not vulgar, heels, and simple, discreet jewellery. These were London's most exclusive escorts, girls you could take to the opera or to dinner at the Connaught or Claridge's, and then back to your hotel suite for whatever sexual services you might require, at much less cost than the expense of maintaining a trophy wife. They were led by their madam, a very old friend of Grigor's, who had, like all good business owners, learned her trade from what you might call the bottom up; Grigor had been an early investor when she had decided to go into management.

He came towards her now with a huge smile, his arms spread wide for a hug, moving slowly in his white fur-trimmed boots, the Father Christmas costume he had been trying on gaping open at the front over his paunch.

'Diane!' he boomed happily. 'You are as beautiful as ever!'

'I bloody well should be,' Diane said, kissing both his cheeks, 'the amount of money I spend on Botox. It's a sodding fortune, I can tell you. Let's have a look at you, Grigor.' She pulled back, taking his hands, surveying one of her oldest clients. 'You're chubbing up, darling. Need to take care of yourself more. What about a nice detox at a posh fat farm after New Year's?'

'We cannot all be thin like you, Diane,' Grigor said, patting his round stomach complacently.

'It gets harder and harder, I'll tell you that for nothing,' Diane said gloomily, looking down the long slim expanse of her body, clad in a navy silk Chloé blouse and matching navy crêpe skirt, balanced on spike snakeskin YSL pumps: if her girls looked like trophy wives, Diane looked like a first wife who had screwed every last penny out of her husband in a historic alimony settlement and used it to become a leading light on London's most elite charity committees. Her hair was expertly streaked by Jo Hansford herself in overlapping layers of pale blonde and ash-browns. Diane had never been beautiful, but she could pass for it with careful make-up, and no one ever caught her without a full face of slap.

'Not like these little tramps,' she said, gesturing at the six beautiful girls hovering at her heels. 'They've got no idea what a diet is, do you, you little sluts? I saw Lori stuffing a whole bag of Cheesy Wotsits down her throat this morning for breakfast.'

'Makes a nice change for her,' another giggled, 'she's usually much too busy stuffing—'

'Oi! Lyndsey! Cut that out! *I* can talk however the fuck I want,' Diane said sternly, 'but you lot are ladies till the clothes come off. Right?'

'Yes, Diane,' Lyndsey muttered a little sullenly.

'Drinks!' Grigor said, clapping his hands in an attempt to lift the mood. 'We must all have some champagne! Sergei, you will pour, please, while I meet these very lovely ladies! Oh, I see we have a very nice mix here!'

'Hello, Father Christmas,' said a slender brunette, fluttering her eyelashes at him flirtatiously; they were a clever blend of her own and individual false ones, applied carefully to the upper lids by Lori earlier that morning. 'I'm Valerie. It's an absolute pleasure to meet you.'

She extended her hand to Grigor, its manicure immaculate, a simple French finish.

Diane nodded approvingly.

'That's more fucking like it,' she said, taking a glass of champagne proffered by Sergei. 'Now, Grigor, what's the set-up here? Do you want the girls to mingle at this party, or keep to themselves?'

'Ah—' Grigor tossed off half a glassful in one swig, and sighed deeply. 'Alas, they cannot mingle. You see, this is a family party at the beginning. Wives, girlfriends, children. But obviously, it is my players I want to keep happy, and this little London home of mine—' He waved his arm expansively around the enormous receiving room with its triple-height ceilings, marble pillars, priceless rugs on the polished walnut floor, and sliding glass doors that led out onto the equally large marble terrace equipped with a huge, built-in Weber barbecue, chrome space heaters and chaises longues – 'luckily for me, is large enough for me to be able to accommodate various different parties at the same time.'

He beamed.

'Directly below us is another apartment that I also own. It is smaller, of course, but it has four bedrooms, and a very nice living room with a big projector screen to show films. What I propose is that these charming girls – Valerie, Lori, and their lovely friends – should install themselves down there when the party up here begins, make themselves comfortable, watch perhaps some films to get them into a romantic mood—'

He gave the girls, who were all furnished with champagne by now, a large, theatrical wink.

' – and then my players will be able to visit them early in the evening, if they feel they can be discreet.' He smiled in anticipation. 'I will be screening *White Christmas* and *It's A Wonderful Life* in the cinema, so they might be able to slip away if their family are settled in and distracted. I have had a staircase put in, of course, which gives access to the apartment below.'

'What about you, Father Christmas?' Lori asked saucily. 'Will *you* be joining us downstairs?'

Grigor looked genuinely horrified.

'I will be screening *White Christmas* and *It's A Wonderful Life*!' he repeated, as if this were answer enough. He polished off the rest of his drink and shook his head in disappointment. Sergei rushed up to refill his boss's glass.

'We will have lots of food, lots of drink, lots of fun,' Grigor continued, a little more subdued now, as Lori bit her lip in embarrassment at having made such a faux pas. 'Gifts for the children, for everyone. And then, night will fall, the children must go home, the mothers must take them, the men stay on to party, and we all come upstairs for a nice get-together.'

'Some of the girls should put on a show,' Diane said decisively. 'Boys always like a show.'

'A Christmas show!' another girl said excitedly. 'With naughty Christmas fairies! We can spank each other with our wands and wear all red and white – and Santa hats! I can get my wings out! Ooh, Diane, can I organise it?'

'Course you can, Kesha,' Diane said with a nod of approval. 'Good girl.'

'Christmas fairies! How charming!' Grigor's smile was back, as big as before. 'I *love* this idea!'

He hooked his finger in the air to summon Kesha, who came over swiftly: taking her red-nailed hand, he kissed it with old-world courtesy.

'I am *very* glad,' he said pointedly to Lori, 'that one of Diane's young ladies fully understands and embraces the spirit of Christmas.'

Dasha

Grigor would have been extremely distressed to realise how little his estranged wife was, at that precise moment, embracing the spirit of Christmas. Dasha Khalovsky was sitting in a hired Rolls-Royce, being driven from Chelsea to Canary Wharf, smoking like a chimney: twin curls of vapour issued from each nostril every time she huffed out a breath. Dasha was the living exemplar of the dictum that rich men wanted their wives to dress like expensive Russian prostitutes; from her hair, bleached and dyed a colour of yellow never found in nature, to the leopard-skin stack-heeled stilettos that gave her an extra six inches of height, Dasha was a triumph of artifice. Her large, round, high, impossibly youthful breasts were of the kind known as 'bolt-ons', because they were so completely out of proportion with the rest of Dasha's body, like a cantaloupe melon cut in half and stuck onto her with Krazy Glue.

As far as the rest of her body went, however, Dasha was old-school. She didn't bother with facial peels or micro-dermabrasion; she simply airbrushed her complexion every morning, building up a layer of foundation that was as heavy as stage make-up and needed the same kind of industrial-strength cold cream to remove. Her narrow, Tartar eyes were heavily outlined in black pencil and fringed with layers of lash-building mascara, her thin lips equally outlined with brown lip pencil and filled in with pale pink gloss. Under her tightly belted Roberto Cavalli zebra-print pony skin coat, her body, though not overweight, was saggy. Dasha's idea of exercise was chain-smoking and scheming; she wore her little pot belly like a mark of pride, considering that it symbolised the two children she had given her husband.

Bastard, she thought viciously now, stubbing out one Sobranie Black Russian cigarette in the built-in ashtray and tapping out another from her antique Fabergé cigarette case, rose gold heavily decorated with yellow gold cartouche in swirling patterns, fastened with a cabochon sapphire. It had been a present from Grigor years ago, and Dasha had not been particularly happy with it. She didn't like old things. She hadn't set her sights on Grigor decades ago, hooked and landed him like a big fish, and then worked like hell by his side to make him one of the most successful businessmen in Russia, to end up with *old things* as gifts. Dasha liked things new and shiny and covered in diamonds: that was the new Russia. You made your money and you flaunted it. She had made such a scene that Grigor, shrugging in resignation, had told her how much it had cost, and Dasha had promptly fallen silent.

Still, that's the last old present he ever got me, she thought in satisfaction, flicking her Cartier lighter, firing up her fresh Sobranie. Dasha usually preferred American or British brands, but no one else made cigarettes like these, black with gold trim, strong and rich. *Besides, everyone knows they're expensive. Which is the most important thing of all.*

Dasha shifted restlessly on the leather seat, impatient to get to her destination. Leaning forward, she banged on the Plexiglas between her and the chauffeur with the back of her heavily ringed hand; it was as if she'd hit it with a knuckleduster. The chauffeur swiftly pressed the button to slide the panel down.

'There's an intercom, madam,' he started. 'You just press the button and—'

'When do we get there?' Dasha broke in; she was just as prone to interruptions as her husband. The new Russia, the Russia of the oligarchs, was in a perpetual hurry, eager to sweep any and all roadblocks out of its way, wanting instant gratification; its citizens had experienced so much deprivation for generations, seen their parents ground down underfoot by the system into bleak grey dust, and were determined not to let that happen to them. 'We should be there by now!'

The driver glanced quickly at his satnav under the peaked cap he was wearing.

'Just a minute more, madam,' he said nervously, as the Rolls swept with stately grace round a corner, past a series of glittering steel and glass buildings, and came to a halt outside a white-painted frontage which, unusually for the area, offered no floor-to-ceiling windows that would allow passers-by to see inside; instead, its windows were smaller and filled entirely with opaque white glass, allowing in light but no vision. The entrance door, grey-painted, had a small, brushed-steel panel beside it, with the lettering 'Canary Clinic' on it in the most discreet font imaginable. If you had to ask what it was, you shouldn't be entering at all, because you certainly couldn't afford it.

'Wait,' Dasha said economically as the driver opened the door for her. She hoicked up her tight Alaïa bandage skirt well over the knee, without which she wouldn't have been able to move, and climbed out of the Rolls, smoothing the skirt down again.

'I'll keep circling, madam,' the chauffeur said, as Dasha walked towards the Clinic door with a visible shrug; she had absolutely no interest in how a driver would manage to wait for her indefinitely on a street completely painted with double yellow lines.

She hit the door buzzer with one terrifyingly pointed acrylic nail, varnished clotted-blood red, and didn't take her finger off it until the door swung open. A nurse Dasha hadn't seen before, square and pale in her white uniform, stood in the entrance: she opened her mouth to say something, but Dasha mowed her down, storming past her. Unbelting her coat, she slipped it off and threw it at the nurse.

A Polack, she thought contemptuously, instantly identifying the nurse's features. *A lazy, stupid Polack.*

'I'm here for Dr Nassri,' Dasha announced. 'You're expecting me.'

'He has only just arrived himself to meet you, Mrs Khalovsky. I'll see if he is ready,' the nurse said politely, her accent confirming Dasha's analysis of her nationality.

'It's *Madame*,' Dasha snapped. '*Madame* Khalovsky.'

Russian aristocrats in the eighteenth and nineteenth centuries had spoken French to each other, rather than their native tongue, considering it a marker of their sophistication. Despite her solid petty bourgeois origins, Dasha had learned to parrot a little French, and insisted on being called 'Madame' for much the same reasons.

'I'll go straight through – I'm in a hurry,' she added contemptuously; *I don't have time to wait around for a lazy Polack nurse to lumber back and forth.* 'He's in his office, right?' She nodded at her heavy pony skin coat, held in the nurse's arms. 'Hang that up, and stay the fuck out. This is private.'

Without waiting for an answer, she strode down the white-tiled corridor, her metal-tipped spike heels clicking loudly on the floor, the beige bandage skirt constricting her movements; long practice enabled her to balance with enviable ease on a potentially slippery surface. The surgeon's office was at the far end, its door closed, and Dasha threw it open with a dramatic slam, bouncing it into the wall and making a picture rattle on its hook.

Hassan Nassri was standing with his back to the room, rummaging through a filing cabinet. He spun round, his heavy dark eyebrows drawing together in a frown.

'Aniela! What on *earth*—' he began in an angry voice.

On seeing Dasha, however, he caught himself short.

'Madame Khalovsky!' he corrected himself, wrenching his mouth, with a visible effort, up into a smile. 'A pleasure, as always! I'm not quite sure why you wanted to see me so urgently – the Clinic is closed until the New Year, as I told you on the phone – I hope it's not some sort of medical emergency?'

His eyes went to Dasha's breasts, outlined in her tight gold-beaded sweater, whose clinging fabric left nothing to the imagination.

'They look excellent,' he observed, giving them a long, assessing stare that only a plastic surgeon could have got away with. 'May I?'

'Sure,' Dasha said with another shrug, dumping her black and violet crocodile Birkin bag on his desk and fishing out her cigarette case. She actually disliked the Birkin; it was stiff, with sharp corners; she preferred a softer bag. But this one had been not only violently expensive, but limited-edition, which meant that women's envious glances followed her constantly when she carried it. That, naturally, outweighed any minor objections she had to the style.

She raised her arms as Dr Nassri came towards her, hands outstretched like a groping drunk on a dance floor, and carefully weighed her breasts in his palms, his fingertips reaching up the sides to feel for any scar tissue.

'They feel very good,' he said, nodding with professional satisfaction. 'Absolutely even, the implants exactly where they should be. What are your issues?' He looked, momentarily, wary. 'You don't want to go bigger, do you, Madame Khalovsky? I couldn't honestly advise—'

'Shit, no,' Dasha said, lowering her arms and lighting a cigarette. 'I can barely find clothes to fit over them as it is.' She stuck the Sobranie in her mouth and cupped her breasts herself for a moment, contentedly, red-tipped nails flashing. 'But I love them. They're what I always wanted.'

'Madame Khalovsky, this is a non-smoking facility,' Hassan Nassri said nervously. 'I'm afraid I have to ask you to—'

Dasha walked over to the open office door, slammed it shut, and turned around to look at the plastic surgeon, dragging on her cigarette with one hand, the other planted on her hip.

'*Also*,' he said, even more warily, 'as a plastic surgeon, I can tell you that smoking is extremely damaging to the skin – you remember that I advised you that healing after your operation would be more problematic because smoking reduces your circulation—'

His voice was tailing off, however, under Dasha's implacable, black-ringed panda stare. Her spider-leg lashes flapped once, a long, slow, dismissive blink, as she watched him trail to a halt.

'Why are you here, Madame Khalovsky?' he asked. 'If it isn't anything urgent to do with your breast enlargement, why have you summoned me out of office hours?'

Dasha took an equally slow inhale on her Sobranie, pinched shut her narrow lips, and exhaled the smoke through her nostrils, looking exactly like a dragon which had been reincarnated as a Russian oligarch's wife.

'I know what you get up to,' she said flatly. 'I know your dirty little secret.'

Nassri might have been intimidated by Dasha's money and power, but he was one of the best plastic surgeons in the world, and he knew it; clients flew from all over the globe to have him work on them, and paid through the nose for the privilege. He turned down a whole third of would-be patients who presented themselves in his office: his philosophy was that the ability to select patients correctly was equally as important as his ability to perform operations successfully. His patients had to be financially secure, and have realistic expectations of what the surgery could achieve. Some people had Body Dysmorphic Disorder, and would never be happy, no matter how much work they had done; others were physically unsuitable. Heavy smokers, people with congestive organ problems, whose lungs were too weak for a general anaesthetic, all of those were absolute no-nos – *though it's the ones you turn down who complain the most*, Nassri thought wryly.

No experienced doctor at Nassri's level of professional expertise had difficulties dealing with conflict; a man who spent a large part of his day rejecting potential patients was not going to be bounced into any sudden response. He sat down behind his desk, swivelling his chair to face Dasha full-on, and steepled his fingers below his chin.

'Madame Khalovsky,' he said quietly, '*anyone* could say to *anyone*, frankly, that they knew their dirty little secret. It is a timeworn opening gambit, used, if you will permit me, by blackmailers hoping to provoke their victim into blurting something out. If you have anything more specific—'

But, without taking her eyes from him, Dasha had stepped forward and pulled something out of her open bag. She tossed it contemptuously on the leather-topped desk.

'Play it,' she said laconically.

It was a DVD in a plastic jewel case, its shiny pale blue surface unmarked by any handwritten label. Nassri shrugged, and said with a small smile:

'Well, okay. I think I can acquit you of trying to give my computer a virus, Madame Khalovsky.'

Unsnapping the case, he took out the DVD and slid it into the appropriate slot on his hard drive, pressing the return key when the prompt asked if he would like to play it. A couple of seconds later, the smile was wiped from his face as he stared at the image; filmed in black and white, but effectively rendered in flickering shades of grey, it was of a woman, lying on an operating table. She was clearly unconscious; her eyes were closed, her body slumped in an unmistakable attitude of total muscle relaxation. Beside her stood a man in a white coat and a disposable mask, which he was pulling down with gloved hands to hang around his neck by the elastic cord which had held it in place. The room was compact, its walls white-painted and blank; it looked not like an operating theatre, but a place for patients to recuperate.

The man, his face exposed now, was clearly Dr Nassri. And now he took hold of the sheet that was covering the woman from the neck down and pulled it to just above her hips, exposing her breasts, huge and artificially rounded, the scar of very recent surgery clearly visible. He peeled off his gloves, one after the other, slowly, like a man performing part of an elaborate ritual, and began to unfasten the top button of his surgical coat.

Sitting behind his desk, the colour draining from his face, leaving his smooth brown skin with an ashy tinge, Hassan Nassri shot his hand out to his keyboard in a compulsive gesture.

Dasha's voice cut him short, its edge diamond-sharp.

'You don't stop,' she commanded, dragging on her cigarette. 'You keep watching.'

Sagging back in his chair, Nassri watched himself onscreen, his expression anguished. The Nassri with the unconscious woman, however, looked serious, as if he were concentrating very hard on something: by now, he had unbuttoned his coat completely, and it hung open as his hands went to his belt, undid the buckle, and began to unzip his trousers . . .

There was no sound coming from the computer's speakers except a low fizz of static, no attempt to zoom in on the scene. It had clearly been recorded on a security camera positioned in the room. A faint moan was audible now, however; it was coming from Nassri, as he watched himself pull his penis through the slit in his boxers, lick his right palm, and start to pleasure himself as he stared down at the unconscious woman lying on the gurney below him. With the other hand, he reached out and touched her nipples, one after the other, back and forth, careful not to pull, or to do anything that might damage the surgery he had just performed; but, all too clearly, he was highly stimulated by what he had just created – the oversized, artificially round bosoms.

He was rocking back on his heels now as his hand moved faster and faster on his cock. His eyes closed, his mouth dropped open, his head bobbed back and forth like the tip of his penis, which was just visible above the tight, stimulating wrap of his index finger and thumb on his shaft. A moment later, he was craning forward, his right hand bending, pointing his penis directly over the woman's rounded stomach. The moans grew louder and louder: a second later, he yelled:

'*Look* at those tits! I'm the best! I'm the *king* of tits!'

Below his cries of triumph was another sound: the moans of the Nassri sitting at his desk, in a hum of denial, shaking his head, as he watched himself come comprehensively over the abdomen of the patient on whom he had just operated.

'I'm the king of tits!' the onscreen Nassri howled happily, as he spunked over Dasha's unconscious body, his entire body shaking in release. 'The *king of fucking tits*!'

The moans stopped, and the Nassri behind his desk covered his face with his hands, unable to watch the sight of himself orgasming on the woman standing in front of him.

'Thank you very much, Dr Nassri,' Dasha said coolly. She dropped her cigarette into the water of the large Lalique vase, containing white winter roses, that stood on the desk: the butt sizzled momentarily, then fizzled out. 'I'm sure that was *exactly* what the doctor ordered. Or should I call you the "king of tits" from now on?'

Hassan Nassri stabbed at the keyboard, managing first to freeze himself in the act of trickling some last drops onto Dasha's stomach, and then, eventually, to fumble the disc out of the drive again. His hands were shaking so badly he could barely hold it: bending it savagely against the side of the desk, he broke it in two and threw the pieces across the room.

'I have *many* more copies,' Dasha said casually.

Nassri's professional assurance had entirely deserted him: he stared up at Dasha, his face a ghastly mask of entreaty.

'You must understand!' he pleaded. 'When I create something so beautiful – like what I did for you – when I work on a
masterpiece of perfect symmetry – when I know how good it
is, I become excited. An unbearable pressure. It builds up, I feel
it so strongly, and then, when it is over, when I know that I
have succeeded, triumphed – I celebrate. It is like an act of
worship, a tribute to beauty—'

But he had to stop, because Dasha was laughing so hard she
had doubled over and was holding onto the desk, her shoulders rising and falling, her cackle like a rook's caw. When she
eventually straightened up, she was red in the face; she took a
tissue from the box on the desk and dabbed the tears carefully
from her eyes, studying the tissue to make sure that her liner
and mascara hadn't run, before tossing it on the floor.

'Oh, very good!' she said, her body still shaking. 'Very good,
Hassan! You don't mind that I call you Hassan, instead of the
king of tits? I feel that we are close now. *Intimate.* After all, we
just watched you jerk your dick and come all over my body.'

Her eyes narrowed, her skin hardened; she might have been
looking through the eye slits of a helmet. Pulling her skirt up a
little, she sat down in the chair facing the surgeon across the desk,
crossing her legs, dangling a Kandee leopard-skin stiletto from her
toes as if she were showing it off for an advertisement shoot.

'I hope you enjoyed that, Hassan,' she hissed. 'I wonder how
much my husband would enjoy to watch you *worshipping* the
beauty that he paid for.'

Hassan's lips were white now with fear.

'*P – please* . . . ' he managed to stutter.

'You should have been more careful, Hassan,' Dasha advised
him, her tone almost friendly now; she could switch back and
forth in an instant. She snapped open her gold Fabergé case
and extracted another cigarette. 'You should have confined
yourself to wanking over women whose husbands won't rip
your balls off with pliers and then feed them to you before
taking a blowtorch to what's left.'

Hassan was trembling now from head to toe; by now, he was beyond speech.

'Have you heard of a man called Arkady Chertkov?' Dasha asked him, her eyebrows rising. 'He was a business rival of Grigor's, long ago. *Long* ago. And he had been given some natural gas concessions—' She smiled, interrupting her story briefly. 'Well, he had *bought* some natural gas concessions from people in the government, for a lot of money. But you see, Grigor had also paid the same people. He had the deal already arranged, and then Arkady stepped in at the last minute and paid them more. I think the word in English is gazumbing.' She tilted her head to the side. 'Gazumbing, gazumding – something funny like that. Anyway, Grigor was very cross, and he went to see Arkady, and he said: "You have not been behaving well, and you must give me the concessions that I paid for." And Arkady said no.'

She stared at Hassan.

'Would you like to know what happened next?' she asked.

Hassan shook his head frantically.

'Fine,' Dasha said. 'I will not tell you.' She smiled. 'I will *show* you.'

She reached into her bag again, and came out with an A4 envelope: holding it open over Hassan's desk, she scattered its contents onto the leather blotter, Polaroid photos with wide white borders. Hassan stared down at them, his expression first incredulous; then, as he slowly took in the reality of what he was seeing – Arkady Chertkov tied to a chair, undergoing exactly the torture that Dasha had described earlier – he went from ashy pale to livid green. Pushing back his chair, he stumbled over to the sink behind the screen in the corner; the noises he made, heaving up his guts, were prolonged and accompanied by a nauseating smell.

Dasha pulled a bottle of Paloma perfume from her bag and spritzed it in a wide arc around her.

'Good,' she said. 'I see you are aware of how serious this is.'

Hassan, having rinsed out his mouth and wiped it dry,

eventually began to stagger back to his desk. All his confident professional assurance had deserted him; he moved as if he were crippled by a savage series of blows, propping himself against the edge of the sink, manoeuvring from there to the back of his chair and thence to a stumbling collapse into his chair again.

'Please ... ' He reached out a trembling arm and pushed the Polaroids away; they tumbled off the edge of the desk, landing on the carpet with a series of soft thuds. 'Tell me what you want from me,' he muttered, unable to meet her eyes.

Dasha leaned forward, propping both her elbows on the desk, all the power and authority in the room now hers. It might have been her office, and Hassan a lowly, grovelling employee.

'I want a hitman,' she said. 'You need to find me a hitman.'

December 23rd

Melody

'*D*arling! Oh my God, just *look* at you! Your poor *face*!'
Felicity Bell, Melody's best girlfriend from their
RADA days, flitted into Melody's temporary home on a wave
of perfume. Belted tightly around her tiny waist was a tweed
coat whose ruffled neckline framed her pretty little face with
fluttering layers.

'It must be *incredibly* sore!' Felicity continued with great
relish, gawking unashamedly at Melody. 'And my God, *so*
swollen! Is it going to be like that for absolutely ages?'

'No, the swelling's going down fast . . .' Melody said feebly,
already wondering whether this visit had been such a good
idea after all. Meeting Aniela yesterday, chatting to her,
showing her the *Wonder Woman* clip, had done Melody the
world of good – at first. But when the buzz had worn off,
Melody had been left feeling lonelier than ever. She'd even
toyed with the idea of ringing Aniela, asking her to come back
and watch a film that evening, and then told herself she was
being utterly pathetic. Poor Aniela would feel obliged to keep
her patient company, and the last thing Melody wanted was to
force her into a fake friendship.

So her thoughts had turned to real friends, girls she'd been
close to since drama school: girls who would understand the

pressure young actresses were under, who would empathise with the decision she had made to have plastic surgery, not judge her.

And girls who know James, who hang out in the same social group, who can tell me how he's doing . . .

Melody was determined not to see James until her face was fully recovered. But the temptation to talk about him, once it entered her mind, was impossible to resist. She'd rung Felicity, who'd been very excited to hear from her; Melody had made her promise that she wouldn't tell a soul where Melody was holed up, and Felicity had sworn, with proper dramatic emphasis, that she absolutely *wouldn't*, on her *life*, for *anything*; but Kathy had been asking about Melody *constantly*, and what if Felicity brought Kathy over too, she knew that Kathy would *love* to see how Melody was doing too . . .

'Mel! Oh, it's so great to see you! We brought you coffee,' said Kathy enthusiastically, following Felicity into the apartment. She was carrying a moulded cardboard tray into which three Caffè Nero paper cups were wedged. While Felicity unfastened her coat and threw it dramatically onto one of the dining-room chairs, walking over to ooh and aah at the view from the huge windows, Kathy placed the coffee tray on the table, took off her own bulky padded coat, hung up both hers and Felicity's in the entrance hall cupboard, and, consulting the marker pen scrawl on each cup, duly distributed them among the three girls.

'Skim-milk cappuccino, no chocolate,' she said, handing Melody hers with a big smile. 'Just like you said.'

'Thanks, Kathy,' Melody said gratefully, taking the coffee. 'I'm really missing these while I'm holed up here.'

It was ironic that Kathy was bustling around, looking after the other girls; it was life imitating art. Melody and Felicity were part of what the papers had nicknamed the 'Corset Crew', a whole group of attractive young actors who were riding the wave of success on the raft of historical TV series that were currently so popular. Melody had, of course, hit big with *Wuthering Heights*; Felicity had just wrapped a TV series called *The Making of a Marchioness*, and both girls had had bit parts in an adaptation of *The Pallisers* straight out of drama school. Slim, pale-skinned and elegant, both Melody and Felicity exemplified the image of upper-class, aristocratic girls whose figures looked slender even in constricting corsets.

Kathy, on the other hand, at size 12, was too large, by the harsh standards of film, to play a heroine. Her skin was too sallow, her hips and bosoms too generously curved. She was, however, a very talented actress – much more so than Felicity, and maybe even more than Melody – and was carving out a good career playing best friends, second leads, and servants; casting considered her figure more suitable for the lower classes. She was currently making a name for herself as Betty, the plucky, working-class kitchen maid with a secret dream of starting up her own bakery, in the BBC Victorian drama series *Howerby Hall*.

Felicity took the coffee cup from Kathy without a word of thanks, just a swift question.

'It *is* soy, isn't it? I'm *so* off dairy.' She curled her tiny little body up in the curve of one of the Ligne Roset leather sofas as confidently as if she were the hostess. '*And* gluten. I feel absolutely wonderful. My digestion's just *ripping* along.'

'Lovely,' Melody said, exchanging a glance of amusement with Kathy, who was perching decorously on the sofa in the small amount of space Felicity's legs were leaving her.

'This place is fabulous!' Felicity went on, looking around her appreciatively. 'It's like fantasy living, up in the clouds! I bet you don't miss Shoreditch one little bit, do you?'

Melody winced. In her impulse for company, for talk about her old London life, she'd forgotten that Felicity had the knack of finding your sore spot and pressing her finger down on it firmly.

'So the surgery's gone all right, then?' Kathy said, seeing Melody's reaction and quickly steering the conversation away from anything to with James.

Melody nodded, peeling off the plastic lid to her cup and blowing on the frothy cappuccino.

'Apparently it went without a hitch,' she said. 'It should have done,' she added dryly. 'It's costing me a fortune.'

'You should have gone to Brazil! It's much cheaper, apparently!' Felicity trilled. 'I read this amazing book recently about Princess Diana not being dead after all – she goes to Brazil to get her face done and then hides out in America – it was *really* fascinating! I'm auditioning for the film, actually.'

'How long do you have to stay in here?' Kathy asked, ignoring Felicity.

'I don't,' Melody admitted. 'I'm just hiding out from the paps. I don't want photos of me looking like this on the front page of the *Express*.'

'Oh no, so you're going to be stuck in here over Christmas? That's a shame!' Kathy said sympathetically, wrinkling up the cute, freckled snub nose that was one of the features which disqualified her from ever being cast as an aristocrat.

'She's lucky,' Felicity drawled, sipping her soy latte. 'Christmas is *so* bloody fattening. She gets to stay in here and eat lovely little healthy meals – and isn't there a spa here as well?'

'There's a Six Senses spa,' Melody said. 'And a wave pool.'

'Oh, I should have brought my cossie!' Felicity exclaimed; she was one of those girls who loved nothing better than to strip off to a tiny bikini while complaining about how fat she was, so that everyone else would tell her she was being ridiculous. She squinted at Melody's body, swathed in her cashmere wrap.

'You got those boob implants taken out as well, didn't you?' she continued. 'They were *really* big in that film of yours.' This was disingenuous; everyone knew the name of 'Melody's film' perfectly well. 'Good thing you got them deflated again. They'd have been *much* too big for anything period. Especially Regency. Unless you were playing a wench, of course.'

She giggled.

Remind me again why I rang her up? Melody asked herself, taking in the maliciously amused expression on Felicity's sharp-boned little face. *She's always been a self-obsessed bitch – what was I thinking, having her round to gloat over me when I'm looking like I fell face-first down a mine shaft?*

Because she's fuck buddies with Piers, James's best friend, she reminded herself. *And she's a terrible gossip – she'll know exactly what's going on with James. If he's seeing anyone . . . if it's serious . . .*

'So! Are you going to catch up with James at all?' Felicity asked, reading Melody's mind with frightening ease. 'Probably not while you're still looking like this, eh?' She giggled. 'Don't want to frighten the horses, do you?'

'Felicity, give it a rest!' Kathy said crossly. 'We're supposed to be cheering Mel up!' She smiled at Melody. 'I'm sure you'll be back to normal soon,' she said in the soothing voice that was making Betty the kitchen maid the nation's sweetheart.

'I hope so,' Melody said with gratitude.

'Are you going to stay on here, Mel, or head back to LA?' Felicity asked, so casually that Melody was immediately on full alert.

'Definitely here,' Melody answered firmly. 'I want to get back to doing stage work.'

'Probably better for a while, because of the close-ups,' Felicity cooed. 'You must be worried about all that scarring.' She looked visibly relieved. 'I'm going over to audition for that Princess Di film in a couple of weeks – you're not up for that too, are you?'

Melody shook her head, carefully, because of the splint on her nose. Felicity's smile was catlike with satisfaction as she propped a cushion behind her shoulders and leaned back on the sofa, handing without a word her discarded waxed-paper coffee cup to Kathy to put on the glass coffee table; Kathy, always nice and helpful, obeyed as dutifully as the maid she played on TV.

'I hear you're doing really well,' Melody said to Kathy, who beamed.

'There's definitely going to be a second series of *Howerby Hall*,' she said happily. 'And they're even talking of giving Betty her own series after that – send her to Leeds to open up a bakery. I dunno, though. I'm a bit worried about being typecast. So I'm doing a new play by Shelley Silas at the Bush – it's really good, very modern, nothing period about it, brilliant part for me – and then I'm looking at something else at the Royal Court. I want to balance things out so casting directors don't just see me as Betty for ever.'

'That's a really good idea,' Melody murmured appreciatively.

Kathy's doing such a good job of managing her career, she thought enviously. *I know she's always wanted to be the next Judi Dench, and she's nicely on her way. Whereas me – well, what am I on track to be? Right now, I'd be lucky to be the next Catherine Zeta Jones! More like Megan Fox, to be honest . . .*

'*So*—' Felicity interrupted, never happy when the conversation wasn't about, or directed by, her. 'You've heard about James and Priya, right? I heard she's going to be doing *Much Ado* opposite him at the RSC, after those *amazing* reviews they got for *Romeo and Juliet.*'

Every muscle in Melody's body stiffened. She had known that the Royal Shakespeare Company had approached James, asking him if he wanted to play the iconic part of Benedick in its upcoming production of *Much Ado About Nothing* next September; but her UK agent had sworn to her just a couple of days ago that the role of Beatrice, who feuded and sparred wittily with Benedick until they were tricked into admitting their love for each other, had not been cast, and Melody was desperate to snag it. Every serious Shakespearean actress dreamed of playing Beatrice. She was a wonderful character, sharp, funny, hiding her feelings behind her rapier tongue, gradually letting down her guard to show the passion she had been concealing, bursting out in a magnificent show of anger against the man who had injured her beloved cousin.

'O God, *that I were a man! I would eat his heart in the market-place!*' she quoted to herself. They were the strongest lines in the whole play, in her opinion, pouring out Beatrice's frustration at not being able to pick up a sword herself and avenge her cousin's honour, her fury that her lover wasn't doing it in her stead: complex, powerful, moving. A world away from having to say 'Suck it and see!' as Wonder Woman, while she seductively ground the heel of her boot into some prone guy's mouth.

She shuddered, pushing away the memory as fast as it had come to her. *But to play Beatrice opposite James as Benedick . . .* it would be the perfect, triumphant return to the British stage for Melody. It would demonstrate that Hollywood hadn't spoiled her irrevocably, that she had her own face and body back, that she was still as good an actress as she had ever been. *And all those weeks of rehearsals, flirting with James onstage, acting the parts of lovers slowly coming together, confessing their feelings in the most beautiful language ever written – that's the best way to seduce back an ex-boyfriend I could ever imagine! Surely he couldn't resist me?*

Melody had tried to get in touch with James after *Wonder Woman* had wrapped, but he wouldn't return her phone calls or emails; she'd sat down and written him a long letter, pouring out her heart, wishing him the best of luck as Romeo, apologising, begging him to forgive her for letting him down, leaving him in the lurch, pages and pages on the elegant stationery of the Hotel Bel-Air.

He hadn't replied to that either.

And I can't blame him. I let him down professionally and emotionally. I broke our pact. He has a total right not to trust me any more. It's my job to convince him that he can.

But Felicity's right – he mustn't see me like this.

Because Melody wasn't just waiting out the paparazzi up here, high in the eyrie of Limehouse Reach like a princess in a tower. She was counting the days until her bruises faded completely, her swelling diminished, so that she could try to persuade the RSC to let her audition to play Beatrice in the New Year. Her agent wouldn't even consider putting her forward until she could prove, visually, that she was once more the Melody who had played Cathy in *Wuthering Heights*, not the Hollywood porno doll.

'I thought they hadn't made their mind up yet about Beatrice,' she said now to Felicity, as casually as she could, trying to pitch her voice evenly, though her heart was pounding a mad syncopation.

'Oh really?' Felicity's features pinched as she craned her head towards Melody. 'Where did you hear that?'

Melody didn't want anyone knowing that she wanted so desperately to play Beatrice. She bit her lip automatically in frustration at what she'd let slip, then flinched in pain as her teeth scraped the scar in her soft inner lip.

'I'd *love* that part!' Kathy sighed. She was a wonderful stage actress; Melody was very glad when Kathy continued: 'But I'll be shooting for *Howerby Hall* next summer – I couldn't do it.'

'I'd imagine Priya's almost definitely going to play opposite James again,' Felicity said, scanning Melody's face for a reaction, but defeated by the bruising and swelling that turned it into a mask. 'They were *such* a success together at the Haymarket! And they *totally* had a thing during the run. Everyone knows that.'

'*Felicity*— ' Kathy whacked Felicity's ankle. 'You don't have to go on about it!'

'It's better for her to know, isn't it?' Felicity was unabashed. She stretched her arms up, pulled out the elastic holding her fine blonde hair into a messy bun, ran her hands luxuriantly through her hair and twisted it up onto the crown of her head again. '*I'd* want to know who my ex was shagging, wouldn't you?'

Upsetting as Felicity's words were, she was undeniably right. Melody *did* want to know, positively craved the knowledge: it was one of the reasons she'd asked Felicity over. She had to be aware of what she was up against.

'And you were fucking Brad Baker in LA anyway, weren't you?' Felicity continued to Melody. 'We all knew that.'

'I was *not*!' Melody snapped angrily, sitting bolt upright. 'That man's a pig! I never let him *touch* me!'

The ring of the doorbell was the most welcome noise Melody had heard in her life. She pushed out of the sofa and shot towards the door, faster than she should have moved, catching her hip on the built-in bar as she went, a judder that ran down her slim frame so that by the time she dragged the door open, she had dislodged her splint; it was hanging sideways from her nose.

'Oh dear, what has happened?' Aniela said, stepping forward and steadying Melody with a firm grip on her shoulders. Melody hadn't even realised that she was shaking until she felt Aniela's wide, warm hands wrapping over her slender frame, holding her still.

'Take a deep breath,' Aniela said gently. 'One, two . . .'

She waited, still holding Melody, as if she could stand in the hallway all day and all night if she needed to, until Melody's ragged breathing had calmed down; then she reached up with the index finger and thumb of her right hand and expertly tweaked Melody's splint back into the correct alignment. The relief of having it in the right place was huge. Melody felt pent-up tears spring to her eyes now that she had someone to lean on, someone to take care of her.

'Let us sit down and look at that nose,' Aniela said, turning Melody round, kicking the door shut and shepherding her patient back into the apartment. 'What has happened to make you so unhappy? Have you had bad news?'

And then, as she saw the two girls sitting on the sofa, she commented:

'Ah, you have visitors.' She surveyed Kathy and Felicity with a clear, observant gaze as she continued, directing her words to them: 'I must please ask you to leave now. I must look after my patient in calm and quiet.'

Kathy was already jumping to her feet as Aniela guided Melody to a chair and sat her down.

'We're so sorry,' she said. 'We never meant to upset you, Mel . . . ' She nudged Felicity, who hadn't made any move to leave at all. 'Felicity, come on! The nurse needs to check up on Mel!'

Slowly, snakelike, Felicity uncurled herself, a tiny smile on her mouth; Kathy was rushing over to the hall cupboard, grabbing their coats. As Felicity stood up, Aniela glanced over at her.

'You are too thin,' she said bluntly.

Felicity, taking her coat from Kathy, preened herself; in her world, this was a compliment. But Aniela wasn't finished.

'It is not healthy,' she continued. 'Your bones will snap like twigs from osteoporosis when you are older. Like this.'

She raised her hand and snapped her fingers in Felicity's face. It was a surprisingly loud sound, and Felicity flinched back.

'Go and eat something,' Aniela concluded. 'A cheese sandwich, perhaps. It will make you more happy. And maybe even nicer. When people are hungry, they are not very nice. Goodbye now.'

She turned to give Kathy a quick smile, making it clear that Aniela knew perfectly well who had been upsetting Melody; Kathy sketched a quick wave at Melody and made for the door. Felicity glared at Aniela but sensibly didn't attempt a retort; she flounced out in Kathy's wake, and could be heard saying: 'How *rude*!' as the door closed behind them.

Aniela smoothed down the strips of tape holding Melody's splint in place, and then took both of Melody's hands.

'Do you want to tell me what the thin girl did to you?' she asked. 'Or would you just like to be quiet?'

A wail, almost like an animal in pain, emerged from Melody's bruised lips: tears flooded from her eyes. She'd suspected that James had got together with Priya during the run of *Romeo and Juliet*, had heard rumours to that effect, but hearing it like this from Felicity was infinitely more painful.

The image of her beloved James, wrapped in Priya's arms, doing with her all the things he had done with Melody, was like a knife in her guts. James, whose body she knew as well as her own; *better*, she corrected herself, *because you look at a lover's body so much more than you do your own. You lie beside him and trace your fingers over his skin, you draw lines connecting his moles, you tickle and tease him and play with the hair growing at the back of his neck, you play Five Little Piggies with his toes as if you were children, you run your palms up the inside of his legs, slowly, watching him start to tremble, arching towards you, knowing exactly where he wants you to touch him, to cup him and stroke him, and you pause, listening to the sounds he makes, the way he draws in his breath in pleasure, and you know those sounds, too, better than you know the ones you make when he's driving you crazy . . .*

With perfect recall, she remembered James's skin, smooth and pale, lightly dusted with moles; the dimpled curve of his buttocks, the hollow at his neck in which she loved to bury her head, the soft vulnerable skin of his stomach, which he always worried wasn't concave enough; she'd always laughed and said that when he got cast as a superhero, he could start doing sit-ups, but till then he'd be fine. In his early twenties, he could eat like a horse and never put on weight, drink beer in the pub with his mates after the cricket or football that were the only exercise he got. He didn't go to the gym, didn't pump up his muscles: his long, lean limbs were perfect for period films.

From the moment Melody had seen James across the room that first day at RADA, she'd fancied him madly; the floppy fair hair falling over his forehead, his sweet expression, his full lips, the way his legs were stretched out in front of him, crossed at the ankle, the careless ease of a public schoolboy, utterly confident in his own skin. He'd sensed her staring at him and lifted his long blond lashes, his blue eyes widening as he took in the sight of her, the black hair framing her beautiful pale face, her slim body in her shabby-chic Top Shop minidress and Converse trainers. Instant, mutual attraction. They'd all gone out to the pub that evening, James manoeuvring to sit next to her, his long thigh in its faded combat trousers pressing against hers; she was really glad she'd worn a short skirt to show off her legs. And she'd made him wait a couple of weeks, knowing that she shouldn't jump into bed with a fellow student the first night, concerned that, as a posh boy, he might shag and run, treat her like a common little chippie.

But he hadn't, of course he hadn't. They'd been in love by the end of the first week, the envy of every other student in their year, ridiculously happy, swinging their linked arms in great loops of celebration as they dashed up and down Gower Street, around Bloomsbury's quiet grey tree-lined streets, running from one rehearsal room to another in a perpetual golden haze of bliss.

They'd moved in together after the first term, into the basement of a house in Highgate owned by a friend of his mother's; the other sharers, also students, had been out most of the time, partying, socialising, but also wanting to avoid the spectacle of James and Melody's overwhelming happiness. They were the example of a perfect couple, two beautiful young people so completely in love with each other that they barely noticed anyone else. They had done nothing that first year, as far as she could remember, but go to classes, have sex, and lie around on the ratty mattress in their room, naked, in each other's arms, learning lines, reading plays, watching films, studying their craft.

And planning their future. They'd get somewhere of their own, as soon as they could afford it, so they'd be able to walk around the place naked, make love whenever, wherever they wanted. They'd get agents, start to make some money, work on their stagecraft, pick their roles as carefully as they could, try to balance their careers with their lives, not to be away from each other for too long. They'd stay faithful; they'd heard all the stories about how actors behaved on shoots – the casual affairs, the drunken orgies – and they'd agreed that wasn't for them. What they had was the best thing ever, the best sex they could imagine, as if their bodies had been designed to fit together perfectly; the first time they'd dragged each other's clothes off and fallen onto Melody's bed together, it had been as if they'd known each other all their lives, a fluid, beautiful choreography; they'd stared into each other's eyes the whole time, their mouths barely parted, kissing and breathing and gasping together as they came over and over again. Neither of them had been virgins; they'd known just enough to realise how incredibly lucky they were to have found a partner who balanced them so perfectly.

And nothing they had ever done together had felt anything but right. They hadn't been particularly wild or kinky; when the sex is naturally that good, you don't have to be. They had just, very simply, made love, over and over again, and every time had bound them together tighter and tighter, made them feel more and more secure. As if they were walking no longer on hard dirty London pavements, but on a springy, resilient cloud that buoyed them up, would carry them through anything.

That had been Melody's undoing. James had come from a cosy, privileged background, his father a vicar in a lovely part of Somerset, his mother's family well-established in the county, with enough money to send all the children to private school and ensure a cushion of security for all of them. With the confidence that his class and education had bestowed on him, he had less to prove than lower-middle-class Melody, who was working so hard to perfect her RP accent, to 'pass' for a lady if she were cast as one, to prove herself to a family that thought

going into debt for *drama school*, of all things, was the stupi-
dest idea they'd ever heard. Ironically, most of the male
members of the Corset Crew had been to Eton; the richer
your family was, the more likely you were, in these recession-
ary days, to be able to try for a career which notoriously offered
only a tiny chance at success.

'I was so stupid! I thought it would be all right,' Melody
sobbed into Aniela's comforting embrace; the nurse had pulled
another chair right next to Melody's and taken her patient in
her arms to let her cry herself out. She had been blurting out
bits and pieces of her story, trying to tell Aniela, between fits
of uncontrollable tears, how wonderful things had been with
James, and how she'd messed everything up, how every single
thing that had gone wrong for her had been entirely her own
fault.

'I left him in the lurch,' she heaved out through her tears. 'I
broke our pact. He was right to dump me, he was right about
me not doing the film, he was right about everything! And
now Felicity's saying that everyone thinks I had sex with Brad
to get the part! I'd rather *die*! I've never cheated on James,
ever.'

She raised her head from Aniela's shoulder, which was damp
now with her tears. Her eyes were as swollen as her cheeks.

'I never wanted to,' she said miserably. 'I love him. I've
always loved him and I always will. I don't want anyone else
but him.'

'Does he know that?' Aniela pulled a tissue out of her
pocket, folded it carefully and began, very delicately, to blot
the tears from Melody's face.

'I want to tell him,' Melody said eagerly. 'That's my whole
idea. I'm going to wait till my face gets better – I have this
audition the first week in January, it's to play opposite him – I
want to get the part, then go to see him, show him that I've
put myself back together, got back on track – my old face, my
old career, everything the way it was when I left for LA—'

'But you need him now,' Aniela said simply. 'Don't you? You are very unhappy without him.'

It was as if all the stuffing had been knocked out of Melody; she slumped back onto the chair, its plastic yielding fractionally, as she stared straight ahead, her whole body acknowledging the truth of what Aniela had just said. She was so used to the flowery language of theatre and film people, the empty flattery, the outright lies, the circumlocutions of people put on the spot who were constitutionally unable to tell the truth, that the nurse's Eastern European straight-talking was like a dash of bracing cold water to the face.

'You know, Melody,' Aniela continued, 'I am a nurse. I do not just work here, with rich people who like to look more young and pretty. I am on wards most of my life with patients who are very sick, very ill. Often dying. And they do not look perfect. Not at all. The old ones especially. If you want to be with this man for a long time, for ever, you will see him get old, get sick, maybe die. And the same for him. You must not try to be perfect for him all the time. Especially now. It is more important that you need him. If he loves you still, he will understand why you look like this right now. And if he does not, you learn that too.'

Melody turned to look at Aniela, but she couldn't say a word. Aniela had left her speechless. And the nurse was already standing up, going over to the kitchen, running Melody a glass of water, shaking out a pill from a phial in her bag, returning to hand it to Melody on the palm of her hand, as if she were feeding an animal.

'Here, a little Valium,' she said, watching as Melody obediently swallowed the pill. 'Lie down now and have a nap. I will come back later to see how you are.'

Very grateful to have Aniela taking care of her, Melody nodded obediently, standing up and going through to the bedroom, pressing the button that automatically closed every blind over the huge windows. She eased her clothes off and slipped under the covers in T-shirt and pants, as Aniela put the Valium back in her bag and came over to shut the bedroom door.

'Sleep now,' she said calmly. 'Rest is what you need. And when you wake, your head will be more clear.'

With great relief, Melody closed her eyes. She hadn't realised how exhausted she was feeling, but Aniela had known; Aniela had seen off Felicity with effortless skill, had calmed Melody down and given her excellent advice, and then sent her to bed to give all that excellent advice plenty of time to sink in.

It's like Aniela always knows the right thing to do in any situation, Melody thought sleepily. *God, I wish she'd been around when I got offered the Wonder Woman part – she might have been the one person who could have convinced me not to take it . . .*

Aniela

Lucky Melody, Aniela thought wistfully as she left the actress's apartment. *Her boyfriend, their relationship – it's what everyone dreams of having. Real love.*

She huffed a laugh at herself. *What do you know about real love, Aniela? You're so good at giving advice, aren't you? What would Melody think if she realised that you're a big hypocrite, that your own love life is a bloody mess? That you haven't kicked out the big useless lump of a boyfriend you don't give a damn about, because you're too frightened of being alone?*

Lubo, Aniela's boyfriend, was the thorn in her side that she knew she had to pluck out. The sooner the better. But the main cause of deaths on battlefields, before guns were invented, Aniela knew from her favourite type of reading, military history, was people pulling out arrows from the bodies of their wounded comrades. You'd have to wrench them to get them out; and often, despite that, the arrowhead would stay stuck inside the wound. Suppurating, driving the dirt and fibres of your clothes into your body, killing you with all the secondary infections even faster than the original wound.

She sighed. *Maybe I read too many books about war and fighting. I just like facts, that's all. You know where you are with facts. Made-up stories can be anything at all: facts, you can rely on.*

Aniela had cut all ties with her family, and she knew that was the right thing to do. She could never trust any of them again. But she still had one link to them: Lubo, the son of her mother's best friend, who she'd known since school. He had moved to London at the same time as her. Having very few acquaintances in the city, they'd found a small place together, a tiny one-bed flat in Seven Sisters. Aniela had been supposed to have the bedroom, Lubo the sofa, but one thing had led to another, a mixture of proximity, loneliness, and convenience, and soon enough Lubo had installed himself in the bedroom with Aniela, starfished over the narrow mattress, farting, burping beer, and grunting out rattling vodka snores.

Aniela had never loved him; she'd barely even *liked* him. It was the greatest source of shame to her that she had taken him into her bed. Much worse than the way her parents and brothers had exploited her – being fooled by your family was allowable, but opening your legs for a lazy, workshy lout you had barely any feelings for, just because he spoke the same language as you, came from the same village and knew the same people – *well, that's fooling yourself. Which really is something to be ashamed about.*

She was desperate to kick out Lubo and live on her own. He didn't even help out with the bills. Aniela, working double shifts and overtime, was perpetually exhausted, while Lubo had to be the only lazy Polish builder in the whole of the UK. *All the bastard does is lie around, drink cheap beer and scratch his balls: he expects me to come home from a ten-hour shift, cook him dinner and clean the house. The sooner I throw him out, the better. Staying at the Clinic over the holidays is like a rest cure.*

Aniela hadn't even turned on the television in the Clinic's reception area: there was never anything to watch, just stupid made-up shows and even worse reality ones. She'd brought a stack of library books with her and was working her way through a book on the Katyn massacre, when twenty-two thousand Polish prisoners of war had been executed in 1940 by the Russian occupiers. It hadn't made Aniela any better disposed to the Russian bitch who'd stormed into the Canary Clinic yesterday, treated her like a serf she could wipe her feet on, and done something to Dr Nassri that had caused him to throw up in his office sink. Then, after she'd left – looking like the cat who got the cream – he'd staggered out, headed for the medicine cupboard and swallowed what looked like half a phial of Valium.

God only know what went on there, Aniela thought, shrugging. Delving deeply into the previous surgical procedures that Jon had undergone was highly unusual for her; she was normally very incurious, something that made her a particular asset to the Canary Clinic, where she did her job with great ability and asked no questions beyond the necessary medical ones. *But whatever went on with that Russian woman and Dr Nassri, I feel sorry for him if that bitch has got her claws into him.*

She shrugged again. *Whatever his problems are, he has enough money to deal with them. He's got a lovely house in St John's Wood, a nice wife, two boys at private school. Not exactly a crappy rented flat over a chip shop on the Seven Sisters Road, with a live-in boyfriend who's nothing but a waste of space.*

The picture of Lubo, as he'd been when she left for the Clinic, lying full-length on the sofa – now so farted-into and stained that the landlady was bound to withhold a large chunk of Aniela's deposit – holding up a can of Special Brew in a goodbye to her, too absorbed in the football he was watching to even take his eyes off the TV screen, popped into Aniela's mind; she shuddered.

And then, as the lift doors opened and she stepped out, the image of the man she was about to see replaced Lubo's. It was even more vivid, and it made her shiver even more, but with a completely different sensation rippling through her. She had looked at Jon's records – pored over them, to be completely honest – and then told herself firmly that she should put them away, that this kind of detailed research crossed over any professional interest and went right into stalker territory. However, by the time she had finally slid Jon's file back into the cabinet again, she had memorised almost all of the details of not only this operation, but Dr Nassri's comments on the previous procedure that Jon had undergone almost a decade ago. He had had not just one, but two facial reconstructions. Which, was, in Aniela's extensive experience, completely unprecedented.

But he's just another patient, she recited in her head as she walked down the silent, plush corridor to the door of his apartment. *Just another patient. With the best body I've ever seen. And something about him that's making me break the habit of a lifetime, snoop into his background, ask all kinds of questions about him that are none of my business. I'm behaving like a stupid teenager with a crush.*

Enough. She rang the bell and, instinctively, put both her arms behind her back, one hand clasping the other wrist. Aniela wasn't a fool; she knew perfectly well what that meant. *I'm not going to touch him apart from what I absolutely have to do to change his dressings. I'm going to be in and out of there as quickly as possible.*

Ten years of training, Aniela. Get it together. You're a professional, so behave like one.

But the unprofessional part of her, the part she had so firmly suppressed for so long, couldn't help hoping that Jon had been exercising again and would come to the door wearing just his sweatpants . . .

Grigor

$\mathscr{A}$ couple of hours earlier, Grigor had been happily enconced on the main terrace of his penthouse, engaged in one of his favourite activities: supervising the positioning of Christmas decorations. He had sent out Andy to purchase a vast amount of outdoor lights, including an enormous Santa with reindeer and sleigh, six foot high, which Andy and two of Grigor's bodyguards were wrestling into place and affixing to the balcony that ran around the terrace. Grigor, wrapped in a floor-length sable coat that made him look like a stumpy beaver, was curled up on one of the loungers, a bevy of space heaters positioned around him to keep him warm, calling out suggestions as the young men struggled to hang Santa off the balcony without dropping the whole thing into the Thames below.

'Careful of my boats!' Grigor yelled cheerfully. 'I like them on the water, not under it!'

Directly below, Grigor owned a private pier jutting out from the waterfront, on which was moored a Princess V62 sports yacht, a lovely sleek white motor cruiser on which Grigor loved to putter up and down the Thames in good weather, sprawled over the white leather sunbed in the cockpit, as his chef grilled on the built-in barbecue on the deck. Beside the Princess was a Blade Runner 35, an insanely curved and torqued white and red racing speedboat with a maximum speed of ninety miles per hour and special suspension jockey seats, which had cost nearly two hundred thousand pounds. Grigor couldn't reach anything like ninety miles per hour on the Thames, for fear of the river police, but it was still the envy of every single man and boy who saw Grigor happily nipping up and down the river, the nautical equivalent of the luxury supercars which Qatari princes and Bahraini playboys with apartments in Knightsbridge kept in their private garages. Every summer, they would come to London to escape the heat at home in the weeks before Ramadan, take the covers off their Ferraris, Bentleys, Porsches and BMWs and park them on Basil Street, outside Harrods, to show them off to the world.

And sometimes they race them too, naughty boys, Grigor thought, smiling. *Up and down Sloane Street or Knightsbridge, at two in the morning.* Grigor's son Alek had been caught out last year, partying with some Middle Eastern friends of his, had fallen out of a private casino behind Harvey Nichols and promptly taken a wager to race his Lamborghini Murciélago against a Bugatti Veyron down the Brompton Road: both boys had been stopped by the police, given on-the-spot fines, and officially cautioned.

Only sixty pounds each, I think it was they had to pay, and some points on their licences. No bribes at all. They didn't even impound the cars so the police could drive them around for a while. What a wonderful country this is!

'How's that, Mr K?' Andy called breathlessly, holding the last reindeer in place, their hooves rearing high above the balcony, as the bodyguards roped the sleigh to the brushed-steel railings. 'Brilliant, eh? Those kids are going to go *mental* when they see this on Boxing Day!'

Andy was already forgetting any deference in his manner with Grigor; after yesterday's Christmas shopping and planning, and today's push on getting up the decorations, he was too absorbed in having unlimited funds to spend on giving Limehouse Reach the most spectacular Christmas imaginable. From being a frighteningly rich and powerful oligarch, Grigor had become, to Andy, a sort of Santa Claus in human form.

'Wonderful!' Grigor boomed cheerfully back. 'I want them to see it from all the buildings around! I want all the office workers and people who live here to take photographs and send them to each other and put videos on the YouTube of Santa landing on my building and say that here is the best Christmas decoration in London!'

A brief expression of sadness crossed his face.

'For a little moment, I think Santa should be landing on the helipad,' he said, gesturing upwards to the helicopter landing site on the roof above. 'But Sergei checks with the shop where we buy the big Santa, and they say no, it is not safe, because it is all empty, there is nothing to tie Santa to but the railings, nothing in the middle to hold him down. And you know, it is not good if Santa and his reindeer blow away and kill someone. No one wants to be killed by Santa.'

Andy frowned thoughtfully, his handsome features creasing in concentration.

'What if we got them to make something specially for next year?' he suggested. 'I bet they would if we paid enough. What about a big, light-up helicopter, with Santa getting out of it? That would look *amazing*!' He smiled, teeth flashing white against his burnished red-brown skin. 'They could make it with lots of extra guyropes so we could tie it down to the railings, round the whole perimeter, to make sure it wouldn't take off in a high wind. *That'd* be all over YouTube and the newspapers and everything. Santa and his helicopter – got to love it!'

Grigor beamed delightedly.

'That is a *great* idea!' he bellowed, throwing his arms wide. 'You hear, Sergei? A *great* idea! Why do you not have great ideas like Andy does?'

The little secretary, huddling inside the apartment in the lee of the sliding glass door, shot a malevolent glare at Andy.

'It's just cos I love Christmas so much,' Andy said hurriedly.

'Santa coming out of a helicopter! It is very funny! And you know what is even more funny?' Grigor demanded. 'We put *antlers* on the helicopter!'

'I *love* it!' Andy said blissfully.

The bodyguards had finished tying Santa, the sleigh and the reindeer onto the balcony by now; with a last couple of vigorous pulls to check that everything was safely secured, they backed away, and Andy ceremonially presented Grigor with the remote control that would turn the lights on. Standing up, the heavy skirts of his coat falling nearly to the ground, Grigor gleefully pressed the power button, and sighed in delight as the entire fixture lit up in full glory.

'Look at Rudolph!' he exclaimed blissfully, pointing to the leading reindeer's nose, which was flashing red on and off. 'And – ha, look at Nestor and Kirill!' His index finger moved to the faces of the two bodyguards, who were feeling the cold; their cheeks were pink, their noses bright red. 'They are both Rudolph too! Very funny! Ho ho ho!' he added for extra comic effect.

The bodyguards, unable to talk back, tramped back into the building, relieving their feelings by glowering horribly the moment they had passed Grigor.

'*You* are very lucky with your nice black skin!' Grigor said to Andy. 'You have no Rudolph nose!'

'That's one way of looking at it,' Andy said tactfully. 'Shall I—'

'Where the *fuck* is he?' screamed a woman's voice in Russian. 'Where the *fuck* is that so-called fucking husband of mine?'

'Oh dear,' Grigor said sadly. 'And we were having so much fun . . .'

He turned to look inside the gigantic receiving room, to see a blur of movement at the far end, where his estranged wife

was struggling between the two bodyguards who were
stationed in the foyer. In her lemon shaved-mink coat, belted
with a wide swath of black leather, her yellow-dyed hair and
her black silk scarf, Dasha looked like a flapping, enraged bee;
from their agonised expressions as they tried to restrain her
without being stung by her nails, the bodyguards were making
a very similar comparison.

'It's okay,' Grigor said, sighing deeply and lifting the heavy
weight of his coat like a ball dress to enable him to step inside
the apartment again. 'She can come in.'

He snapped his fingers at Sergei, who was more than happy
to close the doors behind him and bustle Andy out of the
penthouse. Dasha, released by the bodyguards, shot forward as
if she'd been fired out of a gun, fizzing and buzzing like an
acid-tipped projectile towards her husband.

'Fuck you!' she yelled. 'How *dare* you divorce me? After all
I've done for you – helped you with *everything*, built the business from *nothing* – and now I hear you want a divorce because
you're going to marry fucking Fyodorov's *daughter*? Is this
some kind of *joke*?'

Sergei nobly ran back and tried to interpose himself between
Dasha and Grigor; Dasha shot out one red-tipped hand and
slapped him out of the way.

'Hey, Dasha, that's enough,' Grigor said mildly. 'You don't
hit Sergei, okay? Sergei is a nice guy.'

Undoing his huge sable coat, he stepped out of it, leaving it
like a gigantic hairy puddle on the carpet, the shape of his
shoulders clearly outlined, the lower part sagging downwards.
Sergei scuttled round him, picking up the coat, reeling under
its weight as he heaved it towards the foyer to hang it in the
built-in climate-controlled fur closet.

'Let's have some tea,' Grigor said, walking over to the long
U-shaped silk-upholstered sofa and sinking into the centre
wing, so that he could watch Santa and the reindeers' lights
flashing on and off. 'Nestor, tell Daniel I want the samovar.'

Nestor, who had the lowest status of the bodyguards and was therefore tasked with lugging in the gigantic bronze electric samovar with its elaborately moulded handles and matching teapot, stifled a sigh and headed off to the kitchen to inform the chef that it would be required.

'Why don't you take a seat, Dasha, while we're waiting for the tea?' Grigor suggested.

'Fuck you, Grigor!' Dasha hissed, throwing her own coat at Sergei; nervous of approaching her, he stood as far away from her as he could and dashed forward to catch it at the last moment possible.

'Dasha,' her husband said gently, 'I don't understand you, *moya dorogaya*, my dear. This cannot be changed. The divorce, the new marriage to Fyodorov's daughter.' He sighed. 'I would rather it wasn't, to be honest. It's all costing me a lot of money and time and trouble, and what am I going to do with a new young wife? I'm old and tired, and happy as I am without little Fyodorova running round the place, wanting to make changes to my life. But it's business. You know that better than anyone. Sometimes, for business, one has to make sacrifices. Unpleasant decisions. You yourself have helped me make many of those unpleasant decisions in the past. Look at how you dealt with poor Arkady Chertkov!'

He tilted his grizzled head to the side.

'I would have gone a little easier on old Arkady myself,' he said a little sadly. 'Left him at least – well, *alive*.'

'He begged for death at the end,' Dasha said crossly. 'And I needed – *we* needed – to make an example of him. It worked, didn't it?'

She narrowed her eyes, the false lashes on the upper lids almost closing on the heavily mascaraed lower ones.

'I don't want this divorce, Grigor!' she continued. 'It'll make me a laughing-stock, left for a girl almost half my age!'

Sergei, who had stationed himself discreetly against the back wall of the room, half-concealed behind a Picasso sculpture on a pedestal, gave a muffled snort of sarcastic amusement at this: Dasha was on the wrong side of fifty, and little Zhivana Fyodorova wasn't yet twenty-one.

'I've always boasted about it, Grigor!' She started pacing back and forth on her six-inch Louboutin heels, her hair bouncing on her shoulders. 'I've always boasted that you would never divorce me, that I would be one of the wives who *wasn't* thrown aside for trophy models and beauty queens . . .'

'Ach, *thrown aside*,' Grigor said, flapping his hands dismissively. 'You are not *thrown aside*, Dasha, that is ridiculous! You live like a queen in Monaco, in a mansion by the sea, and you have plenty of pretty gigolos to keep you happy. We haven't shared a bed in years – you can scarcely complain that now we are getting a divorce you will lose your marital rights, eh? But you are the mother of my children! You will always live like a queen for the wonderful boys you have given me! I kiss my hand to you for giving me our boys!'

He did, with a flourish, as Nestor, very carefully, wheeled in the gigantic brass trolley bearing the huge samovar. Daniel, Grigor's chef, followed behind him, supervising the placement, and, when it was successfully installed with its wheels locked, he ceremonially decanted enough tea from the spigot to fill the little teapot that perched on top of the samovar. Placing the teapot on a beaten-brass tray, adding two little cups and a plate of almond biscuits, he stepped towards Dasha, proffering the tray; she waved him aside so furiously that the tray wobbled dangerously in his hands.

'You know I will be very generous in the divorce. You won't want for anything,' Grigor went on, the aromatic scent of the brewing black tea filling the room. Neither he nor his wife had any scruples about airing their dirty laundry in front of the servants; any employee of the Khalovskys knew very well that they would be literally taking their life in their hands were they to gossip about their employers. 'This marriage is a political move, that's all! I'm marrying the Fyodorov girl to consolidate our territory. Come on, Dasha, you know how it is. I'm exiled from Russia – I can't go back without being clapped into prison. Fyodorov wants access to our natural gas concessions, and he can run things from there – he's a real politician, that one, better than I ever was. I let my feelings run away with me sometimes, but Fyodorov, he's a chess player. We're a good balance. It's the way of the future, you know? We all used to be enemies, scrabbling for the monopolies. Now we have to team up, be strong together, because if we don't, the government will pick us off and crush us like bugs, one at a time.'

He raised one hand and squashed his thumb and first two fingers together expressively, then mimed throwing away the insect he had just killed.

'Like that,' he said. 'So be happy!'

'Be *happy*?' Dasha said furiously, hands on hips.

'I will be stronger than before!' Grigor said, sipping some tea. 'And stronger means richer! It will be better for our sons, to have a father who is stronger and richer! And for you; I will always take care of you, protect you, because of the sons you gave me. So your protector will be stronger and richer! You can marry again – some French prince to give you a title. You can buy ten French princes with the money I will settle on you. Or you can keep the money and stay with your gigolos.'

He looked up at her, genuinely taken aback that she was making such a big scene about a highly advantageous business decision.

'You should be happy, Dasha,' he repeated.

Dasha pounded her chest below the huge cantaloupe breasts.

'It's *humiliating*!' she wailed. 'I'll be *humiliated* if my husband divorces me to marry a girl young enough to be his own daughter!'

Grigor heaved a long, deep sigh, and took another sip of tea.

'Dasha,' he eventually said, shrugging. 'What can I say? Most rich men do it eventually. Look at Abramovich,

Berezovsky. I'm not doing it for sex — it's for an alliance. But older men, younger women . . .' He looked straight at her. 'What did you expect, Dasha? It's the way of the world. What can't be cured must be endured, as they say in English. Or,' he added, 'as they say in French, *c'est la vie*. Eh?'

Silence fell: you could have heard a pin drop in the huge room. Sergei was actually hiding behind the Picasso now; even the bodyguards had frozen in place, as if hoping that if they turned themselves into living statues, no one would notice them. Magnificently, Dasha pulled herself up to her full height, poised on the spike heels of her shoes. Her elaborately curled hair, threaded with the gold tinsel extensions that were the rage with rich Arab and Russian women, tumbled down the back of her satin blouse, whose buttons strained over the half-melon breasts as she took in a deep breath of her own.

'Fuck you,' Dasha spat at him. 'I came to give you one last chance, Grigor. Now it's on your own head.'

Holding her head as high as if she were wearing a crown, like the queen Grigor had called her, she stalked with superb hauteur across the vast expanse of the room. A lesser woman would have been daunted by such a drawn-out exit, under the watching eyes of a whole group of men, but Dasha made the most of every step, her hair and breasts bouncing, her heels driving down into the floor like the daggers she would clearly love to drive into Grigor's heart. It was Sergei's job to rush ahead of her and withdraw her mink from the fur closet, but he was too frightened of her nails to do anything but cower behind the sculpture and hope that someone else would do it.

Kirill manfully stepped up to the challenge, but even he held the coat out at arm's length, the metre-and-a-half span of a six foot five bruiser, and couldn't help jerking back as soon as Dasha had snatched it dramatically from his grasp. It was no coincidence that his hands immediately, like those of the other bodyguards, went to his crotch, cupping it protectively. One of the other men had already summoned the lift for her, and they

fell back into a tight, protective, black-clad phalanx, lining her
way as, the yellow mink tossed with glorious abandon over one
shoulder, she stormed into the gleaming chrome interior of the
car.

Dasha

The men who had been struck into absolute silence by Dasha's intimidating scowl would have been very surprised to see that, as soon as the lift doors closed behind her, she wiped the expression from her face. Dasha might have made an exit worthy of Joan Collins in *Dynasty*, but, just like that very experienced actress, as soon as a scene was over, she relaxed instantly, preparing for the next one. Because the entire pantomime she had enacted with Grigor had been just that: an exaggerated piece of dramatic mugging which had gone exactly as she had planned.

Men are so naïve, so ready to believe that a woman's prone to lose her head and get hysterical, she thought contemptuously. *Could Grigor really have credited that I would think that I could plead with him like that and have him call off the divorce, this wedding to the little Fyodorova? Does he really believe I'm stupid enough to and tear my hair to try to make him change his mind about such a huge business decision?*

Apparently. All these years of working together, and he still thinks I'm a complete idiot.

She smiled nastily.

Well, he'll find out soon enough who the idiot is.

Most people would have needed a considerable amount of time to calm down after a confrontation of that magnitude.

But to Dasha, it had simply been a warm-up for the main event.

The penthouse lift went straight to the ground floor, where its doors opened into a special marble recess of its own. Dasha waited for a few moments, holding the doors, judging her timing; then she slipped out, round the corner, hitting the call button on the closest bank of the building's main lifts. The building was almost unoccupied, and most of the lifts were waiting on the ground floor. One pinged and opened almost immediately, and Dasha slid inside, unobserved by the concierge or doorman. She might have been seen on the many CCTV monitors placed around Limehouse Reach, but she knew perfectly well that the less a building's security guards had to do, the less they noticed. On balance, she considered it a very acceptable risk.

Because the entire scene with Grigor had been created to give Dasha an explanation for her presence in the building. Dasha had never needed to see Grigor at all; she had known, when he informed her of the plan to divorce her and remarry his new business partner's daughter, that there would be no possibility of changing his mind. Their sons were grown; the need to keep the family together would not be a factor in his decision. Alek, the eventual heir to the Khalovksy commercial interests, had just graduated from Harvard Business School; Dmitri, the sweet younger boy, had recently done a gap year with VSO, building a school for an African village, and was now volunteering at a workers' collective in Portland, Oregon. Dasha shuddered: she hadn't told Grigor yet about the collective – *Grigor would literally explode with rage.*

She sighed, as she always did when she thought of Dmitri. *He's as wet as the Moskva River and a lot less useful. But at least we have Alek*, she thought, cheering up. *He's a chip off the old block. Hopefully Grigor will be so happy with Alek joining the business that he'll let Dmitri piss around with his hippy-dippy, bleeding-heart career. He should have been born a girl, dammit. God knows where he gets it from.*

Grigor would treat Dasha very well in the divorce; his lawyers had already made that clear. Like the oligarchs he had mentioned, Abramovich and Berezovsky, who had both divorced their first wives, with whom they had not had prenups, he had made a settlement offer generous enough to pre-empt any messy, publicity-ridden court case.

But it's not enough. It isn't half. I was an equal partner to Grigor, and I should have half of all the money we made. Everything he's made, even since we started to live apart, is built on the foundations I created with him. And I don't want this damn divorce! It's humiliating, just like I said.

It was a cruel fact of their world that to have a husband – not a bought French prince, but a real husband, the father of your children, a player on the international stage – gave you much more status. Without Grigor, Dasha would be just another billionairess divorcee, two a penny in her social circle.

He's not going to get away with this. He's not going to throw me aside like a used piece of clothing. He's not going to marry that little nothing of a girl and breed with her – because no matter how low his sex drive is, he's definitely going to fuck her until he knocks her up – and make children who'll grow up to be rivals to my own.

Grigor is the biggest fucking idiot in the history of the world if he thinks I'll stand for that.

Ping! The lift doors opened onto the forty-third floor. Dasha stepped out, consulted the brushed-steel plaque set into the faux-suede wall opposite, and headed down the hallway to the apartment she really wanted to visit. Hassan Nassri, terrified into complete submission by the Polaroids of Arkady Chertkov's poor, abused body, had stammered out the information Dasha had wanted as soon as he could get his lips to stop trembling with fear. Caught between a hitman and a psychotic Russian gangster, there was no meaningful choice. Jon might kill him for giving up the information, but it would be swift and clean. Better that than having his balls ripped off with pliers before his inevitable death at the hands of a vengeful Grigor Khalovsky defending his wife's honour.

Of course, I was actually the one who dealt with Chertkov, Dasha reflected. But it was more frightening to dangle Grigor in front of Nassri, the bogeyman in the shadows. People always fear more what they can't see.

She smiled to herself.

I was so smart. Years before, when she'd scheduled her boob job at the Canary Clinic, wanting even larger ones than the previous surgeon had given her, she'd had the PI she used hack into the computer that controlled the security cameras in the Clinic and download the footage of her operation. She'd wanted to make sure that Dr Nassri was giving her the very expensive implants that she'd paid for, not fobbing her off with inferior products. It wasn't that she had any reason not to trust Dr Nassri; it was much more simple than that. Dasha never trusted anyone.

And when I saw that video, I knew I had complete leverage over him for ever.

It hadn't been a sure thing that Nassri would know a hitman, but it had been more than likely; plastic surgeons of his level were few and far between, and this kind of facial reconstructive surgery was very difficult indeed. There weren't many surgeons capable of giving someone a new identity. *And as it turned out, this one saved Nassri's son from kidnappers! What a sweet story! How upset Nassri was to have to give him away! And what perfect, perfect timing that he happened to be recuperating right now, in this very building. It simply couldn't have worked out better.*

She was smiling with pleasure as she rang the bell on Jon's apartment door.

Jon

Jon didn't have visitors. No cleaning staff either: as a basic security precaution, he didn't use the Four Seasons' room service, and had opted to clean the apartment himself, doing his own laundry, sending the rubbish down the built-in chute in the kitchen. It was a good hour before Aniela, his only visitor, was due. There was absolutely no reason for anyone to be ringing his doorbell.

A normal person would have walked up to the door and looked through the peephole, but Jon was not a normal person. The easiest way to kill someone on the other side of a door with a peephole in it was to wait for them to put their eye to it and then fire a gun through it; the bullet would go right through the orbital socket and into the brain, a sure and certain death shot. Jon should know: he'd killed two people like that himself.

So, with lightning speed, he dropped and rolled along the hallway, arriving in a tight little ball to one side of the door, putting the hallway cupboard between himself and the wall for cover. A bullet from a gun with any kind of kick to it would go right through a modern stud wall with no trouble at all.

'Who is it?' he called, his voice as calm and untroubled as ever.

'I'm from the Clinic,' Dasha said. 'Come to check on how you're doing.'

'Bullshit,' Jon said easily.

'Okay,' she said just as easily. 'I'm not from the Clinic, okay? Let me in, I want to talk to you. You can search me, no problem.'

Jon didn't even bother to answer this one; he stayed exactly where he was, waiting for the woman's next move. *Russian*, he thought. *Damn it. A Russian woman outside my door – this is not good. Women are tougher than men, and a Russian one to boot? Fuck it. This is trouble.*

There was rustling outside; a piece of paper came sliding slowly under the door, folded over. Jon waited until the whole thing appeared. Then he opened the cupboard, pulled down a hanger, inched away from the paper as far as he could, and carefully pushed the paper a little. Enough to see that it wasn't trailing any strings, that it wasn't going to explode when touched, or lifted. Hooking it with the hanger, he dragged it towards him along the carpet, and unfolded it, still using the edge of the hanger.

On it were written two words. Just two words, but they were more than enough.

'Who are you?' he said, staring down at the name he had been using ever since he dropped out of the CIA – Gregory Cunningham – scrawled in black ink. 'And are you alone?'

The questions were a cover. He wasn't expecting her to answer the first, and he already knew the answer to the second; his hearing was that of a sniper, preternaturally acute, and he had heard only one person breathing outside.

'Let me in and you'll find out,' the woman said. 'And yes, I'm—'

Her voice cut off, half-strangled. Because while she was speaking, Jon had unlocked the door with his right hand and whisked it open, fast enough to shock her; with his left, he reached out, grabbed her by the neck of her blouse and dragged her inside, shoving her up against the wall face-first, kicking the door shut and swinging her round so she landed against it, her body a shield between himself and anyone she might have waiting further down the corridor.

The wind had been knocked out of her; she gasped for breath. Jon held her in place with two fingers to her carotid artery, ready to knock her out if she tried anything, as he expertly frisked up and down her body, his hand darting between her legs, her inner thighs, reaching round to circle her back, up into her hair, making sure she had no concealed weapons on her. Wrenching her bag from her shoulder, knocking her coat to the floor, he took three swift steps back, kicking the coat with him as he went. Without ever taking his eyes off her, he searched first the bag, then the coat; then he tossed both of them into a far corner of the living area, stepped back into the kitchen and beckoned her forward.

'Come in,' he said.

'What a nice welcome! You have *very* strong hands,' Dasha purred.

She smoothed down her blouse, tucking it back into her leopard-print silk YSL pencil skirt, taking her time to adjust her clothing until she was perfectly happy with her appearance. Then she sashayed along the corridor, swinging her hips, surveyed the living room, and, hitching up her tight skirt fractionally, took a seat on one of the sofas, swinging one leg over the other, tossing her head so that the heavy yellow tinsel-threaded ringlets fell over her right shoulder.

'Won't you sit down?' she asked, nodding at the opposite sofa. '*Well.*' She looked him up and down, taking in the form-fitting white T-shirt which clung to his body and outlined every ridge and slope of muscle, the bulge of his biceps as they swelled out from the short sleeves of the T-shirt. 'I hope Dr Nassri's made you a face as nice as your body. If that's even possible.'

Jon was a hill boy from Appalachia. He didn't make conversation, he didn't flirt, and he was more than used to women who were tough as nails to be able to take Dasha in his stride. She might be Russian, and clearly richer than Croesus, but to him she was just a more moneyed version of the Mackenzie and Henderson women in Jackson County. They lived in trailers and run-down shacks; they drank home-made applejack and cranberry in jelly glasses, or moonshine and Crystal Light – when they were celebrating, it was sparkling wine and Sunny D, what his Aunt Eileen had called a 'poor-mosa'. This one wouldn't touch anything but Cristal in Lalique glasses: but, as his Aunt Eileen had used to say over her applejack, quoting an old Kipling poem, the Colonel's lady and Judy O'Grady were sisters under the skin.

Jon had learnt young to let women run their mouths off; that way, they'd get to the meat quicker. Sure enough, as he looked at Dasha, she shrugged, seeing that he wasn't going to respond, and continued:

'You're wondering where I got your previous name from, aren't you? And, even more importantly, what I'm going to do with it.'

She paused again, but it was impossible to size up his reaction. His face was so bruised, his eye sockets so swollen, that she couldn't tell anything from his expression, and he had his body utterly under control; the only movement was the shallow rise and fall of his tight firm pectorals as he breathed slowly and steadily.

'Keep going,' he said flatly.

She shrugged once more. 'Very well, let's get to business. My name is Dasha Khalovsky, and I want you to kill my husband.'

Oh, this one's a killer all right, she thought with satisfaction; not a muscle moved as he absorbed this information.

'He's currently in residence upstairs,' she added with a smile. 'In the penthouse. It really couldn't be easier for you.'

'That's convenient,' Jon said dryly.

'And in return,' she said, 'I will tell the private investigators who have been looking into your history for me to go no further. Because they have found something very interesting. They have found that Gregory Cunningham appears from out of nowhere, seven years ago. And already, he seems very experienced in what he does. Mr Cunningham has learned his skills somewhere. It would be *very* interesting to learn where.'

Jon absorbed this without any visible reaction.

'Let's see some proof,' he said equably. 'Dates, places, people.'

Dasha spread her hands wide.

'There's no paper trail. As I'm sure you know already. Everything's hearsay. Believe me, no one wants to talk about you on the record. No one even wants to say your name.'

'Really?' Jon said. 'Then how did you find me?'

Oh, he knows, Dasha thought. *He's guessed already that it was Nassri who gave me his name. And if he decides to take out that pervert in revenge, it won't cause me any sleepless nights.*

'I'll leave that to you to decide,' she said, stretching her arms along the back of the sofa. 'All I really need to say is that my husband needs to be eliminated, and soon.'

Before the divorce goes through, she meant. *So that I can inherit everything.*

'If you agree, I'll call off the dogs. If you don't, they'll keep digging,' she finished. 'It all depends on how deep you've buried your bodies.'

'You're very confident, Mrs Khalovsky,' Jon said, still not moving from his position in the kitchen; here he was perfectly placed to survey the whole area, to keep both the front door and Dasha in full view. His voice didn't change, either. But something altered, in his posture, in his manner. Dasha couldn't have described it, but she knew exactly how it felt; as if a cold wind were sweeping her way, enveloping her in an icy chill. His body seemed tauter, as if on the brink of action, every muscle tightening imperceptibly, making him, if anything, even more still.

This is the most dangerous man I've ever met, Dasha realised. *And I've dealt with some real gangsters in my time.*

'My investigators have instructions that if I disappear, or die in any kind of accident, they're to double their efforts,' she said, managing to preserve her own equilibrium in the face of the tangible threat now emanating from the man she was threatening.

He's twenty feet away, and he could break my neck in half a second, she knew. *I must judge this even more carefully than I anticipated.*

'And what will they do with this information if you disappear?' Jon asked softly.

'They'll take it to my husband,' Dasha said firmly. 'And tell him I was investigating you because I was concerned about your presence in the same building as him. I thought he might be in danger.'

'You're threatening me with your *husband*?' Jon's arms hung loosely by his sides, as they had for the entire exchange; only someone as well trained as he would have been able to avoid the temptation to fidget, to shove them in his pockets or fold them across his chest. 'Somehow, I think you're the scarier one in the marriage.'

Hah! He's no fool, either! He's quite right. Women are always more devious. More treacherous. More unscrupulous.

In this game of verbal chess, he had the advantage of not showing his expression. Dasha couldn't help the corners of her mouth flicking up in a swift, amused acknowledgement of the truth of his observation.

'So, Mr Cunningham,' she said, using his name in a further attempt to rattle him. 'What's your answer? Do you kill my husband for me, or do I let my PIs keep going? I only found out about your existence yesterday. What will they find out if I give them a solid week to work on your riddle?'

'You've got me between a rock and a hard place,' Jon observed. 'Okay. I'll take care of Mr Khalovsky for you.'

Dasha nodded: she hadn't expected him to say anything else.

'Make it look like an accident,' she specified. 'Nothing must come back on me.'

He would have raised his eyebrows if he could.

Lady, you think I'm going to walk in there and shoot him in the head, hitman-style? Are you crazy? Why would I want people looking for a possible murderer in Limehouse Reach? Best thing is a slip and fall in the shower. Happens to hundreds of people every year, and no one ever questions it . . .

But instead, he asked as calmly as ever:

'How do I know this will even our account?'

She stood up, pulling down her skirt. 'I've only spent a quarter of an hour with you, Mr Cunningham,' she said, 'and I have learnt that I don't want to be on your wrong side any more than I am now. You do what I want, and I close the book for ever. And the detectives I've hired will follow along. They're not men of action. Not like you. They won't want to get on your wrong side either.'

Dasha walked towards the door, barely managing to repress a shiver as she passed him. She had met only two other men who had the same ice-cold energy. One was a Chechen contract killer, the other a CIA assassin. And this man made her more nervous than either of them.

Jon retrieved her coat and bag, tossing them to her.

'Don't come back here,' he said shortly as she opened it to leave. 'Ever.'

Oh, believe me, Dasha thought as she left, *you don't need to worry about that. I will do my absolute best never, ever to be alone with you again.*

Jon

*H*e was livid. Absolutely livid. His fists clenched, his jaw trying to set hard, fighting the pain from the recent surgery, he paced back and forth across the living room, up and down the wide expanse. The stunning views of the towers of Canary Wharf, dazzling sunshine glinting off the glass windows, glittering on the water of the Thames in the boat basin below, might as well have been blank white walls. He had managed to keep himself calm and controlled during Dasha's visit, but she had sensed how much danger she was potentially in, and she had been right.

If I hadn't made a vow that I would never kill another human being, I swear to God, I'd have snapped her neck like a twig, cut her up in the bath, dropped her in weighted binliners down the rubbish chute in the middle of the night and then slipped down to dispose of her in the river, he thought savagely. *Blackmailers are the scum of the earth.*

But I made that vow when I became Jon Jordan, and if I don't keep it, my new life literally has no meaning. The whole point of it is that I've stopped the killing. For ever.

In his seven-year freelance career, Jon had made a great deal of money, and he had saved almost all of it. Enough to live on for the rest of his life. His tastes weren't extravagant, and he'd done his sums carefully. A year ago, he'd bought a ranch in Montana. Beautiful country, wide-open – so Jon could see any old enemies coming – but close enough to the Rocky Mountains to make an Appalachian hill-boy feel at home. He was planning to raise horses, maybe pigs too. He liked pigs. They were smart. He'd fly-fish, hike the Rockies, and whitewater kayak. Maybe hunt a little, but not that much. He'd concentrate on ranching. Enough living things had died at his hands; now he'd see how good he was at raising them instead. There'd be more than enough to do, and he was far enough away from town so he didn't have to see a single living soul for months if he didn't want to.

Jon had long ago given up any hope of trusting anyone enough to ever share his life with them. His early years had turned him into a pathologically private, self-contained loner. If the Unit had deliberately set out to create a perfect candidate for their assassin training programme, they couldn't have done better. Jon's mother's refusal to protect her children from their violent, brutal father had been the tipping point; when Jon had begun to suspect that she was actually grateful that her husband was beating their sons instead of her, that was when he really shut down, stopped trusting anyone. Relied solely upon himself.

Even by the standards of the hardscrabble life in the Appalachian hills, Mac Mackenzie had been a brutal husband and father. *The only reason Ma didn't have the usual passel of kids is that Mac kicked her in the womb when she was pregnant for the third time and broke everything in there for good. She should've left then. Aunt Eileen offered to take her in and make sure Mac didn't come by to haul Ma back. Even Mac had to knuckle down to Aunt Eileen if she laid down the law.*

But Ma wouldn't go. And that meant we couldn't either. That was how things worked up in hill country. You stayed with your pa and ma, no matter what kind of job they were doing.

That was when I stopped trying to protect Ma. She was a lost cause. And that's when I started calling him Mac, not Pa.

He'd taken plenty of blows for it, but then he was getting bounced off the walls anyway on a regular basis. When he was thirteen, and Mac was belting him till he bled, Mac had yelled that his older son was just like him, that Mac was beating Jon because he was the spitting image of his father, and that taking the belt to Jon was like hitting himself. *Liar,* Jon had thought furiously. *Liar. And hypocrite. If you wanted to hit yourself, go right ahead. Punch yourself in the jaw. Ask me to take a two-by-four to you if you need a bit more weight behind it.*

Jon shook his head, jerking himself out of the memories of his childhood. *Why the hell did that all come back? I haven't thought about them in years. It's being on my own like this, with nothing to do. Too much time on your hands isn't ever healthy.*

Well, I've sure as hell got something to do now. Figure out how to get out of this mess I'm in.

Dasha Khalovsky didn't realise it, but what she was holding over Jon's head was the worst threat she could have conceivably come up with. The Unit – the highly secret CIA black-ops division for which Jon had been an operative for a decade – was the only entity that Jon truly feared.

If they ever find out that I'm still alive, there'll be hell to pay. As carefully, as meticulously as he had covered his tracks when he faked his own death, Jon couldn't take the smallest, most infinitesimal risk that his old CIA handlers could find out that he was still alive. *You didn't leave the Unit. You couldn't. You died in harness; or, if you were clever and lucky, you got promoted up the ladder to be a handler yourself. Telling them who to kill, setting up targets for assassination. Whole families sometimes, if you couldn't get your quarry any other way.*

Well, no thank you. Not any more.

Jon wasn't confident that he could outrun the reach of the CIA's death squads if they were sent after him. No one could do that for ever.

That Russian woman's got me in a chokehold. Kill or be killed.

I swore I wouldn't kill, and I'm damn well not going to be killed . . . so where the hell does that leave me?

The doorbell rang. For a split-second, Jon thought it was Dasha, and he spun towards the door, a cold rage rising inside him. *Don't let her in,* he knew immediately. *You can't trust yourself right now.*

And then he glanced over at the clock projected on the wall, and realised what time it was.

Aniela. Perfectly on time.

He couldn't help his lips twisting in an ironic smile as he walked towards the door. His slip of the tongue yesterday, telling Aniela he was a kind of escapologist, now paled into insignificance compared with the situation Dasha Khalovsky had dumped in his lap today: *now I have a death threat hanging over my head, I'm not exactly going to let my guard down to Aniela any more . . .*

But as he pulled open the door and saw her standing there, calm and composed in her simple white uniform, fair hair scraped back from her wide forehead, her pale eyes regarding him as seriously as before, he felt the same tilting sense of disorientation that he had experienced before.

What is it about this woman? he couldn't help asking himself. *Why does she get me feeling like this?*

'Come in,' he said brusquely, turning away, determined to look at her as little as possible.

It's because she's a nurse, he told himself. *That whole cheesy fantasy that she'll take care of you, minister to your needs, look after you when you're weak and vulnerable.*

Yeah, that's all it is. I need to deal with this crap, get a handle on it once and for all, and bury it deep. The last thing I need with this crisis on my hands is any sort of external distraction. I'll let her change my bandages and get the hell out in five minutes flat.

Jon strode to the usual chair on which he sat while his wound was checked, turning it at an angle to the door so he couldn't see her enter the apartment.

Ah, crap! he thought. He was deliberately wrenching his thoughts away from Aniela, detaching himself from her physical closeness by working through the consequences of the visit he'd just had: *this means I can't use Jon Jordan after I leave London! It's been compromised. Dasha Khalovsky knows what name I had surgery under. Dammit!*

It would be easy enough for him to get a new passport under whatever name he chose: his contacts were well-established all over the world. But he'd spent a lot of time coming up with the name Jordan, had been really satisfied with its symbolism: the crossing of the river, like a baptism that would wash him clean, let him purge away his sins, make a fresh start. And he had felt confident that the security and discretion of the Canary Clinic – plus the debt Nassri owed him – would keep the name hidden for ever.

Just goes to show – you can't trust anyone. He glanced sideways at Aniela, setting his lips tightly. *Remember that,* he told himself. *You can't trust anyone at all.*

Aniela

'You're agitated,' Aniela said immediately as she closed the door behind her.

She watched him as he stalked to the chair and sat down. It might not have been visible to someone else, but his energy levels were through the roof. His body was vibrating like a tuning fork, sending off a distress signal that she could hear as clearly as if it had given out an audible sound.

'Something has happened,' she stated, frowning. 'Something bad. Is anything wrong with your head? Are you in pain?'

'What the hell are you talking about?' he said, glancing briefly towards her and then away again. His face was so bashed around she couldn't have told from his expression what he was thinking, but she didn't need to see it; the set of his shoulders, the tense lines of his body were telling her everything she needed to know. 'I'm fine.'

'No, you're not,' she said firmly. 'I need to take your blood pressure. I will get the monitor.'

The apartments owned by the Clinic were equipped with basic medical hardware for the nurses' use; Aniela wheeled the trolley with the blood pressure monitor on it from the hallway cupboard and set it up with quick, efficient movements. Jon was wearing another of his short-sleeved crisp white T-shirts, and as she rolled up the sleeve to his shoulder to make room for the blood pressure cuff, she smelt fabric conditioner wafting from it, light and fresh-scented.

He changes and washes his clothes every day, she realised, glancing to the open door of the bathroom, where a rack of white T-shirts, sweatpants and – she blushed – what looked like white boxer briefs were ranged neatly on a drying rack in front of the towel rail. *He's meticulous.* She thought for a second of Lubo, stinky, slobby Lubo, lounging around the apartment, drinking and smoking and eating stinky takeaway food, not washing his clothes for days on end: the comparison between him and Jon was so harsh that she cringed in embarrassment.

Jon's arm was taut and rippled with lean muscle, his freckles distractingly delicate over the bicep that was swollen up like an anatomy drawing, and the tricep that was as hard as iron as she pulled the plastic cuff taut around it and Velcro'd it into place. The image of Lubo's saggy, lardy frame flashed into her mind again, no matter how much she tried to hold it off, and she wrinkled her forehead in a grimace of disgust. She darted quickly behind Jon, ostensibly to pull the monitor into place so that he could see it too, but really so that he wouldn't catch her expression.

'What the hell makes you think I'm agitated?' he asked as she came into view again. He sounded cross now. 'I said I'm fine.'

'Nurse's instinct,' she said, starting to inflate the cuff with the rubber pump. 'Just relax as much as possible, please.'

'I don't get it,' he said, sounding even crosser. 'I don't get why the hell you—'

'Shh! Relax!'

Briefly, much to her own surprise, she reached out and fleetingly laid one finger to his lips. His mouth was the one part of his face that wasn't bruised like a rotting apple. *That was totally unprofessional,* she thought instantly, horrified, dragging her hand back. *He could report me for that. There's something about this man that makes me act like a stupid schoolgirl . . . Oh Jesus, I'm still pumping up the cuff! I'd have cut off his circulation by now if he didn't have such good muscle tone!*

Freezing her grip on the pump, she took a deep breath and read the figures off the monitor.

'A hundred and fifteen over seventy,' she announced with great relief. 'You are perfect.' She gulped. 'I mean—'

'Thank you, ma'am,' he said, and now there was a thread of amusement in his voice. 'You're very kind.'

'Your *blood pressure* is perfect!' Aniela said, her voice rising in a way she never normally allowed. She ripped off the cuff with a frantic pull and dropped it on the monitor, clattering the pump down on top of it. 'This is what we see in athletes – a blood pressure reading this low. It is excellent.'

She took another deep breath.

'I should check your heart rate too,' she said, walking round the trolley, tilting her left wrist to look at her watch as her right hand took his, her fingers sliding round his wrist, finding his pulse with practised ease.

Aniela had been a nurse for almost a decade now; she had taken heart-rate readings so many times that she had often said she could have done it in her sleep. His vein was pulsing beneath the pads of her fingers, a strong, regular beat; it should have been the easiest thing in the world to count them against six seconds and multiply by ten. Automatic, her training kicking in without even exercising her conscious brain; and in fact, her conscious brain was being eclipsed by her body, which was insisting on being heard. Her own heartbeat was pounding, fast and furious, as if her heart were swelling up enough to knock against her ribcage; *that's why I'm having such a hard time taking his pulse – I can't hear it over my own . . . his hand in mine, the intimacy of this touch, it's overwhelming . . .*

'Nearly eighty!' she said, finally managing to take a reading. She dropped his hand as fast as if it were on fire. 'That's a little high – well, higher than I would have expected for such a low blood pressure reading – athletes are usually below sixty-five. Not that I'm saying you're an athlete – well, you're very fit—' She took hold of herself, drawing in a deep breath. 'It's nothing to worry about.'

'Nothing to worry about,' he echoed, looking up at her.

Aniela was standing in front of him, and as she had been taking his pulse, she must have stepped closer than she'd realised; she was between his parted knees now, still holding up her left hand, with its cheap plastic Swatch, staring at it with ridiculous fixation. Lowering the hand, she found herself looking directly down at his upturned face, and for some reason, she couldn't take her eyes off it. She had no idea what he looked like – *and that doesn't even mean anything, because nor does he, nor does anyone. No one even really knows.* In his file, there wasn't even a computer-generated projection of the results of Dr Nassri's work, which was highly unusual: he truly was a man without a face.

But his clear blue-grey eyes, his strawberry-blond hair, his freckled skin, his aura of grace under pressure, those wouldn't change after surgery. Nor would his body, his muscle tone, his flat stomach, his . . .

Aniela realised with horror that her gaze had dropped down his frame, down past his narrow waist to his lower abs, the bulge in his sweatpants . . . Feeling as if all the blood in her body had raced to her head, she backed away as fast as she could in the clumpy shoes.

'I will change your dressings now,' she said quickly, snapping open her bag, putting it on the trolley and shoving the whole thing behind him so that she was completely hidden from view. She tried to kick herself, to snap herself out of the insane state into which she'd slipped, but the moulded toe of her Ultra Lite shoe didn't do much damage; she kicked her calf harder and stumbled, catching the trolley and making the monitor rattle perilously. She dealt with the change of dressings on Jon's head as fast as she possibly could, a process facilitated by the fact that he was healing very swiftly.

'The wound is closing very fast. You have good skin for this surgery,' she said, in an attempt to bring herself back to the strictly clinical. 'This kind of skin – white with freckles – is very good. Dr Nassri says it bleeds a lot, but it heals fast.'

'Oh yeah?' Jon's voice was a soft rumble in his chest; it was as if she could feel the vibrations right up to his skull, under her quick-moving hands. 'I never heard that. What's bad skin for surgery?'

'Smokers,' she said. 'And the darker you are, the more there's a risk of keloids.'

She swallowed hard.

'I don't see the need for more gel dressings,' she lied. Another day wouldn't have hurt, and under normal circumstances she would have definitely replaced them.

But these weren't normal circumstances.

'Great!' he said. 'So I just let the air circulate and it'll heal on its own?'

'Yes,' she said. 'In a few days, when the scar has formed, we will start to put Vitamin E on it to help the healing. And arnica cream for the bruising. It is very effective.'

She started to pack the used dressings into a plastic bag, sealing it and putting it in her medical bag for disposal in the Clinic.

'So does that mean you don't need to come back to check up on me any more?' Jon asked.

Aniela was wheeling the trolley across the room, back into the cupboard, fully in his sightline; she knew that, bending forward a little in the unforgiving white skirt, her bottom must look even bigger and wider than it naturally was. It was mortifying, this uniform; the A-line skirt skimmed her hips, hiding lumps and bumps, but it spread them out as well. And no one but tiny little Melody and her equally thin friends could look good in white.

She shut the closet door and turned to face him, her bag slung over her shoulder.

'I should really come in every day,' she said. 'That's what I'm here for. But if you don't want me any more – if you don't want a *nurse* in any more—' she corrected herself hurriedly – 'you could ring Dr Nassri and tell him.'

'That'd get you into trouble, though,' Jon said acutely.

'Oh.' Aniela was so confused by now by her reaction to Jon that she hadn't even thought of that. 'Yes, yes it would—'

'I won't do it, then,' he said. 'I wouldn't want to get you into trouble.'

Jon stood up, taking a step towards her.

'You seem like a very good nurse,' he observed. 'I mean, I've had surgery before, and nurses have been – I've had quite a few nurses – no, that's not what I meant to say! I haven't had – I mean – *anyway*, you seem very good. As a nurse.'

'Thank you! I try!'

Aniela had no idea what she was saying now, none at all. It didn't seem to make sense, and she had the feeling what he was saying didn't make that much sense either. She stared up at him, at his poor swollen bruised face, and realised that he was holding out his hand to shake hers. She had no idea, either, why he wanted to shake her hand, but she responded, and as his fingers closed over hers she felt them tugging her gently, pulling her towards him. They stood there for a moment, his hand in hers, caught between their bodies, feeling each other breathe, their hearts pounding fast in excitement and utter disbelief.

If I pull away now, if I run out, nothing will ever be said again, she knew, with an instinct as sharp and clear as diamond cutting glass. *I will come back tomorrow at the same time, check him over for five minutes and leave again, and we will never, ever, be this close again.*

I couldn't bear that.

His face was tilting down towards her, a bruised, pulpy mess. And though her eyes closed as she turned her own face up to meet his, craning her neck, it was not because she was in any way upset by the sight of his damaged features, but because being pressed against him, inhaling the scent of his body, was making her too dizzy to do anything else. His other arm closed round her, supporting her, his palm flat on her spine, his touch making her shiver from head to toe, and as it rippled up and up his lips met hers at the crest of the wave, soft and very sweet, gentle and unexpectedly tentative.

It was a true first kiss, or a whole series of first kisses. Each one was slow, each one was a question Jon was asking and Aniela was answering, and each one was gradually more confident, more compelling. His lips parted, and hers did too; with each kiss, they breathed each other's breath, felt the yielding moisture of each other's lips; pulled away fractionally after each one, came back for more, and every time they came back the fragile connection and trust between them grew. It was like watering plants, watching them push up their shoots from the soil, nurturing a tiny little flower into bloom; or sheltering a flame with your hands, nursing it, giving it oxygen without letting a gust of wind put it out, until, all at once, it was big enough and strong enough to survive on its own.

Aniela was flooded with sensation, gasping with it, her body burning up with heat. She touched the tip of her tongue delicately to Jon's lips, exploring them, and heard him groan as he responded, his own meeting hers instantly; his hand slid up her back, slowly, surely; it lifted away, and she moaned in frustration, but it was just to avoid the heavy medical bag on her shoulder. A second later his big palm cupped her head, drawing it even closer, and his tongue drove into her mouth eagerly, so eagerly that she felt a snap of excitement, a firecracker going off between her legs, a tiny explosion which loosened her entire body. She moaned again, leaning into him, dissolving in the kiss, and in response he kissed her so hard that she felt his groin pressing insistently into hers.

His teeth ground with an audible click against hers, one of those little awkward moments that can happen when a kiss is overenthusiastic, and one of the parties hasn't had much practice in making transitions easy and smooth. Aniela pulled back fractionally, turning her head to make the angle of the kiss easier; but Jon was already pushing away, his hands falling from her body.

He took a stumbling step back, turning away from her.

Mortified, feeling rejected and ridiculous, Aniela shoved her bag up her shoulder and fled in an awkward run on her clumsy Ultra Lite shoes to the door.

Dasha

The suite at the Dorchester, where Dasha was staying, was decorated in the lavishly overstuffed English style: swagged and pelmeted yellow and blue chintz curtains, caught back with huge tassels over a whole second set of curtains, a blue which echoed the pattern of the chintz; fringed and layered cushions on big yellow velvet sofas; polished credenzas and desks with unnecessary tiny drawers the inhabitants of the suite would never use; side tables laden with ceramic vases and table lamps. Usually, Dasha enjoyed the décor, which was very similar to the interior of her Monaco apartment. Rich Russians did not do minimalism. The more possessions they had, the better. And all these layers of curtains and cushions that needed to be plumped and dusted, these antiques and framed pictures and mirrors that needed to be polished, spoke also of the money that was available for a stream of staff members to bustle through the apartment, keeping it perpetually pristine.

However, when one was in a hurry, all those side tables and extra armchairs were just a series of obstacles. Dasha navigated through them at high speed, cursing at how many there were, how many stupid *objets d'art* the Dorchester had crammed into the living room. The corner suite had lavish views over Hyde Park, but its trees were bare now, its grass dulled by the lack of sunlight, the low grey sky, and Dasha didn't even glance at the park as she dodged the furniture roadblocks, heading through into the huge bedroom with its king-size four-poster bed, spreadeagled on which was the only view in which she was interested . . .

Muffled, pleading noises came from behind the ball gag as Marcos, Dasha's Brazilian toy boy, saw her enter the room. His big dark liquid eyes opened wide, his thick silky black lashes fluttering as he tried to convey how very much he wanted her to untie him, his head twisting from side to side: since his wrists were lashed to opposite sides of the headboard, his feet to the posts at the foot of the bed, opening his body like a slender, pale-brown X on the yellow shantung silk coverlet, his head was practically the only part of his body that he could move.

Practically, but not quite. Dasha climbed up on the base of the bed, kneeling between Marcos's slim legs, sliding her hands beneath his small tight buttocks; a moan escaped him as he felt her slowly ease out the butt plug which she had inserted before she left him to head off to Canary Wharf. His large, uncircumcised penis, which had been resting fatly on his thigh, stirred as she removed the plug, twisting it as she did so: as it plopped out, his hips bucked, his penis swelling further. Marcos, like all Brazilians, loved the sun, and he loved to sunbathe naked. His foreskin was as tanned as the rest of him, smooth and brown, and, like the rest of his body, it was shiny with the baby oil with which Dasha had anointed him after tying him up.

Pulling back her hand, smiling in anticipation, Dasha slapped his cock. Behind the ball gag, Marcos's moan rose to a buzz, and his hips bucked again, eagerly, wanting more. That was a mistake. He should have stayed still. Dasha never liked to give him what he wanted. Deliberately ignoring his tumescing cock, she crawled up his slippery body, not caring about the oil on her expensive clothes, rubbing herself against him with lubricious relish. Pulling open her silk shirt, she shoved her surgically enhanced breasts against his depilated chest, grinding her crotch into his. When she finally slid the gag out, his pouty lips were swollen and bruised from having been stretched around the rubber ball; deliberately, she crushed them under her own, biting and smushing them down, hurting him, barely giving him a chance to breathe, her tongue driving deeply, invasively, into his mouth.

She kissed him for a long time, as if she were marking her territory; when she pulled back eventually, he was gasping, moaning, his cheeks flushed.

'You hurt me!' he said, his words reproachful but his tone flirtatious. 'You hurt me so *bad*!'

'Hurt? You don't know the meaning of the word yet. D'you want the big dildo, you slut? The one I call Putin's Surprise?' she said, hovering over him, her lipstick smeared now. 'You want me to go and get it now, shove it right up you?

Marcos shivered in fear and pleasure.

'No, Dasha! Not Putin's Surprise!' he begged, trembling from head to toe.

'Maybe later,' she said, smiling evilly. 'Or tomorrow. Maybe, if you are not good today, tomorrow you get Putin's Surprise inside you, not some little butt plug your slutty arse can't even feel by now. And I leave you tied up for twice as long.'

Marcos's big eyes widened still further in anticipation; but then a practical thought struck him.

'Not *too* long. They need to come in to clean,' he pointed out. 'They ring on the door many times while I am here.'

Back in Monaco, Dasha's staff were like the Three Wise Monkeys; the Dorchester's cleaners, however, could not be expected to dust and hoover around the prone, naked, butt-plugged body of a Brazilian gigolo.

'And also, the oil is *all over* the bed,' he added even more practically, jerking his head to look down at the greasy slick of baby oil on the shantung silk. 'You put too much on. They will have to soak it for ages, and it may not come out even then . . .'

But while Marcos had been speaking, Dasha had hoicked up her tight skirt to her waist. All she was wearing underneath it were thigh-high Wolford lacy hold-ups, nothing she needed to remove before she squatted over Marcos's mouth and shoved her bare crotch down onto it.

'You talk too much,' she said. 'I don't pay you to talk.'

She sighed in contentment as Marcos started doing with his lips and tongue exactly what Dasha did pay him for. Leaning forward, she grabbed onto the headboard, manoeuvring herself into exactly the right position, not caring that her knees were digging painfully into his shoulders, that the spikes of her heels were carving divots into his chest. The thrill of confronting first Nassri, then Grigor, then Jon, had worked her up into a high state of excitement and arousal, bringing back memories of when life had been a perpetual adrenalin rush of conflict, aggression, and battling for supremacy.

Dasha's life in Monaco was the acme of luxury, interspersed with trips to the Costa Smeralda to sun herself on yachts, to Chamonix for the skiing, to New York and Paris for shopping binges: she had no need to ever work again.

But part of me misses the old days. Grigor and me, together against the world, fighting back-to-back to carve out the life we'd both always dreamed of.

Pulling out those Polaroids of the lesson Dasha had taught Arkady Chertkov had made her very nostalgic. Russia twenty years ago had been the Wild West, where anything went as long as you had enough money, a free-for-all where the law was on the side of whoever could buy it. Now Putin had clamped down, the law was his; it no longer belonged to the oligarchs. That was why Dasha had nick-named the huge dildo – technically called a Man Rammer – 'Putin's Surprise'. Because it fucked you up the arse when you least expected it.

'Aaah!' she yelled, grinding her hips down onto Marcos's face as he desperately tried to breathe through his nose while still servicing her. 'Yes – like that, you slut, you filthy whore! Eat me out like that! Aaah!'

She was coming, spasm upon spasm, her calves slipping against his heavily oiled chest, her heavily ringed fingers gripping the headboard; her cries were full-throated, utterly uninhibited. All her life, Dasha Khalovsky had taken what she wanted and paid the price for it. Marcos, whom she had poached from a South American oil millionairess in Sardinia last year, was a highly expensive little piece, venal and grasping, with a diamond-studded price tag; but he was worth every penny. Like a pedigree pet, it was important to keep him well-exercised and fully occupied – that had been the Uruguayan millionairess's mistake. Dasha made sure that Marcos was never bored, never knew what was coming next.

As she lifted her lower body from his face, his lips red and dripping now, he licked them lubriciously, staring eagerly at her, knowing that she was deciding whether to let him come or not. If he had begged for it, she would, capriciously, have denied him; but his big cock butted against her buttocks, and she couldn't resist it.

She wouldn't untie him, though. She loved him pinned down, squashed under her. Loved how powerless he was, even when his cock was inside her. Sliding back, she rose and then sank onto him expertly, driving him right up inside her with a single stroke.

'That's right, you whore!' she said gleefully. 'I'm going to ride you for a long time, and don't you dare come before I'm ready – or I'll paddle your balls so you won't sit down for weeks!'

Threats made Marcos even harder; she felt him swell inside her, his girth thickening. For a slim boy, he was hung like a horse: The Uruguayan bitch had been livid when he had left her for Dasha. *But she spoiled him, and that's not what he really wants. Treat 'em mean, keep 'em keen,* she thought complacently, settling in for a long canter: reaching behind her for one of the poles of the four-poster bed, she ripped off the tasselled tie that was holding the curtain looped artistically around it. Leaning forward, groaning in pleasure as his big, thick cock hit a different angle inside her with the movement, she slid one huge tassel under his neck and grabbed it as it emerged on the other side. One end in each hand, the wide chintz strip of fabric running behind his head, it was an improvised set of reins.

'Giddy up!' she said, beginning to lift and sink her hips in a rhythmic, riding movement, dragging the halter taut, forcing Marcos's head up uncomfortably; the muscles in his slender arms strained against their restraints, his narrow hips jerking up to meet Dasha's pounding buttocks. 'Giddy up, little pony!'

Her huge breasts were bouncing with every rise and fall, the sight of them, still in their red lace bra, low-cut to show almost half of their melon-round swell, exciting her even more; they were perfectly symmetrical. Dr Nassri had done a truly excellent job with her boob enlargement. A laugh escaped her as she remembered him, caught out watching himself coming over her, turned on by the sight of the boobs he'd just made.

I got the last laugh, didn't I, Hassan? The thought of the events of that day – of how she had screwed over three men, one after the other – of how she had got exactly what she'd wanted, what she'd planned for – sent her into the first of many rich, blinding orgasms. *Just like the old days – no, even better! In the old days I had to sneak around to get properly fucked, do it behind Grigor's back – and in Russia, they don't have boys like this one, sleek little South American sluts with clever mouths and lovely smooth bodies—*

She looked down at Marcos, whose eyes were shut in concentration now as he tried to last, tried not to let his cock explode inside her until she told him to. He was absolutely beautiful, his lashes long and silky, his skin velvety-soft. She'd definitely keep him around for another few years. A good cock was hard enough to find, as were the deliciously masochistic tendencies that meant that Marcos, though protesting, secretly adored Dasha's rough treatment of him. She remembered the cock and ball torture she'd inflicted on him a few days ago, how she'd made him cry, beautiful tears pouring down his pretty cheeks even as his cock throbbed bigger and bigger with every spank, and the memory made her come yet again, her pussy contracting around him; she leant over, pulling on his reins, and pinched one of his nipples till he screamed.

'Yes, scream, little pony!' she yelled happily. 'You dirty little bastard!'

Dasha was on top of the world. Everything was exactly how she wanted it. In a few days, Grigor would be dead, and she would inherit all their possessions: she would control everything they had built together.

Why didn't I think of this before? Why didn't I have Grigor taken out years ago?

The picture of a life where she ran their business interests much more ruthlessly than Grigor had done was a huge, heady rush. Retirement hadn't suited her. Torturing one Brazilian toy boy was no substitute for the kind of major-league sadism in which Dasha had indulged before retiring to Monaco.

No one's going to know what's hit them! Dasha thought triumphantly. Taking both reins in one hand, she reached back with the other, grabbed Marcos's balls and twisted them hard.

'*Now* you can come, little pony!' she said, watching the expression on his face with relish, pain and pleasure fighting for dominance as he let go and shot his wad, her fingernails digging into his balls, the other hand still dragging on the reins, holding his head up at an awkward angle.

Control. It's what I live for.

And the first thing I'll do when I get full control is have that hitman killed. He's much too dangerous to leave on the loose.

The thought of ordering first the murder of her husband, and then the man who'd killed him, gave Dasha such a rush of excitement that, as Marcos's hot sperm flooded up inside her, she ground her hips down viciously on his spasming cock, forcing it into an awkward angle, making him squeal in distress even as he came. His cries of pain were music to her ears as she wrung out a last, shattering orgasm.

In fact, hearing him scream made her pleasure even more acute.

December 24th – Christmas Eve

Andy

'Merry-nearly-Christmas!' Andy carolled with a big smile as the door of apartment 3512 swung open to reveal a bewildered-looking Mrs Takahashi. Small, plump and with her skin as pale as lightening serums could make it, Mrs Takahashi was like a Japanese version of Imelda Marcos, her hair black, shiny and rolled back from her scalp to give her extra height, dressed in Burberry and Hermès, her pumps classic Ferragamos.

She peered at Andy nervously, confused by the chrome luggage cart beside him. It was stacked high, not with the Vuitton trunk cases favoured by the Limehouse Reach residents, but with evergreen wreaths woven with shiny red and white baubles and bells. Andy bent over to pick one up, jingling it happily in Mrs Takahashi's face, a delicious odour of pine needles issuing forth as he did so.

'Would you like a wreath to hang on your door?' he asked. 'Or some mistletoe?' He gestured to the cart, at a smaller pile of delicate green branches laden with white berries and tied with red ribbons. 'That's for kissing under!'

He grabbed one in his other hand, pursed his full, plummy lips, held it over his head and blew a kiss at Mrs Takahashi.

'You can kiss the mister under it!' he suggested. 'Have a bit of a romantic evening when the kids are in bed, eh?'

'I no understand,' Mrs Takahashi said, her dark eyes wide with a mixture of confusion and fear, backing away from the door. Over her shoulder, she called to her husband in a rapid stream of Japanese; he appeared from the living room, a tumbler of whisky in his hand.

'Ah, yes! *Konichi-wa!*' Mr Takahashi took in the sight of Andy, dapper in his burgundy gabardine uniform jacket and trousers, the Nehru-collared black shirt underneath. 'Merry Christmas! Very nice,' he said, nodding at the wreath and mistletoe in the concierge's hands. 'Very happy.'

'Exactly, Mr Takahashi! Merry Christmas!' Andy jingled the wreath again. 'This is a present from Mr Khalovsky, up in the top-floor penthouse. He's got me to bring them round to all the residents, give a bit of Christmas spirit to the building. He sponsored all the decorations on the tree in the lobby – did you see, we have a theme going? *The Nutcracker!* And all the lovely new lights, that's Mr K too. Very generous, isn't he?'

He beamed, his handsome face gleaming like a polished chestnut. Mrs Takahashi, whose English was limited, looked anxiously up at her husband, asking him, in another stream of Japanese, what on earth Andy was saying: but Mr Takahashi was too deeply impressed by the mention of Grigor Khalovsky to answer his wife.

'Khalovsky-san?' he repeated, his own eyes widening as he pronounced the name of the billionaire oligarch. 'Oh! That is very kind,' he said, bowing deeply in homage to Grigor's wealth and status. 'Very thoughtful of Mr Khalovsky. We must return this kindness with a suitable gift.'

He turned to his wife and let off another stream of rapid-fire Japanese. As she took in the information that they were not being stalked by an over-enthusiastic, Christmas-obsessed concierge, but given a present by the richest, most influential owner out of all the multimillionaires in Limehouse Reach, she relaxed visibly. Her peach-lipsticked mouth broke into a careful smile, and her manicured hands, the peach varnish matching the lipstick exactly, pressed together on her thighs as she bowed too, both her and her husband's bodies lowering at a precise thirty-degree angle.

'Most kind, most thoughtful!' Mr Takahashi said again, taking the wreath from Andy with a nod and then, all too obviously, at a loss as to what to do with it, staring at the concierge in bafflement. 'We hang it on the wall, perhaps?'

'On the front door,' Andy said eagerly. 'If you'll allow me—'

Andy reached out to take the wreath back and then turned towards an uncomprehending Mrs Takahashi, who was between him and the door. Her panic returned as she saw the large evergreen arrangement coming towards her face. Holding up her hand to her neck, she yelped and dodged away, babbling something and shaking her head vigorously; her husband barked back at her just as fast, and then turned to Andy, who had frozen in place, holding up the wreath.

'She thinks you want to put it over her head! Like a necklace!' Mr Takahashi said, very amused. 'I explain to her that no, it is not for that!'

Mrs Takahashi, watching Andy hang the wreath on the door, hooking its ribbon loop over the door number, nodded enthusiastically, mostly with relief.

'Very nice!' she said, clapping. 'Very nice on door!'

'And the mistletoe . . .' Andy held it up. 'May I come in for a moment? It really needs to be hung up inside.'

'Please! Come in!' Mr Takahashi backed into the apartment, his wife following. It was a duplex, large and sprawling, with multiple balconies, and through the living room, on the balcony that led off the high mezzanine, could just be seen a thin, black-haired figure, sprawling on a lounger, seemingly oblivious to the cold, headphones on, tapping away at a handheld games device. The apartment was beautifully decorated with heavy, imposing dark red and black lacquer furniture and a staggering array of built-in electronic and digital devices: Mr Takahashi was the director of a firm specialising in violently expensive cutting-edge

audio-visual equipment, and had kitted out his London apartment with every possible mod con.

'Have you got somewhere that I could maybe . . .' Andy
held the mistletoe even higher, over his head. He looked at
Mrs Takahashi, who was now relaxed and smiling, and decided
not to rattle her again by miming a kiss. 'Um, you need to be
able to stand under it,' he explained.

Mr Takahashi tilted his head back and turned in a slow
circle, looking up.

'No, not turn around—' Andy began. 'Just stand underneath—'

But Mr Takahashi wasn't listening. Dashing over to the
lacquered coffee table, he picked up an iPad and pressed a
couple of buttons. On the mezzanine balcony, the thin figure
jerked as if it had been Tasered, dragged off its huge headphones and spun to glare viciously down at the occupants of
the living room. Mr Takahashi waved his arms, signalling that
the figure should come down; dramatically throwing the headphones onto the lounger, its shoulders slouching, the figure
slumped over to the sliding glass doors, pushing them open
and pointedly not closing them again, the cold air pouring in.
Mrs Takahashi remonstrated, and, with a theatrical sigh, the
figure made a gigantic production of shutting the doors before
it thunked, on its customised DM boots, along the mezzanine
and down the superbly constructed staircase, a series of floating, translucent glass treads that seemed to hang in the air with
barely any visible means of support.

It was revealed to be a male teenager in a tight black sweater
and equally tight grey jeans, so skinny that his legs didn't meet
at any point, not even at the very top. His straight dark hair
hung over his face, his shoulders hung over his ribs. He
mumbled something resentfully in Japanese, to which his
parents both responded sharply.

'Hi, Haruki,' Andy said cheerfully.

'It's Hari,' the boy mumbled in a perfect English accent. 'I
prefer Hari, okay?'

'Great!' Andy hadn't become a successful concierge by adopting anything but a relentlessly positive attitude. 'So, Hari, are you going to help us decide where to hang the mistletoe?'

Hari looked at the mistletoe, rolled his eyes and heaved the world-weary sigh of a vampire who had been alive for hundreds of years and was utterly sick of pathetically enthusiastic humans.

'Yes,' Mr Takahashi said bravely. 'I think we do it as a family. Christmas is for families.'

He glared at Hari, who ducked his head so the hair completely obscured his face.

'You'd *really* get on with Mr K,' Andy observed. 'Honestly, I've been going round the building asking people if they want wreaths and mistletoe – there's barely anyone here anyway, but most of 'em don't even care at all!' He sighed, momentarily disheartened.

'Cool! Who are they? Can I go and hang out with them?' Hari said sarcastically through his hair-veil.

His father hissed a reproach at him as Andy said quickly:

'Oh, teenagers! It's just a phase, Mr Takahashi.'

'In Japan,' Mr Takahashi said coldly, 'we do not have *phases*.'

Mrs Takahashi, tripping to Hari's side, took hold of his hair with both hands and opened it up as if she were drawing back a curtain.

'Handsome!' she said to Andy. 'Look, he is handsome boy! Why he hide handsome face?'

Hari writhed in agony, as if he really were a vampire and his mother, in exposing his face to the light, was scorching the exposed skin. Andy was still holding up the mistletoe, a big, professional smile fixed to his face; he waggled the mistletoe at the Takahashi family like a nanny trying to distract squabbling children with a toy.

'Pretty white berries!' he said. 'Look, they're nice and shiny! Poisonous, though. You'd never think it, would you?'

'Poisonous? Brilliant! How many do I have to eat?' Hari asked, perking up.

Mr Takahashi snapped something furious at his son. Mrs Takahashi backed away as Hari looked at the mistletoe and executed a contemptuous shrug that rippled up and down his body, every inch of his thin frame expressing utter disdain. Grabbing the iPad from his father's hand, he tapped in a command; a speaker high in the ceiling floated down slowly, suspended from a steel wire so fine it was nearly invisible. When it was just within reach, Hari tapped again, shoved the iPad back to his father, snatched the mistletoe from Andy, and twisted the ribbon loop around the wire so that the green branch dangled prettily just below the speaker.

'Very nice!' his mother said, clapping again.

'It's for kissing under,' Andy explained. 'On New Year's Eve, or whenever you feel like it. Your mum and dad could kiss under it right now!' he added to Hari, always the optimist.

An expression of utter and complete revulsion flooded across Hari's face, his nose wrinkling up in loathing.

'God, I really will eat those berries if I catch them doing that,' he muttered. 'If I don't sick them all up straight away just at the *thought* of them snogging. That's *beyond* gross.'

Turning away, he slumped back off upstairs, the hardware on his boots clicking as he went. Mr and Mrs Takahashi looked equally taken aback at the thought.

'We do *not* kiss now,' Mr Takahashi said firmly.

'No,' Andy sighed. 'Well, maybe for New Year's?'

It was obvious that Mr Takahashi was holding himself very still in an effort not to shake his head furiously in denial.

'I'll be off, then,' Andy said. 'I've got Prince Al-Qarashi in the opposite apartment to yours.' This was proving to be a hard day, trying bravely to bring cheer to a handful of people who didn't seem to care about the holidays one way or the other. He grimaced.

'Oh dear . . . I don't suppose he'll be that much into Christmas either . . .'

Jon

Am I going to have to tell Grigor Khalovsky that his wife's plotting to kill him?

Jon was lying on his bed, which was made, as always, with military precision, the pillows perfectly lined up parallel to the mattress, the duvet draped in the exact centre of the bed, the top sheet folded over the edge of the duvet so neatly that you could have measured the margin on each side with a ruler and obtained exactly the same reading. His arms were folded behind his head, a posture that made his triceps bulge out so impressively that Aniela would have gone dizzy if she saw them. He was ostensibly staring at his blurry reflection in the floor-to-ceiling glass windows, a smudgy head rendered in purple and green and pink, like a portrait by Francis Bacon.

Beyond it soared some of the tallest buildings in London, silvery steel monuments to money and power, topped by pyramids, sliced at dramatic angles, the slender, elegant Pan Pacific towers nestled together, the Citigroup red umbrella adding a whimsical touch high up among the big square behemoths. Jon could appreciate their architecture, the effort and risk and sheer hard work that had gone into their construction: but he had already spent way too much time in cities, and if he never visited another one after he left London, he would be perfectly happy.

Could I duck out? I can't leave the island, but could I maybe head up to Scotland, over to Wales, camp out in some shack away from civilisation till my face recovers? I don't need any more medical check-ups, I'm healing fine. Hell, I've been through much worse in the field. I once had to dig a bullet out of my own shoulder with a Swiss Army knife.

But getting anywhere out-of-the-way, with my face like this – how the hell am I going to manage that? Plus, the smaller the place I end up in, the more the locals will gossip. Because it'll be a month, at least, before I can travel somewhere I need to use a passport. This face is going to make me way too conspicuous anywhere I go.

Shit. But if I stay here, I'm caught between a rock and a hard place. If I tell Grigor Khalovsky his wife's out for blood, how will he react? He might try to take me out straight away, or he might believe me and kill her. Or both. It's the definition of high-risk. I need to figure out how he's going to react before I pull a stunt like that. And how do I get to know a Russian oligarch with more bodyguards than God has angels?

In the movies, Jon thought in wry amusement, he'd fake an attack on Grigor's life and then, dashingly, swing in on a rope or ride in on a motorbike to carry him to safety at the last possible moment, thus earning his trust; Grigor would throw his arms around Jon, declare eternal friendship and tell him all his secrets in the space of a few days. *Which is why I don't go to the movies*, Jon reflected.

He swung his legs off the bed and walked through into the ensuite bathroom, a beautiful piece of modern design that was entirely wasted on Jon. The white free-standing Agape Spoon bath with its simple, elegant lines, the Antonio Lupi bowl sink on its polished wood base, and the wall-hung toilet, were cutting-edge, but Jon neither noticed nor cared. The under-heated natural stone floor was pleasantly warm beneath his bare feet, but it was a completely unnecessary luxury as far as he was concerned. The toiletries with which the Four Seasons had stocked the apartment were L'Occitane's finest: and all he registered about them was that they did their job and didn't leave him feeling itchy.

He stared at himself in the silvered-glass mirror. For the first time, it occurred to him to wonder what he might look like when the bruising and puffing from the surgery faded. Gingerly, he reached up to touch his cheekbones; originally, they had been high, craggy ledges. He'd inherited a square, impassive, Easter Island face from the legacy of his Anglo-Scottish ancestors, who immigrated from the poverty-stricken Borders in the eighteenth century, but he'd always thought those cheekbones might have come from some Cherokee ancestor; the Cherokee tribe was still to be found in the Appalachian hills. *Though Mac knocked me across the room when I speculated about it. Kept my mouth shut about that ever since.*

The easiest way to change a face was to take away rather than to add. In his two major reconstructive surgeries, Jon's features had had their edges softened quite a bit. His jaw was still square, but, running his fingers around it, he could tell that it jutted out less than it used to. His cheekbones felt less prominent, less wide, and though his nose was still too sore to touch, he knew it would be shorter and straighter. His ears had been reshaped, some of the cartilage cut off, and they had been pinned back to lie flatter to his head.

I'm all tidied up. All the rough edges have gone. Once the swelling and bruising fade, I might even be good-looking. Have the kind of face a woman might like.

A question popped straight into his mind.

Aniela. Will I have the kind of face Aniela might like?

Taken aback, Jon swung away from the mirror, striding out and into the second bedroom, which he was using as his gym; his hand weights, his chin-up bar, and the mat he used for meditation were neatly arranged inside. Bending his legs, he sank smoothly into a cross-legged pose without needing to use his hands at all, and slid one leg over the other into the full lotus position. He stared ahead at the blank white wall, picturing a small black dot in his mind, then imagining it shrinking to nothing, disappearing into the white background, taking his conscious mind with it, his thoughts of Aniela, his memories of kissing her yesterday, how good she'd felt in his arms—

Shit. This isn't working.

Aniela had come by that morning, prompt to the minute, as she always was: he'd barely been able to meet her eyes, too embarrassed by the events of yesterday, his epic failure to kiss her properly without screwing up. And she'd been embarrassed for him; that had been clear by the way she barely glanced at his scalp for thirty seconds before muttering that it looked fine, grabbing her bag, and shooting out the door again. He'd prepared an apology, an attempt to smooth things over, but at the sight of her all words had fled, and he'd hardly been able to mumble hello and goodbye.

He pounded one fist into the palm of the other. Regular exercise and meditation techniques usually succeeded in banishing any unnecessary thoughts from his mind; yesterday he'd been in such shock after the kiss, so embarrassed by his own awkward failure – that moment when he accidentally ground his teeth against hers – that he'd thrown himself straight into a workout so rigorous that it had left him thoroughly exhausted, his brain temporarily wiped clean of sexual tension. But his dreams had been not only restless, he had woken that morning to find, to his mortification, that they had been even more eventful than he realised; there had been a wet patch on his pyjama bottoms which had leaked through onto the sheet.

I need a woman, he thought, setting his jaw. *I've got to get laid soon – hell, I'd call one in here right now if it weren't for having my face this messed-up. Even the priciest prostitute would run away at the thought of having to fuck a man in this state.*

Besides, the fewer people who see me the better.

Jon had never had a real relationship with a woman; sure, he'd had some teenage fumbling with girls, but after he joined the Army, and was whisked promptly away for black squad training, all his sexual experiences had been bought and paid for. Not only had he never missed what he had never had – his parents' marriage was so hellish it didn't exactly make him want to recreate it – paying women for sex had positively been encouraged by the Unit. The last thing they'd wanted was their killers forming attachments that might make them sloppy and distracted, or less available for shooting off on assignments at a moment's notice and staying away for weeks, even months on end.

So prostitutes had always seemed the safest way to go: a clean transaction where no one was emotionally involved. The Unit had the necessary contacts, madams who'd send over pleasant, friendly girls, regularly tested, voluntary sex workers, no poor junkies or trafficking victims. The entire process was as clean and straightforward as it could possibly have been, and since it was all that Jon had ever known, he'd never wanted anything beyond it.

But those girls were all too skinny, he thought now. *A man wants something he can take hold of, a woman with real curves. Someone to cuddle, to keep you warm at night*. The type Jon liked, the woman his eyes were drawn to, was strong, sturdy, fair-haired, blue-eyed; the kind of girl he'd grown up with, broad-shouldered and full-figured. You didn't see women like that on billboards, selling clothes, and he'd never really understood why; the skinny girls in the ads he saw were pretty enough, but looked more like boys.

Well, Aniela most definitely didn't look like a boy. For a dizzying, tempting second, he imagined offering her money for sex; he could afford to give her as much as she asked for, way more than she made on a nurse's salary. The mere thought of having sex with Aniela was enough to get him hard; his cock was already stiff with excitement, pushing eagerly against the white cotton of his boxer briefs, its head clearly outlined even through the grey marl sweatpants.

Go away, he said to it. *You came already last night, I had to wash the damn sheet. You're like a horny teenager, getting a boner every time you even think about a girl. Have some self-control.*

But his right hand was already sliding down, stroking the head of his hard cock through the sweatpants; it jerked impatiently, too rigid to be teased, demanding a firm hand wrapped around it then and there. He spat on his hand, standing up, dragging down and kicking off his sweatpants; his cock had half-found the slit in his boxers already, was nudging itself through, pink and swollen and insistent; stepping over the puddle of his discarded sweats, he took a couple of long strides across the room, his cock bobbing in the air, thick and full. He made it wait till he reached the bathroom, determined to exercise at least a modicum of authority, but when his hand finally closed around his shaft, it was pointless to deny that his cock was now completely in charge.

His eyes closed, and he heard himself groan loudly, hopelessly, as if it were someone else's hand twisting around his dick, pulling and sliding, fast, slow, then, almost immediately, faster and faster. He couldn't wait, he couldn't do anything but let go completely; frantically, he spat on his other hand and gripped the base of the shaft, cupping his balls, feeling his eyeballs roll right back into his skull with sheer pleasure. His dick was swelling even more, pumping and jerking against his palm, and he couldn't fight it any longer. He slumped forwards against the sink, feeling as if his entire body were concentrated in his dick and balls, all the energy flowing like an arrow between his legs, building up, building up to an explosion, his physical need so insistent that the pressure was painful, desperate, driving . . .

And it was Aniela's face he saw as the arrow raced towards the target: Aniela's wide-set eyes, her soft lips, her naked body, her arms around him, her mouth on his as he slid his cock inside her and heard her moan with pleasure against his lips and – *Jesus God, I've never come so hard in my entire fucking life!*

The hot come shot out of him like a geyser, the delicate skin of his head so sensitive now that the sperm felt scalding, burning, a spray of pent-up desire that spattered with fury against the bowl of the sink, a cloudy, translucent white stream.

Jon's body felt limp, completely drained, like an empty tube. Both of his hands were covered with his own semen. *Genesis, 38:9,* he thought crazily, the image popping into his mind of a Sunday-school teacher lecturing a bunch of small kids about the sin of Onan; *he spilled his seed on the ground,* the teacher had thundered, whacking the desk with her fist to make the point. *Which was a sin! God hates waste! God killed Onan 'cause he was wasteful, you hear me, children? Don't you go wasting what God gave you, 'cause the Bible tells us it ain't right!*

He reached out to turn on the tap, wash his hands, as exhausted as if he'd done a twenty-K run with a fifty-pound backpack strapped to his shoulders.

Be nice not to waste it any more, he found himself thinking. *Be nice to come inside a warm woman's body, then maybe curl up and go to sleep spooning her. Never did that before. Bet it feels real good. Nice and cosy.*

Prostitutes charged a hell of a lot of money to stay the night, and though Jon could afford it, it had always seemed way too much to pay a woman just so's she'd sleep next to you. *What would it be like to sleep next to Aniela? Would she even want to? If I made a move on her again, what would she do?*

If I offered her money, one thing's for sure – she'd want to haul off and slap my face. Only she couldn't slap me, on account of how I'm all bruised up. That'd probably drive her crazy.

He found himself smiling at the picture, of Aniela outraged at his offering her money to sleep with him, though he couldn't really have said why; he supposed he liked the idea of ruffling her feathers. He imagined her putting her hands on her hips, lecturing him, her expression stern, and for some reason he found himself smiling even more.

Drying himself with the hand towel, Jon tucked his satisfied cock back into his boxers, and padded back into his bedroom, throwing himself down on the mattress. It was insanely comfortable, yielding but still firm, the closest thing to bed perfection he'd ever slept on, with its moulded mattress topper and feather-and-down pillows. *Like that Heavenly Bed they have at the Westin hotels,* he thought, his eyes closing. *Maybe I'll get one of those for the ranch. You can buy it all online – the mattress with that nice soft pillow-top, all the pillows and duvet and blankets. Real cosy.*

Jon never slept during the day. He hadn't planned to now; he didn't even realise that he was dropping off, and he didn't realise, either, that as he rolled over, already half-asleep, kicking his legs under the duvet for warmth, he had pulled down a pillow into his arms. And by the time he was breathing the slow, heavy inhales and exhales of deep sleep, every muscle in his body completely relaxed, his body was curled around the pillow, and he was spooning it in utter contentment.

Melody

*I*t looked as if a Christmas shop had exploded inside the lobby of Limehouse Reach. The Harrods of Christmas shops – Harrods, so beloved by the rich Russians and Japanese and Arabs and Italians who came to London for the shopping, vulgar beyond belief with its Egyptian escalator, its gigantic, gold-painted Sphinxes and carvings depicting a journey down the Nile to the Valley of the Kings, and its larger-than-life-size bronze sculpture of Princess Diana and her lover Dodi Fayed dancing like nymphs, Dodi's shirt unbuttoned and hanging open, Diana wearing what looked like a clingy nightdress. They were holding up a huge albatross which, for some reason never quite explained, they were releasing into the sky.

Even with Grigor and Andy's best efforts, the lobby couldn't boast anything quite as jaw-droppingly tacky as a Diana and Dodi bronze statue. But the elegant restraint with which it had been designed had completely vanished, obscured by an avalanche of the biggest, shiniest Christmas decorations Grigor's money could buy. Enormous, gilded, blown-glass ornaments hung from every light fixture. Swags of fairy lights were draped around the entire atrium, dangling down the glass walls in icicle formations, hanging in great swaths from both desks. The white orchids in black rectangular vases, which usually stood on the concierge and doorman's desks, had been replaced by huge, blowsy red poinsettias. Andy had bought oversized clear glass vases and filled them with bright, faceted, red and green baubles, setting them next to the poinsettias, where they caught every reflection and bounced it back like disco balls reflecting thousands of flickering points of light.

The enormous tree was now so thickly hung with even more fairy lights that, as soon as she stepped out of the lift, Melody had to raise a hand to shade her eyes while looking at it. There were so many, they were so bright, that they obscured the ornamental figurines that Andy had suspended from the branches – china ballet shoes, toy soldiers, sugar plums; on the top of the tree was a huge Sugar Plum Fairy in arabesque, from the *Nutcracker* ballet, holding a wand whose tip twinkled brightly. The real presents for Grigor's party were safely tucked away behind lock and key, but Andy had wrapped cardboard boxes in bright gold paper and twirls of ribbon and piled them around the base of the tree to look like oversized gifts. Night had fallen, it was past ten, and the dark sky above the glass roof of the atrium was a velvet-black background to the twinkling, glittering, flashing, multicoloured fairy lights below.

Even the piped music playing in the public areas – normally a tasteful loop of calming selections from Debussy, Bach and Mozart, pruned of any crashing chords or over-enthusiastic high notes – was a Christmas medley. As Melody stared around the transformed, lit-up, shiny lobby in disbelief and wonder, she realised that she was humming along with 'Let It Snow'.

'Your cab's waiting, Miss Brown,' Derek, the doorman, said, using the pseudonym under which the Canary Clinic had booked Melody into Limehouse Reach. 'Is there anything else I can help you with?'

'No, thank you,' Melody said, darting as swiftly across the atrium as she could with her bandaged chest, her head ducked, a felt fedora pulled down to hide her blackened eyes, a soft wool snood wound across her chin and the lower part of her nose, to conceal the bruising and swelling. She couldn't help but stop in her tracks, however, as she passed the fountain and carp pond, and took in the fact that the silvered mosaic tiles of the floor were also scattered heavily with decorative green and red glass stones. Andy had spared no detail to make the lobby as Christmassy as Grigor's wildest dreams.

'Andy checked about putting stuff in the pond,' Derek said chattily as he walked around to hold the door for Melody; there were automatic sliding ones as well, but it was Limehouse Reach protocol that the 24/7 staff always held the door for guests and visitors. 'They won't bother the carp, Andy said. Look lovely, don't they? Very festive.'

'It's all very – shiny,' Melody managed as she pattered towards him on her soft-soled Uggs.

She had picked up the Ugg habit in LA, reluctantly at first, but by the time of the *Wonder Woman* shoot, wearing them had been second nature. You saw photos of actresses on set, between takes, or popping out to run errands, and mocked their ubiquitous, ugly, squishy-soft footwear. But when you had spent the day running and jumping and kicking people in Wonder Woman's tight gold boots, and evenings tripping out of Katsuya or Boa, smiling for the paparazzi, wearing the five-inch heels your stylist insisted upon, you practically cried tears of gratitude for the lovely soft welcoming sheepskin of the Uggs caressing your toes deliciously. Who cared if they didn't give your feet or ankles any support? You were working out like a maniac, starving yourself to stay super-slim, living off skinny lattes and diet bars – you deserved *some* sort of comfort in your life . . .

The rest of her outfit was also perfectly off-duty, trendy young actress from head to toe. Soft grey leggings tucked into the black Uggs, layered T-shirts and a striped grey-and-black oversized angora sweater, topped by a trendy tweed cape. Even the hat and snood over the top looked dashing; if she'd been snapped by paps the photo would have made it easily into *Grazia*'s Style Hunter section.

Apart, of course, from her damaged face.

The cabbie jumped out as soon as he saw his passenger emerge from the building, coming round to open the door. This was much more courteous than most London black cab drivers nowadays, who neither opened doors, helped people in with their luggage, nor spoke to them beyond grunting in disdain when given the address; but not only were Limehouse Reach customers rich foreigners who tipped generously, the doormen were eagle-eyed and wouldn't call a cab company again if they spotted its drivers behaving with any less than perfectly respectful demeanour.

'Where to, miss?' he asked, as Melody settled into the back seat, wrapping her cape around her.

She gave him the address, and he nodded, setting the cab in motion without another word. Again, this was very unusual, a black cab driver who knew how to get to his destination without complaining about the state of the roads, but Melody was in much too heightened a state of nerves and excitement to notice. All her attention, all her anticipation, was focused entirely on her destination. As the cab followed the curve of the road around Limehouse Reach, skirting the edge of the river, she saw a brightly lit boat gliding down the black sweep of the Thames. It was a dinner cruise, heading for the Thames Barrier, people on board laughing and toasting each other over their meals, celebrating Christmas Eve.

Melody stared at the boat with a mixture of wistfulness and envy. She knew that surely, aboard the pleasure cruiser, there must be some unhappy travellers: couples who had been fighting before they left the house, and were still simmering with resentment as they raised their champagne glasses with bright fake smiles; singles, staring at those couples and wishing that they were part of one too, not realising that the relationship they were envying was on its last legs; people frightened of getting old, to whom the end of the year meant a step closer to the grave; immigrants far from home, working on a dinner cruise on Christmas Eve, watching other people laugh and party while they themselves faced a Christmas Day in a bedsit, eating a ready meal, Skype-ing their loved ones hundreds of miles away.

Not everyone on that boat is happy. Not everyone is having a wonderful Christmas.

Melody repeated those words to herself as the boat slid away from view, the cab turning away from the river, heading towards Commercial Road. It was only very recently that Melody had learned this lesson, that not everything was as golden and enchanted as a fairy tale. Because, up until nine months ago, her life had been as blessed as if a fairy godmother had given her everything she could wish for. She was beautiful, gifted, with a sweet, cheerful nature, and she had been loved and wanted from the moment of her birth. One of the main reasons that her relationship with James had been so instantly wonderful, and had continued in such happiness, was that Melody had such a warm, close family.

She had learned to trust, to flourish, to give and receive love, and to expect it easily from others; she had the kind of happy, open nature that meant that she would be attracted to a man like her, one who came from the same caring, affectionate background as her own. Melody had never previously walked past a house in the evening with its lights on, cosy and golden, looked inside to see a group of people eating dinner or having a party, and yearned to be part of them. She had always known where she belonged, that she was loved. It was only when she had gone to LA, and found herself alone, surrounded by people who said they wanted the best for her but actually were only interested in how much money they could make by selling her image, that her bubble had been burst.

No self-pity, Melody, she told herself firmly now. *And no blaming other people. You made your own mistakes. You brought your trouble down on your own head.*

But now, hopefully, you're on the road to changing all that. Getting James back, being cast as Beatrice, having your old face and body again . . .

Melody's lips curved into a smile, even though it hurt her lips.

Just a tiny little list, she thought, amused at herself. *No major New Year's resolutions or anything. Just getting my entire life back, that's all . . .*

The cab had turned right on Commercial Road now, and was heading into very familiar territory. Shoreditch, Spital-fields, Bethnal Green, the most fashionable couple of square miles in London, where she had hung out all the time at RADA, and moved to as soon as they could afford it. They were, of course, members of Shoreditch House, the private club that was Soho House's hipper younger offshoot. Melody had spent long happy summer days lying by the rooftop pool in a Miu Miu bikini, sipping chilled rosé, hanging out with the Corset Crew and their stylist and photographer friends; but much more important to her than the access to the private club, the about-to-be-really-famous names surrounding them, had been looking up and seeing James gazing at her with so much love that it warmed her even more than the sunshine on her body and the wine she was drinking.

That night he threw me in the pool with all my clothes on for a dare, and I pulled him in with me – we were soaking when we got out, laughing and laughing, and we ran home hand in hand, our shoes squelching, my New Balances squeaking so much it made us laugh even harder – and then we got home and didn't even stop to take off all our wet clothes, just fell on the bed and had the most amazing drunken sex . . . and when we woke up the mattress was all wet, because we'd passed out afterwards, and we had to pull it off the frame and lean it up on its side and it didn't dry for days . . .

Under the Overground, down Shoreditch High Street, onto Bethnal Green Road, and right down a little cut-off that led to one of the railway arches.

My God, we're here!

She leant forward and tapped urgently on the Plexiglas panel.

'Pull over!' she said urgently, not ready to drive right up in front of the house. 'Just park here!'

It was a little row of cottages, built to house the silk weavers who had flooded into the area in the early nineteenth century: trade had slipped, French silk had been imported in increasing quantities, and Shoreditch had become a slum. The inhabitants of London were in constant flux, ebbing and flowing, with the East End in particular a shore on which fast-moving tides of immigrants had landed, made some money, and left in their turn as the new rush of would-be Londoners moved in. The weavers had been Irish, driven to London by famine, or Huguenots forced out of France by religious persecution; they would have been unable to even process the information that their little cramped cottages were now worth over half a million pounds. Because, finally, after centuries, Shoreditch was a truly desirable destination, not just a way station for people working all hours to buy themselves a better life.

And a particularly desirable destination in this little street in Shoreditch, tonight, was the house that Melody had shared with James, and on whose mortgage her name still appeared. James had said that he'd make arrangements to take it over, that he'd been asked to shoot an ad for whisky in Japan that would bring in a decent wodge; he'd do that, use the money to pay off Melody's part of the deposit. The paperwork was being drawn up, the lawyers tasked to remove Melody from James's life. It was like a divorce.

But apparently, I'm not grieving at all! I had no idea I was throwing a party! she thought bleakly, staring at the bright square windows of the cottage in question, which looked so densely packed with party guests that it was about to burst. Even with the windows closed against the cold night air, the music was clearly audible: Christmas music, Wizzard singing about wishing it could be Christmas every day. She could hear people inside shouting out the words, laughing as they chanted them; it was very Shoreditch to simultaneously enjoy the song but also mock its cheesiness.

'Um, miss?' The cabbie was looking at her in the rear-view mirror. 'Are you going in or what?'

'No!' she said quickly. 'No, I'm not! Just . . . just wait here, okay?'

The cab had pulled up into a space a few doors down from the house, on the opposite side of the street. It gave Melody a clear view, not only of the front door, but the approach from Bethnal Green Road.

'Wait here?' he echoed.

'Yes! Just – turn the lights off, so no one comes over to see who's inside,' she said.

'I'll have to keep the heat on,' he pointed out. 'Or we'll freeze our knackers off. And the meter running.'

'Okay! Fine! Just *please* turn the lights off!' Melody pleaded, hearing footsteps coming down the street from behind the cab, the high heels and higher giggles that almost certainly meant incipient party guests. She was frantic to avoid detection, desperate that no one should see Melody Dale, her face messed up, huddled in a black cab, waiting outside what was technically still her own home.

Acting like a crazed stalker.

Just in time, the cab driver killed the lights, and Melody ducked against the frame of the cab as she realised how familiar the voices were. Felicity and Kathy, the former in a spectacular fur cape which swirled around her dramatically, the latter in a sensible duffel with the hood pulled up, tick-tocked past on their heels. Felicity was saying loudly:

'Good, it's already going strong! I *loathe* getting to a party too early and having to make dull conversation!'

'That's my favourite bit,' Kathy said wistfully. 'When you can actually hear yourself talk.'

'Oi, gels!' called a male voice behind them with a heavy Cockney accent. 'Give us a photo, eh? It's Felicity, ain't it? And Betty the maid!'

Shit. A paparazzo. Melody shrank even further down in her seat.

'Going to Dr Who's Christmas party, gels? Give us a nice photo on the doorstep!'

The voice was passing the cab now. Melody levered herself up a fraction, just enough to see a burly man in a bomber jacket and jeans catching up with Felicity and Kathy, who were ringing James's doorbell. The cottages were two-up, two-down, no entrance steps or basement areas, and when the door swung open James was clearly visible, light behind him but light on his face too from the streetlight in front of the house.

'James! *Darling!*' Felicity launched herself at him, the cape swinging, kissing him on both cheeks with huge enthusiasm. 'Sweetie, there's a pap out here, can we give him a photo?'

'Um—' James began unwillingly.

Melody knew him so well; he hated that paps knew where he lived, hated the business of posing when he wasn't on a red carpet or doing publicity. But he'd known, when he was offered the part of Dr Who, that he would have to accept this kind of intrusion into his private life as part of the territory. James was a gentleman: he'd made a bargain with fame, and he'd stand by it.

'Go on, mate!' the photographer said chummily. 'Won't take a sec!'

James was already putting one arm around Kathy as Felicity threw herself onto his chest and stared up at him adoringly. The flash snapped, a series of dazzling white flares against the yellow sodium streetlight, and Melody gazed longingly at her ex-boyfriend's handsome face, his long lean body, illuminated so clearly for those brief moments, his high-bridged nose and fair hair flopping over his forehead, his shy, adorable smile. Her hands ached to tear open the cab door, run out, drag Felicity off him, and wrap her own arms around his neck.

That was what I was hoping for. I must have been mad. I've been gearing myself up all day to work up the courage to come here – I had this fantasy that I'd find James all alone, sitting in front of the fire like we used to do, staring at the coals . . . missing me . . .

They'd had to buy small-sized furniture to fit in the dinky little cottage; a loveseat rather than a three-seater sofa, on which they'd curled up together, James constantly, jokingly complaining that his legs were too long to be comfortable, that he'd get a cramp. Melody had bought him a footstool last Christmas, a joke present which he'd actually loved.

I teased him – called him Grandpa, told him that now he had a stool to put his feet on, he'd want a pipe and slippers next – and he just smiled happily and said that sounded lovely, and maybe we could get a dog as well . . .

I should be grateful he's having a party. At least he isn't curled up in front of the fire right now with someone else in my place on the sofa, snuggling up to him, finding things to tease him about . . .

Tears were prickling at Melody's eyes, blurring her vision. Dimly, she saw that James was chivalrously standing to the side of the door, ushering the girls in before him, out of the cold; a cab chugged past hers and stopped in front of the cottage, and he waited for its occupant to pay the cabbie and step out.

'Oi-oi!' the paparazzo carolled, delighted, as the cab pulled away under the railway bridge, giving him a good view of the new arrival. 'It's Juliet! Give us a kiss, you two!'

Priya Radia was less obviously a fame-chaser than Felicity, but she knew perfectly well how to play the publicity game. Flicking her white padded By Malene Birger coat open with an expert tug that popped all the fastenings in one go, revealing an eye-catching peacock-print Mary Katrantzou dress whose acid turquoise, yellow and pink colours set off her warm cappuccino skin to perfection, she took James's hand, leaned towards him on her yellow and orange Kandee patent heels, and tilted up her brightly lipsticked mouth to him for a kiss.

Her thick, glossy black hair was piled on top of her head in a 1960s-style bun, her make-up perfect. She looked amazing.

James's head came down to hers. Their lips met. Priya slid one hand around his neck – the one on the opposite side to the photographer, of course, so that it wouldn't block his shot – and pulled him in for a deeper kiss as the flashes exploded one after the other, the paparazzo, unable to believe his luck, making the most of what would be a very lucrative photo.

'What about Melody, James?' he called bravely, after checking his monitor and making sure he'd got the shot. 'How are things with you two? She still in LA or what?'

James looked thunderstuck by the question, freezing in place. As he stood there, unable to say a word, the music playing inside flooded out into the street: Wham!'s 'Last Christmas', the lyrics feeling horribly appropriate to Melody. Last Christmas, Melody had had James's heart. And as George Michael asked his former lover if he recognised him, Melody felt the most enormous lump building up in her throat. If she stepped out of the cab now, if she ran over to James, would he recognise her? Or would he rear back in horror at the sight of the horribly bruised woman in front of him?

But Priya, who had stepped into the front hall, turned and gave the paparazzo a dazzling smile over her shoulder. She was still holding James's hand; as she pulled him inside with her, the paparazzo snapping away again, she called back:

'Melody who?'

It was the perfect exit line. The door swung shut behind Melody's ex-boyfriend and his new flame; the paparazzo propped his back against the streetlight, checking the monitor on his digital camera; and Melody, in a strangled whisper, said to the cabbie:

'I want to go back – take me back to Limehouse Reach, *now* . . .'

Collapsing onto the seat as the cab pulled away, doing her best not to burst into the raking sobs to which she was dying to give vent, she thought bitterly how true those words were.

It's too late to go back. Much too late. You've been a stupid fool, an idiot. You've thrown away everything you had. You're all alone, on Christmas Eve, watching your ex throw a party and a whole slew of gorgeous girls throw themselves at him. You're the crying woman in the back of the black cab driving around London like a drama queen. In a French film, my character would be beautiful. Eva Green with lots of black eyeliner, mysterious and haunting. But me – I'm in a brutally realistic, low-budget British movie, and I look like shit.

Melody raised her hands to her face. Her greatest fear was that her face would be lumpy or scarred after the surgery, that she would lose her livelihood as well as her lover. *All I'll be fit for if I don't recover properly will be going on* Celebrity Big Brother *with the rest of the drunks and misfits,* she thought wretchedly, winding herself up into an increasingly agitated state. *What else will I be able to do? I'll be a total laughing-stock! The* Wonder Woman *money's running out fast, with the surgery and the stay at Limehouse Reach – I've got some equity in the house, but I can't live off that either, I'll need to buy somewhere else to live . . .*

There was very little traffic on the road back to Canary Wharf on Christmas Eve. Almost everyone was home already, curled up happily with family and friends, and the cab made short work of the drive. Much too short for Melody's liking. It was warm and dark inside the taxi, the engine was ticking away with its loud, comforting rusty purr; she wasn't ready to get out, walk through the bright lobby of Limehouse Reach, a testament to Christmas cheer that was like a mocking reminder of everything she had lost . . .

'Keep on driving,' she said to the cabbie. 'Just for a little while more.'

'It's your money,' he said, shrugging; if a crazy rich woman who looked as if she'd been punched in the face wanted to drive round some of the nastier parts of the East End on Christmas Eve while she cried her eyes out, what did he care? He had nearly a full tank of petrol – he could take her to

Canvey Island and back if she wanted. This was a cabbie's dream fare. Instead of turning off East India Dock Road, he kept going down the A13, the cab chugging along past the Beckton sewage works, past Rainham Marshes. They were fully into Essex golf course territory by the time Melody, slumped into a tear-stained ball of misery, roused herself to look out of the window and panicked at the realisation that she had no idea where she was, alone in a cab with a strange man.

'Back,' she managed to say, her voice thick with tears. 'Back to where you picked me up.'

The road was absolutely empty, a strip of black macadam in the middle of the dark, cloudy night. Pulling a U-turn, the cab duly headed back to London, the high skyscrapers of Canary Wharf soon rising up, bright against the black horizon, their spires picked out in red and green and blue neon lighting, their outlines filled in with tiny white dots. As soon as she spotted the Four Seasons, lower than the other buildings and uplit in a wash of golden lights that puddled out onto the dull dark gleam of the Thames, Melody tapped on the glass.

'You can let me out here,' she said, clearing her throat, trying to sound a bit more in control. 'I'll walk the last bit.'

The fare was a hundred and forty pounds, and she added an extra ten; happy as the cabbie was at this Christmas gift, he rolled down the window and looked at her dubiously as she stepped out of the taxi.

'You ain't going to do anything stupid, love, are you?' he asked bluntly, his gaze passing over her battered, tear-stained face to the dark waters just visible round the side of the hotel.

'What?' Melody said blankly.

And then, realising what he meant, she felt her face suffuse with blood, embarrassed at how crazily she'd been acting. *I must seem like a basket case,* she thought.

'No – no, I'll be fine,' she muttered. 'I just want to walk a bit. Have some fresh air.'

Through the open window, she heard his radio: Chris Rea, singing about driving home for Christmas, and she turned away so that the cabbie wouldn't see her face crumple into misery yet again. It was such a simple song, by a totally unfashionable singer, but since she was a little girl, Melody had loved it: his raspy, lyrical voice, like toffee melting over rocks, the sweetness of the sentiment, the love and yearning to be home, to feel the nearness of the person he loved.

Home. That was with James, almost since I met him. My home was with James. But Mum and Dad, Ashley – that's my home too, and I miss them all so badly . . .

Melody hadn't told her family where she was or what she was doing over Christmas. They'd been desperate for her to come home, knowing that she'd broken up with James, wanting to have her back for the holidays; but Melody had been equally desperate to put back the clock, get back her old face, and she'd known that she couldn't tell them that she'd decided to get even more surgery. After the disastrous work she'd had done in LA, the exaggerated botch-job the surgeon had done on her face, her mother, in particular, would have an absolute panic; Melody could picture all too well the hysterics, the entreaties not to let anyone else mess with her lovely daughter, her mother bursting into tears on the phone, her father getting on the line to ask what was going on, his own horror at the news that Melody was having more elective surgery—

She shuddered at the mere thought as she walked down to the waterfront, taking the narrow public footpath that led between Limehouse Reach and the Four Seasons. It was almost completely dark, shadows thrown by the buildings even blacker than the night sky, but there was not a soul around, and Melody wasn't in the least afraid. It felt like nothing could scare her more than the sight of her own face in the mirror. The weight of solitude pressed down on her, dense as the shadows. And she found herself pulling her phone out of her pocket, scrolling through it and then, impatiently, cancelling that and hitting the dialler instead, her gloved hands slipping on the keypad. She had to drag one of her gloves off with her teeth so that she could input the number that she knew by heart.

The need to hear her parents' voices was rising inside her frantically, a need she'd buried for so long. There had been no one who loved her to accompany her as she went to Dr Nassri, sat through the necessary appointments to establish her psychological stability, that she wasn't suffering from Body Dysmorphic Disorder, the X-rays to determine exactly how the previous work had altered her bone structure, the pulling and prodding at her cheeks where her own fat had been used as a filler, to see where that had settled and if it could be removed evenly. No one to hold her hand as she went under the anaesthetic, no one there when she came to, groggy and disorientated and aching. No one to send her flowers or Get Well Soon cards.

And now, no one on the end of the phone. It rang and rang, on the hallway table, on the kitchen wall, in her parents' bedroom, until eventually a click signalled that it was switching to answerphone. She wished, desperately, to hear her mother's voice, but for security reasons Mr Dale was always the one to record the message, to make it clear there was a man in the house, and it was her father's cheerful baritone that now told her that everyone was out and asked her to leave a message.

It's Christmas Eve! she thought, realisation of what that meant sinking in. *They'll be in the pub, of course. How stupid am I, how out of touch, that I forgot where they always go on Christmas Eve, to the lock-in at the Stroud Arms . . .*

The village in the Cotswolds where the Dale family lived, Little Burghley, was by no means the smartest part of the area, and they much preferred it that way. The trendy actors and politicians and ex-guitarists from Blur had all chosen to settle in the prettier, more picturesque areas, not near the former industrial town of Stroud, which tourists tended to bypass. But the Dale family had no complaints. It was their home, and the fact that the village hadn't been flooded by trendy Londoners meant that it had, to the great satisfaction of them and all the other locals, stayed much the same as it had been for decades.

The Stroud Arms hadn't been stripped down like a ton of North or East London boozers, its carpets and dartboard removed and bare wooden tables and chairs installed, its menu gastropubbed to feature scallops, black pudding, and tomato salads called 'tomato carpaccio' and priced at seven pounds. It was still a cosy, wallpapered haven, with comfy old uphol- stered seats, equally old patterned fitted carpet, games machines, and Scampi Fries or Cheesy Moments sold in packets you pulled off a card hanging behind the bar. Every Christmas Eve, it threw a party for its regulars, with a carol singalong around the upright piano, a raffle for charity, and the local vicar sponsored, also for charity, to wear a costume voted on by the congregation to be as embarrassing as possible.

Last year the vicar had been Pippa Middleton at her sister's wedding, her bridesmaid's dress represented by a long white nightie borrowed from his wife. James had waltzed with him, to the revellers' great delight, and joined the carol singing with gusto. The inhabitants of Little Burghley had taken James to their hearts, followed his and Melody's careers, were genuinely proud of what they'd both achieved.

Melody, picturing the happy scene – James, fringe flopping, dipping a bearded 'Pippa' over the flashing lights of the pinball machine as everyone hooted and applauded – burst into tears again. Her hands were like ice now; she was ringing her moth- er's mobile, but either it had been left at home or the rowdiness in the Stroud Arms was much too far advanced by now for the ring tone to be heard.

The waterfront was completely deserted. Barely any lights were on in Limehouse Reach, and very few in the Four Seasons. No one who could help it was staying in a hotel in the business district on Christmas Eve, miles from any festive nightlife. Not a soul was around, not a single voice could be heard, not a boat passed on the river. Across the black waters of the Thames, the windows of the smaller houses of the new developments on the far bank, by contrast, were all illuminated, cosy, twinkling with tiny dots of colour from the Christmas lights.

To Melody, in floods of tears by now, those cosy little houses, unreachable, separated from her by the wide band of water, were a symbol of the domestic happiness she had lost. She propped her elbows on the railing, staring hopelessly at the distant houses, her head sinking onto her arms as she cried her heart out. She was a sweet, sensible, good-natured girl from a stable and loving family, but she had also chosen to pursue acting as a profession, and, as with most actors, there was a streak of drama in her that was never far from the surface. Right now, absolutely alone in the dark night, hearing the Thames lap at its pilings below her, she sank into an absolute low of self-pity, a black pit of misery and despair.

Her hands were icy, and the phone she was still clutching was beeping now, a mechanised voice saying that her call could not be completed and to try again later. She fumbled to turn it off and it slipped from her fingers, knocking against the railing and sliding right to the edge of the stone pavement, hanging half off the rim, overhanging the water. Melody ducked down and reached her arm through, trying to grab it, but her fingers were so cold that they couldn't close around the phone; worse, she actually pushed it a little further, tilting it perilously closer to dropping into the river and being lost for ever.

When she looked back on the events of that night, Melody found it almost impossible to believe what she had done next. It was the kind of idiotic thing that you did when you were drunk, or high, and thought you were invulnerable.

And even then, you would hope that you'd have friends with you who would pull you back, stop you the moment you swung up your leg and started to climb over the railing that was the only thing that separated you from the drop to the river beyond . . .

She was still fit and supple from all the intensive training that she had undergone for her stunts for *Wonder Woman*; it was the work of a moment for Melody to swing over the railing, land on the other side, and, holding onto the upright metal rail with one hand, lean out for the phone with the other. She was squatting down, and if she had been wearing trainers she might well have managed the whole manoeuvre safely enough.

But the Uggs were her downfall. Literally. As she reached out, extending one foot for balance, the lack of any support for her ankle meant that her foot turned, shooting out from under her, sending her flailing. Her outstretched leg kicked into the phone and sent it over the edge; a second later she heard the splash as it hit the water. She wailed in misery: the phone, at that moment, symbolised her last thread of connection to anyone who loved her. It was as if she had lost everything, every last contact, leaving her completely alone, out here in the dark, utterly isolated . . .

She was too busy sobbing to realise that the hand on the ice-cold metal rail was losing its grip. Her frozen fingers let go and she tumbled back, towards the edge, hitting the pavement with a smack that drove the breath out of her, her knee cracking into the stone, her legs falling over the lip of the bank, dangling dangerously down towards the water into which her mobile had already fallen. Melody flailed desperately, trying to pull herself back, kicking against the stone wall to try to get a purchase, but she only succeeded in detaching one of her Uggs with her frantic efforts; she heard it plummet down, land on the surface of the water with a soft, gentle plop, and knew that it was being absorbed slowly but surely, sucked down by the slow-moving tide.

The image made her even more frantic, panic still more, and, lifting her head, she let out what was supposed to be a full-blooded scream, but issued as a thin wail of terror, more like a seagull being strangled than anything that would alert anyone that she was in trouble. From the hips down, she was hanging over the edge, down towards the water. Her cape was caught under her, her hat was tipped over her eyes; she thrashed around, attempting desperately to grab hold of the vertical metal rail, to pull herself to safety, but the cape was tangled around her, trapping her arms by her sides, and the more she tried to free them, the more she slipped back. She could get no purchase on the smooth stone, and her legs seemed to be inexorably heavy, pulling her down, down to the black waters of the Thames.

It was low tide; if she fell, she would never be able to climb up again and she wouldn't survive for more than a minute in the cold water. The tweed fabric of her cape would saturate with water, pull her down – *like Ophelia*, she thought suddenly. Melody had played her for the RSC; she remembered very well the speech in which Gertrude described Ophelia's death. '*Long it could not be/ Till that her garments, heavy with their drink/ Pull'd the poor wretch from her melodious lay/ To muddy death.*' James had loved the phrase 'melodious lay', had quoted it to her again and again, because it sounded out her name.

But now, writhing frantically, trying to wrestle her arms out from the cape without sending herself down to the shock of the cold waters below, her fingers numb with cold, her breath gasping with terror and panic, all she could think of were the words 'muddy death'. Blood filled her mouth; she must have bitten her lip in the fall. *Soon it'll be water,* she thought, *water filling my mouth, my nose, my ears, my eyes. And then it'll be mud, when I wash up finally under a bridge, when they have to grapple my body with hooks off some stanchion. Will they be able to identify me? Will anyone report me missing? Will James even know that I'm dead?*

Oh God, if they do find me, if they work out when I disappeared, they might track down that cab driver – he thought I was going to do something stupid, he'll tell them I drowned myself, they'll think I committed suicide because I went to my old house and saw him kissing Priya . . . oh God, that would be so awful and humiliating and untrue . . .

This picture was so profoundly sad that Melody heard herself let out another thin stifled wail of utter hopelessness. In that moment, she felt herself sliding back a couple of inches further, the weight of her pelvis now tipping her towards the river, and she knew she was lost. This was it. She was going to die tonight, on Christmas Eve, drowned and swept away, with her body maybe never even found . . .

And then a sharp pain shot through both her shoulders. Something was gripping her, digging in, pinning her down to the paving stones and then dragging her forward, towards the railing. Two hands, grabbing her as best they could, strong fingers sinking into the fabric of the tweed cape, trying to get a purchase on the bones of her shoulders, to haul her by main force back to safety. Craning her head back, her vision half-hidden by the hat that had got jammed down over her eyes, Melody made out two big white blobs in front of her, *like giant marshmallows*, she thought, her vision blurry.

She was jerked further forward, her hip bones dragging along the stone, the cape's twist around her loosening enough so that she could wriggle her arms out a little, use her palms to press to the pavement and writhe closer to the rail, clawing her body along. One marshmallow and then the other stepped back, the hands gripping Melody's shoulders continuing to pull her forcefully back, the person above her breathing heavily with the effort. Melody's head nearly banged into the vertical rail; squirming up, she slid a hand along the stone, and closed it around the rail, the other hand rising up to grab the lower crossbar.

The metal was so cold it was like gripping onto blocks of ice. It took all the willpower Melody had to close her cramped hands around it and hold on. But she did. She held on for dear life. She was no Ophelia: she didn't want to drown poetically so that her ex-boyfriend would feel horribly guilty when he found out. She wanted to live, to get James back, to scrabble one knee under her, kicking away the folds of the bloody cape she was so stupidly wearing, and then to pull up the other leg, kneeling up now, to walk her hands up to the top of the railing, to haul herself up to her feet and, with the help of her saviour, who was still keeping a firm hold on her shoulders, to climb back over the railing once more and collapse, gasping with shock and disorientation, into Aniela's arms.

Aniela

'*M*elody?' Aniela said in disbelief, as the girl crumpled against her. She had assumed, initially, when she saw the figure beyond the railing, slipping down towards the Thames, that it was some poor homeless person, who had either fainted or was trying to kill themselves; she hadn't realised, when she ran over and grabbed hold of the amorphous shape, that it was her own patient whose life she was saving.

Thank goodness Melody's so light, Aniela thought, slipping her arm around Melody's waist, which was narrow even through the layers of cape and sweaters underneath. *It wasn't too hard to pull her up. And thank God she didn't resist me . . .*

'Come on,' she said firmly, helping Melody stand upright. 'It's freezing here. We must go inside straight away.'

Melody started to hop along; Aniela looked down and realised that Melody was missing an Ugg.

'I lost it in the river,' Melody said, her voice muffled, her nose bubbling with snot. 'And my phone. I dropped it, and I was trying to get it . . .'

Aniela kept her voice very even as she repeated:

'You were trying to get your phone?'

'Yes! My hands were cold, and I dropped it – I was ringing

my mum,' Melody babbled. 'And then I climbed over the rail to get it, and I slipped in these silly boots—'

She stopped for a moment, twisting to look at Aniela's expression, but they were in shadow, and it was too dark to see anything.

'That's all! I promise!' she said quickly. 'Honestly! I wasn't doing anything stupid!'

'Climbing over the rail is stupid,' Aniela observed, pulling Melody along again.

'I know,' Melody agreed fervently. 'But, Aniela, honestly – I'd *never* do anything *stupid* – you know, like trying to kill myself – I *promise*.'

It was impossible not to recognise the sincerity in her voice, even though it was trailing off now as Melody sniffed hard. With great relief, Aniela reached in the pocket of her padded Primark coat, pulled out a tissue, and handed it to Melody. She had absolutely no wish to cope with a suicidal, dramatic patient on Christmas Eve; at the least, she'd have to call in Dr Nassri, who would then have to get in a psychiatrist to assess Melody's mental state. And if that assessment didn't go well, Melody would have to be detained in a hospital, to prevent any more attempts at self-harm; it would be a big, exhausting mess at Christmas for all concerned, and Dr Nassri would end up blaming Aniela for not managing Melody better.

'You were ringing your mother?' Aniela prompted, to see how Melody would respond.

Melody was snuffling into the tissue as she hopped along, doing her best to barely touch the cold stone pavement with the sock-covered, Ugg-less foot.

'Yes, I wanted to talk to them,' Melody said simply. 'My mum and dad and my brother. Only they're all out at the local pub. I was remembering what you said, about people who love you. Maybe they can come and see me tomorrow.' She sighed. 'Sod it, I can't remember the last time I backed up my phone – I bet I've lost tons of numbers.'

Good, Aniela thought. There was the ring of truth in this as well; Melody wasn't covering up a dramatic, farewell-to-all-this phone call to her parents. Aniela had dealt, in her time in the NHS, with several failed suicide attempts, and none of them had been in the kind of practical mental state shortly afterwards to be concerned about the loss of phone numbers.

There was still not a soul apart from the two women on the wide boulevard by the river's edge; they shuffled around the Four Seasons, up the narrow path that separated it from Lime-house Reach, and around the front of the building to the Clinic beyond. Aniela, instinctively understanding that Melody wouldn't want the doorman of the Reach to see her in this state – bedraggled, one boot missing – took her on a loop around the curving driveway, with its spur up to the huge car lift in which the doormen would take guests' cars down to the basement parking garage, and round to the main entrance of the Clinic. She entered the code, swung open the door and flicked on the lights; Melody flinched back from the onslaught of bright white fluorescent illumination after all the time she had spent in the dark.

'We will have tea,' Aniela said, 'and I will look at your face. You have some blood on your lip. I hope I do not have to put in a stitch.'

Melody's hand flew to her face. 'I think I bit it when I fell over,' she said. 'I'm *sure* it's fine. Please – I really don't want any more stitches . . .'

'I will check, however,' Aniela said firmly, unbuttoning Melody's cape, taking off her hat, sitting her down under the bright kitchen light and pulling back her lower lip with a firm finger and thumb grip before Melody could even protest.

'It is okay,' she announced, looking down at the shiny pink flesh. 'You have not damaged the surgery, where Dr Nassri takes out the filler. It is a scratch. You will feel a lump for a few days, but no more than that.'

'Phew,' Melody said, sagging back in the chair. 'I *hated* having stitches in there.'

Aniela put on the kettle, and took off her own coat, draping it over the back of one of the chairs. She leaned back against the kitchen counter, looking at Melody, observing her carefully. The girl's face was puffy and swollen from crying, her nose red from the cold, but in the bright kitchen light Aniela's years of experience could see the bone structure clearly outlined beneath the swelling and the fading bruises. She nodded slowly.

'What?' Melody said.

'You are healing well, I think,' Aniela said.

'I went to see my ex-boyfriend,' Melody blurted out, pushing back her heavy black hair. 'Just now.'

'Oh yes?' Aniela turned away, pulling down mugs and a box of tea bags from the cupboards. If she didn't look directly at Melody, the girl would confide more, and Aniela wanted to hear her talk – to make absolutely sure that, by the time Melody went to bed tonight, she wasn't in the kind of mental state that would have her going out to walk by the river again. 'And what happened?'

'He was having a party,' Melody said sadly. 'I saw those friends of mine – the ones who were visiting yesterday, when you came round . . . they went to it, and they didn't even tell me they were going . . .'

Camomile tea was called for. A double dose, with sugar. The kettle boiled, and Aniela filled the mugs, letting them steep.

'And the blonde one – you know, the nasty one that you put in her place—'

Aniela nodded again.

' – she kissed James, right there on the doorstep, practically snogged him for the pap – there was a photographer,' Melody added. 'For the tabloids. And then, this girl who took over Juliet when I went to LA, *she* turned up and she really *did* snog James, and then she made a joke about me and they went inside . . .'

Aniela didn't understand all of this, but she hadn't expected to. In her experience at the Canary Clinic, comparatively famous people always assumed that you were aware of every detail of their lives and careers, and became disproportionately upset when you weren't. In any case, the bones of the story were perfectly clear. Stirring the tea, dunking the bags so that they released every last drop of dark golden liquid, Aniela said over her shoulder:

'That's good, isn't it? He kissed *two* girls. One is maybe serious, but two is just fun.'

She could tell by the arrested quality of the silence that Melody was thinking this over.

'I suppose so,' she said doubtfully.

'You left him alone, and now it's Christmas,' Aniela said, removing the tea bags and spooning plenty of sugar into Melody's mug. 'He has a party, he kisses some girls. Big deal, as you say here. If there is only one girl and no party, then you should worry.'

She set the mug down in front of her patient.

'Drink it all,' she said firmly.

Melody sipped it and grimaced. 'It's really sweet . . .'

'You need sugar. For the shock. And yes, there are calories,' she added, amused, sitting down opposite Melody. 'Who cares? You are thin. Drink it.'

Melody obeyed, cowed into silence.

'You should ring him,' Aniela said. 'Not tonight. Not tomorrow morning, he will be sleeping if he had a party. Maybe tomorrow evening, to wish him happy Christmas. Then you should tell him you want to meet him, and when you meet him, you tell him you still love him. Then you will know if he still loves you too.'

Melody gaped at her.

'You make it sound so simple,' she said feebly.

'It *is* simple,' Aniela said. 'When it is love, it is simple.'

'I always thought that too,' Melody said softly. She drank

some tea. 'You seem like you have everything all worked out,' she observed.

'Me?' Aniela's pale blonde eyebrows shot up. 'No! Not at all! My life is a big mess.'

I hate where I live, she thought, *and I hate my boyfriend. I sent all my savings to my family and they spent them on drink. I kissed a patient who I don't know. And I don't even like my job that much.*

She caught her breath; this was the first time she'd ever thought that.

Maybe I've just been working too hard. Day and night, double shifts, anything to get out of the flat, avoid Lubo. Once I kick him out, I'll be able to relax. It's not like he was helping with the rent.

And I have to kick him out. I just can't do it over Christmas, that would be too cruel. First thing in the New Year, though, he's out.

'What were *you* doing down by the river?' Melody asked suddenly, her dark blue eyes fixed on Aniela's face.

'Walking,' Aniela said. 'Thinking.'

'About what?' Melody persisted.

Despite herself, Aniela smiled. It was the first proper smile she'd ever given a patient, she realised; she was always controlled, professional, friendly but not a friend. But here she was, relaxing in her chair, picking up her mug, sitting back, no longer observing Melody with careful attention, but thinking about her own feelings, her own wants and needs.

Something's changing, she realised. *I'm letting go of things I clung on to before.*

'Just like you,' she answered Melody, and her smile was wry now, 'I was thinking about a man.'

'Really?' Melody's eyes widened. 'Someone you like?'

'Two of them. Someone I don't really even know,' Aniela said. 'And someone I need to say goodbye to.'

'Sounds complicated,' Melody said. 'But you like the one you don't even really know, right?'

Aniela nodded. 'There's something about him,' she heard herself say to her own surprise. 'Something very quiet. I like that. Quiet,' she quickly added, 'but not boring.'

Melody managed a smile as best she could, with her sore lower lip.

'*Well*,' she said, finishing her tea. 'Here's what I think you should do. You should tell him you want to meet him, and when you meet him, you should tell him that you like him. Then you'll know if he likes you too.'

'Very funny,' Aniela said, unable to suppress a grin at having her own words turned back on her. 'You should do more comedy.'

'Oh,' Melody said, irony in her voice, 'I just starred in a comic film. It's only I didn't mean *Wonder Woman* to be *unintentionally* funny.'

Aniela heard herself start to giggle. It sounded strange to her ears; she never giggled.

'Your breasts *were* funny,' she said, remembering Melody wobbling up and down above the tight corset of the skimpy costume. She caught herself. 'I'm sorry!' she said in horror. 'I shouldn't—'

'No!' Melody was laughing too, holding her hand up to her mouth to try to stop the cut in her lip from reopening. 'They *were* funny, you're right. I don't know *what* I was thinking!'

The image of Melody spinning around, her boobs bouncing, filled both of their minds, and they laughed harder and harder, until what they were laughing about wasn't Melody and that tacky Wonder Woman costume at all; it was just an excuse, a release from tension after Melody's rescue from the icy waters of the Thames; her distress at seeing James apparently happy and surrounded by beautiful girls keen to throw themselves at him; Aniela's confusion about Jon, her extreme attraction to him, his rejection of her, the fact that she was unable to stop thinking about him despite his backing away from her, despite the fact that she knew he had had the kind of surgery that was pretty much the province of drug dealers and gangsters . . .

He's not a drug dealer or a gangster, she told herself firmly. *I know he isn't.*

But then what is he?

Melody's laughter had dissolved into an exhausted yawn.

'Ow,' she said, wincing, holding her fingers against her mouth to stop it stretching. 'That hurt.' She yawned again despite herself.

'Good,' Aniela said, standing up. 'You are tired. You will sleep now.'

'I wouldn't have thought – after all that sugar—' Melody yawned yet again, helplessly. 'Ow!' she exclaimed, half laughing.

'The sugar just cancels out the shock,' Aniela said. 'Now you are balanced, and you realise how tired you are. Come on. I will take you back to your flat.'

Obediently, Melody rose to her feet. She looked down at them, one in an Ugg, the other in a damp sock, and managed a little grimace, but Aniela was already handing her a pair of disposable paper flip-flops.

'Better than nothing,' she said. 'Give me your boot.'

She retrieved Melody's cape and hat, took the Ugg that Melody obediently handed her, and headed off to the corridor that led to the Limehouse Reach lobby, Melody slip-sliding after her. They crossed the atrium, the doorman staring after them curiously, but too well-trained to say a word. Melody, overcome by everything she had been through that evening, was as knocked out by the aftermath of extreme emotion as a person in a normal state of mind would have been by two Ambien: *which is why I haven't given her any,* Aniela thought. *Camomile tea and sugar, and she's gone down like a bowling pin.*

She slipped her arm back around Melody's swaying waist as they exited the elevator, and unlocked the door with her own key. Melody's eyes were already closing, almost all her body weight leaning on Aniela now. *She trusts easily,* Aniela noticed. *This is why she made a mess when she went to Hollywood, because she trusted what people were telling her.* She helped

Melody take off her sweater, the paper flip-flops, the socks, and
then guided her to the bedroom, folding back the covers as
Melody climbed into bed.

Aniela had tucked the coverlet under Melody's chin, and
was about to slip from the room, when, quite unexpectedly,
Melody's hand snaked out and gripped Aniela's wrist. The
room was dark, just one bedside light sending a warm, diffuse
glow of light over the silky coverlet. Melody's face was in
shadow, and the fading bruises, the swelling, were barely visible;
Aniela looked down at her patient's wide blue, black-lashed
eyes, the heart-shaped face and symmetric bone structure, and
drew in her breath at how beautiful Melody was.

Melody gazed up at the nurse.

'It's Christmas Eve!' she said drowsily. 'I can't believe it,
really! What about you, Aniela? Can you believe it's Christmas
tomorrow?'

Aniela found herself sitting down on the side of the bed.

'No,' she admitted. 'Not really. It's strange here. We are out
of time. I don't say it right, perhaps . . .'

'Suspended in time,' Melody said, still holding onto Aniela.
'I know what you mean.' She yawned again. 'We're up here, in
this tower, high above the rest of the world. It's unreal. Like a
fairy tale.'

'I hope it is a happy fairy tale,' Aniela heard herself say,
surprised at her own words: *I only ever say positive things to
patients. Why did I just suggest that there might be the possibility
of an unhappy ending?*

But Melody smiled, a lovely, sweet smile, her hand sliding
up to slip its fingers through Aniela's.

'Me too,' she said, her voice heartfelt. 'Me too. Aniela?'

Her eyes were fluttering closed.

'Yes?' Aniela said.

'What would you be doing if you were home in Poland?'
Melody asked. 'With your family? They must be really missing
you.'

Aniela grimaced, but Melody didn't catch the fleeting expression. It was clear, from things Melody had said, that her family was warm, loving, supportive; this was not the time to enlighten Melody about the realities of Aniela's considerably less happy family situation.

'I will tell you about some of the traditions my grandmother, my *babcia*, used to tell me of, years ago, when I was little,' she said instead, squeezing Melody's slender fingers affectionately. 'She came from eastern Poland, and there they think that girls must grind poppy seed on Christmas Eve, if they want to get married soon. And she said that after dinner on Christmas Eve, *her* mother told her to leave the house, in the cold and the snow, and to listen for a dog barking. The first bark she heard was the direction of where her future husband will come from. It was a small village, you understand. Not in the town.'

Aniela smiled.

'I always thought, so you must go and live in a house where there is an annoying dog who barks all night. It made no sense to me.'

'I was just thinking that,' Melody said drowsily, her long lashes lying in semicircles on her cheeks now.

'And the women would have to clean the house, all day, on Christmas Eve, sweeping and dusting. Because evil would stay all year if anything was dirty at the end of the day. Only the women, of course,' Aniela said dryly. 'So they are all inside cleaning, and they must not leave, because the first person to enter a house on Christmas Eve must be a man. If it is a woman, it is a bad omen, because then only heifers would be born on the farm for the whole next year. No bulls.'

Oh dear, she thought. *This is all a little sad. Babcia always liked to tell gloomy stories.*

'They would make twelve dishes for supper on Christmas Eve,' she said. *Everyone likes to hear about food.* 'My grandmother would always cook the twelve dishes for us. And you must try them all, for good luck. The last one is *kutia*, which is wheat, raisins, nuts, honey and spices. It's very sweet, the children love it. You eat the *kutia*, and then you turn out all the lights and blow out the candles, and you look at where the smoke from the candles goes. If it goes towards the window, the harvest will be good. And if it goes towards the stove, there will be a marriage . . .'

There should be a candle to blow out now, she thought. *Like telling bedtime stories, where you blow out the candle when the child has fallen asleep.*

Melody's hand was limp in hers now, warm, soft, slightly damp; Aniela slid her fingers out, very gently, and laid her patient's hand down on the coverlet. Melody huffed out a breath and rolled onto her side, her breathing steady and rhythmical, a little stertorous, because of the recent surgery on her nose. Aniela stood up and leaned over to turn out the light, padding softly from the room.

She was closing the bedroom door, so that daylight wouldn't filter in and wake Melody early; it creaked slightly as it moved, and the noise made Melody stir.

'Aniela?' she mumbled, her voice heavy with sleep. 'Thank you. You saved my life tonight.' She drew in a long, slow breath. 'You're my guardian angel. Like in *It's A Wonderful Life*. You're like Clarence . . .'

Melody's voice tailed off; the words faded, and the breathing turned to a soft, bubbling snore.

Good. She will sleep very soundly, Aniela thought as she closed the door. *I envy her. Tomorrow she'll call her family, and they will come to see her. And maybe the boyfriend will come as well. If not – well, she is beautiful and sweet and talented and nice. She will meet someone else soon.*

But me – I am not beautiful or sweet, and I am not a talented actress. I am not the guardian angel Melody just called me. I'm only a nurse, with no family left that I can trust, and a boyfriend I can't wait to see the back of. And I am stupid enough to be obsessing about a man whose real name I don't know, who hasn't even got a face yet, who kissed me and then pushed me away . . .

She left Melody's apartment, double-locking the door behind her. The music playing in the corridor, piped through the building, was Judy Garland singing 'Have Yourself A Merry Little Christmas', that beautiful, rich, poignant vibrato seeming to work itself inside Aniela's soul, making it vibrate, making her yearn for things that she didn't have, might never have.

I am not nice, either. Not as nice as I pretend. I don't deserve all Melody's kind words. I brought her back here, to her apartment, not just to make sure she was safely in bed, with the door locked properly. I came back because I wanted to have an excuse to be in the building, to be close to Jon.

Aniela found herself wishing desperately that the Canary Clinic had bought its apartments for recovering patients next to each other, or at least on the same floor. That way, maybe, perhaps, if Jon were up for some reason, up late on Christmas Eve, he might, perhaps, hear the women coming past his door, look out through the peephole, see Aniela and wait for her to come back, alone . . .

It was ridiculous. Pathetic. Obsessive. But instead of the button for the lobby, she pressed the button for Jon's floor, four up. When the doors opened, she told herself not to get out, to wait for them to close again; but there she was, stepping out of the lift, Judy Garland still singing, beautiful and melancholy. Aniela walked down the corridor, taking the turn that led to the other occupied Canary Clinic apartment, wondering, crazily, if she could come up with any sort of excuse for ringing the bell at – she checked her watch – nearly midnight.

No. You can't, she told herself, coming to a halt in front of Jon's door. *You can't ring his bell. You can't say you were checking up on him, or thought he'd paged you, or anything at all. Because you'll seem like an insane, psychotic stalker, chasing after a man who's just had major surgery – for God's sake, what is* wrong *with you, Aniela Jasicki, standing outside a man's door, yearning for him like you've never, ever, yearned for anyone in your life!*

She heaved a deep sigh and turned away.

Behind her, the door swung open, and Jon said hesitantly: 'Aniela? Is everything okay?'

She had a moment of such utter embarrassment that she wished the floor would open and swallow her up. If she could, she would have kept walking, pretended she was someone else, made her escape and denied the whole thing tomorrow – *but I can't, I'm still in my uniform. What am I going to do, tell him he must have been hallucinating?*

She turned round, guilt plastered to her face; she felt as she had when the teacher had caught her misbehaving at school. And then, looking at Jon, that guilty expression dissolved into something even worse; a giddy, silly smile. Just as young, just as stupid.

He was wearing a long-sleeved white thermal shirt, the kind that buttons in a placket down the front, and almost all the buttons were open, the soft cotton fabric straining across the spread of his pectoral muscles, silky red-gold hairs twining around the buttons, the V of the open placket drawing Aniela's eyes down, down to the plain khaki boxer briefs that clung to his narrow hips and stopped mid-thigh. His legs were lean and strong, his calf muscles hard; his skin was pale and freckled, and the light from the corridor glowed on the coppery hairs on his legs, which looked just as soft and silky as the hair on his chest. Aniela imagined herself winding those chest hairs round her fingers, stroking them, feeling his skin, running her hands over his perfect body, and her mouth went so dry she couldn't say a word.

He was staring at her, one hand on the doorjamb, the other scratching the back of his head, his lips parted.

'I heard someone outside,' he said eventually. 'Stopping, outside my door.'

'I was bringing back my other patient, from the Clinic,' Aniela managed to say. 'I just thought I'd check on you. Then I realised how late it was. I'm sorry I woke you up.'

'It's okay,' he said. 'I'm a light sleeper.'

'You must be,' she said disbelievingly.

'It's quiet as the grave here,' Jon said. 'You can hear a pin drop.'

And then they stared at each other, conversation exhausted.

Well? Aniela said to herself. *It's up to you now. You can't tell Melody to be brave and then not follow your own advice. He must know why you're really here, after all. And he's still standing there, waiting . . .*

Slowly, Aniela stepped towards him. She found herself wishing, fervently, that she wasn't dressed in her unflattering nurse's uniform; *but then, what could I wear that would look better on me? I'm pear-shaped, so I don't look good in jeans – I don't like my legs very much, so skirts aren't much better . . . at least if I were in a nice pair of court shoes, my feet wouldn't look so big—*

She was close enough to him now that their bodies were almost touching. She could smell his natural scent, warm and musky, with that clean soap smell overlaying it. There was no point looking up at his face; how could she read his expression when he didn't have one? So, feeling as if she were taking her life in her hands, she reached out and touched his chest, something she had been longing to do from the moment she saw him.

He could get me sacked for this. Okay, he kissed me yesterday, but Dr Nassri won't care about that. Private nurses get paid more: we're expected to smile and put up with patients being a little frisky from time to time. A Corsican gangster, having a nose job at the Clinic, had been famous for his wandering hands, and all Dr Nassri had told the nurses when they complained was to move faster.

But showing up at a patient's apartment in the middle of the

*night . . . initiating contact, rather than just letting him kiss me –
that's completely out of bounds. One call from Jon and I'll be
kicked out on my big bum faster than you can say Happy Christmas.*

Unless . . . unless . . .

*Unless he puts your hand over his, big and warm and surpris-
ingly rough with calluses, and slides your fingers underneath the
border of his thermal shirt, against his skin. Over his heart,
which you can feel beating, fast and hard. And then lets you
move your fingers further, tangling them in the hair on his chest,
which you've also been longing to do ever since you first saw
him . . .*

His hand over hers gave Aniela the confidence to look up.
His mashed-up face didn't bother her at all. She was so used to
seeing patients in various states of recovery that his bruises, his
splinted nose, were just another part of her job. What she saw,
as she gazed at him, was that his eyes were very earnest, and
very clear, and maybe even – which sounded mad even to
think, with the strength she was feeling beneath the palm of
her hand, the musculature and poise of his body – maybe even
a little frightened.

Without hesitation, she reached up with her other hand,
tilted his head towards her and kissed him.

It was just as immediate as it had been the day before, just
as sweet. And just as tentative. Aniela had another crazy
thought, which in itself was crazy; she had gone for years being
nothing but sensible and practical and working all hours that
God sent, saving almost everything she made. And now, ever
since setting eyes on Jon Jordan's extraordinary body and
damaged face, it felt as if she was doing nothing but having the
most insane ideas.

But she couldn't help it. She was remembering a film she'd
seen months ago, an old film, on late at night, which she'd only
watched because she was so dazed from an eighteen-hour shift
that her library book on Napoleon's unsuccessful campaign in

Russia had failed to settle her down for sleep. The film had been called *Starman*, and it was beautiful and sad, about an alien who came to earth and became a gorgeous, blue-eyed man, the dream of the lonely heroine; the kind of man who could have any woman he wanted, but was so new in the handsome body he'd taken on that he hadn't had any women at all.

Because Jon Jordan might have been given a whole new personality along with his new face, or at least had his memory of any contact with a woman wiped clean. He kissed her with the sweet eagerness of a teenage boy with a girl he really liked, and the caution not to give offence, not to have her withdraw her favours because he had gone too far, presumed too much, pressured her too fast. There was a space between them, Aniela sensed intuitively, that was hers to fill.

And she realised, with the same flash of intuition, why he had pushed her away before. It hadn't been rejection of her; it had been his own fear of doing the wrong thing, embarrassment at the brief clumsy moment when his teeth grazed hers.

She pushed him very slightly, backing him into the apartment, giving him a cue that he immediately picked up upon; his arm locked around her, holding her closer as they moved inside. He kicked the door shut with a swift efficient movement. Her head tilted back further, and she dragged her hand from his chest and slid it round his shoulders, pulling his head down even more, kissing him with everything she had, showing him vividly, wordlessly, how much she was enjoying it, how much she wanted his tongue to slide into her mouth, his arms to wrap tighter and tighter around her, his erection, hard as the muscles of his chest, as the leg pressing insistently between hers, tilting into her, making her dizzy with excitement and the sheer heady rush of being wanted so much.

Aniela pulled her head back, a sudden thought striking her even in the middle of the best kiss she'd ever had in her life.

'We have to be careful,' she said, trying for some reason to sound professional and serious instead of a lust-crazed stalker.

'Of course,' Jon said instantly. 'But I don't know if I have anything—'

'No! Of your *face*!' she said, giggling in a way that made her sound like a silly teenager. 'You mustn't strain your *face* – you've had major surgery, you mustn't do anything too strenuous—'

'Aniela—' Jon's hands framed her face, holding it, stroking her cheeks with his thumbs. Again, it was the oddest thing not to be able to see on his face how he was feeling, and he seemed to sense this; he shook his head impatiently, as if in frustration.

'I don't know what to say,' he managed. 'I'm not really good with women. I haven't had much – I haven't been—' He swallowed, his Adam's apple bobbing. 'If this is your way of telling me you've changed your mind about being here, that you want to stop, please, for the love of God, just be honest with me! I don't think I can take much more of this – you must know how I'm – the reaction I'm having to you—'

He cleared his throat, arching his lower body away from her.

'No – I really did mean your face,' she said, half-laughing, half-desperate with the urgency of her need. 'I want to fuck you, I promise. I want to fuck you more than I've ever wanted anything in my life.'

He froze. She couldn't tell why, but she didn't care; she just wanted to convince him to keep going. Determinedly, Aniela slid her hands down his back, just above his buttocks, pulling him close again, a moan rasping from her as she felt his hard cock once more against her inner thigh. Beneath her palms, the small of his back was damp through the thermal top, and his body jerked in response as she pulled the top up, stroked his bare skin, traced the declivity of his spine down to the cleft of his buttocks, felt his own hands grip her own bottom, lifting and grinding his cock against her even harder, his strength immense, effortless; he was lifting her off her feet, something no lover had ever done in her life. Incredulously, solid, big-boned Aniela felt her feet leave the ground, and she squealed in surprise, clinging to his neck for dear life, sure that he would stagger and slip under her weight.

But there wasn't the slightest hesitation in the strong arms that were holding her up, the thighs that were braced for counterbalance. She felt him swivel, turn their bodies so that her back was to the wall, and then, even more amazingly, he shifted, one hand now taking her entire weight as her legs wrapped round his waist, the other hand sliding between her legs, clumsily but surely unbuttoning the lower part of her dress, reaching up, and closing, awkwardly, firmly, around her crotch.

The world stopped. She buried her head on his shoulder, clinging to him even tighter, the sheer heat of his palm between her legs overwhelming; she realised she was rocking against him, moaning into the damp smooth skin of his neck, as he rubbed her like Aladdin did his lamp, not with any skill or experience yet but finding his way, listening to the sounds she was making, concentrating hard, using the heel of his hand till she was completely beyond words, and then, wanting more, wanting to touch bare skin, rising up to pull inexpertly at the waistband of her tights.

She couldn't bear him touching her at her waist, especially with her leaning forward like this, the bulges and rolls of solid flesh even more apparent. Reaching down, she managed to grab his arm, to push it down again, to whisper in his ear:

'Rip them – just rip them—'

He never needs telling anything twice, she realised, as his fingers twisted into the crotch of her cheap, 40-denier, off-white uniform-approved tights, pulled and tore it open; he snagged the lace trim of her pants, hesitated for a moment, and then, as she thrust her hips at him in mute approval, beyond words again, he ripped the cotton too, the strong muscles of his forearm flexing easily, making light work of tearing the fabric.

'Can I—' He pulled back his head, looking down at her, and she couldn't look up at him, was too far gone already, could only moan a 'Yes' into his shoulder, dragging the thermal top aside so she could kiss his skin, lick him, taste the salt of his sweat, brace herself, shuddering, for the feeling of his hot hand between her legs again.

'You're so *wet*,' he said in wonder. Two fingers slid inside her, and his gasp was louder than hers. 'So wet—' he groaned, 'so wet and *hot*—'

Aniela was sandwiched between him and the wall, her arms around his neck, her legs around his waist, spread wide, spread wider as he fumbled at his boxers and stepped into her even more tightly, his cock springing up through the slit he'd unbuttoned, up and into her, making her scream into his shoulder and then bite down in sheer primitive excitement as he slammed his full length into her. He was right, she was dripping wet, her body open, completely and utterly ready for him. Both his hands cupped her buttocks, bracing them, lifting her even a little more as his thighs rose and fell, like pistons driving. She thought, as she clung to him, as she felt her pelvis shudder under the impact of his strokes, of the *Starman* image again, but now, ridiculously, she was imagining another alien, the Terminator, all tensile steel and titanium, strong enough to lift anything, to fuck her so hard she thought she was going to faint, and she sank her teeth again into the sweating skin of his shoulder, kissed the salt trail, reminded herself that he was flesh and blood, her hands sliding down his arms and wrapping around the hard, round apple bulges of his biceps, feeling the flexing strength with each stroke.

He yelled something she was too far gone to hear, one last, even more frenzied thrust slamming her head back against the wall; the next thing she knew, something hot was trickling down her inner thigh, and Jon was collapsing against her, squashing her against the wall, his face mushed into her, her legs spread so wide now that her groin was hurting. Her heart was pounding so fast she couldn't do anything, couldn't say anything, for several breaths; but finally, when he didn't move, her cheek was being crushed against the paintwork and her hip flexors were screaming in agony, she managed to push gently at his shoulders, easing him back.

'Sorry—' he muttered, instantly responding. He lowered her to the ground; she winced as her legs unwrapped from his waist, keeping her arms around his neck as she regained her balance.

'Are you okay?' he said. 'Was it too much? It was too much, wasn't it? I'm sorry – shit, I'm so sorry. Did I hurt you? Oh shit, I got some on you – I'm *so* sorry, Aniela – come to the bath-room—'

The door to the guest toilet was opposite them in the hallway. Dazed, her head still spinning, holding onto him to keep steady, she let him lead her in, grab tissues from the silver box on the top of the toilet, dampen them in warm water and wipe down her leg. He dried it with a hand towel, very care-fully, and then stood back and looked at her. She could see her own reflection in the big glass mirror over the sink; there were plenty of mirrors in the Limehouse Reach apartments. Rich people seemed to like to look at themselves a lot.

I actually look almost pretty, she realised with disbelief. There was a bright red flush on her cheeks, and her eyes were an equally bright blue, shining and clear; some of her hair had come loose from its bun, and was hanging down over her face, blonde and straight, softening its round shape. Her lips were red, too, red as her cheeks, a colour she had never thought to paint them. *I look like a Dutch doll.*

I look like a woman a man might actually find attractive.

'I hurt you, didn't I?' Jon sounded frenzied now. 'I'm so sorry! I got carried away, I treated you like a prostitute – can you forgive me?'

In the mirror, Aniela saw her lips move, saw them break into a smile, and then into a laugh. She looked down at herself: half the buttons on her dress had come unbuttoned, and it was hanging off her. Her tights were ripped and crumpled around her ankles. Her pants hadn't come off completely, but they felt very loose: Jon must have fatally stretched the elastic. She laughed again, taking in the sight of herself, the absolute disorder into which she had been reduced after a mere few minutes. She did look ravaged.

'That,' she said, 'was the best sex I've ever had in my life. And I didn't even *come*.'

'It *was*?' Jon shook his head in disbelief. 'Wait, you didn't come? Fuck!' He slammed one fist into the palm of the other hand, taking a couple of steps, pacing to the rim of the toilet and then back again. 'I'm sorry! I'm so sorry! But really?' He stopped in front of her, looking at her face with what seemed an intent stare. 'The best sex you ever had in your life?'

'Jon,' Aniela said softly. 'Stop saying sorry.'

'Okay,' he said immediately. 'Sorry. I mean—'

She held out a hand to him.

'I need to lie down,' she said. 'My legs are still very wobbly. Let's go to bed.'

Jon took her hand; then bending down, he picked her up, swinging her into his arms and carrying her out of the bathroom.

'You make me feel like I don't weigh anything at all,' Aniela sighed happily, resting her head on his shoulder again.

'Well, you weigh more than a hundred-pound kitbag,' Jon said seriously. 'But you're much easier to carry.'

She giggled. 'Thank you.'

'Thank you? You're thanking *me*? I didn't even make you come!' Jon shook his head incredulously as he strode through the living room and into the main bedroom, laying her down on the bed. Her shoes had long since come off; she relaxed gratefully onto the soft, yielding mattress and duvet.

'Oh, this is *lovely*,' she said, stretching out.

'You like the mattress?' he asked.

She nodded.

'I thought you might,' he said, sounding satisfied.

She didn't understand, but then there was so much with Jon that she didn't understand that she supposed she'd just have to pick her battles. He was still standing by the edge of the bed, staring down at her, his face unreadable. She patted the duvet next to her.

'Do you want me to show you how to make me come?' she asked.

The mystery of where he'd come from, why he didn't know how to kiss or, seemingly, how to give a woman an orgasm, could be set aside for now. Her legs might still be like jelly from the impact of him fucking her so hard, but she wasn't remotely tired, and she wanted him close; not just to make her come, but to lie beside her, on top of her. She wanted to feel his weight pressing her into the mattress, to settle his hips into hers, to have sex all over again, no matter how sore her groin was; they'd go slow this time. He'd fucked her like an express train, and now it was her turn to drive. To stop at all the stations, she thought, smiling with anticipation.

He was already settling onto the bed beside her, looking down at her for clues. She took his hand and ran it over her breasts in the cotton uniform; he was swift to respond, stroking her, unbuttoning the last couple of buttons that were still holding her dress together, pulling it open. Aniela wished, very much, that she was wearing anything but the nasty old Playtex bra that she'd bought from the local market, Cross My Heart in a battered box that had knocked around the back of plenty of lorries, a picture of a woman with 1980s teased hair on the front. Sitting up, she unhooked the bra swiftly, throwing it on the floor, not even waiting for him, just wanting it off, for him not to see how unflattering it was. If she had only known, she would have gone to Marks and Spencer, or La Senza, some nice high street shop, bought a matching set, trimmed with pretty lace, maybe a bra with underwire and a little padding to give her some more up top than nature had.

But his hands are holding me, stroking me, tracing circles around my nipples, just as if I were the prettiest thing in the world, as if I were wearing a silk negligee like a film star . . .

Jon's hands slid behind her, up to her hair, pulling out all the big grips that Aniela used to keep it tidy, carefully unwinding the rubber band that held her bun in place, easing it out with minimal tangling. Seriously, intently, he drew her long blonde hair forward, a straight skein down over one shoulder, reaching to the curve of her breast, and stroked her hair and her skin together, her pale pink nipple; then he did the same on the other side. It was as if he were learning her, every slope of her body, and somehow his concentration on her was easier precisely because his face was so bruised it was impossible to read its expression.

Aniela would have been embarrassed by open appreciation, a stare of lust or admiration. But the post-surgery swollen mask that his face currently wore made her able to bear his long slow scrutiny. He drew the white dress off her shoulders, pulling it off her, and traced his hands slowly down her arms, to her waist, and then her stomach, which she was sucking in for dear life. But he didn't seem to move faster over its convex curve, to mind that hers stuck out while his was a ridged, hard washboard.

Jon's hands went to the waistband of her underpants, and started to pull them down. She lifted her hips eagerly, and heard his indrawn breath as he saw her soft fair pubic hair; he grazed it with his thumbs as he went, as he drew off her pants, and with them what was left of her tights, dropping them to the floor.

And then he stopped. He stopped, looking down at her naked body, and instinctively, Aniela knew that he was panicking because he didn't know what to do next. His cock was pressing against his boxers again, nearly making it through the slit; but it was her turn now, and she held her hand out to him again, pulling him to lie down next to her, then pressing his fingers between her legs.

'You're still so wet,' he murmured almost shyly.

She huffed a little laugh.

'It doesn't go away,' she said. 'Or it won't, not when you're here.'

Bending her fingers round his index and middle ones, she guided them just inside her, hearing him gasp, and then pulled them out, following the ridge of her pubic bone, just to where she wanted him to concentrate on, bucking the moment he touched her swollen clitoris.

'Is that—'

'Yes . . . Oh *God*, yes . . .'

She was so overwhelmed with the need to come that, despite her best intentions, she couldn't wait for him to do it, to slowly learn how: *but if I push him away he'll be mortified*, she knew. *I can't make him feel rejected . . .*

'Shall I show you how I do it?' she asked, thinking quickly. 'How I make myself come?'

Jon nodded so fast that his face blurred momentarily; his lips parted but he couldn't get a word out, the idea excited him so much. He propped himself up on the bed pillows, one hand shyly returning to stroke her breasts, his breath coming quick and shallow as Aniela started to work on herself, slipping her fingers inside herself, moistening them, then dragging them back out to stroke her wet cleft, making little circles, faster and faster, her hips bucking against her fingers.

She grabbed Jon's hand, which was much too gentle now, squeezing it around her breast, her back arching to push herself further into his palm, and felt her eyes rolling back in her skull, her lids closing, her head arching back too as she started to make the noises that meant she was about to come. Aniela had never been embarrassed about the human body; her family were all blunt and direct, never using a euphemism where a straightforward word would do instead, and

her years of nursing had obliterated any stray fragments of
shyness that might be trailing around her psyche. The idea
that a man might be put off by her face, her cries, when she
reached orgasm would never have occurred to her; she would
have burst out laughing if another woman had confessed to
her that she was worried about looking pretty in the throes of
sex.

So she was quite unselfconscious as her voice dropped,
becoming almost guttural, sounds flooding out from deep in
her throat, one hand thrumming between her legs, the other
still tight around Jon's, as the orgasm hit her with full force,
release streaming through her, one spasm after the other, like a
series of electric shocks. She could still feel Jon's cock inside
her, still remember the sensations that she had felt when he
fucked her, and that sent her even further over the edge, dropping down to a long soft landing. Her hands loosened, fell
away, and she lay there, eyes still closed, her chest rising and
falling, feeling as if her face was suffused with blood, burning
hot, burning up . . .

Beside her, Jon shifted, his fingers sliding between her legs,
making her jump. She was overstimulated, almost wanted a
moment to recover, and she was about to tell him so, to ask
him to wait a moment or two; but then the sensation of his
fingers inside her became so overwhelming that she turned
towards him, put her arms around his neck and clung to him
again in mute encouragement. Dazedly, she thought that she
was already beyond anything she'd ever experienced before,
that maybe there was no such thing in this new world as
overstimulation, that she should just let go completely, that
she could certainly trust him to be strong enough to catch
her . . .

He pulled his fingers out to the tips, sliding them up to her
swollen centre as she had done, copying the movements he
had watched her do, and the next second Aniela heard herself
groaning again, gasping for breath, her hips pumping into his

fingers, coming over them; they were lying facing each other, and as Jon started to make her come he kissed her, his tongue driving into her mouth now so confidently that she would never have recognised him as the man who had been so tentative with her yesterday, or even in the hall a little while ago. His tongue in her mouth, her own kissing him back eagerly, his fingers inside her, it was as if she were completely suffused with sensation, as if she were coming not only between her legs but all over her skin, the orgasms spreading and spreading like heat pouring out from her core and over her entire body.

Elated with the power he had, his success at this new skill, Jon didn't stop for what felt like a very long time. Aniela could feel his cock between them, her hips rocking against it – *nothing*, she thought, her head swirling, *no feeling better in the world than a man's dick that's this hard for you, nothing better in the world* – but his control was amazing, his ability to keep making her come exceptional. Unlike every other man she had been with – *and that's not many, so what would I know?* – Jon had worked out almost immediately that less was more. By this stage, he was simply flicking his thumb lightly around her clitoris to make her explode to climax. Aniela had the sense that he was experimenting now, as if she were a toy he was playing with, like a little boy with a top he was spinning, sending in circles, pushing to see what he could do with it next.

When he stopped kissing her and whispered something against her mouth, she couldn't even hear the words for the crashing pumping of her heart, the blood racing through her veins; without waiting for an answer, she felt him lying back, stripping off his thermal top and his boxers, now both soaked with sweat. His hands closed round her hips, lifting her as effortlessly as always, settling her over him. His cock was so hard and springy that it found its way into her without either of them having to touch it; it ran between her legs, paused over her wetness and then plunged deep, making her scream, her hands braced on his arms.

His whole body tensed, immobilised, as if they were playing an X-rated version of Musical Statues.

'Is it—'

'Yes! Yes! It's good!'

'You just screamed so loudly—'

'It's *good*!'

Aniela looked down at him, at the torso that had made her heart stop and her eyes widen in disbelief and admiration the moment she had seen him, bare to the waist, just a couple of days ago, opening the door to this apartment, his sweatpants hanging loosely on his narrow hips, his chest lightly filmed with sweat. Then, she'd averted her gaze after a brief, incredulous stare; now she could gaze at him all she wanted, at the red-gold hair on his chest, its pattern interrupted by a couple of fading white scars that slashed across his torso, the hair narrowing to a darker, coppery line that led down his stomach, his belly button almost flat to his abs, the hair starting again after it, darkening and deepening into a deep rusty tangle.

'Just a couple of days ago,' she marvelled, raising her eyes to meet his. 'We just met a couple of days ago.'

He was propped up on a couple of pillows, looking at her naked body just as intently as she was surveying his; she was hugely grateful that she had shaved her legs that morning. His hands were behind his head, his triceps so big and swollen in that position that once her attention was called to them she couldn't look away. He cleared his throat.

'Is that – is that normal?' he asked.

Aniela frowned, not understanding.

'What do you mean?' she asked.

'Is it—' His stare dropped to her small breasts now, not wanting to meet her eyes. 'I mean, I felt really – when you came in, two days ago, I felt really easy with you.'

'*Easy*,' she repeated in disappointment.

'Aniela—' He sat up with a swift flexing of his abs, driving his cock at a sharper angle inside her, making her gasp with pleasure and momentarily lose track of anything else. 'I never feel easy with *anyone.*'

'Really?' She felt herself flush with pleasure.

'Really,' he said simply.

'What did you mean, normal?' she asked.

It was becoming increasingly hard – *difficult*, she corrected herself quickly so she didn't completely lose it, *difficult* – to focus on what he was saying. But she knew, with absolute instinct, that if she didn't, she would miss something very important. Jon was like no other man she had ever met, or ever would, a man who was able to have a serious conversation while still maintaining a rock-like erection inside her. To ask her a question that obviously meant a lot to him. She needed to concentrate on the answer. After all, his hard dick obviously wasn't going away.

'I don't have much – I haven't much – at all—' He cleared his throat again. 'You're the first – not the *first*, but—'

He was looking even more intently at her breasts. *Well, they're small, but at least they're not saggy*, she thought with relief.

'I haven't really, ever, what you'd call dated – well, what *I'd* call dated, you don't say that really in the UK.' He was almost babbling now. 'So I don't know if this is normal.'

'Does it *feel* normal?'

Aniela allowed herself to lift up, just slightly, and then push down, taking his whole length into her again. Jon shuddered in pleasure.

'It feels a *lot* better than normal,' he said.

'Does it feel better than when you've had sex before?' she asked, greatly daring, rising higher up, pushing back down more strongly. His tip butted against her cervix eagerly, a moan issuing from his lips.

'It feels better than *anything* before,' he said honestly. He looked up now, and she could see how earnest his eyes were. 'Aniela—' He swallowed. 'I've only ever paid for it before.'

'*What?*'

She hung suspended for a moment, impaled on him, unable to take in what he had just said. And then she burst out laughing. The laughter rippled all up and down her, making her body sway and rock, sending tiny spasms through her clitoris, rubbing against his rough curls of pubic hair, a delicious tickling sensation. She threw her head back and laughed her head off. When she finally managed to catch her breath, he said blankly:

'I didn't think you'd *laugh*.'

'It's just . . .' She was still giggling.

'I'm completely clean,' he said anxiously. 'Fully tested. I promise. And the women were all – you know, willing. Not trafficked. Nothing like that.'

'Oh good!' She shook her head in disbelief.

'So why did you laugh?'

Aniela shook her head again.

'*Look* at you,' she said. 'Why would you ever have to pay for sex? It's crazy! You're crazy!'

And yes, you have the best body I or almost anyone else will ever have seen in their life – but even if you didn't, anyone with a cock like this should never have to pay for sex, she thought, unable to resist moving any longer, beginning to describe circles with her hips, sighing at how good it felt. She realised that Jon was still staring at her incredulously.

'No,' she panted. 'This isn't normal.'

And then she screamed again, because he had lain back on his pillows and was fucking her from below. This, definitely, a hundred per cent, was not normal. Lubo had just lain there when she got on top; sometimes she'd even suspected him of watching the TV over her shoulder, the sliver of the screen that he could see through the open bedroom door, into the living room. *He might as well have been a dildo I nailed to the mattress,* Aniela thought, another crazy giggle rising up inside her. *I had to do all the work myself. And I didn't even mind that much, because it was better than having Lubo's fat, hairy stomach smacking against me, and he lasted longer that way.*

But this . . .

Jon was flexing his hips, each pelvic thrust slamming his cock up inside her; it was like sitting on a pile driver. Aniela screamed and leant forward to grab his shoulders and held on for dear life as her entire body juddered with delight. He had realised by now that her screams – at least this kind – were to be interpreted positively, and he seemed to be trying to provoke more and more of them: if that was his goal, he was succeeding, because Aniela, by now, was screaming her head off in ecstasy and disbelief. She ground herself back against him, and Jon responded eagerly, tilting his hips at more of an angle, sliding out a little each time and then back in again, slick and hard and lubricated.

And she realised, with great pleasure, that he was beginning to make noise too. Before, he had been completely silent apart from his panting breath; now, he was starting to grunt in time with his strokes. He grabbed her hands from his shoulders and held them up, his arms bracing easily, taking the weight of her torso, the hair in his armpits damp rust-red, the skin of his chest flushing, beads of sweat standing out in his chest hair.

'Be careful of your face!' Aniela exclaimed, seeing it go redder as his strokes grew faster and more frenzied.

'Too . . . late . . . now!' he panted, and his hands around hers tightened, pulling her towards him, pulling her off him, tumbling onto his chest, not a moment too soon, as behind her his cock spurted into the air a stream of hot milky come, a long, blissful, final grunt of complete satisfaction issuing from his lips.

'Ah, God,' he moaned, rolling her to the side, his arm falling over her, pulling her next to him. 'Ah, *God*, that was so fucking good . . . *fuck* . . . '

'But was it normal?' Aniela asked into his shoulder, licking his sweat, pushing her body in utter contentment against his.

He huffed out a laugh, his arm heavy around her. 'You make me come like a geyser,' he said. 'That was amazing. I feel like I took LSD or something.'

'What's a geyser?'

'American hot springs,' he said drowsily. 'Bigger than anything you've seen in Europe.'

Aniela smiled.

'*Everything* in America seems bigger than anything I've seen in Europe,' Aniela said, still throbbing all over from the aftermath of sex.

'Did any get on you?' he said anxiously, reaching for a pillow, ripping off the case and wiping himself and the wet patch down with it.

'It's not acid, you know,' Aniela said, kissing his shoulder now, tracing her finger in awe down the line where the muscle separated. 'It won't burn me.'

Jon tilted his head to look at her face. 'Are you okay about what I said?' His mouth twisted in an embarrassed grimace. 'You know—' He pushed ahead bravely. 'About the prostitutes.'

'It's not my business,' Aniela said. 'I mean, you said they were willing, not trafficked—'

'Oh yes! They were very nice girls – well, you know what I mean. And they—' He broke off. 'I can't believe I'm telling you all this.'

Aniela reached up to stroke his hair.

'How does your face feel?' she asked. 'Does anything feel strained, or painful?'

'Are you kidding?' He took her hand and kissed it. 'I never felt better.' He paused. 'Will you stay the night?'

She smiled. 'In case you need medical attention?'

But Jon was too serious a person to pick up on the

opportunity to make light of his request: he said what he meant and meant what he said.

'No,' he said simply. 'I just want you to stay the night.'

Warmth enveloped Aniela as if he'd drawn the duvet round her. It would have been so easy for him to pick up on her cue, to joke with her instead of making a straightforward declaration of his feelings.

'The mattress is very comfortable,' he added solemnly.

'Oh, good,' she said, not quite sure what he meant by this.

'It has a mattress topper,' he went on. 'You can feel it, right? It's really nice.'

'Yes,' she said firmly, though all she could concentrate on was Jon, how his naked body felt against hers, his scent, the freckles on his arms. 'It's really nice.'

'Well, okay. I'm glad you like it.'

He picked up the remote control and turned off the lights.

'Is the heat okay for you?' he asked.

'Yes, it's fine,' Aniela said, beginning to realise that he had never slept the night with a woman before, and that he took his new responsibilities as a host very seriously. 'Lovely,' she added, hoping that he would stop soon.

'I'll get the duvet – here – you should cover up—'

They wriggled the duvet out from under them, pulling it up; Aniela snuggled back against Jon, still unable to believe that she got to lie next to a man with a body like his. *It's shallow of me,* she knew, *but can't I take some pleasure in that? Aren't I allowed, after years with Lubo and his big hairy bottom, to enjoy having had sex with a man like this?* She examined her conscience, and found it clear. *Even if this is just a one-off, if this never happens again, I've had sex with the most amazing man I've ever met.*

Because it probably won't happen again. His face will heal and he'll disappear, to wherever mysterious men who have complete facial reconstructive surgery go. If I'm lucky, we'll have an affair while he's here. I'll get to have the best sex in my life a few more times. And I'll remember it for ever.

Next to her, Jon let out a deep yawn of release.

'I have to buy some condoms,' he said sleepily.

'I expect the prostitutes always brought them,' she said, but her heart rose as she thought: *that means for me. For us, to have sex more while he's here*.

'They did,' he said seriously. 'They're pretty keen on condoms. What kind should I get?'

'Extra large,' she said, giggling.

'Don't tease me,' he said, but he was laughing too. 'Seriously, what kind? It was really hard to pull out in time. I don't know how people do that.'

'They don't,' she said sleepily. 'They get pregnant, or STDs.' A sudden thought occurred to her. 'You mean you never – even when you were a teenager – you really mean you *never* had sex without a condom and had to pull out?'

'Uh-uh,' he said, turning on his side, pushing her gently so she did too and he could spoon her. 'Oh, this is nice,' he said contentedly, as he fitted his soft penis and balls against her bottom, his feet finding and twining around hers. 'I thought it would be.'

'You haven't—' *He* is *like Starman*, Aniela thought in wonder. *He's like some sort of virgin from outer space.* 'What planet do you *come* from?' she couldn't help asking.

'Appalachia,' he said, with a glimmer of humour in his voice. 'Ever heard of it?'

She shook her head, and then felt him stroking her hair, smoothing it into a skein over her shoulder as he'd done before.

'Pretty,' he said drowsily. 'Pretty hair. Soft.'

There was a clock by the bedside, its dial illuminated: it was past one in the morning. Aniela realised what that meant.

'Merry Christmas,' she said softly.

Jon's hand slowed on her hair.

'Hey, you're right. Merry Christmas,' he echoed.

And then, the very next thing, as if he could simply flick a switch and fall asleep, she heard his breathing slow and change, grow calm, steady. His hand rested on her shoulder, heavy, completely relaxed.

He's fast asleep, just like that, Aniela thought, amazed. *Maybe he really is from another planet. Planet Appalachia, somewhere in a galaxy far far away.*

Aniela smiled to herself. *Well, if he is, and if he wants to take me back there with him in his spaceship, I might even go.*

December 25th – Christmas Day

Andy

'We wish you a Merry Christmas, we wish you a Merry Christmas, we *wish* you a Merry Christmas, and a Happy New Year!'

Grigor was in his element. Wearing his full Santa Claus costume, his belly protruding happily in a satisfyingly round sphere that pushed against the red fabric, a white beard hooked around his ears and a red, fur-trimmed hat pulled down over them, he looked, from a distance, the perfect Father Christmas figure, round and jolly, if a little shorter than usual. It was only when you got closer to him that you realised the costume was custom-made to fit him, that the legs of the trousers ended perfectly just below his ankles rather than puddling over his shoes, that the red material was the finest merino wool, and that the fur trim was real: white mink, softer than soft.

Mr K, Andy thought respectfully, *takes Christmas* very *seriously.*

Grigor had got hold of a wreath made entirely from red metal bells woven together, and was rattling it like a tambourine; he capered around the lobby, shaking his jingly bells, a huge smile on his face. Two bodyguards, one on either side of the lobby, stood as stony-faced as ever, more than used to seeing Grigor give his high spirits full rein. The bodyguards had enough self-control not to react to Gregor's bell-ringing, but the three reindeer stationed around the lobby were not so well-trained. They shifted their hooves nervously whenever Grigor and his wreath came anywhere near them, their heads, each heavily laden with a full rack of antlers, bobbing back, away from the crazy man in red jumping around and making loud noises.

Grigor's capering was really the last straw as far as the reindeer were concerned. They were used to appearing at events, having been bred on a farm for that specific purpose; but those events were almost always outside. Even the generous glass doors of Limehouse Reach's lobby had not accommodated the height of their antlers; Grigor, naturally, had insisted upon hiring full-grown adult males, and the handlers had had quite a job getting them to duck as they clopped inside the building.

The reindeer didn't like the shiny floors, the bright lights, and the fact that they were separated. Reindeer were sociable animals, who liked company, but even in the huge lobby there wasn't room for an entire herd of reindeer to be grouped together. They didn't like the fact that their handlers were dressed in weird green outfits, which smelt new and odd, and they *particularly* didn't like the wide, glittering collars which Grigor had commissioned from Swarovski for them at great expense, huge stones in green and red and white, cold and unfamiliar. The crystals reflected the illumination of the lobby, the positive blaze of lights emanating from the gigantic tree, and, of course, each other's collars: the more they fidgeted, the more their unease grew, the more they looked to each other, and the more their collars flashed emerald and ruby and diamond into each other's eyes, dazzling them and making them even more uncomfortable . . .

Grigor, naturally, was oblivious to the reindeer's growing distress. He had paid a great deal of money to hire them, and it was their handlers' responsibility to keep them quiet as he danced around and sang gleefully.

'So bring us some figgy pudding, so bring us some figgy pudding . . .' he carolled. He dashed over to Andy and threw one big meaty arm around the concierge's shoulders. 'Sing, Andy! Sing with me!'

'So bring us some figgy pudding, and a cup of good cheer!' Andy sang along happily.

This was more fun than he'd ever imagined having at work. He was already blissed-out, dazzled with the sheer amount of money that Grigor had thrown at making this Christmas more lavish than Andy could ever, remotely have imagined; the last few days had been like living in a fantasy, as if Grigor really were Father Christmas come to life, a magical creature who only had to click his fingers to make any dream come true. Armed with Grigor's credit cards, Andy had decked out not just the lobby but Grigor's penthouse within an inch of their lives, with the most expensive Christmas decorations money could buy, and he was very keen to see all Grigor's guests ooh and aah at the sight of them.

'Wow! Look!' Andy broke off singing the carol to point towards the huge curving glass walls of the foyer, where, through the exquisite spray-on snow stencils he had spent all yesterday carefully creating, the yellow flash of a Lamborghini Aventador could be seen rounding the drive and pulling up in front of the doors.

'It is Wayne!' Grigor roared cheerfully, striding towards the sliding doors. 'Hello, Wayne! Happy Christmas!'

The short, rather squat figure of Wayne Burns, the star striker of Grigor's football team, Kensington, hopped awkwardly out of his two-hundred-thousand-pound car, manoeuvring uncomfortably under its door, which lifted up at an angle like an opening wing. Pulling down his suit jacket, he walked towards the building, leaving his keys in the ignition for the doorman to park the car in the basement garage.

With his pug nose, cauliflower ear and small, rather piggy eyes, Wayne was no David Beckham, Fredrik Ljungberg or

Ashley Cole. Calvin Klein were never going to ask Wayne to
pose in his underpants or hold a bottle of aftershave sugges-
tively. He didn't even move well; his walk was clumsy, his legs
too short for his frame, his arms too long, swinging like an
orang-utan's from his wide shoulders. But on the pitch Wayne
was transformed. If not precisely graceful, he was poetry in
motion, sheer footballing genius in action, the kind of skill that
could not be taught, merely coached to polish it to perfection.
Wayne had been a child prodigy, and just like Suzuki-method
six-year-old violinists or pianists, he had been spotted young.
He might not have the looks of a male model, but he didn't
need them; he already had more money than even a footballer
could ever spend, a mansion in Elmbridge, Surrey, near the
Kensington training ground, a large collection of the most
expensive cars available to humanity, and a gorgeous glamour
model girlfriend, Chantelle, who was the subject of many
inventive chants by the fans of Kensington's opponents.

It helped, of course, that her surname was Bitts.

''Ello, Mr K,' he said, smiling shyly as he entered Limehouse
Reach. ''Appy Christmas and all that.'

'Wayne! It is so good to see you!' Grigor enfolded his star in
a warm embrace. 'And the lovely Chantelle? She is not here?'

'No, she's gone to see her mum,' Wayne said. 'And I'm
staying in the London flat tonight. Y'know, to be here for the
big game tomorrow.'

He looked around the lobby, and jumped at the sight of the
reindeer.

'Bloody 'ell! Are they real?' he said nervously, backing well
out of range of the antlers.

'Of course!' Grigor boomed, throwing his arms wide. 'I am
Santa, so of course I have reindeer! See, my elves are looking
after them for me . . .'

The handlers, who were not enjoying wearing their green
felt elf costumes with matching ears one little bit, stared
sullenly at Grigor as he waved expansively at them, turning on

his heels in a happy circle, gesturing at the reindeer. The reindeer, sensitive animals, picked up their handlers' bad moods and whinnied unhappily.

'And here is Andy, my main elf!' Grigor said, dancing over to Andy and pulling him forward.

Andy beamed at Wayne: unlike the handlers, Andy loved the elf costume he was wearing. The bright green colour was not only festive, but suited his dark skin to perfection, much more than the burgundy uniform. If he'd been short, it might have been embarrassing, but Andy was tall enough for the outfit not to be a comment on his height, and the tabard, belted tightly at his waist with a big leather belt, actually flattered his slim figure. The elf ears, fixed onto a headband and wired so they bobbed when he moved, were the final touch.

'Nice to meet you,' he said to Wayne. 'Happy Christmas, and welcome to Limehouse Reach.'

'Andy, you must take Wayne upstairs,' Grigor said, 'and give him some mulled wine! My chef has made a special recipe. It is very good. I must wait here for the rest of my guests. Ho ho ho!' he roared unexpectedly in one of Wayne's ears, shaking the wreath next to the other one.

'Jesus, Mr K,' Wayne said, backing away. 'You trying to deafen me?'

Wayne grinned at Andy, who realised he was smiling back. Wayne might have a face only a mother could love, but his smile was very sweet, and his demeanour completely unlike the swaggering stance that Andy would have expected from someone whose two-hundred-thousand-pound car represented merely ten days' pay.

'I call him Mr K too,' Andy heard himself say.

'I know! He said to call him Grigor,' Wayne said, 'but it don't seem right when he pays my wages.'

'Off! Upstairs!' Grigor shouted happily, grabbing both young men's shoulders and shoving them in the direction of the penthouse lift. 'Make sure to show him our Father Christmas on the terrace! When I come up, there will be *two* Father Christmases! Ho ho ho!'

'Don't worry,' Andy said as they walked off. 'You can't miss Father Christmas on the terrace. He's ten feet high.'

'The reindeer aren't coming up too, are they?' Wayne asked. 'I wouldn't put it past Mr K to try to get 'em in a service lift.'

Andy sniggered.

'*Please* don't suggest that to him, okay?' he said. 'Or he'll give it a go. It was hard enough getting them in here. One of them had a bit of a freak-out and did the most enormous poo you've ever seen. Poor old Kevin had to shovel it all up.'

Wayne rolled his eyes.

'That's Mr K all over,' he said affectionately. 'Always got to do bigger and better. Sky's the limit when he gets a bee in his bonnet. 'E's been banging on about 'is big Christmas do for months now.' He glanced sideways at Andy. 'I see 'e's roped you in as well, eh?'

'To be honest,' Andy admitted, 'the costumes were my idea. I *love* dressing up. Did you see Derek, on the front desk? I got him antlers.'

Wayne shook his head.

'Nah, I didn't. Should look out for that when I go back down.'

'If you could sign something for him,' Andy said tentatively, 'he'd love it. He and his kids are all big Kensington fans. I'm sorry, I know you're off duty—'

'Nah, it's fine. I really don't mind.'

Wayne gave that sweet smile again. It took Andy quite by surprise; Wayne's demeanour was so stolid when he was playing, and when he agreed to a rare interview, that Andy had barely ever seen the striker smile; it lit up his face, transforming it, turning his small, ugly features into something almost charming.

'Especially if it's for a kid,' he added. 'I really like kids.'

'Oh, me too! There'll be lots tomorrow, at the Boxing Day party,' Andy said happily as they stepped into the lift. He had been up and down in it multiple times in the last few days, but its sheer level of bling always made him blink. The tiny, glittering Italian mosaic tiles interspersed with the gold-framed mirrors were polished daily to a high sheen, and the Up and Down buttons were made of giant Swarovski crystals.

'Wouldn't like to get in this with a hangover, eh?' Wayne said.

'At least there isn't a disco ball hanging from the ceiling,' Andy said unguardedly.

Wayne burst out laughing.

'We should get one!' he said. 'Be a laugh on Mr K!'

'*You* could do that,' Andy said, pressing the Up Swarovski. 'Somehow, I don't think *I'd* get away with sticking a disco ball to the ceiling of Mr Khalovsky's thirty-thousand-pound lift with Blu-tack.'

Wayne laughed even harder.

'You're funny,' he said, when he had caught his breath. 'And I must say, you've got balls, dressing up like that. Suits you, as well.'

'Oh! Um, thank you,' Andy mumbled, not sure how to respond.

The lift whooshed up to the penthouse; as the doors opened, the scents of Christmas swirled towards them – spicy mulled wine, clove-studded oranges, mince pies warming, roasting meats. It was heady and welcoming, quite unlike Sergei, who, standing there to greet the guests, glared at the sight of Andy.

'Mr K told me to bring Mr Burns up here,' Andy said quickly; Grigor's secretary was becoming increasingly jealous of Andy's rapport with his boss.

'That's right,' Wayne chimed in, taking in the situation with surprising swiftness. 'Andy's supposed to show me the decorations on the terrace. Mr K said that loud and clear.'

Sergei hissed something vicious under his breath. Then, plastering on a teeth-baring smile, he took a gold-chased, enamelled punch glass from a silver tray held by a waiter standing beside him and handed it to Wayne. Wayne promptly passed it to Andy and held out his hand for another glass.

'Call me Wayne, mate,' he said to Andy. 'Mr Burns is my dad, and I fucking 'ate the old sod. Ain't seen 'im or me mum since they sold a story on me to the *News of the World* years ago, and I ain't planning on seeing them ever again.'

'Oh, that's really sad,' Andy said, taking the glass and avoiding Sergei's enraged glare. He had known this, of course; anyone who even occasionally glanced at the tabloids was aware of Wayne's problematic family and their attempts to make money off their son's talent. 'Especially at Christmas.'

'Yeah,' Wayne said, shrugging. 'But in a way, I was sort of glad, y'know? It was just a stupid story on me getting in trouble, bunking off school when I was a nipper, getting pissed on shandy. But it gave me the excuse to cut 'em off. Me dad's an alkie and me mum's not much better. I've set them up for life, and if they blow through what I've given 'em, that's their business. I just can't be doing with it no more.' He looked a little surprised. 'Listen to me, running me mouth off! Sorry, mate! Bit of a depressing thing to be talking about at Christmas!'

'Oh no,' Andy said quickly, 'it's fine. I was brought up in care, and I didn't even know my mum. Believe me, I had a lot of shitty Christmases. So this—' he gestured around the lobby of the penthouse apartment – 'is *beyond* amazing. I feel so lucky to be here.' He giggled. 'Even if Sergei's just waiting to shove me back downstairs again where I belong.'

''E's a miserable sod,' Wayne agreed, darting a glance back at Sergei, who was standing by the lift to greet the next arrivals, glaring at Wayne and Andy's backs. 'Let's wind 'im up, shall we?'

He clinked glasses theatrically with Andy.

'Merry Christmas, Andy!' he said loudly. 'Sorry to hear your family's even crapper than mine, but here's to us both being on top of the world for Christmas!'

He smiled at Andy. Sergei seethed in impotent rage as they walked into the gigantic great room. Wayne stopped dead, blurting out in shock at the sight that met his eyes:

'Fricking *'ell*! Are you *fricking joking or what?*'

'Isn't it amazing!' Andy said joyously. 'It's a train set! I got it from Hamleys! *But*, instead of a train – it's Santa's sleigh! All electric! The kids can sit in it tomorrow and go round!'

'Bloody *'ell*,' Wayne said with huge respect, staring at the sleigh with its following carriage, decked out within an inch of its life, sitting on the wide train tracks which looped around the entire perimeter of the enormous room and disappeared into Grigor's 'library' beyond. Stationed at intervals around the room were tables covered in red fabric, decorated with gold and green bows, gilt candelabras at their centre, heavily laden with food and drink; it was like something from a fairy tale. 'I never seen anything like this in my *life*.'

Automatically, Andy burst into song, singing the words Wayne had just spoken: then he clapped one hand over his mouth, horrified. 'Sorry! That's a song from—'

'*Dr Doolittle*,' Wayne said completely unexpectedly. 'I *love* that film. Blimey, will you look at this?'

He stepped cautiously over the train tracks, his short legs having some trouble crossing their girth, heading for the dining table. 'Old Mr K really done us proud.'

The long table – a twenty-foot slab of ancient dark oak which would never have made it up to the penthouse if the builders hadn't sensibly made the service elevator double-height – was already groaning with bowls of clementines, apples, nuts and dried fruits, cheeses, quince paste, and canapés. Huge ice buckets bearing magnums of Dom Pérignon were stationed at intervals behind the big, elaborately carved, leather-upholstered chairs, and deep insulated glass bowls on the table held mother-of-pearl shells in which tiny, pale grey beads of Beluga caviar and gold Osetra royal caviar were piled up in as generous quantities as if they were boiled sweets in a jar.

'I did the table centrepieces,' Andy said proudly, gesturing with his glass at the gold and red candles, the vases full of candy canes tied with green silk ribbon, the tinsel twisted around the poinsettias. 'Well, I helped.'

'It looks amazing,' Wayne said appreciatively, as a waiter bustled over and presented Wayne with a tray loaded with tiny mince pies, each one decorated with fragile, trembling gold leaf.

'Nice,' Wayne said, taking the plate the waiter was proffering with his other hand and loading it up with pies. 'What about 'im, then?' He nodded to Andy. 'Mr K told 'im to show me round. I can't stand 'ere eating if 'e ain't. Not manners, is it?'

'Oh, I'm all right,' Andy said quickly, but Wayne Burns, Kensington star striker, merely had to express a wish for it to be instantly executed, and in thirty seconds Andy had a plate and was taking a couple of gold-leaf-covered mince pies.

'Diet starts after Crimbo, eh?' Wayne said, biting into one and scattering shards of pastry layers all down his ill-fitting four-thousand-pound suit. '*You're* all right,' he said wistfully through a mouthful, looking at Andy, slim and elegant in his tight-fitting elf costume. 'I chunk up really easily. Me mum used to call me Chunky Monkey when I was little.'

Andy sputtered out pastry over the plate that he was sensibly holding just below his mouth.

'Yeah, I know,' Wayne said resignedly, wrinkling his small pug nose. 'It's funny cos it's true.'

'You're very strong,' Andy said firmly. 'I've seen you play. You move really fast. I bet you're solid muscle.'

'I wish!' Wayne patted his stomach gloomily. 'More like lard.'

Andy giggled.

'Oh, come *on*,' he said. 'With the amount of exercise you do?'

'Yeah, but then I eat a pie and it all piles back on straight away . . .' Wayne finished the mince pie he was eating and chased the pastry down with some mulled wine. 'Mmm,' he said. 'This is top stuff. I don't usually like 'ot drinks, but this is well tasty.' He nodded to the terrace. 'Shouldn't you be showing me the Father Christmas, then? Be something to do.' He glanced around the room, which was empty apart from three bodyguards and two waiters. 'I know I'm early. I always am.'

'All right, here we go,' Andy said, leading the way onto the terrace, holding the door for Wayne. 'Next year we're going to do a giant Father Christmas getting out of a helicopter on the roof, but this is all right for now.'

Wayne's eyebrows shot up at the sight in front of him.

'Yeah,' he said respectfully, taking in the reindeer rearing up, four feet up from the top of the balcony, the sleigh, Santa Claus at the reins, the entire contraption dwarfing even the big space heaters and enormous built-in Weber grill. 'I'd call this all right for now. The kids are going to go mental over this. Wait—'

He looked down at the snow underfoot.

'Did it *snow* 'ere? But 'ow come there ain't any on the roads?'

Andy giggled again. 'We got a snow machine!' he said gleefully. 'It was my idea! Brilliant, isn't it? You should see it coming out, it's *so* much fun. Even the bodyguards were dying to have a go.'

'Mate, that's *excellent*,' Wayne said seriously, turning round 360 degrees to take in the spectacle of the snow-covered terrace. 'So that snow on the Santa Claus—'

'Yeah! It's all real! Mental, eh?' Andy said. 'Why don't you have a go on the snow machine after lunch? It'll be ready for a top-up by then.'

'Love to,' Wayne said with great enthusiasm. 'I must say, you and Mr K *definitely* know 'ow to throw a party.'

Andy finished the rest of his mulled wine. It was rich with port and brandy, and tasted as richly crimson as it looked; he felt his head spinning, and took it as a warning. Reluctantly, he said:

'I should be getting back downstairs, I suppose. That's really where I'm meant to be.'

'Oh.' Wayne finished his own glass, looking straight ahead at the reindeer. 'Yeah. Sorry to keep you.'

'No, it's been really nice! And thanks for making them give me some food. Sergei'd never have let me have anything if you hadn't said so.'

'Plenty to go round,' Wayne said, still staring ahead, his nose like a little snubbed button in profile, a slight double chin showing under his small round jaw.

A waiter bustled out onto the terrace with a fresh tray loaded with the largest prawns Andy had ever seen in his life.

'River prawns, sir?' he asked, extending the tray to Wayne.

The door to the great room had been propped open, and raised, jovial voices inside made both Andy and Wayne look towards their source. A large, bullet-headed man loomed into view, wearing a very expensive suit; he was clearly Russian. Next to him was a thin, pale girl with her hair scraped back into a ponytail, dressed in a navy Chanel couture wool frock with a beaded Peter Pan collar, flat pumps with grosgrain bows on her long narrow feet. Sergei was practically bobbing and scraping to the man, babbling questions about his flight and his comfort; the man was flapping his hand dismissively at Sergei, who was buzzing around him like a small, annoying insect.

'That's Grigor's fiancée. And her dad,' Wayne observed, biting the tail off a gigantic prawn. 'Seen 'em round the club last week. Tiny little thing, ain't she? 'E'd better not get on top. Snap 'er in two.'

Andy cracked a laugh.

'*That's* Miss Fyodorova?' he asked under his breath, as the waiter shot over to offer food to the high-status new arrivals. 'I thought she'd be more . . . more . . .'

'You and me both, mate,' Wayne said dryly. 'Oh well. Her dad's stinking rich.'

'He'd have to be,' Andy said without thinking, looking at the slight, droopy girl, her face bare of make-up, her persona of any sex appeal. 'She looks like a wet piece of spaghetti in a two-thousand-quid dress.'

Wayne laughed so hard he spat out some prawn into his hand. Everyone turned to look.

'I really should go . . .'

Andy dashed off, nodding respectfully at the father and daughter as he passed. Sergei hissed again, his head jerking forwards like a cobra, making it clear that Russian near-royalty was his exclusive territory, and that Andy should not stop to introduce himself; Andy wouldn't have dreamed of it. But Sergei must have decided on reflection that Andy's obedience wasn't enough. As Andy waited for the lift, he felt a sharp poke on his shoulder, two fingers jabbing into him; he swivelled round to see Sergei, almost a foot shorter than him, glaring up at him with absolute fury.

'Who do you think you are?' Sergei spat out, so viciously Andy almost expected to see venom dribbling from his lips. 'You are nothing! A stupid concierge! You are no one! So you and Mr Khalovsky both like Christmas? Big fucking deal, as you say here! Tomorrow, Christmas will be *over*, and Mr Khalovsky will forget all about you, but *I* will still be by his side! Looking after everything for him, *everything*! You know what I did for him, just this morning? *Do* you?'

Sergei's narrowed eyes were completely black, like the people in horror films who are taken over by demons. Andy shook his head dumbly, terrified of both Sergei and the answer to his own question that Sergei was about to give: *if he's going to tell me he tossed off Mr K as a Christmas treat,* Andy thought in panic, *I'll burst out laughing – I won't be able to help it – and then this little freak will probably have me killed . . .*

'I made him a Christmas stocking!' Sergei hissed. 'With his name on it! And presents inside! Hanging on the foot of his bed, when he woke up! He was so happy he cried and said that he was the luckiest man in the *world*!'

'Oh, that's lovely!' Andy exclaimed quite spontaneously. Sergei stared at him with deep concentration, trying to make out whether Andy had spoken satirically, but Andy's face was an open book, and it was perfectly clear, even to a suspicious Russian, that Andy had meant what he said.

'Yes!' Sergei eventually said triumphantly. 'Yes it was! He *loved* it! And though he said Father Christmas had come, he knows it is really *me* who comes! Sergei!' The secretary pounded his scrawny chest so hard with his clenched fists that Andy was concerned he might actually dent himself. '*Me! I* do this for him! *I* take care of him! So *you*—' One hand shot out and stabbed Andy again in the chest; if Andy hadn't been wearing the elf costume, which was made of heavy felt, Sergei's finger would have left a bruise.

'Ow!' Andy said, jumping back, frowning now. 'Enough with the poking!'

'I poke you every time I want!' Sergei said, foaming at the mouth with rage. 'You are just a pathetic concierge! You stay downstairs, where you belong, and I stay up here, with Mr Khalovsky, looking after him, taking care of *everything* for him! You think because you make a fool of yourself, dressing up like that, he will like you! Well, you are stupid! You just look like a big green frog! *Stupid!*'

The lift pinged. With huge relief, Andy shot through the opening doors.

'Don't worry, I'm going!' he said, noticing with horror that Sergei's back had hunched over, his fingers extended like claws; he looked rather like Gollum defending his 'precious'. Andy glanced at the bodyguard stationed by the lift; even that impassive Slavic professional, for a second, rolled his eyes back in his skull to show the whites. It was a clear indication that he also thought Sergei was barking mad.

The doors slid shut again: Andy found himself looking at his own reflection in their steel surface. His handsome dark face was blurred in that distorting mirror, but he could see the whites of his eyes, the paler purple of his lips, and a little of his equally white teeth; he found himself turning round, staring at his much clearer reflection in the antique gold-framed mirror set into the mosaic back wall. He shook his head in wonder at the bizarre confrontation he had just had with Sergei – or rather, that Sergei had just had with him.

But, crazy though that had been, its memory dissolved almost immediately. There was something much more pressing on Andy's mind. His brain was racing with speculation. And then he shook his head slowly once more, his brown eyes wide, still watching his face in the mirror, the elf ears on his head wobbling as he did so.

'No,' he mouthed to himself. 'No. Not possible.'

Melody

She was crying again. And to do Melody justice, she was totally sick of it. Melody was not one of those actresses who thrived on perpetual excesses of emotion and drama; she was basically a sensible girl who didn't need to create chaos around her to feel alive.

'I'm sorry, Mum! I don't mean to be so pathetic! It's just so lovely to see you!' she wailed through her tears, clinging to her mother.

If Melody's face hadn't been so bruised, she would have looked exactly like a smaller, more delicate version of the older woman; Sonia Dale had passed on her striking colouring, the black hair and triangular, cat-like blue eyes, to Melody, and in her youth had been just as slim as her daughter. Age and soft living had layered and padded more flesh over the fine bones, but her hair was piled up on top of her head to give her height, her make-up thorough but discreet, and her print wrap dress hid her pleasantly plump body in all the right places. And, like all good mothers, she had that crucial item in her handbag – a packet of tissues.

'Come on now,' she said, easing her daughter back, trying not to grimace at the bruising on Melody's face; it was faded yellow now, the colour of dirty nicotine stains, and the swelling was also going down. But it was still unpleasant enough to be a shock for a mother who had had no idea, until Melody rang her first thing that morning, that her daughter had undergone yet another gruelling round of plastic surgery.

Reaching for a tissue, Sonia dabbed at Melody's face with extreme caution.

'Do you think you could put on some foundation, love?' she asked. 'You know, just so you don't frighten the horses.'

'Literally,' commented Ash, Melody's brother, who was standing by the window staring out at the stunning view beyond. Actually, he was craning his head down as much as possible, trying to give himself vertigo. 'You better not wander around the village looking like that, Mel. Not near the riding school, anyway. With a face like that you'll spook a whole string of horses at one go.'

'*Ashley Dale*,' thundered his father crossly. 'Don't you make fun of your sister like that!'

'It's okay, Dad,' Melody said, sitting up, but still leaning against her mother on the sofa, where she had collapsed into Sonia's arms almost as soon as her family had walked in the door. 'I did it to myself. It's my own stupid fault. Ash can take the piss as much as he wants.'

'Ah, bollocks, Mel,' Ashley said, turning round from the view of Canary Wharf's skyscrapers, bright in the clear sunny winter sky. 'Way to take all the fun out of it.'

'Sorry, Ash,' his sister said, managing a smile. 'Bet it doesn't last long.'

'This is a brilliant place,' Ash said, looking around him. 'Like, *amazing*. Are you going to live here now?'

'No!' Melody said instantly. Apart from the suite at the Bel-Air in LA, she'd never been as unhappy anywhere as she had here at Limehouse Reach. 'I can't *wait* to get out of here!'

Twenty-one-year-old Ash sighed audibly as his dreams of visiting his sister, even moving into the second bedroom of this amazing shag pad in the sky, fizzled and died.

'It even has a built-in *bar*,' he complained in frustration, going over to the free-standing white unit with its smooth grey Corian top. Behind it, against the wall, was a cupboard with glass doors, its glass shelves stocked with martini glasses, hi-ball tumblers, brandy snifters and champagne flutes; Ashley bent down to open the doors below the glass shelves, revealing a drinks fridge on one side and a wine rack on the other. '*Well* cool!' he exclaimed.

'That *is* lovely,' Sonia Dale cooed, craning her neck to look at the set-up over her daughter's head. 'Phil, do you think we could do something like that in ours?'

'Where?' her husband asked bluntly. 'We haven't got room for that, Sonia!'

'Maybe if we knock through, like I've been talking about – do an L in the kitchen and put it on the far side—'

'Sonia! We are *not* having an L in the kitchen, and that's that! It'll cut the room in half!'

'Not if we knock through to the utility room—'

Sonia's attention was temporarily diverted to her husband; this particular battle had been raging between them for ten years now and saw no signs of abating. It was the unstoppable force meeting the immovable object. Melody's eyes met Ashley's, and they both smiled in recognition of the decade-old dispute kicking off between their parents. It was hugely comforting, because it was so familiar.

Melody slipped away from her mother on the sofa, came over to her brother and enfolded him in a hug, careful not to squeeze too tightly because of the bandages on her chest. Ashley didn't have Melody's ethereal beauty; he was more solid, less striking, a nice-looking, averagely built young man who was close enough to his older sister to hug her back warmly.

'You've been through the wars, Mel love,' he said, patting her back. 'All sorted now, though, eh? It's been a weird old time of it. We haven't known what to think.'

'Hopefully I'm all sorted,' Melody said, giving him a last cuddle and then pulling back.

He looked down at her.

'You got your tits done as well, right?' he asked hopefully. 'Mum said you said you'd had all this surgery to get everything back like before.'

'Yes!' She grinned. 'They should be all fine – the implants weren't in for long, so the doctor said I'll still be—'

'Aah! Sorry I asked!' Ashley covered his ears. '*Last* thing I want to hear is details of my sister's boob job! I'm just glad you won't be, you know, bouncing around like that any more. That Wonder Woman outfit—' He shuddered. 'I dunno how brothers of glamour models manage, seeing their sisters with their tits out all the time. It's enough to give you a complex or something.'

Phil Dale came over; sensibly ignoring any discussion on the size or bounciness of his daughter's breasts, he hugged her in his turn, stroking her hair and saying how worried they'd been.

'It just wasn't like you to disappear like that over the holidays, Mel,' he said over and over again. 'I know you were so busy, and we hadn't seen much of you in the last year, with all the filming and being in California, but we really did think we'd get you back for Christmas ...'

'I'm sorry, Dad!' she mumbled. 'I just thought I'd hide away for the holidays, get the work done and start the New Year all back to normal ... it seemed like such a good idea at the time ...'

'Well, no harm done,' Sonia said sensibly, standing up and smoothing down her skirt, picking up the blue suede handbag that matched her eyes and one of the colours in her print dress. Sonia was very big on things matching. 'Melody's come to her senses, she's given us a ring and we've dashed down first thing on Christmas morning to come and bring her home. I must say, at least there wasn't a soul on the roads. Natalie next door's keeping an eye on the turkey I've got in the oven, but we should really be getting back. Phil, do you want me to drive? And Melody, do you want to pack your stuff now? There's room in the car, and we've got the roof rack. You won't need to be coming back, will you, love? Not to stay, I mean.'

'I don't know,' Melody said, thrown into confusion. 'I mean, I've got the nurse here, and the doctor's on call if there are any complications—'

James is in London, is what she really meant. *I need to be close to him, work out what I'm going to do. If I pack up and leave, I'll be really far away from him . . .*

'Come on, Sonia love, don't rush her like this,' her father said, coming to her rescue. 'Melody, why don't you just get yourself an overnight bag for tonight, and me or Ash can bring you back tomorrow or the day after. Do you need to check with that nice nurse?'

Aniela had just come in for Melody's daily check-up when the Dales flooded in to see her; she'd promptly left them to have their happy reunion, telling Melody to page her if she wanted her to come back later.

'Not for my face,' Melody said unguardedly. 'She says I'm healing fine. This place—' she gestured around her at the stunning flat – 'is more for the privacy, you know. I was scared to death of the paps seeing me like this.'

'They'll know you had more surgery,' her brother said frankly. 'I mean, if your lips don't look like a goldfish's any more, and your boobs aren't the size of—'

'*Ashley!*' both his parents yelled furiously.

A momentary silence fell: Ashley hung his head. It was the first time the Dales had all been quiet at the same time, and into the momentary lull there slid a seductive voice which was familiar to everyone in the room, and, at this point, most people in the country. It was a woman, cooing in velvety tones:

'Mmm, this tastes *wonderful*! Maybe it's just me, but I *love* to lick gravy off the spoon – I bet you do too, when it's this good. It's that dash of Madeira that gives it a delicious extra kick . . .'

'*Ma cosa fai, Devon?*' The woman was interrupted by an Italian male, impatient and bossy. '*Che schifo!*'

As one, the Dales turned to look at the big flatscreen TV, which Melody had been watching before the arrival of her family. A beautiful, curvy brunette, her white bosom wobbling as delicately as two luscious mounds of blancmange above the low-cut neckline of her festive red cardigan, was turning to frown crossly at a skinny, large-nosed Italian man whose hair was a mass of wild curls; he was removing the wooden spoon she had just licked sexily, throwing it in the sink of the kitchen in which they were standing.

'I wash that *now*,' he said severely. 'It is deesgusteeng to leeck the spoon!'

'Ooh, it's the Christmas special of *Devon in Paradise*! I *love* Cesare,' Mrs Dale sighed. 'He's *so* sexy. That Devon's a lucky woman.'

'As you can see,' Devon was saying to the camera, frowning horribly at Cesare, 'Italians are incredibly bossy and think they know *everything*, even when they don't. And one thing they *definitely* don't know how to make is Yorkshire pudding.' She turned around and bent over, presenting her rounded bottom to the camera as she opened the huge oven and removed a tray of mini-muffin tins, each one containing a golden, puffed-up, perfect Yorkshire pudding.

'She's lost weight,' Phil Dale commented appreciatively. 'Looks great, doesn't she?'

'It's Cesare,' Sonia informed him. 'He's been teaching her about healthy Italian eating. Small portions and no snacking between meals. He yells at her if she tries to sneak down to the kitchen in the middle of the night.'

Devon McKenna, the undeniably gorgeous TV cook, had been at the centre of a soap-opera scandal last year, when she had left her rugby-player husband and run off to Italy with an Italian aristocrat; the scandal had been compounded when her younger sister Deeley promptly moved in with and got pregnant by the discarded husband. All four parties seemed fine with the new arrangement, and however, Devon had been even more of a fixture on the pages of *Hello!* and *OK! Magazine* ever since – especially as her comeback TV series, *Devon In Paradise,* which featured her and Cesare squabbling viciously as he lectured her on how to cook Italian food properly, had become a ratings hit.

'Ooh, Phil! Did we record this?' Sonia asked anxiously.

'It'll be on Catchup, Mum,' Ashley said, pulling a face. 'Honestly, the way you lech over that Cesare's a bit disgusting, if you ask me.'

'Oh, your dad doesn't mind,' his mother said cheerfully. 'He likes looking at Devon, don't you, love?'

'Who doesn't?' Phil Dale said, unabashed. 'But that Cesare'd better not ban her from licking spoons – it's half the fun.'

'Oh, you!' His wife elbowed him, giggling.

On screen, Devon had extracted a pudding from the tin, and, holding it in one hand, she filled the little dent in the centre with a dribble of rich gravy.

'Here,' she said to Cesare. 'Open wide.'

She winked at the camera. 'Even fussy Italians like Yorkshire pudding!'

As Cesare's lips closed over Devon's fingers, Mrs Dale sighed in pleasure.

'God, I *can't,*' Ashley muttered to Melody, turning away. 'It's like watching your parents look at porn.'

Mercifully for Ashley's sensibilities, the doorbell rang just as Cesare was grudgingly pronouncing the pudding 'not bad for your Eeengleesh food'. Melody, going to answer the door with her brother behind her, couldn't help a brief flash of fantasy taking over – James tracking her down, turning up on her doorstep with a huge bunch of flowers. Melody knew it couldn't be him, but still, her heart rose as she unsnibbed the lock and swung the door open—

– to see, to her enormous surprise, a burly, squat Father

Christmas standing there. A pair of big padded elf ears reared over one of his shoulders; Melody tilted sideways to see Andy's face below them, smiling reassuringly.

'Ho ho ho! Happy Christmas!' bellowed the Santa Claus in a distinctly foreign accent. 'I see you have your wreath on your door! Very nice!'

He raised one he was carrying and jingled it furiously; involuntarily, Melody took a step back.

'This is Mr Khalovsky from upstairs,' Andy said swiftly. 'The penthouse, I should say. He's the one that kindly bought the wreaths I brought round.'

'Oh yes! Of course! Um, Merry Christmas!' Melody said, hoping that Mr Khalovsky wouldn't blanch at the sight of her face; little did she know that Grigor was very familiar with the signs of plastic surgery damage from his wife's various operations, and had instantly jumped to the correct conclusion as to why the young woman in front of him had two fading black eyes, a nose splint and more bruising round her chin.

'Mr K would like to invite you all to Christmas lunch!' Andy announced cheerfully. He and Grigor looked so totally unselfconscious in their costumes that they might have been wearing them their whole lives.

'Please!' Grigor said expansively. 'You *must* come! There is so much food. I look at my table and I think, we must have more guests for this feast! So I pop down, as Andy says, to invite you. I am the Father Christmas for the whole building today!'

'Oh, I don't know,' Melody began. 'My family's come to take me back to theirs, and I haven't seen them in months, so—'

'*Mr Khalovsky? Grigor Khalovsky?*' His eyes so wide they looked as if they were held open with invisible toothpicks, his mouth equally round, Ashley elbowed his sister out of the way. 'The owner of *Kensington*? No *way!*'

Grigor beamed. 'You like football, young man? Then you must join me for lunch! You would maybe like to meet Wayne?'

'*Wayne Burns?*'

Ashley's voice had risen to such a high squeak that soon it would be only audible to bats and dogs.

'Did you say – *Grigor Khalovsky?*' Mr Dale had come up next to his son; Melody was being squashed against the side of the door, completely forgotten by her sports-crazed father and brother. 'Sir, it's an honour—'

Shyly, he put out his hand: Grigor grabbed it with both his and pumped it up and down as if he were working an old maintenance handcar on the railways.

'Grigor! Please! You will all come to lunch, yes? To meet Wayne?' he added, smiling widely at Ashley.

'Yes *please*,' Ashley said devoutly.

Melody had a split-second to decide how she felt about it: she didn't know if she was ready for Christmas lunch with a lot of strangers. Ringing her family had seemed like a huge deal yesterday, and now the cosy reunion had turned, in the speed of light, into a major social whirl. *But I can't tell Dad and Ash that they can't go to lunch with Wayne Burns!* she realised, taking in their excited expressions. *And besides, I want to audition for Beatrice as soon as I can – that'll mean getting back into real life with a vengeance, letting everyone have a good look at me. This might be just what I need to toughen myself up a bit.*

And as these thoughts raced through her head, the chance to hold back her male relatives passed: they stampeded past her to follow Grigor down the corridor. She turned to look for her mother.

'Mum? You all right with this?'

But her mother, bright-cheeked with excitement, was already closing her phone and slinging her bag over her elbow, hurrying towards her, eager not to be left out.

'It's all right, love,' she said, words flooding out of her in a stream of consciousness. 'I've texted Natalie and told her to take out the turkey when it's done. The veggies are in the warming oven, and they'll probably all be dried to a crisp by the time we're back, even if she turns it off now, but who cares! I can make turkey sandwiches for dinner – if we're hungry, which, let's face it, we probably won't be, after eating at a Russian oligarch's! And there's Terry's Chocolate Oranges at home, *plus* a big Milk Tray selection box *and* a tin of Quality Street – *lots* to snack on tonight if we get peckish! Ooh! Natalie'll be *writhing* with jealousy! Just imagine! Lunch with the owner of Kensington *and* Wayne Burns! I must say, Melody, I wasn't over the moon about you wanting to be an actress, but we *do* end up meeting famous people whenever you're around, dear!'

She took a deep breath of excitement.

'Melody, I never thought I'd say this,' she continued with utter seriousness, 'but this is *even better* than the time you took me to the BAFTAs and Daniel Craig backed into me and spilled my wine all over the carpet.'

A sudden thought struck Mrs Dale.

'I don't suppose you ever get invited to anything with Devon and Cesare, do you?' she asked hopefully. 'Ooh, I think I'd *die* with excitement if I was in the same room as him!'

Jon

*H*e had absolutely no idea what he was supposed to do now.

It would help, of course, he realised, *if I had any idea of what I actually wanted to do.*

Aniela had been gone by the time he woke up that morning. That, in itself, was an extraordinary occurrence; he had no experience, naturally, of having a woman sleep over, but he was so highly attuned to his surroundings, even when asleep, that he was still amazed that she had managed to get up, dress and leave without his stirring in the slightest. God knew what time it had been: his internal clock, which woke him without fail at six-thirty, no matter what country he was in, had also failed him. He had slept almost till ten, which was unprecedented.

And it must have been the sleep of the dead. Jesus. Anyone could have broken in, and I'd've slept through that as well.

Jon cringed. Last night, he had been dozing on the couch when he'd heard her soft footsteps come down the corridor and pause outside his door; he'd been sure it was her without even knowing why. And once she was inside, he had let down his guard completely.

He shook his head in disbelief.

It isn't even as though I'm holing up here with no one knowing where I am but the medical staff, he thought. *I have this whole Mr and Mrs Khalovsky mess to sort out, and I haven't made a lick of progress on that. Which is insane, considering that crazy bitch is going to make a whole mess of trouble for me if she doesn't hear soon that I've offed her husband.*

And I'm damned if I'm going to do that. I made a vow, and I'm not breaking it for some bloodthirsty Russian woman, no matter how tough she is.

So why've I barely spent a minute trying to figure out how to get my ass out of this trap she's put me in?

Jon sighed. He knew the answer perfectly well.

It's her. Aniela. The moment she walked in here, everything went haywire. I only met her seventy-two hours ago, and I've done more stuff differently in those seventy-two hours than I have in the last ten years.

'Stuff differently'? he repeated to himself. *Nice euphemism, Jon. One day you're fantasising about her, wondering what it'd be like to sleep over with her – the next day you're doing it. All over the damn apartment. And then passing out after like she hit you over the head with a brick.*

In five minutes, she's going to ring that doorbell. And what the hell are you going to do then?

Aniela was a professional through and through. He had no doubt that she'd turn up for the scheduled appointment that she was contractually paid to keep. But what if she just checked his scar and left again? What if she thought it was up to him now to be the man and make a move?

That sounded pretty reasonable, actually. It was how Jon had been brought up – that the guy should be the guy, and court the woman. Aniela and he might have got down to it without a lot of preliminaries; he realised ruefully that he was getting hard just remembering that. *I can't open the door to her with a hard-on! Or can I? Would a woman like that? Would it be a compliment? Or would she get really pissed instead?*

'Dammit!' he said out loud, striding across to the Smeg freezer, dragging it open, pulling out the full ice tray and slapping it onto the back of his neck. The shock at least took the edge off his erection.

Though really I should be jamming it between my legs, he thought, furious with his body. *I train it, I feed it right, I work it out, it does whatever it's supposed to. Until now.*

He'd actually considered trying to get in some flowers to give her, flowers or chocolates; Jon had absorbed that from popular culture, knew that you were supposed to give women bouquets and candy. But it was Christmas Day, and everything was closed, and though he'd have bundled up, wrapped his face in a scarf and gone out, he'd called down to the doorman who'd told him that nothing round here was open, nothing at all. It was the business district; he'd be lucky to find a corner shop, let alone somewhere to buy a bouquet or box of chocolates decent enough to give a woman you'd just had quite a lot of sex with.

And though I'm sure the concierge could get me anything I needed, I'd be way too embarrassed to ask him to get me presents for a lady. Aniela's the only female who comes to visit me – cause no one knows about Dasha Khalovsky. The concierge'd be bound to guess, and that'd be awkward for both me and her.

Plus, even if a store was open, I'd probably just have got the wrong thing anyway, he thought despairingly. *How the hell am I supposed to know what Aniela would like? Or, maybe she's just going to want to pretend that nothing happened between us – in which case, thrusting a bunch of roses at her'll go down worse than a bucketful of wet sick—*

The doorbell rang. He swallowed so hard his Adam's apple thrust almost painfully against his throat. For a moment, he had an impulse to run and hide in the bathroom, lock himself in, not answer the door, wait it out till she left again . . .

Jesus, Jon, pull yourself together! You've done some of the worst things a man can do – you can confront a woman you had sex with!

Putting his shoulders back, he marched to the door like a private on parade, taking hold of the lock and wrenching it open so hard that he nearly slammed it into the wall behind.

'Hey,' he said, looking down at Aniela and swallowing again even harder.

'Good morning,' she said, as poised as ever, her hair perfectly smooth, her uniform freshly ironed.

For a moment Jon wondered crazily if he'd hallucinated it all; could he really have kissed this woman, ripped her tights and her panties off, pushed her up against the wall and thrust into her? It seemed inconceivable, something that could only happen in a parallel universe. The distance between them was huge, terrifying; but he was backing away to let her in, making even more of a void between them. Why was he doing that, when what he really wanted to do was step towards her?

He turned and walked towards the living room, totally confused, and all too aware that his erection had popped up again just at the sight of her. *No more talking*, it yelled at him impatiently. *You know what you want. Just do it.*

'How is your head today?' Aniela asked him politely, settling down her bag on the coffee table.

Jon had no idea.

'Uh, fine. I think,' he said at random.

'Shall I look at it?'

She stood there with her hands folded in front of her, demure and composed. He wanted to reach out for her more than he'd ever wanted anything in his life. To sink into her, to feel her warmth and softness wrap around him, to fuck her and to fall asleep with her again.

Jon wished, with every fibre of his being, that she'd do

something, give him some sort of hint, one way or the other. At least put him out of this misery.

Surely she knows I need some help here! I was real honest with her about my past. If she wants me to do something, act in a way she wants, she should help me along a bit—

He stared at Aniela, trying desperately to read her mind. When the doorbell rang, he honestly didn't know how he felt; relieved or impatient at the interruption. *Or on high alert, in case it's that mad psycho Russian come back to threaten me all over again—*

'Who is it?' he yelled, not moving; there was an internal wall between him, Aniela and the door. If someone started shooting, God forbid, they were much better off here. Plenty of kitchen furniture to use as a shield.

'Hello! Mr Jordan?' called a man's voice. 'It's Andy, the concierge. I'm here with Mr Khalovsky from upstairs. He was wondering if you'd like to pop up for Christmas lunch – he's inviting everyone in the building—'

Aniela had jumped back, because Jon had dived towards her as soon as Andy had identified himself, snapping open her medical bag and rifling through it. He dragged out a wide roll of elastic bandage, swiftly wrapping it twice round his head, from his crown around the base of his chin and up again, covering his tell-tale scar; then he flipped it, binding it round his forehead, and then the sides of his face. In a mere thirty seconds, he had concealed most of his features; he kept going till he had used the entire roll, tucking the end in, dashing towards the door as he finished. By the time he had reached the door, he looked as if he were playing the Invisible Man in a game of charades.

A quick glance through the peephole, and Jon was opening the door, his eyebrows rising as much as they could at the sight of Grigor's looming bulk in a red Santa suit. Andy was too well-trained to exclaim at Jon's bandages, but he did stare at them, momentarily struck dumb, as Grigor trotted out his invitation, complete with wreath-jingling.

'You are all right to come?' he asked. 'My chef will make you soft food if you have problems to chew—'

'Yeah, I'm good,' Jon said, making a snap decision. 'Well, it's very kind of you, Mr Khalovsky. I'm very happy to accept your invitation. I'd just need my nurse to come with me. Aniela?' he called.

She emerged into view at the end of the corridor.

'You okay with—' Jon started.

'Of course! Of course! A nice nurse to come too! Very nice!' Grigor clapped his hands, the wreath jingling, his beard waggling. 'Miss Nurse, you are invited to lunch with us!'

'Cool,' Jon said smoothly, gesturing to Aniela to join him.

Well, this was good improvising. I get Aniela with me, so I can take some time to figure out whatever the hell is happening with her. Plus, I can scope out Grigor's situation, his security, the penthouse layout . . . get a sense of what kind of man he is. Work out how to finesse this whole damn mess, how I can get out from under Mrs Khalovksy's ultimatum without killing her husband.

'Cause though all I can think about is Aniela, this whole Dasha Khalovsky situation is the only thing I should be focusing on right now. It's way more urgent.

Get it together, Jon. Start thinking with the head on your shoulders, not the other one.

And if anyone asks about the bandages, my story'll be that I was in a nasty smash-up. Four-car pile-up. Went through the windshield – that'll tear a face to pieces.

Aniela was coming towards him, a frown on her face, her pale eyebrows drawing together, and as soon as he looked at her, he felt a goofy smile trying to plaster itself over his bruised and messed-up face. The cool, rational part of his brain that had just swiftly calculated how to handle this new development faded away as quickly as it had snapped into action.

No killing, he reminded himself. *Not even if you see the perfect opportunity to break Khalovsky's neck and fake it as a fall. After all, you've got a nurse as your lunch date!* he thought with a flash of humour, as he stepped back deferentially to let her precede him out of the apartment. *You can't be killing anyone with an angel of healing by your side!*

Aniela

Completely confused, Aniela trailed after Grigor's wide red back as he stamped happily down the corridor in his big fur-trimmed boots. Andy was just behind him, green costume luminously bright, elf ears bobbing merrily. They were in a file, behind her was Jon, and behind Jon was one of Grigor's bodyguards, bringing up the rear. A second bodyguard led the procession, speaking quickly in Russian into his head mike, though he was handicapped by having to look round every few seconds to see if his master was following or had stopped suddenly to pound on a door. Grigor came to a sudden halt by the bank of lifts, and everyone did their best not to cannon into each other like dominoes as they all stopped abruptly too.

'You,' Grigor boomed, pointing at Jon and Aniela, '*you* will go down to the lobby, and then Nestor will meet you and show you into my own lift! Ilya has told him you are coming. And *we* will go up to find . . . who is left, Andy?'

'Well, we could try the El-Khalabis, Mr K,' Andy said. 'Though I'm not sure if they'll really be into the whole Christmas thing. I mean, Prince Al-Qarashi *really* didn't get the wreath.'

'Nonsense!' Grigor said dismissively. 'Christmas is for everyone! I am a Jew, and I love Christmas!'

'Oh, that's *such* a good attitude, Mr K,' Andy sighed. 'If we all thought like that, we'd have world peace!'

'*Hahahaha!*' Grigor's deep chuckles reverberated around his ribcage as if it were an echo chamber. He reached up and patted the top of Andy's head, in front of the padded head- band that secured the elf ears, just as if Andy were a favourite pet. 'You are a very funny boy, Andy. Very funny. World peace! Ha! How would we ever make any money?'

Lifts pinged, Grigor, Andy and the bodyguards stepped into one going up, and Jon and Aniela into the down one. Aniela had been hoping for a moment alone with Jon, but inside the car was Melody with her family.

'Aniela!' Melody exclaimed. 'Are you coming to Mr Khalovsky's too?'

'It seems so,' Aniela said, shrugging in disbelief. 'It is all very strange.'

She looked closer at Melody.

'You have put on foundation,' she observed. 'You see, I told you the bruising would be easy to cover.'

'Foundation, and just a little mascara,' Melody's mother said briskly. 'I decided to pop back in to do a little bit of touching up on her. Poor lamb, she doesn't want to be sitting there at a posh lunch looking like she just went ten rounds with Mike Tyson. No offence,' she added quickly to Jon.

'Not at all,' he said easily. 'Believe me, you don't want to see what's under these.' He raised a hand to the bandages. 'It'd put folks right off their food.'

Mrs Dale tutted sympathetically.

'Very sorry to hear that, I'm sure,' she said. 'What was it, a car accident?'

'Went through the windscreen face first,' Jon said coolly, his other hand reaching out, touching Aniela's with an almost infinitesimal movement. 'Airbag malfunctioned. Real nasty business.'

'Oh, *dear!*' Mrs Dale said sadly, as her husband added:

'You should sue them, mate. The car maker.'

'My insurers are dealing with all that,' Jon said. 'But my lovely nurse says that I'm making a good recovery.' He smiled at Aniela. 'And she seems to know exactly what she's doing.'

Aniela felt herself going red. *I have no idea what* you're *doing*, she thought angrily. She had been convinced that Jon had accepted Grigor's invitation as a way of avoiding being alone with her, and had been hugely hurt by that; all that morning, nipping back to the Clinic to shower and change, then visiting Melody, she had been buoyed up by the knowledge that she was going to see Jon again at noon, that he would be expecting her to keep her regular appointment. She'd had no idea what to expect; just the thought of seeing him again, being close to him, alone with him, had been so exciting that she couldn't look beyond that—

God, you're a liar, she told herself crossly. *Of course you looked beyond that. You were hoping to spend the day with him, not go back to the Clinic alone; to order in some food, curl up on the sofa, maybe watch a Christmas film—*

Oh please, there you go with more lies! Even more than that, you wanted to fuck his brains out all over again!

Whereas he didn't seem to be in that much of a hurry to be alone with her; *quite the opposite,* she thought crossly. *And now I feel like an idiot. He couldn't have rushed out of there any faster.*

But he made sure I was coming with him – and he just called me lovely—

There was no point looking at his face to try to read anything there, but strangely, that didn't even worry Aniela that much. She was very accustomed to reading people's body language as much as their facial expressions. It wasn't a skill all nurses had; Aniela had worked with plenty of what they called in England 'chatty Kathys', a term she loved, people who were too busy gossiping to take a moment to silently take in how their patients were doing.

Aniela wasn't one of those. She liked to quietly absorb a

patient's energy, to form a sense of how healthy they were, to study her own reactions to them for signals as to what kind of approach they needed. And now, standing next to Jon, whose fingers had left hers but were still close, she realised that she wasn't feeling insecure. Unsure of what was going on, confused as to what he was doing and why he had bandaged his face, slightly nervous at his ability to lie so easily and quickly, yes: but not insecure.

Interesting, she thought as the lift came to a halt on the ground floor.

The men politely waved the women out first: Melody gasped at the sight of the reindeer in their gloriously shiny Swarovski collars as she came out into the full atrium.

'My God!' she exclaimed. '*Reindeer?* I thought for a moment I was seeing things!'

'I got photos on the way up,' Ashley said eagerly. 'I tweeted them already. People are totally not believing they're real.'

'Dasher! No!' said one of the handlers, who was dragging on the leash of his enormous charge; the reindeer in question had decided that what it wanted to do, urgently, was to drink some water from the carp pond. He was ducking over, his huge head, laden with the rack of antlers, perilously close to the surface, as the handler tugged futilely on the harness, trying to pull him back.

'Oh dear, aren't there fish in there?' Mrs Dale exclaimed.

'They won't *eat* them, Mum!' Ashley said impatiently. 'Reindeer are veggies!'

'They can scare them within an inch of their lives, though, can't they? How would you like a big thing like that sticking its tongue out right into where you lived, looking all hungry?' his mother pointed out indignantly, walking over to the pond. 'Look!' She stuck out a finger, indicating the orange shapes of the carp, which were all huddling together at the far side of the pool, in the shadow of the gigantic head looming over them. 'The poor little fishies are terrified!'

Striding right up to the reindeer, she tapped him on the bridge of his nose.

'Cush!' she said firmly. 'Cush!'

'Mum! What are you *doing*?' Ashley hissed.

'Come on, you,' Sonia Dale said to the reindeer. 'Cush!' She tapped him again.

'I'm projecting calm-assertive energy,' she explained over her shoulder. 'Like the Dog Whisperer says to do. I'm being the pack alpha.'

'But that's *dogs*, love!' her husband said. 'Not reindeer! And isn't "cush" what you say to camels?'

'To get them to lie down,' the handler muttered savagely. 'Not to back off a flipping carp pond—'

'Cush!' Sonia said loudly to the reindeer, who snorted, and then, miraculously, raised his head, making her jump back as the antlers swung up. Obediently he took a few steps back from the carp pond and the annoying woman who kept hitting his nose.

'See?' she said triumphantly. 'It worked! It's all about the energy you're projecting, just like I said!'

The reindeer, presumably cross at being thwarted, let out another snort, and then gave vent to his feelings even more practically by squeezing out a series of droppings onto the shiny marble tiles.

'Look,' Phil Dale said, very interested. 'They're like giant Maltesers.'

'Bet they don't smell like giant Maltesers,' Ashley said, as Derek resignedly came out from behind the desk with a broom and dustpan.

'It's *unbelievable* how much they can shit,' he muttered crossly.

'So did you break the windscreen with your face?' Ashley said to Jon as they crossed the lobby to the penthouse lift. 'Actually, like, plant one on it? That's *mental*.'

'Ugh, Ash is so gruesome,' Melody said to Aniela, wincing.

'He loves gore. I hope that poor man doesn't mind. He seems very brave about it.'

'Oh no,' Aniela said. 'He won't care at all.'

And she realised that she had spoken about Jon with as much casual assurance as if she had known him for years, rather than a mere three days.

'Did your nose break first?' Ashley was continuing eagerly. 'Or did it all sort of happen at once? Did you feel all the bones smashing? Did it hurt a lot, or were you in shock?'

'Are you in touch with James at all, love?' Melody's mother questioned her daughter, now that she had a brief girl-to-girl moment. 'You don't mind my asking, do you?'

'Felicity says he's seeing Priya now,' Melody said, her voice sad. 'You know, the girl who took over Juliet when I dropped out. She got really good reviews.'

'Oh, *Felicity*!' her mother sniffed, effortlessly ignoring anything but the crucial part of the information Melody had just given her. 'I wouldn't trust a word that young lady says! I'm always reading interviews with her in the papers about how she's naturally thin. *Well*, do you remember when *I* came to visit you when you were filming *Wuthering Heights*? That nice young man who did your make-up, Gary Jordan, very kindly set my hair for me when he had nothing else to do, and we had a lovely gossip. *He* told me that Felicity actually lives on Big Macs and laxatives. *And* that she was jealous of you because you had the lead and she had to play that soppy Isabella,' her mother added.

'She had *lovely* costumes,' Melody said, momentarily distracted. 'But yes, it's quite true about Felicity and Big Macs.' She grimaced. 'We call it her Macs and Lax diet.'

'Macs and Lax!' Aniela repeated, shaking her head. 'That is *not* healthy!'

The bodyguard stationed by the penthouse lift recess, having described the arrivals into his head mike, received confirmation that he was permitted to let them up; he pressed the button and held the doors for them as they all filed in.

'God, Aniela, you wouldn't *believe* what actors and actresses do to stay thin and young,' Melody continued, throwing herself into this new subject to steer away from the painful issue of James. 'And movie execs too. Brad Baker, who directed my film, injects human growth hormone into his tummy every day. Demi Moore used to go off to Switzerland to have leeches suck her blood.'

'No *way*,' Ashley said, shivering happily. '*Leeches?*'

'And I had a snake venom facial in LA,' Melody recounted. 'That one's quite common.'

'They put a *snake* on your *face?*' Aniela and Sonia Dale said in horrified unison.

Melody giggled again. 'No, it's in a serum. It's sort of tingly. Apparently the venom stings you gently, and that sends signals to the nerves, and *they* send out signals to produce chemicals that strengthen the facial muscles and smooth out wrinkles.'

Aniela was beyond speech at this: Jon, looking at her, chuckled quietly.

'Aniela's about to tell us all how dumb this is,' he said, amused.

'Did you see any difference?' Sonia asked.

'Not really,' Melody said. 'It's so nice when you have a treatment, though, you feel better afterwards and that relaxes you. I'm sure that's all most of these things do.'

'Cost a fortune,' her father muttered. 'Stupid women, these places see 'em coming.'

'Oh, lots of men in LA have facials too, Dad,' Melody assured him. 'You'd be surprised.'

'I bloody would!' Mr Dale said as the lift doors opened. And then, like everyone else but Jon, he gasped audibly at the sheer glitz of Grigor's apartment.

Like Donald Trump, Grigor liked shiny. Like Trump, Grigor's money was brand-spanking new. And neither man had any problem with anyone knowing it. Other extremely rich men and women might invent or buy illustrious ancestry, or marry into impoverished aristocracy desperate for an investment to prevent them having to sell their stately home to a hotel chain; they would go on to furnish their house with antiques which they would insist were family furniture, buy up old silver at estate sales and claim the crests as their own.

But neither Trump nor Grigor Khalovsky had any problem whatsoever showcasing their happily vulgar, *nouveau-riche* tastes for shiny, glitzy, and gilded. Trump's New York apartment had a gold-leaf and diamond door, marble lining the walls and the floors, and every single item in it that could be gilded had been: it was as if Louis XIV, the Sun King, had been reincarnated as a Saudi prince.

Grigor's taste was less ornate than Trump's, but just as shiny. Rays of light flashed off the gigantic crystal sculptures of a swan on one side of the room, and a bear on the other, both six feet tall, anchoring the twin Breccia Pernice marble pillars, a deep orange-red flecked heavily with mica. Three more pillars were positioned at intervals at the back of the giant reception room, giving it an imposing, palace-like air. The floor was also in the red Breccia Pernice marble, but the lighter shade, a gleaming reddish-pink. It was normally strewn with Bokhara rugs, oversized white suede recliners and conversation sets, but most of these had been removed to allow access for the train tracks. The painted sleigh was front and centre, and the Christmas decorations hanging from every available surface were blinding; Andy had twined lights around the swan and the bear, and it was impossible to look at them directly without the reflections of the fairy lights on the cut-crystal surfaces blinding you in five seconds or less.

Combined with Grigor's fondness for huge, carved, dark oak furniture that looked as if it had come straight from a medieval banqueting hall, the effect of the giant crystal sculptures and marble pillars, contrasted with the hyper-modern sofas, was as if a sci-fi film had tried to meld historical periods unsuccessfully. His decorator had cried in private even as he cashed the cheques.

'Mulled wine?' asked a waiter, materialising at their side with a tray of exquisite glasses.

The Dales made oohing and aahing sounds of appreciation as they took their wine; Aniela hesitated, unsure as to whether she should or not. Jon reached for a glass, and she was surprised, though not knowing why, until he handed it to her and drawled:

'You're not on duty. Miss Melody and I don't need you looking after us – do we, ma'am?'

'No!' Melody smiled at Aniela, who could see, in a flash, how very beautiful Melody was going to be when the last swelling on her face went down. 'Really, I'm fine. And what about you? I'm so sorry, I don't know your name.'

'It's Jon,' he said, stretching out his hand to shake hers. He was wearing his usual T-shirt and sweatpants, and Aniela jealously noticed Melody's cat-eyes widen as she took in Jon's veined, muscled bare forearm, his superb physique. 'Sorry, ma'am. Forgot my manners there.'

'Oh, it's *fine*,' Melody said, still staring at Jon's body, her eyes dropping to look at his flat stomach and narrow waist. 'Lovely to meet you, Jon.'

Aniela realised that she had downed her mulled wine in one go. Putting the empty glass back on the chased silver tray, she said firmly to Jon:

'I would like to check your bandages before we all sit down to lunch.' She glanced at the waiter. 'Is there a bathroom we could use?'

Stupid question: there are probably fourteen, fifteen bathrooms in this place, she thought as the waiter led her and Jon down a corridor with zebra-wood flooring and indicated a door to their left. Her heart was fluttering like a stupid teenager at the prospect of being alone with Jon, even briefly, and she could only hope that one of the reasons she'd created this opportunity was to get him away from Melody's intense scrutiny.

I'm jealous of the way Melody was looking at him, she realised. *Which is ridiculous. I have no right to be, none at all. Melody's clearly still in love with her ex-boyfriend. I can't blame her for staring at Jon's body – anyone would. I'm behaving like an absolute idiot.*

The wine had gone straight to her head, lighting her up, making her brain feel as warm and glowing as one of the many Christmas ornaments hanging around Grigor Khalovsky's apartment. Determined to seem professional, she said as the door of the bathroom closed behind them:

'I thought I should tighten those bandages. You did a very good job putting them on so fast, but—'

She stopped talking. She had to: Jon's hand was covering her mouth, lightly, but firmly. The last six words had been said against his palm, inaudible to anyone but him. Looking down at her, he shook his head, his eyes watching her carefully through the bandages. And then he stood, waiting, until she slowly nodded her own head to show that she'd understood the message he was trying to convey.

Aniela wanted, very badly, to kiss his fingers; it was a release from temptation when he removed his hand and sat down docilely on the toilet seat, tilting his head up to give her access to his bandages.

'I'll just rewrap them,' she said, careful now of what she said, after Jon's warning that a Russian oligarch was perfectly capable of bugging his guest bathrooms. 'Make sure they don't come loose.'

'That sounds like a good idea,' he said as she began to unwrap the stretchy fabric. The bathroom was just for guests, and not even the most favoured ones, who would be ushered into Grigor's private quarters, but it had been done out more expensively than most of London's five-star hotels. Dark and luxurious, its suite – basin, bidet and toilet – was black, with gold-plated taps, its wallpaper chocolate shantung silk and its floor tiles darker chocolate marble. An oversized Millefiori diffuser in a recessed shelf – narrow reeds in an elegant bottle full of pale orange, mandarin-scented oil – perfumed the room exquisitely.

But for all Aniela noticed of her luxurious surroundings, they might as well have been a grimy, mould-stained loo in the back of a cheap café, smelling of drains and damp. She was standing between Jon's spread legs, touching his scalp, his face close to her breasts as she bent over him, and all she could see, all she could smell, was him.

It's this he wants to hide, she knew as she wrapped the bandage lightly but firmly around his scalp and under his chin. *That was the first thing he did, cover this scar.* It was a giveaway, that scar, the way it ran from ear to ear around the top of his skull; *not impossible that his face should have been so messed up in a car accident that he had to have total reconstruction, but still, it draws a lot of attention. It makes people wonder. And remember it, years after.*

Whereas a face wrapped in bandages is just that. Much less hard to recognise or identify. Jon thinks really quickly.

It took her a bare minute to redo the bandages, twisting and tucking the end in so deftly that she was sure it couldn't be dislodged except if it were done deliberately. She allowed herself the luxury of waiting, just a moment, after she'd finished, hoping that he would pull her close, hold her tight, take this opportunity to snatch a kiss, but he didn't, and she stepped back just in time to avoid looking as if she'd been waiting for one.

'There you go,' she said, turning to leave the bathroom.

She didn't even hear Jon move, but the next second he was beside her, reaching out to open the door, his American manners much better than the average Englishman's. As she passed, he took her hand and lifted it to his lips.

'Thank you for taking such good care of me,' he said softly.

'You're welcome,' Aniela muttered, and felt herself go red

all over again. She shot down the corridor as fast as she could go on her clunky shoes, resisting the urge to lift her hand to her own mouth, to kiss her fingers where his lips had just been. It was with huge relief that she saw a waiter stationed at the entrance to the great room with a tray of champagne glasses; eagerly, she took one and drank a third of it in one swift pull, trusting to her hard Polish head to keep her relatively sober.

Across the room, a Japanese couple, standing beside the swan and looking very smart and very uncomfortable, stared at her, exchanged a swift babble of words and then politely bowed to her, presumably in respect for the uniform. Out on the snow-covered terrace – *did it snow when I wasn't looking?* – she made out the small, stocky figure of Wayne Burns, chatting to the Dales, and a large, bullet-headed man smoking an enormous cigar; two bodyguards were hovering beside them, looking a lot more interested in the conversation than they were focused on protecting the man who clearly had to be their employer. On the far side of the terrace leaned a slight girl in a navy dress, slumped over the balcony rail, looking as if she had no interest in any of the jolly revels that were about to unfold, and inside, lying on one of the recliners, was an equally thin Japanese boy, black straight hair tumbling over his pale face, thumbing away at some kind of tiny, hi-tech, streamlined game that Aniela had never even seen before.

These people are all super-rich, she thought. *It's probably some prototype that'll cost thousands when it finally comes out.*

Another group of Russians were being ushered in by a small, deferential man who was practically bowing and scraping as he organised the removal of their lush fur coats and furnished them with drinks. The men were short, ugly, and authoritative, the women tall and statuesque in tight Alaïa bandage dresses, their hair long and flowing. They were either models of twenty-five and under, or first wives who from the back looked thirty, and from the front – and a discreet distance – forty-five. *Which*

probably means they're fifty-five, Aniela thought from her experience working at the Canary Clinic.

'Merry Christmas everyone!' Grigor's entrance, trailed by
Andy and another couple of bodyguards, was focal, dramatic:
he strode in, the Santa hat giving him a few extra inches of
stature, the red and white widening him, making him look like
a large post-box trimmed in fur with a big white beard and an
even bigger white smile. 'God rest ye merry gentlemen! And
ladies!' he said happily.

His arm was thrown around a slender young man whose
straight hair was parted in the centre and fell around his
face. The nouveau-hippy style only chimed with his simulta-
neous attempt at mutton-chop whiskers if you were living in
one of America's counter-culture hipster centres – Portland,
Seattle, or Brooklyn. The young man's concave chest, vegan-
pale skin, loose, baggy shirt and inexpensive dark trousers all
added confirmation that this was the look at which he was
aiming. Anything more of a contrast with Grigor's opulent,
fur-trimmed, custom-made suit could not have been imagined.

'Look who is joining us! Such a nice surprise! My son,
Dmitri, all the way from America!' Grigor announced, much
like a king presenting a crown prince to the assembled court.
'How happy this makes me!'

The people on the terrace had come inside, summoned to
greet their host by Sergei, who had dashed to call them in. The
Russians all exclaimed delightedly in their native language,
coming forward to kiss Dmitri or clap him on his back; he was
so narrow-shouldered and thin that he visibly wilted under
some of the men's enthusiastic shoulder-slaps. Mr Fyodorov
was particularly vigorous, sending Dmitri staggering forward a
good foot.

'We are all here!' Grigor threw his arms wide. 'Family,
friends, neighbours, strangers who will become friends! How
nice this is!'

He repeated this speech in Russian, and beckoned everyone to the table. Then a flash of green, heading for the door, caught his eye: Andy, having brought all Grigor's guests upstairs, was exiting to resume normal concierge duties.

'But what is this? Andy, where are you going?' Grigor exclaimed, his wide-thrown arms now circling to encompass the sleigh-train, the decorations, the snow outside. 'My favourite elf, who makes Santa's dreams come true – you must stay here and celebrate with us! Sergei, make a place for Andy at once!'

The little secretary, who had been beaming with pleasure at the sight of his boss's happiness, his face turned worshipfully up to Grigor's, darkened like a storm cloud on hearing these words. He stared at Grigor in shock, as if hoping that he had just imagined what he had been told to do.

'Go! Quick!' Grigor barked, flapping at him.

Sergei turned to shoot Andy a glance of utter loathing, before scuttling over to a waiter and rattling off a series of swift instructions. Andy, Aniela noticed, looked genuinely taken aback; he clearly hadn't expected the invitation, and hesitated, suddenly looking embarrassingly conspicuous in the green costume. Sergei, zipping around as quickly as a buzzing bee, made sure that all the guests whose invitations were of long standing found their seats at the upper part of the table.

Grigor, of course, was at the head, with Zhivana Fyodorova at one side and the tallest, blondest, most Donatella-Versace-resembling Russian woman on the other. Dmitri was next to Donatella Versace, Mr Fyodorov the other side of his daughter, probably because she looked too fragile and shy to be able to make conversation with anyone else. The huge dark carved chair dwarfed Zhivana: she looked like a child in an adult's seat, her spindly legs not quite reaching the floor, a pale little Alice in Wonderland without Alice's forceful personality.

Muttering furiously to himself, Sergei did a surprisingly good job of arranging the motley crew who were sitting at the lower end of the table. Mr and Mrs Takahashi were next to each other, with their son Haruki beside Ashley Dale, with whom he might have been assumed to have something in common. Melody, being young and pretty and a celebrity to boot, had been placed next to Wayne, who had the best English speaker of the young model girlfriends on his other side. Aniela and Jon, who had the lowest status of all, were at the very foot of the table, facing each other.

'You! Stupid elf! Here!' Sergei snapped, picking up the oversized silver charger that marked each place setting and smacking it down on the heavily embroidered tablecloth. 'You sit! Mr Khalovsky says you sit, so you sit!'

He stalked off, his skinny frame vibrating with rage, as Andy gingerly came forward, sliding into the chair that the waiter had pulled to the foot of the table, creating an extra place. Aniela smiled at him welcomingly, very happy to be seated beside him. She had no social ambitions of any kind, and would have been perfectly happy with this lowly position in any case, especially as it meant she didn't have to make conversation with anyone who might look down on her for being a mere nurse. But since Jon had been seated opposite her, she was in bliss. She gave Jon a shy smile as one of the waiters came around to push in her heavy chair and place her red linen napkin on her lap.

'Well, this is a turn-up for the books,' Andy said a little nervously. He saw Wayne, higher up the table, grinning in welcome, and mouthed at him: 'I just hope Sergei doesn't tell 'em to poison my food . . .'

'He does not like you,' Aniela observed.

'You're not joking! I'll be watching my back,' Andy said, winking at her. Always polite, he turned to greet Jon, to whom he had not yet introduced himself. 'Hi,' he said. 'I'm Andy, the concierge. You must be the other Clinic patient. Nice to see you out and about. You've been in the wars, mate!'

'You have no idea,' Jon said, his lips twitching in a smile.

'D'you know who that is?' Ashley, face ablaze with excitement, the spots on his neck now blending into the overall flush of pleasure, nudged Haruki Takahashi. 'It's only *Wayne Burns*! Is this the best Christmas ever, or what?'

'I do not know who Wayne Burns is,' Haruki said coldly.

'Mate! He's a footballer! Best footballer in the country, in my book! Where have you *been*?'

'I don't care about sports,' the boy said even more coldly. 'I like noir comics and '90s trip-hop.'

'Ooh, comics,' Ashley said gamely, a well-brought-up and amiable young man. 'I love 'em. What do you read?'

'You wouldn't have heard of them,' Haruki said with a curl of his lip. 'I like *Yummy Fur*. And *Chew*. And *Red Colored Elegy*. That's manga, of course,' he added with the specific, sarcastic pleasure a teenager takes in citing references he knows that stupid adults will never get.

Defeated, Ashley slumped back in the enormous chair as a waiter slid a gold-bordered china plate in front of him, on which several blinis were arranged, each topped heavily with caviar. Cut-glass bowls of crème fraîche were being placed along the table wherever the waiters could find room between all the decorations.

'And that's my brother Ashley,' Melody was saying easily to Wayne; she had met plenty of famous people in her short career and was quite comfortable chatting to anyone. 'He's a *massive* footie fan.'

'Oh yeah?' Wayne, who had been looking surprisingly daunted by the prospect of having to make conversation either with a Russian model or an upcoming young actress, perked up instantly on hearing this. 'Who d'you support then?' he asked Ashley.

Five minutes later, Wayne, the Dale men and even Mr Takahashi were engaged in a lively conversation. Melody, happily sure that her brother and father were in total bliss, winked at her mother – *at least my face can manage that without hurting,* she thought ruefully – gestured at Ashley to slide his plate towards her, and ate all his caviar as well as her own, scraping it off the blinis. He'd hate it, and it was almost calorie-free.

Meanwhile Mrs Takahashi and Mrs Dale were finding some common ground; Mrs Takahashi was stinking rich, but Mrs Dale had a celebrity daughter, which gave them a more or less level playing field on which to engage.

'Aww, everyone's getting on well, aren't they?' Andy said delightedly, cutting off a piece of blini, topping it with a spoonful of crème fraîche and putting it into his mouth. He chewed and swallowed with a thoughtful expression. 'This is *really* good,' he said with the content of a satisfied gourmet: as a luxury concierge, he was used to being entertained gratis by the best restaurants in town, so that he could recommend them to his clients. 'Only the absolute best for Mr K.'

'I like it,' Aniela said, rather surprised. 'I have only had the salmon caviar before. You know, the big red eggs. Like plastic bubbles. They are not so nice.'

'Don't get used to it!' Andy said, grinning, his handsome face so infectiously charming that it drew glances from all down the table. 'This'd cost an arm and a leg if you tried to get it at Harrods.'

Aniela smiled back at him.

'I will finish it all,' she said contentedly. 'And say thank you very much to Mr Khalovsky.'

'Here,' Jon said, handing his plate to her across the table decorations. 'Knock yourself out. It's not my thing.'

'Really?' Her face lit up, both at the extra treat and at Jon's consideration. 'Are you sure?'

'Absolutely,' he said, smiling back at her.

I must try not to be too happy, too excited, she told herself, taking the plate, unaware how excitement had put a sparkle in her eyes, on which Jon's lingered appreciatively. *But still – when a man kisses your hand and gives you food from his own plate, that is a sign that he likes you, I know. Not just that he wants to*

have sex with you. I may not have a lot of experience with men,
but I know how to read people. Maybe he does actually like me.

'Penny for them?' Andy said.

She started.

'Sorry?'

'Penny for your thoughts, love!' he said. 'You were away
with the fairies!'

Aniela's English was very good, but her command of slang
had temporarily deserted her, driven out by speculations about
Jon's feelings for her. She stared at Andy, totally confused as to
what his question meant.

'I think he's asking what you were thinking about,' Jon said.
'But I could be wrong. I'm not that up in British slang expressions.'

'Sorry!' Andy said contritely to Aniela. 'Your English is just
so good, I didn't mean to confuse you. Hey—' he lowered his
voice – 'is everything all right with Melody? I was meaning to
ask. Is it okay to use her real name now? And Kevin told me
she was in a real state last night and you had to bring her back
in and spend the night at hers. She seems a lot better today . . .'

That had been the excuse that Aniela had used that morning,
passing Kevin, the doorman on duty, who had been naturally
curious about why she was going back to the Clinic at six in
the morning; Melody, who had been escorted back in a state of
disarray the night before, had provided the perfect excuse.
And it seemed fair, because without Melody's having a minor
breakdown, I wouldn't have been in the building at all. I mean,
even I wouldn't have just gone to stand in front of Jon's door
without any reason at all to be in Limehouse Reach . . .

Or would I?

'Yes!' she said quickly, and it came out loudly enough to
make Mr Dale, sitting on her other side, glance over for a
second, briefly distracted from the football talk that was
flying back and forth up and down the table. 'Yes,' she
repeated, hoping she wasn't blushing, turning her shoulder to

Mr Dale and completely avoiding meeting Jon's eyes. 'She's fine. It was just – well, it was late – *very* late – and I just thought – *we* just thought – I was really tired, and there was a spare bedroom, so I—'

'Those mattresses are real comfy, aren't they?' Jon interrupted. 'I've done a lot of travelling in my time, and mine's one of the best I ever slept on. Did you like yours?' he asked Aniela.

She narrowed her eyes at him for trying to embarrass her like this. *So unfair!* she thought crossly.

'It was okay,' she mumbled.

'Just okay?' Jon said, shaking his head. 'That's a shame. I can't think of one I've found better, except of course for the Westin beds.'

'Oh, those are *famous*, aren't they?' Andy agreed, turning to Jon. 'I've had *lots* of clients rave about them.'

The waiter was filling Aniela's wine glass with red wine, removing the now-empty vodka that had been served with the caviar. Their appetiser plates had been taken away, and now huge, loaded dinner plates the size of platters were being set in front of them. The chef had clearly taken the position that he had made enough food to feed a small village for a week, and thus served all his employer's guests portions large enough for a whole family. Turkey, cranberry sauce, soufflé potatoes, green beans sautéed with garlic, herb and wild rice stuffing, a gratin of Brussels sprouts in cream and bacon served in a matching gold-rimmed ramekin.

Aniela's eyes widened. Even back home in Poland, where portions were huge, she had never seen a feast like this. She glanced up the length of the table, and was very amused to observe that all the men were licking their lips, tucking their napkins into their shirt collars and looking down at their plates with greedy anticipation, while the woman, without exception, were either overwhelmed or downright disdainful. Mrs Takahashi and every single one of the Russian wives and girl-friends were actually rearing back from their plates as if they expected to be summarily force-fed from them if they didn't immediately register their unwillingness. Zhivana even reached out a slender pale hand and pushed her plate a little away from her.

She probably lives on air and water, Aniela thought meanly.

No one had started to eat; they were waiting for their host to give them the signal to begin. Pushing back the oaken throne on which he was sitting, Grigor scrambled to his feet, hoisting himself off the pile of velvet cushions which gave him extra height at the table.

'Ladies and gentlemen,' he began, holding up his cut-glass goblet of Romanée-Conti – it was much too heavy a red wine to be properly paired with turkey, but it was one of the most expensive wines in the world, which was all that Grigor really cared about – 'Happy Christmas! It is a wonderful time of year for me, and especially this one, because I have with me my beautiful fiancée, Zhivana, who will make me the happiest man in the world when we marry in the New Year . . .'

A stir of excitement ran round the room at this information: everyone who didn't already know this news strained to get a look at Grigor's bride-to-be, and a tiny sigh of disappointment issued from their lips when they realised that the limp celery stick of a girl between Grigor and her beaming father was the chosen one. Zhivana's pallid, drooping face did not change expression in any way as Grigor continued:

'And my younger son, Dmitri, has also come to join us! My older son Alek has sent his best regards to all – he is skiing in Verbier with the Casiraghi children.'

He smiled complacently at this reference to the scions of the Monaco royal family. The guests, already half-tipsy with mulled wine and champagne and vodka, murmured in appreciation of the name-drop.

'So let us all raise a toast to family and friends, present and absent,' he continued, waving his glass with dangerous abandon, 'and—'

If Dasha Khalovsky had been waiting in the wings, ready to make her entrance with the most perfect dramatic timing possible, she could not have done better. Everyone had raised their glasses and had their heads turned towards Grigor: as Dasha launched herself, screeching, into the great room, the guests snapped round as if they were watching a soap opera come to life.

'You fucking *bastard*!' she shrieked. 'Merry fucking Christmas to you too, you *pig*! Sitting here and toasting with our friends and not giving a shit about me, *alone*, *rotting*, for all you care! After all those years together, all I gave you, you throw me aside like a used old jacket when something younger comes along! How fucking *dare* you!'

The first wives at the table shivered, almost imperceptibly, as if a cold wind had blown over their bare shoulders. The models looked even more confused than usual. And Grigor turned bright purple with fury. He had taken off his beard and hat to eat, so his whole face was visible, and his ability to switch instantly from genial host to livid husband was impressive and frightening in equal measure.

'What the *hell*!' he yelled back. 'How the *fuck* did you get in here?'

Dasha was wearing her yellow fur coat, and her hair was loose, its tinsel extensions glinting among the almost equally yellow locks. Theatrically, she ripped the coat open and placed her hands on her black silk-clad hips, standing with her legs a little apart, tossing her hair back; *she's crazy, but she does look very powerful*, Aniela thought, unwillingly impressed by Dasha's sheer presence. *I wouldn't like to get on her bad side.*

Jon eased his chair a little back from the table. It looked as if he were merely trying to get a better view of the unfolding confrontation, and no one but Aniela paid any attention to the small movement.

'I still have a key to the lift, you idiot!' Dasha yelled. 'And you can't stop me coming in here any time I want! I own this place too!' One hand still on her hip, the other traced a sweeping, magnificent gesture in the air that encompassed the entire penthouse.

'Not for long!' Grigor shouted, pounding his fist on the table so hard that the glassware and cutlery rattled. 'You're not getting this in the settlement!'

'I don't bloody want it, the way it turned out!' Dasha shrieked, more than equal to this. '*Look* at it! It's a fucking mess! Nothing goes with anything else! I can't believe you bought that stupid, six-foot glass *bear*! I told you it was ridiculous, and so did the decorator!'

'You *bitch*!' Grigor clutched his chest, wounded to the quick. He glanced quickly at the giant crystal bear, as if to confirm for his own benefit how nice and big and shiny it was.

'What the hell do you want, Dasha?' he demanded angrily. 'Why are you ruining Christmas like this? You're getting a huge settlement!'

'I don't *want* a fucking settlement!' Dasha's voice was as high as a castrato's by now. 'Fuck you! I want our life back the way it was! Now you're marrying that little *nothing*— ' She practically spat at Zhivana, who didn't even react to this; it was her father who bellowed like a bull at the insult to his daughter, waving a fist at Dasha. 'And you'll have *kids* with her! Kids who'll disinherit *ours*!'

She swivelled on her heel and pointed at Dmitri like a murder suspect trying to cast suspicion on another one in an amateur dramatic production of an Agatha Christie play. Her rings flashed.

'I am here for *you*, Dima!' she said poignantly, switching gears like a skilled soap-opera actress, using the diminutive of his name. 'I was not going to come, to make a scene! But when you texted to say you were having lunch here and would come to me later – when I realised you would be *here*, with *him* and *her*, when all she's waiting for is to marry your father and have children with him to take your inheritance away, I could not control myself!'

Zhivana was huddling back in her chair now, her eyes wide, looking like a terrified little girl: whether she was more frightened of Dasha's wrath or the prospect of giving birth to Grigor's babies it was impossible to tell.

'Mama, I really don't care about the money,' Dmitri said timidly. 'I'd give most of it away to charity anyway.'

'You'd *what*?' his father yelled, turning to look down at his son.

'Don't pick on Dmitri! He's a good boy! A moral boy!' his mother screamed. 'Things *you* don't know anything about!'

Jon's chair slid back another foot. Aniela stared at him curiously.

'Dasha, there's enough for everyone!' Grigor turned back to her in frustration. '*More* than enough! You'll be fine, Alek and Dmitri will be fine, I could have twenty kids with Zhivana and *they'd* be fine—'

Zhivana let out a tiny wail of protest at the mere idea of having twenty kids: and the number also tipped Dasha right over the edge. Her black-lined eyes bulging in fury, lips bared, she let out a banshee wail and dashed full tilt at Grigor, hands up like claws.

Every single bodyguard stationed around the room pulled out his gun automatically at this threat, even Fyodorov's; their employer was a mere two seats away from Grigor. But it was pointless. They couldn't fire. Dasha was Grigor's wife. Without a direct command, they couldn't possibly have shot her. And even if she had been a total stranger, it was much too dangerous with so many dignitaries in the line of fire.

So while they hesitated, it was Jon who sprang into action. Even Aniela, sitting opposite him, was blindsided by the speed with which he moved. Later on, she would try to reconstruct everything he had done, replay what she had seen: everyone else's eyes had been entirely fixed on Dasha, but Aniela had been half-watching Jon, and the moment he jumped from his chair, she knew it.

After that, though, it was partially blurred, because he had moved so very fast. Unbelievably, she realised that he had vaulted right over the table, like a gymnast on a pommel horse, both hands smacking down onto the table, sending glasses flying, his legs tucking up into a tight ball, his waist twisting to send his legs driving together like a piston over the far side of the table, his feet shooting between her and Mr Dale, landing square on the ground. But he must – how, she couldn't imagine – have grabbed something from the table en route, because the second he landed his right hand flashed out and sent something flying towards Dasha, a narrow missile, silver and sharp and deadly-looking. A knife.

Women screamed. The bodyguards dashed forward. But no one could have prevented the knife from taking Dasha square between the shoulder blades: she went down as if poleaxed, the wind hit out of her, the knife itself clattering to the ground. Jon had spun the knife in the air, reversed it, so that it was the handle, not the sharp blade, that had struck her. She fell to her knees, gasping, hitting the marble floor with her hands in the next moment for balance, and Jon shot past her, reaching an amazed Grigor in two strides, grabbing him and pushing him down into the chair, shielding him with his own body.

A round of terrifying clicks sounded through the room, the noise reverberating off the marble pillars; every single armed man in the room was cocking his gun. Jon was surrounded by them, all aiming their lethal armoury directly at him. Bodyguards of Russian oligarchs didn't do subtle. The Glocks were, frankly, unnecessarily large and overblown for the job they had to do. But they certainly had their effect. The Russian guests and their wives didn't bat an eye at the sight of all the wide blued-steel barrels pointing at Jon's head, but the models screamed, as did Melody, Mrs Takahashi and Mrs Dale: the men gasped.

Aniela screamed too. But she was so terrified that nothing came out. She had pushed back her chair too and jumped to her feet, though she had no idea why – she couldn't possibly have helped Jon in any way. It had just been a confused, frantic impulse not to be trapped at the table when the man she cared about was putting his life in danger. And now she stared hopelessly at the scene, something from an action film, as every single terrifying-looking gun targeted Jon's back as he pushed Grigor down into the chair, and there was nothing she could do if someone's finger trembled on the trigger . . .

Desperately, she watched as one of Grigor's hands appeared, spatulate and hairy, grabbing onto Jon's forearm. And then the other hand, on the other forearm, Jon stepping back as Grigor hauled himself to his feet once more and pushed his rescuer aside, flapping his hand impatiently at the semicircle of bodyguards surrounding him.

'Put those things away!' he barked angrily. 'You're frightening the ladies! And what the hell are you going to do with them?' He clapped Jon on the shoulder. '*This* is the only guy who did anything – the one who's just had *surgery*, for fuck's sake! Look at him! And I don't even *pay* him!'

Fyodorov let off a stream of Russian at his own guards; they all backed away, holstering their weapons, heads ducked in shame. The guests, released from fear of their lives, turned to each other and babbled their relief. Grigor had been generous in his assessment of who had been petrified by being surrounded by armed oligarchs' bodyguards; it hadn't just been the women. Mr Dale and Mr Takahashi were both still trembling, and the former, uninhibited by Japanese reserve, had grabbed his wife, clinging to her in delayed shock. Wayne Burns downed his entire glass of Romanée-Conti in one go and shook his head violently afterwards, as if in denial of what had just happened. Ashley Dale and Haruki Takahashi, however, had finally bonded and were chattering to each other furiously about exactly what kind of guns the bodyguards had pulled, how Jon had vaulted over the table, and which Tony Jaa Thai action film was their favourite.

'What the fuck did you just *do*?' Grigor said to Jon, his hand still resting familiarly on his shoulder. 'I never saw anyone move so fast in my life!'

'I'm a stuntman, Mr Khalovksy,' Jon said smoothly, as Aniela held her breath waiting for his answer. 'That's how I got injured – staging a car crash. Hope I didn't freak you out, slamming you into your chair like that. I wasn't sure if the lady was carrying or not.'

Grigor snorted.

'You did the right thing. That bitch is *crazy*,' he hissed malevolently at his wife.

Dasha, who was being helped up, one bodyguard on each side of her holding her elbows while a third frisked her expertly for concealed weapons, hissed back:

'*You* make me crazy, you *fucker*! And I don't need a fucking gun to take you out! I could strangle you with my bare hands!'

'Yeah? *Yeah?*' Grigor thrust his burly head at her, his hands rising to pull the fur-trimmed collar of his Santa costume from his neck. 'Try it, you mad bitch! Try it and I'll kill you first!'

'*Papa! Mama!*' Dmitri Khalovsky pushed back his own chair with a visible effort – he was thin and it was very heavy – and stood up. His tenor voice was high and strained, but his sincerity and decency were painfully obvious, and everyone in the room fell silent, including his warring parents.

'*Stop it!*' he yelled passionately, his accent without a hint of Russian inflection. 'What's *wrong* with both of you? You're supposed to be adults and you're behaving like a pair of kids! No wonder I want to stay in the States and never come back!'

'Dima—' His mother started towards him, shaking off the bodyguards impatiently, her eyes flashing. 'Darling – it's all your father's fault, he's trying to turn you against me—'

'*Mama, ne nado*! Stop! It's *both* of you! You're just as bad as each other! I can't take this any more!' Dmitri pushed back his curtains of hair with both hands. 'I've been doing a lot of work on myself in the States. I've joined an encounter group, and

I'm realising that my upbringing has been fundamentally toxic on almost every level. I doubt that either of you is evolved enough to even understand what I mean by that. But it must be obvious that this is a totally unhealthy situation, and it can't go on. I wish you two would consider some sort of relationship therapy, conflict resolution, to help you mediate your differences and—'

'*I'll* show him therapy!' Dasha screamed at Grigor, lunging at him again: Jon grabbed her around the waist, ducking her swinging arms, spinning her round and throwing her into the grip of the nearest bodyguard, who lumbered back under the impact.

'*She*'s the one who needs therapy!' Grigor yelled at Dmitri. 'At the end of a Kalashnikov!'

His wine had spilled down the front of his Santa suit when Jon had tackled him into his chair, but there was some left, and Grigor polished it off defiantly and slammed his glass onto the table.

'Coward!' Dasha retorted, wrestling in the grasp of the bodyguard. 'Typical! A *real* man would do it with a knife – with his bare hands!'

Grigor opened his mouth to reply, turned blue, clutched his chest, and collapsed to the ground.

'Oh my God, he's having a heart attack!' Mrs Dale shrieked. 'RICE! RICE! No, that's for when you strain something! Phil, what is it? We did this in the Red Cross course at the WI!'

'Stayin' Alive!' Mr Dale said. 'No, that's to get the right speed for CPR—'

'FAST!' Ashley yelled. 'Face! Arms! Speech! Time!'

'But that's for a stroke!' his mother said. 'He's fallen over – that's not a stroke, is it?'

Jon, kneeling by Grigor's prone body, called:
'Aniela!'

But she was already there, pushing her way through the massed bodyguards, dropping to her knees, loosening Grigor's costume even further at the neck, pressing her fingers into the big vein there to check his pulse.

'Back off!' Jon snapped. 'Give the lady some room to do her job.'

The bodyguards, clustered tightly around Grigor, obeyed Jon's air of authority instinctively, though a couple of them, the more intelligent ones, exchanged glances of surprise that they had automatically followed his orders. They remained circling him, apart from a couple who split off to flank Fyodorov's chair.

Dmitri ran over to his father's side, throwing himself down next to Jon, tears in his soft brown eyes. Dasha, however, took advantage of the bodyguards' momentary distraction to twist free and dash away, fleeing the great room in the direction of the lift; they hadn't been instructed to detain her, and though the two who had been holding her started to go after her, they hesitated, unsure of whether grabbing the boss's wife and dragging her back would be overstepping their bounds. Unused to acting on their own authority, they shrugged and let Dasha go.

'Dad!' Dmitri said frantically. 'Dad! Is he all right? What's happening?'

Gently, Jon put a hand on Dmitri's chest, easing him back till Aniela had finished. Grigor was unconscious; she lifted one eyelid to check, ducked her head to listen to his breathing, and eventually looked up again.

'He's okay,' she said, and the entire room sagged with relief. 'It's just a syncope. A faint,' she clarified, seeing everyone's faces remain blank. 'His heart rate is absolutely fine. It was probably stress,' she said to Dmitri, 'but you should advise your father to tell his doctor what happened and have a thorough check-up. It can be caused by a reaction to medication, for instance.'

'Thank you!' Dmitri wiped his eyes with the back of his sleeve, Fyodorov snorting at this sign of male weakness. 'I was so scared!'

'Let's pick him up and take him into his bedroom,' Aniela suggested.

Fyodorov barked some commands, and the bodyguards jumped forward to pick up Grigor. Halfway across the room, however, his recumbent form started to jerk in their arms.

'Whaa . . .' Grigor said faintly. 'Aaaah . . .'

His legs thrashed, kicking out, catching one of the men a glancing blow in his face; to his credit, he took it, barely flinching, and didn't drop his employer.

'*Postav'te menya!* Put me down!' Grigor mumbled.

Fyodorov strode across the room, his heavy body loud on the marble floor, and slipped an arm under his friend's shoulder as he was lowered to the ground.

'Come on,' he said gruffly. 'Back to the table. We're celebrating, old friend.'

'He should really—' Aniela began, but Jon's hand closed on her shoulder and she took the hint, falling silent as one oligarch helped the other back to his seat in pride of place at the table.

Fyodorov settled Grigor in; the latter was a little grey around the gills, but his breathing was steady, and he smiled at his assembled guests as one of the bigger bodyguards heaved the chair up to the table again.

'Eat!' he said, waving magisterially down the length of the table. 'Drink! Be merry!'

'Jesus,' Jon said quietly to Aniela. 'I hope to hell no one else knows the end of that line . . .'

'What did you mean?' she asked Jon two hours later, as they finally made their exit from the penthouse, laden down with gifts.

Grigor had had Sergei bring round what he lightly called 'party favours' for everyone, but which were predictably lavish gifts. The Russian guests, of course, had received individually custom-made presents, whose glitter and sparkle had been visible right from Aniela's viewpoint at the foot of the table;

but even the extra guests, the ones invited that morning to swell the numbers, had received eye-widening gifts from a store Sergei kept for just this kind of purpose. The men had been given exquisite white-gold and *cloisonné* enamel cufflinks in the Kensington football team's navy and burgundy, commissioned especially from Fabergé by Grigor, while the women had pendants – mercifully, not in the team's colours – decorated with diamonds and the same enamel for which Fabergé had become famous.

But as well as receiving these 'party favours', Jon and Aniela had, on announcing that they were leaving, been whisked into the library and presented, by a beaming Grigor, with a Patek Philippe watch for Jon and another pendant for Aniela, an eighteen-carat-gold modern Fabergé egg, pale blue enamel studded heavily with diamonds, which hinged at its centre to reveal a gold butterfly set inside, its wings also covered with diamonds, hanging from a matching gold chain studded at intervals by long pale blue enamel ovals with a diamond at each end.

'It matches your eyes,' Grigor had said, and when she had protested that it was much too much he had put it into one of her hands, taken the other hand and closed it over the egg with a firmness that brooked no more attempts at refusal. She was still clutching it now, unable to believe how pretty it was. She had shown it briefly to Andy on the way out, passing him slumped on a sofa, smoking cigars and drinking brandy with the famous footballer, both of them laughing their heads off. Andy had waggled his eyebrows and laughed even harder and said something she hadn't quite understood but seemed to mean that she should have fun. Have fun wearing it, he must have meant.

Well, that'll never happen. I'd be too scared someone would mug me. Besides, what do I need with something this expensive? I'm going to sell it as soon as I can and put the money into something safe. An ISA, maybe. Nothing risky.

'What do *you* mean?' Jon asked, repeating her words back to her. They stepped out of the penthouse lift, into the lobby.

'Oh!' Aniela, a little tipsy now, realised that she hadn't explained what she was talking about. 'When we were going back to the table. After Mr Khalovsky fainted. He said eat, drink and be merry. And *you* said I hope no one knows the end of that line.'

'Oh yeah!' Jon smiled, his lips curving, his neat white American teeth flashing. Aniela was so used now to looking at him with the bandages wrapped round his head that she didn't think anything of it, but she noticed Kevin, the doorman, glancing sideways at Jon with a look in which curiosity and horror mingled. 'It's from Ecclesiastes. Eat, drink and be merry, for tomorrow we die. Kind of ironic,' he added, his smile twisting now into something more sardonic.

Aniela didn't understand the part about being ironic, but she caught her breath at the 'tomorrow we die'.

'Oh no!' she exclaimed. 'It would have been very bad if someone had said that!'

'Right.' Jon grinned at her. 'Lucky I know how to keep my mouth shut, eh?'

'You know much more than that,' Aniela said.

She had meant that Jon had the kind of whip-sharp reactions that had impressed Grigor sufficiently for him to offer Jon a job as a security consultant as soon as his face had healed; Jon had thanked him and said that he would seriously think it over. But as soon as the words were out of her mouth, she felt herself blush. *He'll think I mean sex*, she thought, and turned away towards the door that led to the Clinic.

'Well, thank you,' Jon said lightly. 'Uh, where are you going?'

'I was just . . .' Aniela tailed off. She looked back, over her shoulder, hoping that he would ask her up to his apartment, but too proud to suggest it.

But he didn't. He just stared at her. She felt herself growing even redder; the alcohol she had drunk was making her a little dizzy, but no less self-conscious. She was still vividly aware of how awkwardly she was standing, twisted round with her head at an odd angle, probably showing a double chin, her body not in a flattering position either, widening her hips.

And I ate so much! she thought, panic rising in her. *Caviar, turkey, potatoes, mince pies and chocolates* . . . She was carrying an extra box of chocolates – they had been given to all the guests, each one hand-made by Daniel, the chef, and gilded with edible gold leaf. *If he tries to pick me up now, he'll break his back.*

'Aniela?' he said hesitantly at last. 'Um, I was just think-ing—'

'Yes?' she said quickly. *Too quickly. Too keen.*

'That maybe you should check me out, you know? My scar!' he added just as swiftly. 'Check my scar out! You know, I was jumping round back there – I might have strained something – ripped some of the scar tissue—'

'Oh! Yes!' Relief flooded through her, stronger and more intoxicating even than the amazing red wine she had drunk at lunch, wine that she would never be able to afford again. 'Yes, I probably should have a look at that . . .'

'Great!'

Jon scooped her armful of gifts from her and strode off towards the lifts without looking back, the presents hostages, surety for her following him. Aniela scampered after him, unable to say a word. She had never been skilled at making conversation, at plastering over moments of social difficulty with an easy flow of words, and now she was completely tongue-tied. She pressed the button for the fortieth floor, because his arms were full, and they stepped into one of the cars, turning as one to look at the closing doors, standing there in silence as it rose. Aniela was more grateful than she'd ever been for the piped music in lifts; without it, he would have heard her breathing, been aware how fast and shallow it was at her excitement at being alone with him.

Looking down, she realised that her nipples were hard, hard enough to show through both the fabric of her bra – *thank goodness I put on a slightly nicer one today, just in case* – and the heavy cotton of her uniform. Normally she would have been mortified by this, by her body's clear evidence of her attraction to Jon; *it's as if my nipples are actually reaching out to him*, she thought, and the urge to giggle rose in her, sudden and forceful.

I'm drunk, she realised. And though, immediately, she wasn't sure if that were true after all – she'd been careful at lunch, had eaten lots of food to balance the wine that had flowed so freely, had a hard Polish head – she grabbed onto the excuse with a wild surge of eagerness that quite replaced the rising giggles.

I'm drunk – I can't be held responsible for what I do next, not really – it's the wine, not me—

Aniela couldn't wait one more minute, one more second. He had asked her up to his apartment – they were alone together, and the lift was ascending with unbearable slowness – forty whole floors, how could she possibly wait that long—

She launched herself at him like a missile, her arms around his neck, her mouth on his, her whole body pressed gloriously against his. The presents he was holding tumbled to the floor, landed on both their feet, and she was giddily happy that he had dropped them at once, without hesitation, to wrap his arms around her instead. She pressed herself tightly against his narrow waist, his lean flanks, his cock, which was already stirring for her. She ground herself against him, letting herself go completely, the disinhibiting effects of the champagne and vodka and wine now thoroughly kicking in, the leash she had been keeping herself on kicked away like the Fabergé egg and pendant and cufflinks, like the Patek Philippe watch.

They were just things. But this, with Jon, was way beyond anything that money could buy, the best Christmas present she could conceivably imagine . . .

Aniela kissed him with every drop of pent-up passion she had been nurturing all these years of working day and night, all the frustration of barely having had sex, all the delight of having, even briefly, found a man who was absolutely amazing at it. She practically mounted him. And, as she had already realised, Jon was a fast learner. His hands wrapped round the back of her head, his tongue drove into her mouth, kissing her back as confidently as if there had never been a clash of teeth just a couple of days before, as if he had always known, instinctively, how to angle his head so that he could kiss a woman as deeply as he wanted to. The bandages rubbed against Aniela's cheek, reminding her that he was still a patient in her care, that she should be careful with his face; and then she thought: *I just saw this man vault over a table, throw a knife at someone but leave them unhurt, protect an oligarch with his own body when the guards didn't – I think I can trust him to look after himself.*

The relief was delicious, a yielding up of any last vestiges of responsibility. She forgot, completely, about being a nurse, about anything but wanting, very badly, to feel him inside her again, straight away, *immediately*. His cock, now hard as a steel pole, was shoving excitedly against her crotch; it seemed just as on board with this prospect as she was. He was lifting her, pulling her even closer against him, and she moaned, her eyes closed, completely shameless. *I'm drunk*, she thought delightedly. *I'm drunk, it's Christmas Day, and this is my present, right here, Jon's cock between my legs—*

Something pinged. She was so out of it, so dizzy with sex, that she thought for a second that it was a microwave. It was a moment more before his hands reluctantly slid from around her, moved her a little back from him; Aniela's eyes opened equally reluctantly as she realised that the floor below her feet had stopped moving.

The doors had slid open, and were now beginning to close again: Jon shoved one foot into the gap to hold them, ducking to scoop up the gifts from where they had tumbled over the carpet. Aniela didn't help. She couldn't. Her head was spinning, her legs were wobbly; she reached out a hand to steady herself against the wall before heading out of the car, Jon following closely behind.

Inside the apartment, Jon dumped the presents onto the kitchen counter, took her hand and pulled her towards the bedroom; kicking off her shoes as she went, she followed eagerly. All she wanted to do was throw herself down on the bed and pull him on top of her, and when they reached it, she promptly sat down on it, only to have him drag her up again and keep towing her into the bathroom.

'I don't think—' she began nervously.

She didn't want acrobatic sex in the bright lights bouncing off the marbled and mirrored walls of the bathroom; that was for when you didn't feel full and tipsy. She wanted to roll around on the lovely soft mattress, have delicious, not-completely-sober sex; the bathroom could come later, after they'd slept off the huge lunch.

But what Jon was doing was so odd that she broke off. He had let her go and was reaching into the shower to turn it on full blast. He did the same with the basin, looked down at the bidet and shrugged, and turned that on too: then he leaned past her to close the bathroom door.

'I need to tell you a couple of things,' he said.

'*Really?*' Aniela's face fell comically. 'You want to *talk?*'

In her tipsy state, she felt a big giggle working its way up to her throat. *It's like he turned into the woman and I turned into the man.*

'Aniela! Are you even *listening?*' Jon asked crossly.

She realised she had been miles away, staring at his chest, at the perfect curve of his pecs, lost in a haze of anticipation.

'Sorry!' she said quickly, snapping back to the moment.

Look interested, she told herself firmly, *or you might not get laid . . . he might get offended and storm out . . .* She felt the giggle again and had to take her lower lip between her teeth and bite down, hard, to stop it coming out.

'Why is the shower on?' she asked, when she had herself back under control. 'And the sink? And the *bidet*?' She knew she was slightly drunk, but she was sure it wasn't normal, even for a very clean American, to turn the bidet on before you had a serious conversation.

'Can't be too careful,' Jon said. 'No way anyone could hear what we're saying with all this water running. I'll do a sweep for bugs later.' He shrugged. 'There weren't any before. But someone could have dropped down while we were chowing turkey and planted some.' His eyes flickered. '*I* would have. So, better safe than sorry.'

Aniela's legs gave way under her; she sat down on the edge of the bath. Despite the steamy heat in the bathroom, a cold chill ran down her spine as the seriousness of the conversation they were about to have sank in. *What do they call it in English? Oh yes. Reality check.*

'You're not a stuntman,' she said flatly.

'No,' Jon said wryly. 'I'm not.'

She looked up at him, silently waiting for him to answer the real question she was asking. A man more experienced with relationships, with talking to women, would have known to sit down next to her on the wide rim of the freestanding granite bath, to take her hand and look at her reassuringly while he told her what he was, or what he had been. But since no one had ever done that with Jon, he had never learned how.

So he propped himself against the basin instead, folded his arms over his chest, and said:

'Okay, here it is. For some reason, I don't seem to be able to do anything but tell you the truth. Don't ask me why, because I don't know. And don't ask me why I trust you, but I do.'

Reaching up, he began, slowly, to unwrap the bandages from his head, baring his scalp, his features. Jon wasn't himself aware of the significance of this gesture, that as he began to tell Aniela the truth about himself, he felt the need to remove any physical layers of concealment from his face, but Aniela noticed it. She sat quietly opposite him, sobering up fast, her years of nursing experience giving her the ability to stay calm without registering any emotion at the story he was telling her.

The only omission Jon made in telling his story was the man he had killed, the true reason why he had had to leave Jackson's Hollow and never go back. Instead, he alluded to a rough, violent upbringing, the need to forage for food that had made him an expert sniper, and told the story of how he had been headhunted from the Marines to be turned into one of the CIA's most effective black ops agents.

'Which means that I killed people,' he said simply, beginning to roll up the bandages around the fingers of his hand. 'A lot of people. But I was just a dumb kid then. I thought they were all the bad guys, enemies of Uncle Sam – you know, truth, justice, democracy, the American way. And then I found out that they'd got me to kill some of the good guys. Worse. They wanted me to blow up a whole family, just so they could pin it on some folks they wanted to drop in the shit. So I looked back, and I started to wonder. I asked myself how many of those guys I'd killed that they told me were bad really *had* been bad enough to need killing. And I started educating myself. I never had anything like proper schooling – I could read and write, but not much more than that. I never read much about our history, I just believed what I saw on Fox. I started finding out about a lot of shit that the CIA pulled in Latin America, for instance. Training death squads, running 'em. Mining harbours, torturing people – *nuns*, for Christ's sake. Bad, bad shit.'

He put the bandages down on the basin. The mirror above was completely fogged up with steam by now.

'It put the lid on the idea that I could trust that the folks who sent me out on missions were always in the right,' he said. 'And when you're hurting people, maybe even killing 'em, you have to be right. You're probably thinking I was a fool to believe 'em in the first place, and I can't blame you. All I can tell you is that a kid's lucky to leave the Hollow able to read and write at eighth-grade level.'

He shrugged.

'Well, I couldn't keep doing what I was doing, but I couldn't quit either,' he said. 'I knew too much about all sorts of stuff. No way they'd ever let me go. So I planned it out, faked my own death and drove off a cliff.' He smiled. 'Or that's what they thought. I bought a new face in Brazil, and I turned myself into what you might call a gun for hire.'

Aniela still didn't say a word; neither of them was the kind to talk if it wasn't necessary. If there was more to come, he needed to be allowed to tell it in his own time, when he was ready. She wouldn't prompt him or push him in any way.

'And yeah, I killed more people,' he continued. 'Like I said, I can't lie to you. Only they were a hundred-per-cent certified bad people this time around, because I could pick and choose my jobs now. Gangsters, kidnappers, pimps. I got to save the good ones and take out the bad people, for a change. But I always knew it wasn't going to be for the rest of my life. And it's not like I actually enjoy it.'

His mouth twisted wryly.

'I've worked alongside enough people who do to know the difference. So I got myself a nice little retirement plan, bought myself a ranch, and I'm going to settle down and work my land. And getting out of the gun for hire business. I went kinda Old Testament about that. Made a vow to put it behind me for good and all.'

He raised a hand to his face.

'Got Dr Nassri to work me over. Last time I ever go through that,' he said ruefully. 'I tell you, there's something real strange about not knowing what you're going to look like for months on end.'

He looked straight at Aniela, his eyes clear and frank.

'How much of this is a surprise to you, Aniela?'

She stared back at him.

'Perhaps not so much,' she said simply. 'One facial reconstruction is not normal, not without significant damage to correct. But two? To put yourself through that not once, but twice?' She saw Jon register that she knew about his previous surgery, and swept on quickly: 'Don't worry, it is deep in your file. Dr Nassri is always very careful.'

'But you found it,' he observed.

'Yes.' She blushed a little. 'I was curious about you.'

'Good,' he said, surprising her. 'People should be careful about who they hang out with. They should use all the information they have. You were right to check up on me.' He nodded approvingly. 'So you thought . . .'

'Only someone with a lot to hide would do what you have done,' she said. 'And you were so brave about the surgery. You refused painkillers or sleeping pills afterwards. You wanted to be fully conscious. That was interesting too.'

Jon's eyebrows were raised as high as they could currently go.

'*Very* good observation,' he said.

She swallowed. She didn't feel at risk from him, not at all. She didn't have any problem with what he had just told her. And yet she was about to ask him something that she thought he might react to very badly indeed.

'Okay, you got a question. So spit it out,' he said, his voice calm.

Taking a deep breath, she said bravely:

'Did you put something in Mr Khalovsky's glass when you grabbed him and pushed him down into his chair?'

Jon froze. Not a muscle in his body moved for a good minute as he processed this. A vein pulsed at his throat, and Aniela watched it in morbid fascination. She was afraid. Not of what he might do to her, but exactly the opposite: that her acute powers of observation where he was concerned might have made him so wary that he would want nothing more to do with her. She had a sudden image of a train she'd seen in a film, unstoppably tearing down the tracks, the driver desperately trying to apply the brakes to no avail, sparks flying from the metal wheels. But she knew that she wasn't capable of putting on the brakes right now. If someone did it, that person would have to be Jon.

He opened his mouth, clearly still deciding what to say.

'What makes you think—' he began, and then he caught himself. His chest rose and fell as he made his decision. 'Okay. Yes. Yes I did.'

He shook his head slowly.

'I better tell you the rest of it. Did you see me do it?'

'No,' she said. 'I guessed. What did you give him?'

'A little concoction they used to give me back when I worked for the Unit,' he said. 'I have a chemist make it up for me now. There's a tiny bit of Rohypnol to knock 'em out and a couple of other little bits and bobs. Works a treat. I had a capsule in my pocket. You just break the top off and pour it into a glass in a second. Tasteless, odourless, very efficient.'

'And you just happened to have it with you?'

'Nope,' Jon said. 'I was looking for an opportunity to use it. So here's what happened. Two days ago, Dasha Khalovsky rang my doorbell . . .'

He told her the whole story.

'Damned if I know what she has on Nassri,' he concluded, 'but it's sure as hell got to be big to make him go against me.'

'It is,' Aniela said seriously. 'I was in the outside office when she went in to see him. He threw up in his sink. Twice.'

Jon's eyebrows raised a fraction. 'Well, there you go. She's what my Aunt Eileen would've called a holy terror. Knocking Grigor out like that'll give me a couple more days to figure out what to do about this mess. I calculated she'd see him go down, think I'd done the job and take to her heels to make sure she wasn't tied in to me in any way, and I bet right. This way, she'll think I made a good-faith effort and give me some more time to pull it off.'

'But you're not going to do it,' Aniela observed, staring at him intently.

'No, I'm not!' He sounded genuinely surprised. 'I told you, I made a vow! A man's word's only as good as his bond.'

Aniela didn't know that expression, but she could understand the sense of it perfectly well. She stood up and walked towards him.

'I believe you,' she said seriously. 'But what are you going to do now? If you can't kill Mr Khalovsky?'

He laughed bitterly. 'Damned if I know! It's a hell of a mess, isn't it?'

She stared at him in wonder.

'You don't seem worried,' she commented.

He shrugged. 'I've been in worse spots.'

Looking down at her, he framed her face gently with his hands.

'So now you know,' he said. 'I had to let you know what you were messing with.' He caught himself. 'I suppose I had to let you know about Mrs Khalovsky as well, come to think of it. She made some nasty threats, and she's more than capable of following through. You could be in danger if you're spending time with me.'

'I just saw you in action,' Aniela said, smiling. 'I think I can trust you to take care of me.'

'Whoa,' Jon said. 'That's a big responsibility.'

She stayed absolutely still, her eyes on his.

'Do you want me to go?' she asked, and felt her ribcage tense, her breath clamped in her lungs, waiting for his answer.

She knew that he was thinking it over, considering his options, that the answer might be 'Yes': she could sense it from his touch, his stance. And though his body was signalling eagerly to his brain that no, it didn't want her to go at all – in fact it wanted her a lot closer, *now* – she was aware, too, that it would be Jon's brain that would make the decision. She didn't say another word; she just stood there, letting his cogs turn and engage, giving him all the time he needed.

'No,' he said softly at last, just when her lungs were beginning to burn. 'Don't get me wrong. I think you should go. But I don't *want* you to.'

It was all she needed to hear. Reaching up, she looped her arms around his neck once more, pressed herself against him, kissed him with huge relief and delight. By now the steam was filling the room as if they were in a Turkish bath, the aquamarine mosaic tiles beaded with moisture, their clothes damp and sticking to them. She started to pull up his T-shirt and he helped instantly, pulling the neck carefully up and over his face and scalp, Aniela's breath catching yet again in her throat as she took in the sight of his bare chest, the light scattering of coppery hair darkening as it trailed down to his waist; greedily, she ran her hands over him, tracing the lines of his muscles as they flexed and curved in again, shaking her head in wonder at the hardness of his waist and abs, counting each ribbed swell of his abdominals on her way down to the waistband of his sweatpants.

Untying the cord, she pulled them down, his briefs too, and wrapped her hands around the rising pole of his hard cock with such satisfaction that she sighed loudly in pure pleasure. Jon groaned, his head arching back, his hips tilting forward to drive himself even more firmly into Aniela's hands. But it wasn't enough for her just to grip him, stroke him, run his velvet-soft skin over his stiff core; she sank to her knees, cushioned by the floor mat, licked off the drops of liquid that had collected at the tip of his cock, and then, drawing her lips back over her teeth, closed her mouth over him.

He filled her completely, his thick shaft pushing against her tongue, the roof of her mouth; it was overwhelming. Aniela's eyes closed so that she could concentrate completely on what she was doing, her lips tightening around his cock even more firmly as she felt him respond, swelling even more. She heard herself moaning deep in her throat, her index finger and thumb in a tight ring around his base, holding him as she began to suck up and down, flicking him with her tongue as she went, clinging with the other hand onto the edge of the basin for stability. Hot hard flesh in one hand, cold hard ceramic in the other; the contrast was oddly erotic. And everything was moist now: her skin, her uniform, the sink, the mat beneath her, his cock in her mouth, his hands twisting in her sweat-dampened hair, his balls bouncing against her fingers . . .

She realised, dizzily, that he was pulling her off him, off her knees and up to face him.

'You shouldn't,' he said, his voice blurry with desire. 'That's what prostitutes do – you don't have to do that with me—'

Aniela laughed in his face.

'I like it,' she said, kissing him. 'I *love* it. You have a gorgeous cock, I love to suck it.'

'You're *kidding*,' Jon said disbelievingly. 'Women *like* to do that?'

'Not just women,' she said, laughing again.

He would have blushed if he could.

'You can eat me too,' she said, high on excitement, as he started unbuttoning her uniform. 'But not now. Now I want you to fuck me . . .'

'Oh!' Jon bent down and rifled in the pockets of his sweatpants, which were puddled on the floor. 'I got these from Andy!'

Proudly, he held up a three-pack of condoms. Aniela, pulling down her pants and tights and unhooking her bra – she assumed that he wouldn't have had much practice at that, and she couldn't wait another moment – took in the sight and whooped in sheer delight. Grabbing the packet from him, she ripped one open, pulled it out and slid it onto him proficiently.

'*Jesus*,' he said. 'I really want to – how do we – where's the best—'

He looked around him desperately, having no experience with this; but she was already pulling and pushing him into position, manoeuvring herself in front of the basin, facing the big mirror recessed into the sea-blue mosaic tiles. Behind the mirror was a built-in anti-fog mat; everything around them was blurry, water droplets hanging in the air, pouring down like heavy rain in the walk-in shower, pounding onto the tiles below, creating a mist, but in the mirror they could see themselves clearly. Drops of water clung and beaded to their naked bodies, making the surfaces slick enough to slip and slide against each other as Jon took his cock in his hand and eased it between Aniela's legs. She was as wet inside as out by now, and he drove up into her faster than he'd meant, making both of them scream in pleasure; he gripped her hips frantically, bracing his legs as she clung to the edge of the basin.

'I can't last too long,' he groaned in apology, 'I can't hold out, I just want to fuck you so hard – I'm sorry—'

She stared at their reflection, her white Polish skin, her blonde hair plastered to her scalp, her eyes starry, her cheeks red, her nipples pink: yes, her breasts were too small, her hips too big, and she couldn't even bear to look at her stomach, but who cared? Jon obviously didn't. Jon, his head bent, was kissing her neck as he drove in and out of her, his hips juddering, his cock huge inside her, the tight curls of hair at his crotch rasping against her, a delicious tickling sensation that built and built, faster and faster, Jon gasping deep and gutturally, his fingers holding her like clamps as he pulled her even closer to him, and she screamed again in delight as he bent her over more and, in a last surge, rammed himself to climax, raising his head to watch their wet bodies slamming together in the steam.

'Yeah!' he yelled. '*Hell* yeah! *God – yes*—'

Aniela, her entire body rocking with delight, feeling Jon coming inside her, his cock jerking with his spasms, watched her own face break into the biggest smile she had ever seen.

'Happy Christmas,' she said in utter contentment.

December 26th – Boxing Day

Melody

'*A*re you sure about this, love?' Melody's mother asked as the Dale family's Volvo turned into Commercial Road. 'It's not too late to change your mind and come back with us, you know! You've got some clothes in your old room, and we can always find some extra bits and pieces for you. I'm sure I've got a few things that you can wear.'

'Right, Mum,' Ashley chortled beside his sister. 'Most of your stuff'll go round Mel twice.'

'Ashley Dale! Don't you talk to your mother that way!' his father said furiously, swinging round from the front passenger seat and clipping his son around the head.

'I've got some leggings she could wear,' Sonia Dale said comfortably, unoffended by Ashley's comment.

'And if I hadn't had my boobs reduced,' Melody said, relishing the opportunity to tease her brother, 'I could probably borrow Mum's bras too—'

'Agh!' Ashley clapped his hands over his ears. '*Double* disgusting! Sister and Mum's lady lumps!'

'Melody?' Sonia asked, very used to ignoring her son where necessary. 'Sure you want to do this, love?'

Melody nodded resolutely, leaning forward to put her arms around the headrest of her mother's seat, catching sight of herself in the mirror. She had slept in a heavy layer of arnica cream the night before, and that morning Sonia had spent a good deal of time carefully patting cover-up and foundation onto Melody's face, using liquid eyeliner which wouldn't pull her skin, and mascara on upper and lower lashes. It would have taken stage make-up, or the kind used to cover up actors' tattoos for film, to completely conceal the bruises, and Melody's cheeks were still lumpy, her lips swollen from the aftermath of the surgery; but at first, even second glance, she looked much better than she would have thought possible.

She was going to visit James. She'd led her parents to believe that she'd rung him, that he'd agreed to see her, but the truth was that Melody hadn't had the nerve to call James; what if he simply refused, point-blank, to meet her? She couldn't have coped with the rejection.

So she was trying again to turn up on his doorstep – still, technically, *their* doorstep – and see what his reaction was. Maybe it was unfair, one-sided; she knew she was coming, while he would be taken completely unawares. And maybe it was cowardly, but right now she felt stupidly, recklessly brave . . .

'Drop me on the corner, Mum,' she said quickly, seeing that they were coming up on the little street that led towards the railway lines. 'That way you won't have to do a U.'

'Oh, I don't mind,' said Mrs Dale. But there was a convenient place to pull in at the corner, London being quiet still on Boxing Day, and she slid the Volvo into the space.

'Say hello to James from us,' Mr Dale said, opening his car door; Melody hugged her brother briefly before getting out.

'Hope it goes okay, Mel,' he said, patting her arm awkwardly. 'And thanks for yesterday. I can't believe I got to hang out with Wayne Burns. Best Crimbo *ever*.'

She couldn't help smiling; both Ashley and her father were still on Cloud Nine from Grigor Khalovsky's party the day before. After the huge scene with Grigor's wife, and Grigor's collapse, the merriment had continued even more cheerfully than before. Grigor's engagement to the shy little mouse girl had been toasted once more, as if to draw a line under Dasha's home invasion, and the name of the wife Grigor was currently divorcing had not even been mentioned again.

With the host making an unexpectedly fast recovery, and Fyodorov yelling at the waiters to bring even more of the Hine cognac to serve with the brandy-soaked pudding and mince pies, the celebration had re-started surprisingly easily, and by the time the Dales staggered out at around seven, no one was in any state to drive. The four of them had watched television for a while, happily drink-sodden, Phil and Ashley reeking of expensive cigars to boot, and then Phil and Sonia had taken the second bedroom while Ashley crashed on the sofa.

'Can't argue with having cameras on mobile phones now,' her father said, enfolding Melody in a warm embrace. 'Wait till I show everyone at home the pics of me and Ash hanging out with Wayne Burns, like we were best mates! I know your mum loves meeting the actors, but this was a top treat for me. Thanks, love.'

'I can't really take credit, Dad,' Melody mumbled into his sweater, but she was smiling; she'd caused her parents a great deal of worry and stress over the last year, and although it might have been total chance that Grigor Khalovsky had invited them all to Christmas lunch, it couldn't have been a better present for the Dales.

'You'll be all right, won't you?' her mother said, hugging her tight and kissing her on her forehead, the one part of Melody's face that hadn't been bruised by her surgery. 'I'm sure you will,' she said firmly, answering her own question, stepping back and holding her daughter's shoulders.

Her mother was smiling, but Melody could read very different emotions under the prettily made-up, well-groomed surface. Sonia was very concerned, her forehead creasing, her lips tightening even as she forced them to curve upwards. She knew how much her daughter loved James, how happy they had been together, and what an awful mistake Melody had made when she had been seduced by the siren song of LA.

Mrs Dale started to say something and promptly caught herself; she had always been very good about not interfering too much in her children's lives, which was one of the reasons that, as adults, they were so close to their parents. Instead, she said gently:

'Take care of yourself,' squeezing Melody's shoulders and then releasing her daughter with visible reluctance. 'And give us a ring very soon, won't you, love? Maybe you could come to visit for New Year's Eve . . .'

If this meeting with James doesn't go so well, was the subtext, and Melody could hear it as clearly as if her mother had said it out loud. *If you need to come home to your family and curl in a ball and cry your eyes out, you're always welcome. I'll tuck you up and make you cheese toasties until you feel better.*

'Thanks, Mum,' Melody said with huge gratitude. 'You should get back in the car now, it's freezing.'

'Snow in the next couple of days,' her father said. 'They've been saying it on the news.'

'Have you got the chains in the car, Phil?' said his wife, as he held the driver's door open for her.

'Of course I have,' he said, rolling his eyes. '*And* the safety triangle, *and* the hi-vis jacket . . .' Winking at his daughter, he closed his wife's door and went round the car to his own. 'All I need now is a St Bernard dog with a nice little barrel of brandy round its neck to pull us out of drifts if we get stuck . . .'

Melody stood on the corner, pulling her coat tightly around her; she watched the car pull away, waving at it, her father's hand sticking out of the window, waving back at her; only when it disappeared did she take a deep breath, turn, and march quickly down the little side street which was still so very familiar to her, to the cottage which had once been her home. Before she could lose her nerve, she raised her hand and pressed the doorbell which had once been hers. It rang out loudly, particularly audible on such a quiet day, with few people around; *and now it's done,* she told herself firmly. *I can't run away, like a kid dropping something nasty on a doorstep and then making a dash for it. I have to stay here and give him time to answer . . . if he's in . . .*

She was in such a heightened state of nerves that she honestly couldn't have said whether she wanted James to be in or not. When she heard footsteps tumbling down the polished pine floorboards of the narrow little staircase, which she had jokingly called the Stairs of Doom when she lived there, she caught her breath. Because even through the closed front door, she recognised James's particular way of taking a flight of stairs, the way he jumped the last three and then padded barefoot to the door—

'*Melody?*' he said in surprise and disbelief as he opened the door.

It's a very odd thing to be in a relationship with someone whose face is plastered on billboards, flashing on TV ads, staring thoughtfully from the covers of glossy magazines. Previously, Melody had been completely insulated from this effect, because she had known James for years before he had become Dr Who, had fallen in love with him just as James Delancey, just another aspiring actor. Now he was not only a heart-throb, but a cultural icon. The outfit that he wore as Dr Who – the artfully disarranged hair, Hoxton-trendy skinny jeans, tight-fitting patterned knit cardigan, and Converse sneakers – weren't James's personal style at all; he was much more conventional. But his slim figure carried them off perfectly: he wore the clothes with dashing ease, and looked so handsome in them that teenage girls, waiting outside the stage door to get his autograph after seeing him as Romeo, had screamed, stormed the door and fainted with such regularity that the theatre had had to hire extra security staff.

However, when James came back from Cardiff after a bout of filming the show, he wasn't Dr Who in any way. He was the James he had always been, with his holey sweaters and his fringe flopping naturally over his forehead without the hair wax his make-up artist used to work and piece his blond locks so they looked as if they were arguing with each other. Melody had never been bothered in any way by the status James had developed since they had been together.

Not until now.

Melody froze, staring up at him. She couldn't even remember a time when James's face, James's body, as familiar to her as her own, hadn't been hers to touch, to stroke, to nuzzle against. They had always been very tactile, hugging, kissing, walking down the street with their arms linked, curling up together on sofas or armchairs, happiest when physically connected to each other. Now, it was as if a force field existed between them. Melody yearned to reach up her hand, to wrap it around his neck, stroke his soft silky hair, pull his head down for a kiss: but she couldn't. James was no longer an extension of her. And his fame made it even stranger, to be so close to him but no longer with the right to hold him close to her. For a second she felt like a crazy stalker, as if their years together had never happened. It was surreal, horrible, disconcerting.

And yet James hadn't changed at all. He was in his flannel pyjamas, one of his old navy sweaters from school pulled on over them; he hadn't changed in any way. *It's me that's changed*, she knew, watching James's expression as he took in the contours of her face, visible below the layers of foundation. He raised a hand to push back a lock of her black hair, staring at her with great concentration, one thumb gently stroking her cheek for a moment as he did so, making her tremble.

'You're cold,' he said, misunderstanding the reason for her shiver, backing away from the door so that she could come in. They had knocked through all the internal walls in the small cottage before moving in, wanting to make the space look as big as possible; even the Stairs of Doom were open-plan, without a railing. One step inside and Melody was in the sitting room, glancing over at the fire, which was ready to be lit, the ash scraped out from the grate and a few pieces of newspaper bunched up in balls beside it.

'Melody—' James couldn't take his eyes off her. 'Did you – your face—'

He couldn't even get the words out to ask why her face had some tell-tale swelling over its contours. *He said he couldn't bear to think of me letting people cut up my face . . .*

'I put it back!' she said quickly, urgently. 'I put it back the way it was! Everything!'

'I don't understand,' James said, looking confused.

'I showed the surgeon a picture of me,' she said eagerly. 'Not a head shot, a proper one. The one you took of me when we were on holiday in Goa. And I said that I wanted my old face back, like that. Exactly as it was. He even did a tiny implant on my chin where it'd been shaved down—'

James winced, flinching back.

'James, I was such an idiot,' Melody went on, grabbing his hands, looking up at him. 'I made one mistake after another. I wish I could explain to you how I got caught up in it all, how it happened. Brad was really convincing – he sort of sucked me in, he told me I was going to be the new Ava Gardner, and he made the film sound amazing – and the screenplay *was* amazing, you *know* it was, you read it . . .'

James flinched again at the mention of Brad, and Melody thought she knew why.

'Nothing happened,' she insisted, her voice rising with the need to convince him, remembering the snide gossip that Felicity had so gleefully passed on. 'I promise, nothing happened at all. *Ever. I promise.*'

James looked shamefaced; he ducked his head, his hair hanging in his eyes.

'But it's okay if you – I mean, I left you hanging, not knowing when I was coming back, even *if* I was coming back – I messed you around – I'd understand if something happened with you . . . ' Melody tailed off.

She was lying: it wasn't okay, not at all. The thought of James twining his body around another woman's, his smooth skin against hers, the delicate salt of his sweat on her tongue, his arms holding her, his hair falling into her face as they made love, was inexpressibly painful to her. She had always thought that she and James would never be unfaithful, would be together for the rest of their lives, no one ever coming between them. Perhaps it was a ludicrous dream for an actor to have, with the travelling and temptations on set and in the rehearsal room, a profession where a marriage lasting ten years was considered a Hollywood lifetime, but she had truly thought that she and James could be the ones to beat the odds. They had the connection everyone dreamed of, a love that had flamed into life instantly, but hadn't burnt out as quickly as those fast affairs usually did, settling instead into a real companionship.

Never in my wildest imaginings would I have thought that it would have been me who ruined it.

'I left you,' she went on bravely. 'I went off and left you in the lurch – not just with everything here in the house, but the play too.'

'It was our *dream*, Mel,' James said passionately. 'To play Romeo and Juliet together in the West End. And now that's gone for ever! We can never get that back!'

'I know, I know . . .' Tears were forming in her eyes. 'That's all my fault, I know it is. And I know you might be seeing Priya, and I can't blame you for that, not at all . . .'

'It was just a fling!' James said swiftly. 'Barely anything at all! I was so lonely and miserable – I was saying all these lines to her but I kept imagining you – it was always supposed to be you as Juliet! It lasted less than a week. We both knew it was a mistake. And then we went back to being friends and it was actually so much easier afterwards . . .'

Melody dabbed at her eyes, frightened not so much of her mascara running but that the tears would wash away the foundation and show James the fading bruises below. It wasn't that she needed to look perfect for him; they'd spent whole weekends holed up together without her putting on a scrap of make-up. But she knew how much he loathed the idea that she had had plastic surgery, and she didn't want him to see the evidence, not so soon.

'So you're *not* seeing Priya?' she asked, her emotions utterly confused. She hated that he had been with Priya, even for a few days. But the relief at hearing that it had been so short-lived, that Priya had failed to replace her in James's heart – and she believed him, because James had never lied to her – was overwhelmingly positive, a huge rush of happiness.

'No! No, I'm not!' James assured her urgently. 'We're mates – I had a party a couple of days ago, and she came along, which was nice – she snogged me, but that was just 'cause a pap was there—'

'Oh!' Melody threw herself into his arms in a total release of tension. She wrapped herself around him, breathing in his sweet smell, his woolly sweater, his almost painfully lean body whose hollows and curves and bones were even more familiar to her than her own. 'I love you so much,' she said, the tears starting up again. 'I missed you so much. I've been so unhappy without you, I'm so sorry for messing up so badly . . . *please* say you forgive me and we can go back to where we were before!'

Her chest was hurting, pressed against James so tightly, the scars from the removal of the breast implants aching. But she didn't care. She wondered if James would even realise that she'd had those taken out too. He was used to feeling her body this way, he had never hugged her with those awful spongy balls attached to her front. He would have hated them, and she had hated them too. Not being able to sleep on her front, not knowing what clothes to wear over them, being embarrassed by her own cleavage, by the looks men would give her, as if they thought that she'd had the boob job for their especial benefit. *And not only that – as if they had the absolute right to leer, because I did such a stupid thing to myself deliberately, turned myself into some sort of Barbie sex doll, making my boobs their property.*

I was such an idiot to mess with my body like that. What was I thinking?

And then she remembered the corset fittings, everyone fussing around her, the moulded plastic cups jutting out in front of her chest, unfilled, Brad and the costume designer in a huddle, muttering about how DC Comics would react when they saw the test shots ... the comments that padding wouldn't do it, that Wonder Woman was supposed to be much more curvaceous ... her feeling of total failure as she looked down at her too-flat chest, that she had been let down by something completely out of her control ...

'All I want is to go back to where we were before!' She was sobbing now. 'We were so happy, we can be that all over again, like nothing's changed—'

'Mel—' James pulled back, holding her shoulders, looking down at her, his eyes wide and serious. 'There's something I have to tell you about—'

'Something? Don't you mean some*one*?' came a high-pitched, upper-class voice from the top of the stairs, and Melody swung round in horror to see Felicity standing there.

A born actress, Felicity knew exactly how to make an entrance, and how to dress for this crucial scene. She was wearing one of James's shirts, a faded old denim one, and, apparently, nothing else at all; it was unbuttoned to where cleavage would have shown, if she'd had enough flesh for cleavage. Her long pale legs, glossy with just-applied body lotion, were almost entirely visible under the ragged hem. She had managed to tousle out her sparse blonde locks into a very impressive bedhead, and either she had applied a couple of coats of mascara and lip gloss, or the make-up she had on the evening before was actually as miraculous as the advertisements said, and had lasted perfectly without a single smear or smudge.

As she started down the stairs, kicking one leg elegantly forward without looking down, her eyes fixed on Melody's, she could have been a Miss World competitor in a bikini, finding the next step expertly, able to hook her heels backwards just enough to make her entire descent without taking her gaze from her rival.

'Well, this *is* a surprise!' Felicity said lightly. 'Boxing Day morning, of all times for you to show up, Melody! Has James offered you some coffee yet? He was just going to make us some . . .'

Bile rose in Melody's throat. She looked at James, her blue eyes pleading with him to tell her that Felicity was here because she had got drunk last night at some party, that he'd let her crash here in the spare room, that nothing at all had happened between them—

But she could see from his guilty expression that this swift, innocent explanation for Felicity's presence in their house was nothing but wishful thinking.

'You're seeing *her*?' Melody blurted out, as Felicity paused on the second step above the ground floor, keeping the tactical advantage of height.

'There's no need to say it like that!' Felicity said icily. 'Look at yourself! Go on, look!'

Reluctantly, despite herself, Melody turned her head to stare at her reflection in the mirror over the fireplace. The room was small enough that she could see herself very clearly. And the picture wasn't pretty. The side of her face that had been smushed into James's sweater had been wiped of make-up, the yellow-green bruising now lividly chartreuse. Black smudges were smeared around that eye; bizarrely, the other side was still perfect, which just made the effect look even worse.

'You look all mashed up!' Felicity continued implacably. 'What on earth were you thinking, running off to LA to make that ridiculous film, getting your boobs all pumped up like balloons? You've made yourself into an absolute laughing-stock!'

Everything Felicity was saying was true. Her words were cutting and cruel, but they echoed precisely Melody's own thoughts about herself. The nastiest ones, the voice that spoke to her in the middle of the night, when she woke up and couldn't get back to sleep. The voice that told her that she'd lost everything she'd worked so hard for, her lover, her career, and that she'd never get them back.

'Honestly, you really are nothing but a laughing-stock now,' Felicity was repeating gleefully. 'Nobody takes you seriously. Those fake boobs, bouncing up and down in that outfit of yours! James was horrified. Weren't you, darling?'

Judging her moment, Felicity descended the final two steps and stepped elegantly over to James, resting a manicured hand proprietorially on his shoulder, tossing back her hair seductively. Melody backed away, all too aware of what her face looked like.

'You said that you'd lost all respect for her,' Felicity said, leaning in to James. She must have sprayed on perfume before she came downstairs, because Melody smelt it in the air; with increasing misery, she realised that it was one of her own favourites, which she had left here when flying out to LA: with horrible irony, it was called Clinique Happy Heart. 'You said that you couldn't possibly ever think of her in the same way again. You said that it felt like you'd never really known her at all . . .'

It was too much. James's expression was even more guilty, his lips pinched together as if he wanted to deny the truth of what Felicity was saying, but couldn't. Ironically, considering that he was a professional actor, in his personal life James couldn't lie, absolutely hated doing it; it was one of the qualities that Melody loved in him most of all.

But now it meant that he couldn't even come out with a comforting denial, couldn't salve the wound that Felicity had slashed in Melody's self-esteem. It was clear that James had made all those comments to Felicity, and Felicity's sweetly satisfied smile underlined it; she was too clever to put words into James's mouth that he had never spoken.

Felicity had turned so that her back was to the rest of the room, blocking Melody from access to the rest of what was still, technically, half her property. The sun from the window behind Felicity streamed in and backlit her flatteringly, striking glints in her hair. She stretched her arm across James's slim shoulders, easing her hip into his, so that now they looked like a couple confronting an interloper in their house. Melody took another step back; by now, she was at the door. She glanced sideways, to the line of pegs on which coats were hung, seeing James's old duffel coat, his leather jacket, his nicer tweed coat for smart evenings out. Before, the pegs had been crammed with Melody's various coats, capes, jackets, hats, scarves – James had often complained about the amount she had loaded onto them, how there was no space for his things.

But now there was plenty of space for all his coats. And next to them was hanging the fake fur cape Felicity had been wearing on Christmas Eve, which Melody remembered that she'd seen swirling around Felicity as she posed next to James for the paparazzo, its hood pulled up to frame her face flatteringly.

Has she been here all the time since then? Hanging out, celebrating Christmas with him, as if she were his girlfriend?

Maybe she is his girlfriend, and they assume I know it. Maybe Felicity agreed to come round a few days ago to see if I realised that she was with James, hoping that I'd bring it up . . .

The thought of Felicity replacing her, moving into the house Melody had bought with James, in such excitement and anticipation of happiness – the bed they had chosen, the mattress they had bounced on in John Lewis, giggling their heads off – made Melody feel that her heart was being squeezed so tightly that she couldn't breathe, couldn't speak. Turning, she fumbled at the door, her hands shaking, barely managing to get it open and fall out, running down the pavement as if she were being chased.

And I am, she thought bitterly. *I'm being chased by the ghost of myself. The way I was before I fucked everything up, before I went off and left a huge gaping hole in my life, the size of my own body, into which some other woman could jump and get together with my gorgeous, eligible, famous boyfriend . . .*

She was pulling out her phone as she reached the corner, about to ring her father.

They won't have got that far. And there isn't much traffic, it'll be easy driving. Mum can just turn round and come and get me, take me home, and look after me. I can curl up in my old bed, eat cheese toasties, put myself back together, come to terms with the fact that James is with someone else . . .

And then, setting her jaw – which made her wince, because of the cartilage graft there – Melody pushed the phone back into her pocket again.

No. I've got to grow up. I pretty much went straight from home to playing house with James, and then, in LA, the producers and Brad put me up in a hotel, got me to do what they wanted, convinced me to make terrible decisions, one after the other.

Well, I'm standing on my own two feet now. I'm putting back all the surgery I had, I've been brave enough to go and see my ex-boyfriend, and now the last thing I should be doing is running back home so my mum and dad can treat me like a little girl.

A black cab came past, its light off, but without a passenger inside; Melody stuck out her hand and it pulled up in front of her, the driver leaning over from his seat, staring in concern at her face.

'You all right, love?' he asked, grimacing at her bruising and the smeared make-up.

'Yes – *no*,' Melody said quickly, desperate to get away from here. 'I just need to get back to Limehouse – Limehouse Reach, next to the Four Seasons – do you mind?'

'Yeah, jump in,' he said, nodding behind him. 'Ain't that far, there's no one on the road.'

She could see him staring at her in the rear-view mirror, but he was kind enough not to ask any more questions, limiting himself to a friendly:

'Take care of yourself, eh?' as he deposited her outside Limehouse Reach. 'And Happy Boxing Day!' he called as the cab pulled away.

Holding her wallet, Melody paused outside the building, looking up at its rippling glass façade, the curving balconies that wrapped around the upper floors, the clear winter light pooling elegantly on the clean lines of the skyscraper.

It wasn't home, or anything like it. But it was new, and bright, and shiny, and at that moment, it looked to Melody very much like a place where she would be able to make a fresh start.

Jon

A niela was still asleep. Jon eased himself out of bed, not wanting to disturb her. It had been a hell of a long day yesterday; that crazy Christmas lunch at Grigor Khalovsky's, his spilling his guts to Aniela afterwards, and then the sex. Jesus, the sex. He'd never known anything like it. Some of the women he'd been with before had been damn good at pretending that they were enjoying themselves; who knew, maybe they even had been, just a little bit. But there was nothing like doing it with a woman who wanted it just as much as you did.

They'd done it again in the middle of the night, and Jon couldn't have said whose idea that had been. He'd been spooning her, and he'd woken up with a stiff cock, that much he knew; but had she woken up first? Had she been arching against him, reaching back to stroke him? Had he pulled her towards him, or had she guided him where she wanted him, holding him, stroking him? It didn't matter, of course. It didn't matter a damn. But this was all so new to him, so unprecedented, that he found himself playing back all the details after each time they had sex, trying to remember every single moment, as if he were making sure he had a complete picture, storing it up in his memory . . .

He grimaced. *That's* exactly *what I'm doing. Storing it up for the lean years to come.* Because soon – when his face healed – he'd be gone, off to Montana, to set up his ranch, lie low for the rest of his life. He was a loner, and he'd always be a loner; he hadn't given a moment's thought to the idea of having female company, certainly not full-time. He had needs, of course. He'd assumed that there might be some nice discreet escort in Butte. Jon's experience of travelling the world had taught him that there wasn't a place on this planet where you couldn't find a woman who was willing and ready to trade no-strings sex for cash.

The trouble is, after this, it's going to be a lot harder to settle for less. He pulled on his sweatpants, looking down at Aniela, her blonde hair covering her face, her skin as white as the sheets. Carefully, he pulled the coverlet up over her round shoulders, not wanting her to be cold, and padded out of the bedroom to make coffee. It was nine-thirty, and he knew she had to see the other patient in Limehouse Reach at eleven, that girl who'd had her face done; he should wake Aniela up, make sure she had a bite to eat before she had to head on out.

But what the hell do I give her? Coffee, for a start. That was easy enough. The apartment came furnished with one of those Illy coffee machines, big, shiny, red and chrome, which came with a bunch of pods that you dropped into a slot and threw away afterwards, no muss, no fuss. Hell of a waste, as far as Jon was concerned, and hell of a cost too. All those little plastic pods must cost a fortune. He was old-school American: nothing beat a good old drip coffee maker, stained a little from years of use, sitting on the kitchen counter so's you could just pour yourself a mug whenever you needed one, giving you a slow steady buzz throughout the day.

Still, if you made a double espresso shot, dumped it into a mug and topped it up with boiling water, he had to admit that you got a pretty good cup of joe. That was okay; if she wanted coffee, he could make her some. But for the rest? Jon was no chef. He'd never really cooked for himself in his life, never had a home in which he'd needed to; he'd vaguely assumed that, on the ranch, he'd throw together home-made chilli and pretty much live off that.

He opened the fridge and stared at its contents dubiously. A huge tub of margarine, another one of peanut butter, quarts of long-life milk. That was it. The freezer was crammed with ready meals, bags of mixed vegetables and pre-sliced bread; he'd stocked up before the surgery, to make sure he never needed to go out for supplies.

Briefly, he considered picking up the Four Seasons room service menu and ordering Aniela breakfast, but he had to nix that idea. If Dasha Khalovsky hadn't been roaming the halls, swearing bloodthirsty vengeance on her husband and trying to drag him into her plans for revenge, he'd have done it, taken the risk of having a room service waiter come over. He'd been living on protein shakes till yesterday: Christmas lunch with Grigor Khalovsky had been his first taste of solid food in a fortnight.

But as it was, no way could he let anyone he didn't know into the apartment, or even open the door to sign for the food. Dasha Khalovsky was complicating his life, big-time, and the only way he could see to deal with the threat she presented was to set up a meet with her, record her instructing him to kill her husband, and then turn round and take the information to Grigor Khalovsky.

Jon had been racking his brains to figure out a way round this dilemma that didn't involve telling Grigor. Because he knew that the consequence would be Grigor promptly taking out his estranged wife. And Jon hadn't made his vow not to take another human life lightly; he wanted to keep it in the spirit as well as the literal intent. If he went to Grigor Khalovsky with evidence that Dasha wanted him dead, he might as well shoot Dasha in the back of his head himself and save Grigor the trouble.

I still don't see any other way round it. Once Dasha was dead, the threat she posed would dissipate. No way would her PIs go on digging up info on him after their client disappeared or died in mysterious circumstances. They'd assume, if they had any sense, that Jon had been at the back of Dasha's death, and that he'd come after them if they didn't drop the investigation into his background like a heavy stone. The last thing any investigators savvy enough to be hired by Dasha Khalovsky would want was a hitman with a slate to wipe clean targeting them as his next victims.

'Jon?'

Aniela, rubbing the sleep out of her eyes, stood in the doorway to the bedroom. She had pulled on a T-shirt of his, which came down to her plump upper thighs, and her fair hair was tangled around her face. She never wore any make-up as far as Jon could see; certainly she looked no different when she had just woken from sleep than she did when she came in to see him on her rounds, apart from the fact that her hair was loose. He liked that a lot.

'Sure looks pretty like that,' he said. 'Your hair, I mean.'

'Oh!' She blushed. 'Thanks! I have to tie it back for work.'

She looked over at the clock projected on the living-room wall.

'I need to be at Melody's in an hour,' she said. 'Would you mind – if I go back down to the reception and then back again, they'll know I've been sleeping here – if I could get a coffee, maybe, and something to eat—'

'I was just going to make one,' Jon said quickly. 'And toast? Toast okay?'

She nodded.

'Uh, with peanut butter or without?'

Her features softened into a smile. 'Are those my only choices?'

'Pretty much,' he admitted. 'Unless you want a protein shake? I got frozen fruit – I could rustle you up one.'

'No, coffee and toast are fine. No peanut butter. Thanks,' she added. 'I'll just go and shower, is that okay?'

'Yeah, sure. Feel free to use all the fancy stuff in there,' he said, thinking that he must sound like the biggest idiot in the world. 'You know, the stuff they give you with this place. Shampoo, conditioner, the works. I got them to leave me a whole bunch when I moved in.'

He was babbling. Thank God, she nodded, turned and went off to the bathroom, sparing him from any further embarrassment. He had no real idea how to talk to a woman who'd spent the night, for free. So far, he wasn't doing much of a job.

At least I said I liked her hair, he thought, turning to the Illy machine. *That's got to count for something.*

He heard the water running in the bathroom and pictured her, naked, skin as white as milk, with generous curves but small breasts, like an oil painting he'd seen somewhere. *I should look that picture up on the net,* he thought. *Tell her she looks like a painting. Can't go wrong telling a woman that, can you?*

He was hard again at the thought of her nude in the shower, the water pouring down on her, remembering them going at it yesterday, watching her face as they did it, feeling her wet slippery skin beneath him, her wide hips filling his hands very satisfyingly. The escorts Jon had been with in the past had been built on very different lines to Aniela. Most men, it seemed, wanted women who were too skinny for Jon's taste; he liked women who had more than a handful of flesh to hold onto, who'd keep you warm at night. And the escorts, without exception, had had their boobs done. He didn't get that either. A woman shouldn't mess with what nature gave her, in his opinion. Those fake boobs looked and felt just that – fake. Why a guy would want that instead of the real thing, he had no goddamn idea at all.

But if women didn't do unnecessary stuff to themselves, Aniela wouldn't have a job here at the Clinic, he thought. *So she wouldn't be in my shower right now, soaping herself, running her hands all over her body—*

His erection was painful, rubbing against the seam in his pants; he was dying to go into the bathroom, drop the sweatpants, step into the shower and kiss her and touch her until she melted and parted her legs and let him in. *Shit, I can't. I'll make her late for work. Dammit.*

Briefly, he actually considered tossing himself off into the sink, the pressure in his dick was so intense, his balls heavy and swollen with spunk. But what if she came in while he was doing it? How could he explain it? Closing his eyes, he pictured Dasha Khalovsky, with her dyed hair, big fake tits, bright gaudy clothes, her faceful of make-up and puffed-out, over-filled lips: that image was enough to soften his cock, disperse the bursting, urgent need for Aniela.

He distracted himself further by making coffee, and was taking out frozen slices of bread and dropping them in the toaster, putting together a place setting for Aniela at the breakfast bar when she emerged from the bedroom again, dressed once more in her uniform and those funny white shoes, her hair washed and scraped back from her scalp, looking all professional once more.

'I guess you don't need to come back after,' he said as she climbed up onto the white leather stool and took the coffee mug between her hands gratefully. 'To check up on me, I mean.'

She froze for a moment, her light eyes meeting his above the rim of the mug, and then dropped her gaze to the surface of the coffee instead.

'Fine,' she said flatly. 'No problem, I leave you alone.'

'I just meant—'

Yeah, what did you mean? he asked himself. *Why did you just tell her not to come back, when ten minutes ago you were desperate to fuck her?*

It just seemed really fast, he realised. *She'd go, sure, but then she'd be back in an hour – I wouldn't even have time to catch my breath. And yeah, we'd fuck practically as soon as she walked in the door, but then what? What would we do after that?*

Horribly, he remembered a joke another guy in the Unit had told him once, years ago: that you didn't pay a hooker to have sex with you so much as you paid them to leave afterwards. He didn't want to think of Aniela like that, as if he were using her for sex. It was more that he didn't have the first idea what they would do if they weren't having sex or sleeping. *What would we do – talk? I have no idea how to talk to a woman.*

Be honest, Jon, he told himself. *With this one, you pretty much rattle away. You may babble on, but you have no problem talking to her.*

So it's not that you worry you won't get a word out. It's something else, isn't it?

Aniela was eating her toast now, washing it down with sips of the long-life orange juice. He looked at her head, bent over her plate to avoid meeting his eyes, at the precise parting she must have made with his comb, straight as if she'd used a ruler to measure it, running down her scalp, the skin delicately rosy-white, a few short fine blonde hairs coming free at the roots. The feelings that rose in him, staring at her so intently, were a mass of confusion: but one thought pierced through, more painful than the rest, like a stab right through his heart, skewering it with exact precision.

I can't seem to control what comes out of my mouth when I'm around her. So sooner or later, I'll end up telling her about my childhood. My cosy, loving family and my sweet, caring mom and my big, strong, protective dad, white picket fence and all . . .

Bile rose in Jon's throat at how different his upbringing had been from the perfect fantasy one of his imaginings. He choked it down with a huge effort.

How can I ever tell her what I did when I was seventeen, back in the Hollow? How could any woman hear that and want to spend another moment with me?

No. Better to push her away first. So I never have to see the expression of contempt on her face when I blurt out the truth about my past.

I can't be anything but honest with her. I've figured that much out by now. But I can't tell her the truth about myself either. So where does that leave me?

He knew the answer already, had lived with it his entire adult life.

Alone.

He just hadn't realised how sad that damn word sounded before.

Andy

'*A*ndy! My friend!' Grigor, overcome with happiness, threw his arms around Andy and hugged him as closely as he could in the Santa suit he was wearing.

Does he sleep in it? Andy wondered; Grigor loved the suit so much it was hard to imagine him taking it off at night. Despite Grigor's expensive aftershave, the fur-trimmed wool was beginning to smell faintly of oligarch sweat. Certainly, after today's partying, it should be sent off by courier to a specialist dry cleaner and given a thorough laundering.

'This is the *best* Boxing Day party I have ever had, thanks to *you*, my friend!' Grigor bellowed. 'It's the most wonderful time of the year!' he sang: Andy was so used to Grigor bursting into song now that he didn't even flinch as Grigor's bass rang out right next to his ear.

Zhivana, in a cream silk Lanvin dress trimmed with guipure lace, drifted by like a droopy little ghost: Grigor caught her, enfolded her in an equally enthusiastic hug and placed two smacking, avuncular kisses on each of her hollow cheeks.

'My pretty little fiancée!' he said happily. 'What is your favourite Christmas song, pretty little Zhivana Fyodorova?'

Zhivana didn't need to think this over; it was clear she knew immediately. Her muddy brown eyes lit up with rare pleasure as she said with relish:

'"The Cat And The Mouse". I love to listen to it. Do you know this song?'

Grigor shook his head, smiling down at her indulgently.

'It is *very* sad,' Zhivana began, and Grigor's expression crumpled in comic disappointment. Andy bit his lip, trying not to smile, as Zhivana continued:

'The cat cannot get into its house at night, and it is snowing, so it is cold, but then a mouse comes along—'

'And the cat eats the mouse!' Grigor suggested, patting his tummy. 'And that makes him feel better!'

'The cat *protects* the mouse,' Zhivana said coldly. 'It curls around the mouse all night, in the snow, to keep it warm. And then Santa comes—'

'Ho ho ho!' Grigor carolled.

Zhivana's narrow brows drew together in a frown. Andy, greatly daring, elbowed Grigor in the ribs as a signal that his responses were not going down like a house on fire with his fiancée, but Grigor was oblivious. *High on the Christmas spirit*, Andy thought with a sigh.

'Santa comes,' Zhivana continued firmly, her mouth set in a straight line that matched her eyebrows, 'and they find the cat is dead. It is frozen to death – it died to protect the mouse, keeping it warm.'

'Oh *no*!' Andy exclaimed, shocked. Zhivana nodded, a little smile playing around her lips.

'And all the reindeer cry,' she said with satisfaction. 'They cry a *lot*, because they are very sad to see the poor dead cat, all cold and frozen. They put the mouse in the sleigh, and then Santa lifts up the cat, the dead cat, and puts it in the sky like a star, and says that every Christmas the cat star will shine brightly to remind the mouse that it still has a friend—'

'Please! Stop!' Andy was sobbing by now. 'Please! No more!'

'I told you it was very sad,' Zhivana said, nodding seriously. 'To me this is the true feeling of Christmas. Sacrifice. Death. Jesus Christ died to save us, and Christ is like the cat, who dies to save the mouse, so cold there in the snow, frozen to death—'

'*Please!*' Tears were falling down Andy's face. He rubbed his face on his sleeve, but since he was wearing his felt elf uniform, the fabric didn't do anything to absorb them.

'Here.' Dmitri, Grigor's son, came over, taking a linen napkin from a passing waiter and handing it to Andy. 'What's happening? Dad, are you making Andy cry?'

'No, it was me,' Zhivana said, turning to him. Her light brown hair was done in a series of small plaits pulled into a loose bun at the back of her head, making her profile surprisingly pretty. 'I am telling him the story of the Christmas song "The Cat And The Mouse". It is my favourite. Because it tells the true story of Christmas, how Jesus is only born so that he can die in pain to save the world.'

'Oh my God, Meryn Cadell!' Dmitri exclaimed. 'I love that song! It's so totally poignant.'

Andy, very grateful for the napkin, blew his nose so vigorously that the big pointy elf ears he was wearing on a headband jerked back on his smooth skull.

'Sorry,' he muttered, turning away and readjusting the ears.

'No! It is not your fault!' Grigor said, patting him on the shoulder and making the ears wobble again. 'It is Zhivana who makes you cry.'

He frowned severely at his fiancée. 'We are *happy* at Christmas,' he said firmly. 'It is a *happy* time.'

'But, Dad—' Dmitri pushed back the straggly of hair that fell over his thin face – 'don't you think that's, like, really bogus? I mean, you can't just *declare* that we all have to feel a given way at a given time. In my opinion—'

'*Pomolchi!* Shut up!' Grigor yelled at his son. 'Christmas is more important than your opinion!'

'Mr Khalovsky, you should be careful with yourself,' Sergei said solicitously, zipping up behind him. 'You must not become agitated, not after yesterday.'

'I'm fine,' Grigor said impatiently. 'The nurse who was here and the doctor who came this morning said I was fine, didn't they? No one knows even why it happened.' He gestured magisterially with one red-gloved hand. 'I am in tip-top health!' he announced. 'And it is the most wonderful time of the year!'

His furious stare at his son rather belied his words; luckily at that moment the brightly painted sleigh-train chugged past, its open carriages filled with screaming, excited children dressed in Burberry and Gucci, waving madly at Father Christmas. It couldn't have been a better interruption; beaming cheerfully, Grigor waved back at them. The train came to a halt, and the children piled out and descended on Grigor, begging for presents.

'What do you say, Elf?' Grigor asked, putting his hands on his hips and turning to Andy. 'Is it time to give the children their gifts?'

Andy pretended to think it over.

'Maybe just a few minutes more, Santa—' he started, winking at the children.

'No! Now! *Now!*' shrieked a particularly demanding and entitled little six-year-old girl, the daughter of a footballer and a glamour model. Called Princess Chastity, she was dressed as Jasmine from *Aladdin* in a custom-made pale blue silk outfit, her nails immaculately silvered. 'I want presents *now!*'

'Okay! I like a little girl who knows what she wants!' Grigor smiled down at her. 'Gather round, children . . .'

'Boys over here,' Andy said loudly, to be heard over the screams and the Christmas music being played over Grigor's sound system. 'Girls over there.'

Dmitri clicked his tongue in disapproval as the small

children thronged around. Both boys and girls looked like
miniature versions of their fathers and mothers; the boys were
in obscenely expensive designer sportswear and the very latest
trainers, the girls done up to the nines in tight, shiny party
dresses, their ears pierced, their nails done, their shoes
sequinned and boasting heels of at least an inch.

'It's a real shame that the presents aren't gender-neutral,'
Dmitri observed. 'This would be a very good opportunity to
strike a blow against the gender stereotyping our society seems
so desperate to propagate—'

'Capri! London! Stop pushing, you little horrors!' screeched
one mother, tottering over on her six-inch stacked heels, her
bandage skirt only allowing her to take very small steps. 'I can
see you shoving Mitchell! She's only four!'

Mercifully, Dmitri's father was too busy chortling 'Ho ho
ho!' and handing out presents passed to him by Andy to hear
his son's words. Dmitri turned away to see Zhivana climbing
into one of the carriages, her small body fitting neatly inside.
She smoothed down her dress over her knees and looked
around her hopefully to see if the train was going to start again.
Catching Dmitri's eyes, she gave him a small, melancholy
smile.

'If I go round and round,' she said, 'I don't have to talk to
anyone.'

'I'll get it going,' Dmitri said, and was rewarded with
another small smile as he went off to find the console that
sent the train chugging round its circuit. He threaded his way
through a group of wives and girlfriends who ignored him
completely, seeing his brown corduroy suit and mutton-chop
sideburns and assuming that he didn't have a penny to rub
together; none of them realised that he was their host's
younger son.

The women's cascading hair extensions, plumped-up lips
and breasts, Hervé Léger dresses and Louboutins made them
look like parodies of femininity. They would have fitted in

perfectly at any drag club. Dmitri averted his eyes as he went past: they were the absolute pinnacle of the exaggerated gender roles to which he strongly objected on ideological grounds.

'Happy Christmas!' Andy said cheerfully to the children as he handed gift after gift to Grigor.

'I want a *big* one!' Princess Chastity shrieked, rather belying her name. 'A really *big* one!'

'Like mother, like daughter,' quipped the mother of London, Capri and Mitchell, making Andy give a snigger which he quickly suppressed. 'Ooh, talking of big ones, look at you!' she observed, noticing Andy for the first time and looking him up and down. His costume – a tight green jerkin with a big white collar, belted over equally tight red trousers, the hems and cuffs pinked into sharp points – showed off his well-set shoulders and slim figure very well, and his chestnut skin was not washed out by the bright colours.

'I never thought I'd fancy an elf,' she went on. 'First time for everything, I s'pose.'

She looked over at the group of WAGs.

'Oi, Chantelle, look at this hot elf!' she shrieked.

Chantelle, Wayne Burns's long-term girlfriend, her strawberry-blonde locks done in a 'Kate Middleton' – smooth and voluminous, with the ends tonged into loose curls – glanced over. She was wearing a dark pink stretch satin dress with a mullet hem, more suitable for a night out at one of the London clubs footballers frequented, Mahiki or Bunga Bunga, than a daytime party with children present. Diamonds gleamed in her low-cut neckline and in her ears; her skin was an even, glossy tan and her teeth blindingly white. She noticed Andy and broke into a very sweet smile.

'Ooh, Corinne, he's *lovely*,' she cooed. 'You know what they say – big ears, big . . . heart!'

She burst into giggles, turning to the rest of the women to pass on her witticism; they all turned to stare at Andy, looking him up and down as if he were a Chippendale dripping with baby oil. He writhed in embarrassment.

'Don't get too close to him,' shouted another woman. 'You don't want to be reported to Elf and Safety!'

Andy had heard, and used, the expression 'fall about laughing' many times before, but he had never actually seen it happen. Chantelle and the second woman found this wisecrack so hilarious that they actually collapsed with laughter, staggered on their heels and had to grab at each other for balance.

'Elf and Safety!' spluttered another one. 'Louise, that's fucking hilarious! Oops!' She slapped one hand over her mouth. 'Sorry,' she said guiltily. 'Trying to watch it round the kids.'

'It's not like they don't hear it round their dads all the time,' sighed Louise, staring out at the terrace, on which most of the footballers were gathered, smoking cigars with Mr Fyodorov, drinking cognac or beer, and roaring with laughter. 'When they're bloody home, that is.'

'*Mum! Look!*' Princess Chastity rushed up to her mother, her eyes blazing with acquisitive delight. She was so excited she was hyperventilating, her breath coming in frenzied pants; with her bulging brown eyes and heavy breathing, she resembled a chihuahua in blue harem pants. '*Look!*' She waved her unwrapped gift frantically at her mother.

'Omigod, it's one of the Loub Barbies!' her mother exclaimed, taking the box. 'Well, I call that really nice of Mr K.'

'It's Dolly Forever!' her daughter gasped, barely able to speak with excitement.

The Barbie, one of a limited edition designed by Christian Louboutin, had copper-coloured locks and wore a safari dress that laced up the front. But the *pièce de résistance* was the pair of thigh-high, pink suede boots, entirely covered in fringe, with miniature five-inch heels: a Baltimore street-corner prostitute would have rejected them as being a little too overstated. All the WAGs, however, cooed over them, Chantelle declaring that they were the prettiest things she'd ever seen in her life and that she was gagging for a pair.

'Look what Mitchell got!' Corinne, Mitchell's mother, showed off her daughter's present. 'Another of them Loub Barbies! I think all the girls have 'em.'

'What's that one?'

'Amen – Amen – no, that's not right—' Corinne puzzled over the name.

'Sound like you're in church,' Louise giggled.

'Yeah, right. Chance'd be a fine thing,' Corinne said sourly. Her long-term boyfriend, Patrice, was happy to have children with her but so far had refused to tie the knot: she'd snagged an engagement ring off him last year, but was finding it harder to seal the deal than she would have done to run a mile in high heels.

'Anem – fuck, what *is* this?' Chantelle took the box, looking at the Barbie, who had the same copper hair, and was wearing a lime-green satin evening dress with an oversized satin bow attached to the back that swept into a train. A diamond bracelet glittered on her wrist, and her lavender shoes were tied around her ankles with big bows.

'Anem – it's a bloody tongue-twister!' Louise made an attempt.

'It is A-nem-oh-nee,' said Zhivana, riding past in the carriage, her posture as straight-backed and perfect as if she had just come from a Swiss finishing school – which, in fact, she had. 'Like the flower. Anemone.'

The train carried her away, across the room, and all the wives turned to stare after her crossly.

'Who the fuck is *she*?' Louise, on whom copious free champagne did not have a calming effect, asked with an angry scowl.

Chantelle wriggled over and spoke swiftly and urgently in Louise's ear.

'Oh,' Louise said. '*Oh*.'

Zhivana's carriage had completed the loop at the far end of the room, and was traversing back, past the Christmas tree.

'Ta!' Louise called, waving the Anemone Barbie at her. 'Anemmy-whatsit! Got it!' She handed the Barbie down to Mitchell, who promptly ran off to join the group of feral little girls on one of the sofas, tearing their boxes open and arguing viciously about whose doll was best.

'Stupid bloody name for a Barbie, though,' she muttered, turning back to the WAGs.

Andy drew a deep breath. The avalanche of children had abated; they had all retreated to various areas of the gigantic apartment to gather over their spoils, leaving a ragged, shiny pile of paper and ribbons behind them.

'I'll clear this lot up, Mr K – erm, *Santa*,' he said gamely.

'Thank you, Elf!' Grigor said jovially. 'You are a big help!'

He leaned into Andy.

'And when you are done, would you like to go downstairs? To the second apartment?' he asked *sotto voce*. 'Some of the men here have been already for a quick visit, and they say the ladies are *very* good at what they do. I am pleased to hear that.'

'Oh!'

The offer of an encounter with the escorts whom Grigor had installed in the secret second apartment below the penthouse came as a total surprise to Andy.

'Well, Mr – *Santa* – that's a really nice offer and I'm very grateful,' he said carefully, 'but, to be honest, it really isn't my kind of thing.'

'No need to tip!' Grigor assured him, patting him reassuringly on the back. 'It is all taken care of. Very beautiful girls!'

'Thanks,' Andy said, 'but—'

Grigor's expression changed from jovial to fierce in a split-second. It was at moments like this that one could clearly tell that behind Grigor's happy, charming façade was still the oligarch who had made billions through very unsavoury practices in the Wild West environment of post-*glasnost* Russia.

'Andy, I must ask you something,' he said, and the very few hairs on the back of Andy's neck stood up in fear, as if an icy wind had blown through the room. Grigor's hand closed on Andy's shoulder, a firm grip, and despite the fact that Grigor was in a red Santa suit and Andy in a green felt elf outfit, Andy wasn't fooled in any way about how serious the situation had suddenly become.

'You do not have any plans to do anything with one of *those* ladies, do you, Andy?' Grigor asked, jerking his head towards the giggling cluster of WAGs. 'I hear what they say about you. They are very pretty, and they think you are very handsome.'

'I—' Andy started, but Grigor cut right across him, his voice quiet and vehement.

'But they are not for you. You understand? I do not care what they do, how drunk they get, what they say to you, how much they shake their tits at you like cheap prostitutes. *They are not for you.*'

Andy's face was a picture of shock, his mouth open to a near-perfect O.

'Mr K, I would *never*,' he babbled with the utmost sincerity, his voice shaking. '*Honestly*. It hadn't even entered my *mind*. Cross my heart and hope to die!'

Grigor looked at Andy's horrified face and nodded several times, each nod a weighty bob of conviction.

'I see that,' he said, and Andy let out a sigh of relief that was almost a squeak. 'Good. Good. I believe you, Andy.'

'*Honestly*,' Andy babbled. 'I would *never.*'

The hand on his shoulder released, became a pat of approval.

'Very good,' Grigor said. 'You understand, they are the women of my men out there.' He nodded to the footballers on the terrace. 'I know that some of them behave worse than the ladies downstairs, okay? But they still belong to men who work for me.'

'I *totally* get it, Mr K!' Andy said fervently.

Grigor patted him once more.

'I see you looking at Melody yesterday, many times,' he observed. 'You like her? You like Wonder Woman? She is too thin, but very beautiful.'

'Oh, she *is*,' Andy agreed instantly. 'I mean, she *is* too thin, but they all have to be nowadays. She's got that real Old Hollywood glamour, though, don't you think? Reminds me of Ava Gardner. Or a young Liz Taylor.'

Grigor, seeing Andy's eyes light up as he pronounced these iconic names, smiled at him tolerantly.

'It is beautiful,' he said, 'to dream about a beautiful actress. Very romantic. You are a pure boy, Andy. I see that I can trust you completely with the women of my men.' He patted Andy once more in approval and reassurance. 'Soon we will put on *It's A Wonderful Life*,' he said, the cheerful Santa once again.

'Oh, lovely!' Andy's body was still shaking from that moment when he had felt in real danger from Grigor, but the prospect of one of his favourite films perked him up. 'I'd *much* rather watch *It's A Wonderful Life* than pop downstairs, to be totally honest.'

'Hah! This is why I like you so much, Andy!' Grigor called. 'I agree! Me too!'

Andy was very grateful to drop to his knees and start piling the wrapping paper into a series of big black rubbish bags; his legs were wobbly. *It's one thing sort of being aware that he could have you shot as soon as look at you,* he thought, looking down at his trembling hands. *It's another to actually see that look in his eyes.*

'Want a bit of help, mate?'

Andy would have jumped if he hadn't been on the floor. Turning, he saw the friendly, freckled, slightly spotty face of Wayne Burns at the same level as his own; the footballer had knelt down too and was collecting stray flowers of shiny ribbon, handing them to Andy.

'Um, yes! Thanks! That's very nice of you,' he said weakly.

'You all right?' Wayne's brow was creased. 'You look a bit peaky.'

'Oh yes,' Andy said quickly. 'Or no. I mean, I'm fine. There's just a lot to do, that's all.'

'I bet. Major party, this is,' Wayne said. 'Here.' He took the black binliner from Andy and opened it wide. 'I'll hold this, you stuff. We'll go quickest that way.'

'Ta.' Andy flashed him a smile. 'You having fun, then?'

Wayne shrugged. 'It's okay. I get a bit tired of hanging round the lads, though. I mean, we're together a lot of the time, you know? It's not like I need to see them in my time off too. It was better yesterday. You know, different people. Bit of a laugh.'

'It *was* fun yesterday,' Andy agreed. 'Lots of drama, too.'

'Chantelle was sorry she missed it,' Wayne said, looking over at his girlfriend. 'She loves a good fight. But I dunno, maybe it was for the best. She doesn't do classy when she goes out, you know? I mean, there are limits to how tight your dress ought to be. She can't 'ardly walk in most of hers. I ask 'er to cover up a bit sometimes. It doesn't seem respectful, specially for Christmas.'

'She does look very – smart,' Andy managed, looking at Chantelle in her pink satin dress.

Wayne sighed.

'It's like, when they all get together,' he said, glancing around the group of bosomy, rake-thin WAGs, 'they have some sort of competition to see who can get their tits out most. You know what she calls 'ers? Baby 'eads.'

Andy gaped at him.

'You *what*?'

'Yeah. Baby 'eads. Like there's two bald 'eads sticking up over the top of 'er dress.'

Andy looked over at Chantelle again, at the two melon-sized mounds rising majestically above the low-cut square neckline of her stretch satin dress, her diamond necklace wedged into the lavish cleavage.

'They *are* a bit like—' he started, and then he started to laugh. 'Sorry!' he managed to say.

'See what I mean? Baby 'eads!' Wayne was grinning. 'I mean, where'd she even come up with something like that?'

'Women,' Andy said daringly. 'I never know what's going on in their heads.'

'You and me both, mate,' Wayne agreed, tying up the neck of one bag and pulling the next one open. 'God, this paper's 'eavy, innit? You could, like, print a book on it or something. When I think of the cheap Woolies stuff my mum used to use . . .'

'I know, seems a waste, really,' Andy said. He debated something in his mind, wondering how best to approach the subject.

'Um, Grigor just asked me if I wanted to pop downstairs,' he started, keeping his voice low. 'D'you know about that? Did he ask you too?'

Wayne rolled his eyes.

'Course,' he said shortly. 'It's all part of the deal, innit? Why d'you think all the lads are so keen to come to this do? Patrice and Dave've been down there already, and that's just the starter, y'know? They'll be at it big-time when the girls've gone. Threesomes, foursomes, spit-roasting, train-pulling. All sorts.'

'What about you?' Andy asked casually. 'It's not really my kind of thing.'

'Not mine neither,' Wayne said just as casually, and Andy's brown eyes and Wayne's hazel ones met for a brief moment.

They went on filling the bin bags.

'Mr K's going to be putting on *It's A Wonderful Life* soon in the screening room,' Andy said.

'Oh, I love that film,' Wayne said.

'Me too.'

The wrapping paper and ribbon were almost all bagged up by now. They filled the last binliner and tied it up. Andy stood up, picking up a handful of bags, and Wayne followed suit with the rest.

'Oh, you don't have to—' Andy demurred, but Wayne shrugged nonchalantly.

'Might as well give you an 'and with the rest of it,' he said.

'Well, if you're sure – we can dump these in the kitchen waste compactor,' Andy said. 'And then I could give you a bit of a tour round the apartment, if you'd like? Mr K likes me to do that for VIP guests, show off all his gadgets and gizmos.'

'Okay,' Wayne said just as nonchalantly. 'That sounds like it'd be fun.'

'And this is the fur closet,' Andy said excitedly, heaving open the heavy, cedar-backed door. It had a keypad on it, which secured the furs inside when Grigor was not in residence; when he was here, though, the lock wasn't used.

Wayne put a hand on the door as he followed Andy inside.

'God, it weighs a ton!' he exclaimed.

'Yeah, it has to be, cos it's all climate-controlled,' Andy explained. 'It's got an air-purification system, it's all cedar-lined – the coats have to be separated a bit so the air can circulate around them – isn't it amazing?'

The heavy door swung shut behind Wayne, who was standing, gawping, at the sight before him. On either side, open rails gleamed dully against the rich dark cedarwood panelling of the fur closet, illuminated by deep-set lights that were deliberately kept low to avoid damaging the precious contents of the long walk-in cupboard. It was more like a Knightsbridge furrier's boutique than a private home: jackets, coats, capes and wraps made of Russian sable, mink, Siberian fox, chinchilla, astrakhan, and blue and golden sables. Shaved smooth, trimmed into burn-out designs, dyed all the shades of the rainbow: Dasha still kept many of her coats and hats here, and her tastes ran to bright colours – viridian greens, lemon yellows, glowing fuchsias, jewel tints of ruby, emerald and sapphire. Built-in drawers held fur-trimmed gloves, and along high shelves that ran above the rails was stacked an equally dramatic range of fur hats and ermine tippets with dyed, dangling tips.

Wayne walked along the carpeted floor slowly, looking from side to side, reaching up to touch one of the tippets, which was trimmed with a whole fringe of little tails.

'Bloody 'ell,' he said at last. 'There's a *lot* of dead animals in 'ere.'

'I know,' Andy said. 'Look.'

He was right at the end of the closet, lifting down a leopard toque from the shelf.

'It's real,' he said. 'Real leopard. Can you believe it?'

'Bloody *'ell.*' Wayne reached out a hand and stroked the fur, marvelling. 'It's unbelievable, really. I didn't know that was even legal. Aren't they protected or something?'

'Oh, this is vintage,' Andy assured him, and then caught his breath as Wayne's fingers touched his, brushing against them.

'Vintage! That's just a way to charge more for second-'and gear, ain't it?' Wayne said, grinning. 'Cracks me up.'

'I *know*, right?'

Heart racing, Andy put the hat back on the shelf, taking his time, arching his back so that Wayne could get a good look at the round, tight buttocks of which he was justifiably proud. He was hoping that Wayne might be tempted enough to reach out and stroke them, but no such luck. Swallowing hard, Andy swivelled round again, looking Wayne up and down, taking in the round pink dots of blush on his cheeks, the unmistakable swell in his suit trousers.

Now or never, Andy told himself. *There is a tide in the affairs of men. Which, taken at the flood, leads on to fortune—*

It was Shakespeare. He'd always liked that quote, the phrase 'affairs of men', but now it took on an even more significant meaning: *make your move or lose it for ever. But you'd better be bloody sure he's not going to freak—*

Andy realised with horror that he was still wearing his elf ears. Reaching up, he dragged them off and chucked them away, taking a step up to Wayne: greatly daring, he slid one hand behind Wayne's neck, pulling him towards him for a kiss. Wayne's mouth was narrow, and Andy's full, plump lips engulfed it, like a delicious soft cushion, delicately moist at first, and then deep and wet, his tongue sliding past Wayne's lips, filling his mouth. Wayne moaned deep in his throat, his hands eagerly clutching Andy's buttocks, pulling him as close as possible, his big, sturdy thighs parting to draw Andy between them, shoving him right into his crotch so that Andy could feel Wayne's cock thrusting through his trousers and rubbing against his own.

'Fuck, that feels good,' Andy groaned, reaching down, unzipping Wayne's trousers and pulling out his cock. It was thick and stubby, like its owner, which was a big relief to Andy: he was so turned on by Wayne, it would have been a huge disappointment if his cock hadn't been up to scratch. *And I always go for girth over length*, Andy thought happily as his fist closed over Wayne's dick and started to work the foreskin up and down the shaft. *Well, who doesn't?*

Wayne was kissing Andy like a madman now, his hands rising up to wrap around Andy's smooth skull, tilting his head up to kiss the slightly taller man, as enthusiastic as a puppy. They staggered back, against the rack of coats behind them, kicking aside the fur boots neatly arranged below.

'Let's get in the coats more,' Wayne muttered, still kissing Andy frantically. 'It's freezing in here . . .'

The fur closet's climate controls kept the interior at twelve degrees centigrade, to ensure the coats were at optimum temperature and did not overheat the natural oils in the fur overheating. It had been chilly from the moment the two men had entered, but their rising excitement at being alone together had heated their skin, made them temporarily oblivious to the cold. Now, however, that flesh was being bared, Wayne's trousers falling to the ground, Andy's following suit, they were feeling the chill. Andy reared back, gasping as Wayne pulled down his briefs and grabbed his cock with gusto, if not a great deal of skill, and looked frantically around him.

'Put this on!' he commanded, dragging a huge man's Russian sable overcoat from a heavy padded hanger.

'But I won't—' Wayne began, confused.

'Just do it!' Andy threw the coat at Wayne, prised Wayne's clutching hand reluctantly off his throbbing cock, and dropped to his knees. A second later, he was deep-throating Wayne, who practically wailed with pleasure as Andy's hot, full, wet lips wrapped around his dick. Obeying instructions dutifully, Wayne shrugged on the overcoat, its weighty folds tumbling around him and Andy, who knelt between his splayed legs. Understanding now, Wayne wrapped the coat around his lover, keeping him warm as Andy sucked Wayne's cock harder and harder in his heated mouth. Complete darkness engulfed Andy, darkness that smelt richly of fur and male sweat. It was incredibly erotic. He closed his eyes and sucked even harder, wanting to drive Wayne insane, to give him the best blowjob he had ever had, to make Wayne's head explode with pleasure when his cock finally shot its load.

Wayne's back was to the cupboard wall, the huge footballer's muscles in his thighs and calves keeping him upright; Andy ran his hands with absolute relish over the hard, swollen, pumped legs, the thighs only lightly hairy, much of it rubbed away by the constant chafing of his exercise shorts. His calves were much more thickly covered in hair. Wayne's cock was pushed right to the back of Andy's throat now, battering against it, the wide stubby dick desperate for release; Andy licked a middle finger, ran it between Wayne's legs, up to his hairy buttocks, and, with a deft twisting motion, eased it into his bottom, feeling expertly for the little trigger he knew would drive Wayne over the edge.

Above him, he felt Wayne's entire body go into spasm, his legs trembling, his hips locked rigid as his cock bounced like a ball against the roof of Andy's mouth, spurting out his come. The ring of muscle around Andy's finger tightened like a vice; he waited until Wayne eventually gasped a long wail of what sounded like incredulity as well as orgasm, and his body slackened all at once, and then, gently, guided his finger out again even as he swallowed down the come that Wayne had pumped into his mouth. It took several gulps to get it all down; Andy licked his lips in relish. And then, yielding to impulse, he reached out and wiped his mouth on a fold of the sable coat. The fur was exquisitely soft on his lips; he wondered, with a rush of blood to the groin, what it would feel like wrapped round his cock—

Suddenly, Wayne dropped to his knees, his back sliding down the wall, more a collapse than a deliberate decision. Choking under the heavy coat that had flopped over him, Andy parted the folds and stuck his head out of the top. He was laughing, exhilarated by the sheer thrill of sucking off Wayne Burns – there was no denying the extra frisson of servicing the most famous English footballer currently playing.

But when he saw Wayne's face, his laughter stopped dead.

'What?' he said, confused.

Because Wayne looked as if someone had hit him over the head. His cheeks were bright pink, he was breathing stertorously through his mouth, and, unless Andy was very much mistaken, his little piggy eyes were brimming with tears.

Andy caught his breath, wriggling free of the coat to sit next to Wayne. Instinctively, he took in his arms the man whose cock he had just sucked, cradling Wayne's head on his chest.

'What *is* it?' he asked, absolutely baffled. 'Is something wrong? I could've sworn you had a really good time . . .'

'I did!' Wayne sobbed into his chest. 'That was fucking amazing! *You're* fucking amazing!' He raised a tear-stained face to Andy's. 'I just never – well, almost never did anything like that. I spend all my time with all these fit blokes – on the pitch, the showers, all their kit off, wandering round the locker room tugging on their willies, and I'm always so panicked about getting a stiffie, about them realising I want to fuck the lot of them . . .'

Andy stroked Wayne's sparse reddish hair, kissed his mouth softly, then his eyes, kissing the tears away.

'Do you not – I dunno, go to clubs, order in someone every now and then— '

'I don't trust anyone,' Wayne said miserably. 'You know what it's like. Every single guy I know who plays away's been dobbed in by the slapper 'e cheated on 'is missus with.'

'They're the slappers just as much as the girls,' Andy couldn't help pointing out. 'They're the ones cheating.'

Wayne drew in a deep, shuddering breath and sat back against the cupboard wall. Wrapped in the black, inch-thick fur coat, he looked as if he was wearing a bear costume.

'Yeah, you're right,' he said. 'I'm worse than them, cos I'm faking it. You know? I try to talk like them, sound like them, talk about chippies and slappers. Pathetic, isn't it? And the mental part is, they all take the piss out of me cos I'm the only one not cheating on my girlfriend.'

'Chantelle? Do you do it with her?'

Andy knew he ought to have put this question considerably more tactfully, but for some reason he was burning up with the desire to know the answer. When Wayne shook his head, the relief that ran through Andy was ridiculous. *What's it to me? I'll never be alone with him again anyway . . . as soon as he stops venting, he'll shove me away and call me a fag to make himself feel better . . .*

'Are you joking?' Wayne's small eyes widened as much as they could. 'No way! I mean, she's a nice girl and all, but I'd rather shag a—' He caught himself, clearly not wanting to be rude. 'Anyway, she's a minge-diver. She and Corinne 'ave a thing going. I said to 'er once, if Patrice knew 'e could watch you and Corinne at it on a regular basis, 'e'd marry 'er like a shot.'

Andy was giggling with relief. A watery smile illuminated Wayne's face, making him look very young. Andy blotted the last tears from his eyes with the tips of his fingers. Wayne reached up, took Andy's hand and pulled it to his mouth, starting to suck each finger in turn. Andy moaned.

'Tell me you're going to do that to my cock,' he pleaded, watching his dark fingers slide between Wayne's pale, freckled lips with a shudder of excitement. 'Tell me you're going to suck me off, let me spunk in your mouth . . .'

Wayne's face was bright pink at the dirty talk.

'I really want to,' he said, his voice blurred by Andy's thumb, which he was licking like a lollipop. 'But I might not be as good as you – I 'aven't done it that much—'

The admission had cost him a lot to make; he was pillar-box red by now.

'Pretend it's an ice cream,' Andy said, leaning back, dragging down another fur coat, sprawling on it, widening his legs, raising his knees; deliberately, he started pulling on his cock with one hand, cupping his balls with the other. 'Pretend I'm a Magnum, and you've got to lick it all up till it's gone . . .'

'Fuck, this is like being in a porn film,' Wayne said devoutly, heaving himself up, divesting himself of the sable coat with a huge effort, and kneeling over Andy. 'God, you've got such a big dick—'

'Suck it all,' Andy said, watching Wayne's face, how red it got with the sex talk, how eagerly he was licking his lips as he bent over Andy. 'Suck my big dick and swallow every last drop . . .'

Andy could tell that Wayne wasn't that experienced by the combination of keenness and tentativeness with which he handled Andy's penis. *Right now, he really is a puppy*, Andy thought, propping himself up on his elbows so he could watch Wayne kissing his cock with the same wet, slightly sloppy,

completely charming kisses with which he had been covering
Andy's mouth some minutes ago. The sight made something in
Andy melt, a warm tenderness engulfing him, this internation-
ally famous footballer, whose posters covered millions of
Kensington fans' walls worldwide, whose skill on the pitch was
considered a gift from God, now, inexpertly, but with great
concentration, trying to deep-throat Andy's cock.

Andy reached out a hand and stroked Wayne's head, running
a finger round one of his small round ears, caressing his neck;
encouraged, Wayne redoubled his efforts, and Andy started to
pump his hips up, fucking Wayne's mouth.

'Yeah, take it all,' he murmured. 'Take it all and drain me
dry . . . yeah, that's good, that's so good, suck me hard now,
suck me really hard, make me come—'

It was the point of no return. Andy's slightly curved cock
was fully engorged now; he'd have loved to last for ages, to
have Wayne suck it as long as possible, to feast on the sight of
Wayne Burns going at his dick as if it really were an ice cream.
But his balls were tightening, his arse was too: he was going to
shoot, there was nothing for it, he couldn't hold out a second
longer, the pressure was too much: he groaned deeply, and,
with sheer delight, he let himself go, heat streaming out of his
cock, feeling like a bowstring arching and snapping back,
driving the arrow of his dick so deeply into Wayne's mouth
that he gagged on it—

The door of the fur closet swung open.

Fuckit, fuckit, fuckit! Andy thought desperately, sperm shooting into Wayne's mouth as muffled footsteps sounded on the
carpet, and a man's voice said something in Russian, a higher,
fluting woman's voice answering him in the same language.

There was nothing either Andy or Wayne could do but keep
going. Wayne was swallowing desperately, his eyes bulging
with the effort; he looked like a white, freckly tree frog. Andy's
lips were clamped shut to make absolutely sure that not a
peep escaped him, that no sound made by him would betray

the lovers' presence. He kept his hips rigid; only his cock still moved, pumping away, shooting its hot load into Wayne's mouth, as the woman came down the aisle between the coat rails, paused, started pushing hangers to one side . . .

We're right at the back of the room, Andy told himself in utter panic, his head spinning. *Nobody would hang their coat right back here; it would be near the door, where she could get to it easily.*

But what if she's blown away by all the amazing furs? What if she starts having a nose around, trying some on, seeing what's here?

Ah, fuck—

His cock was drained now. Wayne eased back fractionally, licking the last drop from the tip, his expression a comical mixture of satisfaction and fear. The woman took something off a hanger; Andy managed to ease the side of his head around the coat hanging next to him. *At least it's a dark brown mink,* he thought with wry humour. *She won't notice me against it sticking out like a sore thumb.*

It was Zhivana Fyodorova, pulling on a white chinchilla coat, belting it around her tiny waist, stick-thin even in its fur wrapping. She took down a matching hat from the shelf above and settled it on her head. Andy was just relaxing in the assumption that she was all done, when she paused, pivoted on her slim kitten heel, and came quickly towards him and Wayne.

He froze, his head still protruding from the mink coat but aware that now he couldn't pull it back, in case the movement alerted her. Awkwardly stuck at that angle, he waited, holding his breath, as Zhivana walked right to the back of the closet, her thin calves, in sheer pale silk stockings, almost next to him.

Please let her not bend down to get some boots! he pleaded to everything he'd ever held sacred. *Cher, Madonna, Kylie, I beg you – you're the patron saints of gay men – please let her not want to get some boots from where we're lying—*

Whichever deity heard him and answered his prayers, he couldn't know. But what Zhivana did next was totally unexpected. As if her legs had been kicked away from her, she collapsed in a heap, her light, fragile body landing almost soundlessly on the thick carpet, her furs puffing out around her. Her head was ducked down, the nape of her neck just showing, slender as a stalk; it had barely any more colour to it than the white furs she was wearing. Her arms were folded around herself. On her hands were suede gloves of the most delicate pale pink, immaculate, gloves that had never touched a surface that hadn't been cleaned minutes before by an invisible army of servants.

Andy stared at her helplessly, not knowing what to do. *Has she had too much to drink?* he wondered. *She's such a tiny little thing, she could get hammered on one glass of champagne.*

He could hear Wayne breathing behind him, feel Wayne's hot breath on his cock. In the silence, it seemed incredibly loud. Andy himself was only daring to take tiny little sips of breath, and that was difficult enough, because his heart was still racing with the excitement of his orgasm, his cock still throbbing.

And then he heard something else. It was Zhivana. Still curled in the ball into which she had sunk, still with her arms wrapped round her waist, she was whispering to herself. He couldn't make out the words, and was pretty sure they were Russian anyway. They were soft and sibilant, like an incantation. Or a prayer.

Clearly, she assumed she was completely alone. Andy was horribly embarrassed to be spying on her, even inadvertently. He didn't move a muscle, terrified of making his presence known, getting caught with Wayne Burns, fucking in their host's fur closet; but also of disturbing this very odd girl – Grigor's fiancée – in the middle of some intensely private ritual. *It's like she's casting a spell,* he thought. *And if it doesn't go exactly right – if she realises me and Wayne are here – she'll blame us, turn us both into pigs or something . . .*

It was crazy to even think like this, of course. But there was something about Zhivana Fyodorova that was eerie and unreal enough to make you think of fairies, spells, otherworldly creatures. When her arms loosened their grip around her waist, when her head, crowned with the wide, snowy fur hat, lifted again, Andy half-expected to see her face different somehow. *Transformed*, he thought wildly. *God, I have to stop watching all those teen witch and vampire series . . .*

Because Zhivana, of course, looked just as she had before, the small features as composed as ever. She stood up with the swift, graceful movement of a very young woman, and paused for a moment in front of a dangling display of fox masks, hanging in a line from a cedar rail; reaching out one slender, pale-pink hand, she stroked one of the foxes, running her finger down its nose, as if she were caressing a live animal. There was something hugely poignant in the gesture.

And then, retracting her hand, she turned and walked very quickly towards the door, her heels barely audible on the lush carpet. She didn't try to drag open the heavy door herself; instead, she tapped on it, as lightly as a fairy knock, and instantly a bodyguard on the other side swung it open for her. Without a word, she tripped through with a last rustle of her chinchilla skirts.

The door swung shut again. Andy and Wayne collapsed in a tangled heap, puppets who had had their strings cut all at once.

'I thought—' Wayne hissed.

'I know!' Andy hissed back.

'We should get going, they'll be wondering where I am—' Wayne dragged up his trousers.

'Yeah, of course, me too,' Andy said, not to be outdone in the rush to cover up and run away from the intimacy of sex. He pulled up his elf trousers and stood up, smoothing down his tunic, reaching a hand to Wayne to help him up. He was feeling the cold again, after the heat rush of orgasm and fear;

he shivered, and Wayne did too as he stood. They pushed their way through the coats and towards the door.

'Give it a bit,' Wayne said. 'In case she's hanging around in the corridor and wonders where we were when we pop on out.'

Andy nodded. He knew he was being a fool, but he was wondering what would happen now. *Nothing*, he told himself firmly. *Nothing at all. It's over, it's done. You know how this works, Andy.*

'Hey,' he said, wanting to lighten how he was feeling, because he had a sudden, stupidly sentimental lump in his throat. He reached down to pick up his elf ears and slid the headband back on. 'You ever sucked off an elf before?'

To Andy's absolutely delight, Wayne, whose colour had returned to its normal pasty state, instantly went pink all over again, and even emitted a little giggle. Andy leaned forward and planted a kiss on Wayne's lips; he meant it as a farewell, but Wayne kissed him back so fiercely that he smushed Andy's lips against his teeth.

'It was *ace*,' he whispered, pulling back. 'Fucking *ace*.'

Andy stroked Wayne's cheek for the last time, drew in a deep breath and dragged open the heavy, insulated door.

'It was, mate,' he said tenderly, looking back for a final glance at Wayne's deliciously pink cheeks. 'It really was.'

And then he cleared his throat, flipped a switch in his head, and raised his voice to the enthusiastic, professional tones of a concierge giving a VIP a special guided tour.

'Amazing, but just a little on the chilly side!' he said, for the benefit of anyone who might be outside, holding the door for Wayne to pass through. 'The walk-in red wine fridge in the kitchen maintains a constant temperature of fifteen degrees – that at least would be a bit warmer.'

But no one was paying the least bit of attention to them. Further down the hallway, rather like a properly organised ship evacuation, the women and children were leaving first, in a stream of kisses and farewells to their menfolk, the children overstimulated on sugar and gifts, screaming and red-faced in their nannies' arms, the wives flushed with champagne and carrying the blinged-out Jimmy Choo gifts which Andy had carefully selected for them. The men were already returning to the great room, practically rubbing their hands with anticipation after having said a cursory goodbye; Wayne went over to kiss Chantelle, a careful peck on either cheek that barely touched her skin, and helped her chivalrously on with her padded, fur-trimmed, pink coat that made her look like a giant version of the Barbies all the little girls were clutching.

'Get home safe, love,' he said.

'Oh, I'm crashing with Corinne tonight,' Chantelle said, looking at Corinne and winking. 'You don't mind, do you? You won't even notice I'm gone!'

'Nah, you girls have fun,' Wayne said.

'Oh, don't you worry about that!' Corinne trilled. 'Laters!'

Andy stayed in the hallway, ostensibly to help everyone out, make sure nothing was forgotten, but really to be able to give Grigor the signal, when he returned to the huge reception room, that the coast was clear.

'Now the party begins!' Grigor bellowed, throwing his arms wide.

It was the cue everyone had been waiting for. 'I Wish It Could Be Christmas Every Day' blared out at full blast over the sound system, bodyguards and waiters stationed strategically around the room fired big plastic guns into the air that shot fake snow right up to the high ceiling, and a stream of beautiful girls in underwear ran squealing with excitement into the living room from Grigor's study, where they had been waiting to make their entrance. White snow and glittering tiny silver snowflakes descended in a glorious cascade over their bodies, and they all had handfuls of glitter which they threw up into the air as they ran.

Andy couldn't help thinking that the escorts hired by Grigor were, in general, much prettier and better-dressed than the actual wives and girlfriends of the football players. Yes, they were in skimpy underwear, negligees and basques, but it was all very elegant and beautifully made – *much better taste than some of those tacky dresses the WAGs were wearing, frankly*. One Chinese-looking girl with long black hair and a burgundy silk corset set that showed off her miniature waist was the spitting image of Gong Li, a Chinese actress whom Andy considered one of the most beautiful women in the world; the girl could have been a model if she'd only been a few inches taller. *And not a glamour model, like those tarty types who were here all afternoon – a real fashion model.*

'You like the girls, yes?' Grigor clapped Andy heavily on the back. 'I see you looking at them!'

'They're *very* pretty,' Andy commented, looking at a black girl with legs up to her armpits, who was already draping herself over Patrice. She was wearing a white 1950s-style two-piece bra and knicker set which looked superb against her dark skin, the knickers fastened on one hip with an oversized white silk bow. *If I were her, that's exactly what I would wear,* he thought approvingly. *She looks stunning.*

'Which one do you like most?' Grigor asked jovially.

Sergei, at the gigantic table, was supervising as the staff brought out big bowls of Viagra and Ecstasy; a silver salver, three feet long, contained one huge line of cocaine, which had been piped out from a three-kilo bag; it spiralled out from the centre round and round, following the oval of the salver, finishing in a last enormous loop.

'The girls or the drugs?' Andy asked, grinning.

'Ha! You are so funny, Andy!' Grigor had been hitting his favourite orange-scented Muscat quite heavily by now, and his eyes were glazed, his breath, close to Andy's face, smelling pleasantly of sweet dessert wine.

Girls were already pulling men off to the various bedrooms,

others straddling their clients on sofas. Patrice, just as Wayne had said, had beckoned over a luscious blonde and installed both her and the black girl on his lap, kissing and fondling each other as, between them, he reached down to unzip his trousers.

'Mr Khalovsky?' A particularly pretty girl with ridiculously long eyelashes, wearing a red satin teddy and a pair of huge white butterfly wings, sidled up to him. 'Shall I start the show now? You know I was saying I'd do a little Christmas show for everyone – like a sexy panto – Jaycie, Val and me have been working on it for ages—'

'Oh, how nice!' Grigor beamed on her. 'But I think in a little while. Right now, the gentlemen are all enjoying themselves now that their ladies have gone. I think we let them have a nice time, and then in a while – at half-time, let's say – you can put on your show.'

The girl reached up and ran one finger down the front of Grigor's Santa costume.

'What about we go somewhere more private, then?' she cooed. 'I *love* a man in red! I don't know why, it always really turns me on . . .'

'Thank you, my dear,' Grigor said, 'but I was just about to put on *It's A Wonderful Life* in the screening room. Maybe later.'

'Ooh! Haven't seen that in years – I'd love to see it again!' Andy exclaimed. 'I'll join you if you don't mind, Mr K.'

'Excellent!' Grigor glanced at the table. 'Do help yourself to anything you want.'

'I think I'll skip it,' Andy said. He was dying for some X, but simply didn't trust himself on it in this company, let alone with Wayne around; *I couldn't keep my hands off him*, he knew. Grigor had ordered Sergei to sort Andy out with one of the staff bedrooms, so he was crashing in the penthouse that night, and he'd probably watch the film and then go to bed; *what am I going to do at a straight orgy?*

He allowed himself a short, blissful moment to picture him and Wayne sneaking off to the small staff room where Andy had changed out of his day clothes into the elf outfit. They would strip off, climb onto the single bed, laughing at how narrow it was, how they had to cling onto each other to avoid falling off. Andy would gently turn Wayne over, pull up his broad, muscled buttocks, lick him and tease him about how hairy he was, what a freckled arse he had—

'Oi, elfy!' yelled Vince Martin, the goalie, who was leaning against the dining table, sniffing from a line of coke he'd just done, as the beautiful Gong Li lookalike, kneeling between his legs, sucked him off. 'Like what you see? You've got a right old stiffie there! You want her to do you after? She's got a mouth like a hoover attachment!'

Andy looked down; his cock, hard from imagining a completely naked Wayne, was tenting out the front of his trousers, visible below the pointy hem of his tunic. Raising a hand feebly at Vince, he turned and scampered away, through another, smaller sitting room and into the screening room.

Then he stopped dead. Grigor was ensconced in the front row of custom-made red leather recliners facing the screen, his feet up on the footrest, a waiter refilling his glass with Muscat; but that wasn't what had made Andy freeze. Beside Grigor was Wayne, sprawled in another lounger, a pint glass of Guinness in his hand, a gigantic container of popcorn wedged between his legs. *Exactly where I'd like to be*, Andy thought wistfully.

'Come in! We are just starting! Sit here!' Grigor smacked the seat of the recliner on his other side. 'How nice and cosy – two men who love Christmas as much as I do!'

Two poofs running away from a lot of prostitutes, Andy thought ironically. His eyes met Wayne's, seeing the same wistfulness in them as he was feeling. *Honestly, I just want to be on a bed with him with the door locked and all the time in the world . . .*

Oh well, what can we do? He shrugged resignedly. *Lucky we're not sitting next to each other. No way could we keep our hands from going where they're not supposed to . . .*

'This is lovely, Mr K,' Andy said, sinking into the chair Grigor had indicated. 'Any chance of getting some more popcorn?'

December 27th

Melody

'Anthony, I'm *more* than ready!' Melody said fervently into her phone. 'I *promise*! Honestly, I'll be off the book for the audition! I'm sitting here with a copy of the play, learning lines already.'

'Oh, Melody, I don't know if that's such a good idea,' her agent Anthony said. She could hear his concern as clearly as if he were in the room with her, frowning deeply. 'You're running away with this a bit, pinning all your hopes on it—'

'I've got nothing else to do but read *Much Ado* and practise line readings,' Melody said. 'Anthony, this is *exactly* what I need – something to focus on. I feel better than I have in months. I'm starting to work out, I went to the gym already this morning—'

'Is that okay? You've just had surgery!' Anthony sounded worried now. 'You don't want to rip anything, Melody.'

'I'm just walking on the treadmill,' she assured him. 'The nurse said that was okay. But I feel so much better, honestly.'

'And how's—' Anthony hesitated. 'How is everything, um, healing?'

Bless his British tact, Melody thought, smiling. *In LA they'd cut right to the chase. My LA agent told me not to get back in touch until I was 'a hundred per cent pretty' again.*

'It's doing well,' she assured him. 'Not good enough for film and TV for a while. No one would look at me like this, not till I can go in for an audition without a scrap of make-up. But if I wear lots of foundation, I'm fine for doing a stage audition. They'll be able to see already that my face is going to be okay by the summer.'

'Do I need to come over there and have a look at you?' Anthony asked. 'Tell me honestly, Melody. I don't mean to be rude, but last year—' He paused, choosing his words. He wasn't in his office over the holidays; Melody had rung him on his mobile, without any notice, giving him no chance to prepare for this awkward conversation. 'Last year, you went completely off the rails,' he said at last. 'No one could say a word to you. You were so set on going the whole LA starlet road, you had absolute blinkers on. Please don't be offended, but I would like to be sure, before I start bothering the RSC, that you haven't done anything else to your face . . . you know, any more big changes . . .'

'Okay, look,' Melody said swiftly, putting him on speaker, pressing buttons on her phone. 'I'm going to take a photo right now. Ignore the bruising, I can cover that all up. And most of the swelling's gone down. You'll see, my lips are back to normal, the fillers are out of my cheeks – I've had my nose and chin put back too, but you won't see that as much—'

Standing by the floor-to-ceiling window, daylight streaming in, she held her phone away from her and snapped a photograph of her face. She checked it: even the bruising wasn't so bad now. Her nose splint had come off yesterday, before the visit to James, which was why Aniela had cleared her for mild exercise. All things considered, she thought this should reassure her agent sufficiently to convince him to put pressure on the Royal Shakespeare Company producer and director.

'I'm sending it to you now, okay?' she said. 'Look at it and tell me what you think.'

'What, now, while we're still on the phone?' Anthony, who was from the older generation and not technologically gifted, sounded genuinely amazed at the thought that this might be possible. 'Oh God, my phone's beeping! Is that the photo coming in? I might cut you off if I try to look at it . . . oh no, hang on, I've got an idea . . .' His voice became muffled as he turned away from the handset, taking on the higher tones of someone talking to a small child. 'Romy? Darling, come here and help Daddy, there's a good girl! Can you show Daddy a photo that a friend just sent him on his phone? Oh, you're so clever! Thank you, sweetie!'

His voice came back, clear again.

'Romy's seven,' he said gloomily, 'and she can work my phone so much better than I can – it's terrifying. Right! I'm looking at it now!'

There was another pause: Melody held her breath. Anthony exhaled gustily.

'Fine,' he said. 'Goodness. Fine. Well, Melody, this isn't bad at all, is it? You look like yourself again!'

She relaxed, sinking into the white leather Eames chair below the window. Anthony was old-school posh: *not bad at all*, in his language, meant *very good indeed*.

'I do, don't I?' she said happily. 'It *really* isn't bad! The surgeon was absolutely brilliant.'

'And, erm, the other thing? Things?' Anthony asked, sounding very awkward. 'Romy, darling, can you just pop somewhere else for a moment? Daddy needs to talk to his friend in private . . . why don't you go and bother Mummy for a little bit? God knows, you've been bothering me for ages. Ow! Don't bite Daddy!'

Melody was giggling.

'My chest area,' she said demurely, 'is back where it was. No more balloons.'

'Well, frankly, that's a huge relief,' Anthony said. 'Leading ladies at the RSC don't have, erm . . .'

'D cups,' Melody finished.

'I don't quite know what those are,' he admitted, 'but I get the general idea. So basically, I can reassure Martin that you've totally reversed everything you had done in LA?'

'I'm the Melody from before,' she assured him firmly. 'Just like in *Wuthering Heights*.'

'Okay. Leave it with me,' Anthony said briskly. 'I'll ring you back as soon as I have any news.'

'Sorry your daughter bit you,' she said, smiling, as she heard Aniela's knock on the door; getting up, she went to open it.

'She's obsessed with pretending to be a spaniel for some reason,' her father sighed. 'I keep telling her spaniels are good dogs and don't bite their owners. I think she has them confused with pit bulls . . .'

Melody gestured Aniela in as she thanked Anthony, said goodbye and clicked off the phone.

'You look very good,' Aniela said with thorough approval, looking Melody up and down. 'Not just your face, though that is healing very well. All of you. Your energy is very good and high.'

'I've been up since eight, had a smoothie and porridge, then I went to the gym and walked for half an hour on the treadmill, came back, had a shower and rang my agent to tell him to put me up for the lead in *Much Ado About Nothing* – for the Royal Shakespeare Company next summer,' Melody said, all in a rush. 'He's getting on with it right away – the auditions are happening this week.'

'Wonderful!' Aniela said approvingly, following her into the living room, leaning against the breakfast bar. 'And the boyfriend? You have seen the boyfriend? How was that?'

'You do get right to it, don't you, Aniela?' Melody said, smiling wryly. 'Would you like a cup of tea?'

She went into the kitchen and filled up the kettle.

'That would be very nice,' Aniela said.

'And yes, I've seen the boyfriend,' Melody said, pulling a box of English Breakfast tea from the cupboard. 'He's screwing someone else. That blonde cow who was here a few days ago.'

'The one who made you cry,' Aniela said, remembering. 'She is not nice at all.'

'No, she bloody isn't,' Melody sighed.

'You know,' Aniela said seriously, pulling up one of the stools and sitting down on it, leaning her elbows on the counter and steepling her fingers, 'it is easy for nasty girls like that to get hold of a man when he is sad. I have seen it many times.'

'God, thanks, Aniela,' Melody said faintly, as the kettle started to boil. 'That's not exactly—'

'You will have to fight her for him, if you want him,' Aniela continued.

'Well, I'm going to be fighting her for this part in the play,' Melody said. 'I know she wants it too.'

'Who is better?' Aniela asked. 'Her or you?'

'Bloody *hell*— ' Melody coughed out a laugh. 'You don't beat around the bush, do you?'

She dropped tea bags into mugs and got the milk out of the fridge.

'But what is the answer? Who is better?' Aniela persisted.

Melody writhed. 'Aniela, I'm English. We don't talk about how good we are, we're not like Americans . . .'

She met Aniela's clear, direct gaze, and gave up.

'Honestly,' she said, '*I* am. I really think I am. I was the up-and-coming star in our year, I beat out every actress of my age in the UK for *Wuthering Heights*. I have much better comic timing than she does, and I work an audience better, too. If it were between me and Felicity, I should totally get this part.'

'Good!' Aniela nodded with approval. 'It's good that you are confident. You must be confident like this with the boyfriend. You must be sure that you are better for him, nicer than her. You *are* nicer than her – you are not someone who makes people cry. Then you must go to see him – *soon*,' she specified. 'Because women like that move very quickly with men. She will have him engaged to her before you can turn around, to make sure of him while he is still confused.'

The kettle had boiled; Melody, filling the mugs, nearly let one spill over, she was so struck by the truth of these words. She could picture the whole thing. Felicity, having latched onto James – recently, it must be very recently, or Melody would have been told by someone eager to see her reaction to the unpleasant news – would immediately try to consolidate her position as the new girlfriend of Dr Who. She'd make sure the two of them were papped together at every opportunity, use the publicity to catapult her up to the next level of fame. It would have been naïve to pretend that theatre, TV and film producers weren't acutely aware of an actor or actress's public profile; in order to cover their costs, put more bums on seats, as the expression went, they would almost always pick the most well-known face that they could.

Melody couldn't blame Felicity for wanting to make sure the viewing public recognised her name and her face. *But I can when it means she's trying to push me out of the way with James by making horrible comments about my surgery. And if she tries to take advantage of his being lonely without me, pushing him into an engagement* – the mere idea made Melody livid. James was that very rare thing in their profession, a young man who truly wanted to settle down, happiest living in domestic bliss with a woman he loved. *And someone unscrupulous could definitely exploit that, rush him into a commitment before he realised what was happening. Aniela's absolutely right.*

'Aniela, you're really good at giving advice,' she said, bringing the tea over to the counter. 'Making people see things clearly. You should be a life coach or something.'

Aniela's smile was crooked, twisted at one corner, as she pulled the milk container towards her and poured some into her mug.

'I am good at giving advice, yes,' she said. 'But that is easy, to give advice. I must also tell myself what to do, and follow it.'

She took her time spooning some sugar into her mug and stirring it in, three teaspoons; like most nurses, she had a sweet tooth. Melody had the good sense not to prompt the other woman; she waited, eyebrows raised – she was getting more and more movement in her forehead now that the Botox was wearing off, it felt wonderful – for Aniela to continue.

'I tell you to go to your boyfriend – ex-boyfriend – and tell him you love him, you want to be with him,' Aniela said finally. 'I tell you to be brave. But I must be brave, too, with the man I like.'

She blew on her tea.

'It's hard to do,' she concluded. 'Very hard.'

'It is,' Melody said determinedly. 'But we're both going to do it, aren't we?'

Aniela's chest rose and fell.

'I want to,' she said. 'I want to very much.'

The mugs had cooled down enough to pick up by now. Melody took hers by the handle and clinked it against Aniela's.

'We'll make a pact,' she said, her sapphire eyes shining. 'Okay? Nothing ventured, nothing gained. We'll both be brave.'

Slowly, Aniela picked up her own mug and clinked it back against Melody's.

'Okay,' she said. 'We will both be brave.'

Aniela

It's all very well, Aniela thought forty minutes later. *Melody can take her time, work out how to approach her ex, strategise a way to win him back. While Jon, I have to see right now.*

Melody had no idea, of course, that there was something between Aniela and Jon. Why would anyone guess that a sane, sensible nurse like her would be obsessed by a patient with a face like a plateful of meat? *Not to mention the fact that he used to be a hitman, and that Dasha Khalovsky's trying to blackmail him into killing her husband. I should be running away from him as fast as I can.*

Every single health professional that Aniela had ever worked with had considered her one of the best nurses they had ever encountered. She was serious, proficient, extremely hard-working and completely unsentimental, quick-thinking and unflappable. She'd lost count of the times she'd been told approvingly by doctors and managers that she had a good head on her shoulders, an English expression that she had never quite understood.

And here I am, with my good head, about to throw myself at a man without a face who used to kill people for a living. Very good decision, Aniela. Very sensible.

She couldn't help smiling. *In my work, I do everything right. And in my private life, I do everything wrong.*

It was one minute to noon. She waited until her watch read exactly the right time, both hands clicking together, before she raised her hand and pressed the bell button on Jon's door.

He wouldn't hide from her, she knew. Even if he didn't want to see her, he would open the door and tell her so. He was a man; he wouldn't behave like a child.

Sure enough, the door swung open. Jon stood there, his entire affect as awkward as a man who can barely move his face can look.

'May I come in?' she asked, feeling suddenly very formal with him.

'Sure.' He stood back to let her pass. She went into the kitchen and sat down at the breakfast bar; it was the same stool, the same Corian counter, in exactly the same position in the apartment as Melody's, which never stopped being strange to her.

'Can I get you something?' he asked, padding up behind her. *He's being formal too*, she noticed.

'I am okay, thank you,' she said politely. 'I had some tea at my other patient's.'

'The actress,' he observed. 'How's she doing?'

'Very good. She is healing very well, her swelling is going down fast. Dr Nassri is excellent at what he does,' Aniela said approvingly.

She looked at Jon, who was leaning against the fridge, hips propped back, his arms folded across his chest. This made his biceps swell, the corded veins on his forearms stand out, and Aniela stared at his body longingly, but she knew that his stance wasn't a good sign; crossed arms clearly indicated defensiveness.

'How is your head?' she asked. 'Shall I look at it?'

He shook it. 'I'm fine,' he said simply. 'Healing good.'

Well, that's the preliminaries over. Now you leave, or you get down to it.

Be brave.

'I know you will be gone soon,' she said, wishing now that she'd asked for a glass of water, a cup of tea, so that she had something to do with her hands while she struggled to get out what she wanted so badly to say. 'I know you will go to America and live on your ranch and never come back. I understand that. I understand that after you go, I will never see you again. But while you are here, I would like to be with you.'

She couldn't look at him directly: she wasn't that brave. But out of the corner of her eye, she saw him shift at the last words, as if he'd been surprised by them.

'I like being with you,' she went on. 'You are very peaceful. And you are very good at sex.'

Jon made a choking noise; when she glanced at him, she saw that he was coughing in shock.

'My – my ex-boyfriend—' Aniela didn't know how to refer to Lubo; he didn't really qualify as a boyfriend on almost any level – 'he was loud. He had the TV on all the time, he talked, he burped, he farted. But you are very quiet. I like that. And like I said, you are very good at sex.'

Jon's coughing fit was only slowly abating. He put one hand up to his throat, easing the soreness.

'You know, Aniela, I haven't hung out with many women,' he said. 'There weren't that many in the Unit. But somehow I think that even if I'd met a ton of 'em, you'd be pretty damn unique.'

'Is that good?' Aniela asked, looking him in the eyes now.

He pushed off the fridge and took a couple of steps towards her; her heart raced in excitement. *This is good . . . surely this is good . . .* But his trajectory took him to the other side of the breakfast bar, putting its width between them. *Not so good.*

'Aniela,' he said simply, 'I don't know what to say to you. I've got no experience of being with a woman, apart from the ones I used to pay to be with me.'

Another woman would have burst into reassurances about how great he was. Aniela retorted instead:

'You can pay me. If you want. I'm very poor – I've lost all my savings. So I could use the money. I bet prostitutes make much more than nurses do,' she added thoughtfully.

Jon stared at her incredulously. She felt dizzy, light-headed; as if she could say anything, anything at all, throw words up into the air and let them fall in showers all around them both. And then she realised why she liked spending time with Jon so much, why she was putting her pride on the line for him; because with him, and only with him, she felt utterly and completely free for the first time in her life.

Jon was speechless at this point. His eyes were goggling, his mouth open. The livid bruising on his face was, she saw, slowly beginning to fade, the purple around his eyes lightening to a pinky-mauve, and she could see their colour more clearly, the grey-blue of Atlantic waters.

'I could bring the condoms,' she suggested, almost giggling now with her own audacity. 'I would include that in the price.'

Jon's lips moved: he was trying to say something and failing utterly. Instinctively, Aniela pushed back her stool and slid off it.

'I will leave you to think about it,' she said. 'You can page me whenever you want.'

She walked towards the door, hoping for some stupid romantic gesture, and knowing that it was idiotic. Jon wasn't going to run towards her, sweep her off her feet, cover her face with kisses, tell her he was madly in love with her; she wouldn't have trusted it if he had. And yet, she didn't want to leave like this, not without him having said another word—

'Aniela?' Jon said behind her, and she turned a little to look at him. He was standing in the corridor, hands shoved into the pockets of his sweatpants, shaking his head very slowly in disbelief.

'I don't think I've ever been as confused in my life as I get around you,' he said.

'Good,' she said, smiling.

She walked out, closing the door firmly behind her. And then she did something just as stupid and romantic as the gesture she'd been imagining; she leaned back against it, the smile still on her face.

He thinks I am unique. I confuse him. And I make him laugh. Not bad, Aniela. Not bad at all.

Jon

Maybe I could tell her. Maybe she's the one woman in the world who'd understand. I mean, look at the stuff she comes out with! She sure has a different way of seeing the world!

Hands still stuffed in his pockets, he walked to the far end of the living room and stood there, staring blindly at the extraordinary view of the skyscrapers surrounding Limehouse Reach; they seemed almost close enough to touch. But Jon wasn't seeing them at all. His eyes were open, but the scenes that were scrolling before his eyes were from almost twenty years ago, when he'd been seventeen. He was remembering the last night he had ever spent in the Hollow, the last time he had ever seen his family. The night that had changed his entire life, and made him who he was: a man who not only had no relationships, no human contact, but managed very well without them.

That night – *well, more like four in the morning* – his father Mac, who'd been out drinking and playing cards with the local moonshiners, had staggered home, crazed on meth, moonshine and bootleg Hennessy, and yelled for everyone to wake up, because he had something real important to tell their stinking asses. And when they clambered out of bed and made it through to the kitchen, wiping the sleep out of their eyes, they'd found Mac loaded for bear.

Young Drew, as Jon had been then, had spent his childhood doing whatever he could to be a bulwark between Mac and his younger brother, Davey. Drew had taken blows that were meant for his younger brother, stepped in when Mac was picking on Davey, diverting his anger, provoking the wrath in Drew's own direction. He'd learned to ride the blows as best he could, dodge the worst ones and take the lesser full on. He'd watched and he'd waited, he'd grown stronger and more alert. Because Drew had known that, one day not too long distant, a reckoning would come between him and Mac, and Drew would need to be ready.

Drew didn't have much time for a mother who had wilfully refused the offer of rescue by her sister Eileen, who had turned down her only chance to save herself and her children from her violent husband, and let him beat them and her into pulp. But he wouldn't let Mac kill Ma, and he sure as hell wouldn't let Mac kill or cripple himself or Davey.

So that night, when Mac, yelling abuse and threats, set off by the devils inside him and the drugs and alcohol coursing through his body, had picked up a poker and gone after Davey with it, Drew, seeing the madness in his father's eyes, had stepped in, as he did so often, and wrestled Mac for the weapon. He'd got the poker out of Mac's grasp, and backed away, panting for breath, holding it like a baseball bat, more than ready to slug Mac if he came for him.

Mac had been on the verge of lunging for his older son, ready to wrest the poker from his grasp, furious at this challenge to his authority. Mac had age, weight and experience on his side; he was in the prime of life, muscled and strong, and Drew was a stripling by comparison. But there had been something in Drew's stance, the set of his feet, planted firmly on the dirt floor, the steady look in his eyes, that had made his father hesitate. For the first time, he wasn't sure if this was a fight he could win.

And like all bullies, Mac only picked on targets weaker than himself. The idea that he was no longer able to hit his older son with near-impunity – and worse, that there was full rebellion, because both Davey and his wife were sheltering behind Drew now – sent him over the edge to true insanity. Grabbing for the loaded Winchester rifle propped by the door, Mac had started to level it, aiming squarely at Drew.

His wife screamed. Davey yelled:

'No, Pa! Don't do it!'

Mac's eyes were crazy, but his hands were steady. He was going to shoot his own son. Drew had stepped forward and, in one fluid movement, swung the poker, cracking Mac across the face with it, sending his father flying back into the stove.

Whether it was the blow to the face or the crack of his skull against the cast-iron stove that killed Mac Mackenzie, no one ever knew. There certainly wasn't an autopsy. As his mother fell to her knees, wailing in grief over the dead body of her abusive husband, Drew had bent down, moved her aside, hauled the corpse over his shoulder in a fireman's lift, and carried it miles uphill to the open mouth of a long-disused mine.

Never even heard him hit the bottom of the shaft, it was that deep, Jon remembered now. *But then I went back and hauled up bags of lime and chucked 'em down too, just so's he wouldn't stink and make someone wonder where the hell the smell was coming from if the wind blew in the wrong direction.*

Under the rough law of the Appalachian hill people, the killing was considered justified. Mac Mackenzie had been out of his mind on drink and drugs, turning a rifle on his own son for no reason beyond what Drew's Aunt Eileen called 'sheer bad-dog cussedness'. No one would turn Drew in to the police, of course; that would have been unimaginable. If retribution had been called for, it would have been exacted by the clan leaders, and Drew would have disappeared for ever, along with Mac. The verdict, however, was banishment. What Drew had done, though justified, could not be sanctioned. He was a patricide, and he could not be allowed to stay in the territory.

Drew was banned for life from setting foot in Jackson County; his aunt had been deputised to tell him the news. He'd known it was coming, had already been packing a tattered old backpack with his meagre possessions. All he'd done was shrug and say that in that case, his mother'd have to come with him to the Marine enlistment centre, because he was seventeen and needed the permission of a parent to sign up.

I never looked back. For the first time in my life, I was completely free. Ma never protected me, and Davey didn't stand up for me at the family council. I heard tell he never even argued I should be let stay. Aunt Eileen's the only one who spoke up for me staying in the Hollow. She's the only one I gave a damn about in the end, and she passed ten years ago, when I was still working for the Unit. That's my one regret, that I never got to say goodbye to her.

Aniela kinda reminds me of her, he thought suddenly. *Tough, uncompromising. Never afraid to speak her mind. And no one messed with Aunt Eileen.*

Jesus. No wonder Aniela scares me shitless.

Andy

*H*is head was screaming, his mouth dry as a sandpit. He heaved himself off the bed and into the ensuite shower, standing under water as cold as he could bear for a good five minutes until the throbbing in his skull subsided; then he towelled off, drank three glasses of water, one straight after the other, brushed his teeth, and pulled on his clothes, bundling the elf outfit up for the laundry collection. Grigor's staff bedrooms didn't have windows, just vents to circulate the air; it was weird, not being able to see daylight when you woke up. *Like living on a ship*, Andy thought. *Only there someone else wakes you up, don't they? Bells ringing all the time. Here I could've slept for twenty-four hours and no one would even notice.*

He looked at his watch: ten o'clock. *God, if I'd been at home I'd've slept in till my head stopped hurting;* the shower had helped, but he definitely needed a paracetamol or two. But the single bed had been uncomfortable, he had thrashed around, all the drink he'd taken the night before making his rest uneasy, and all he could think of now was how much he wanted to jump on the DLR and get started on the journey back home to Chingford.

Well, not quite all. Andy had drunk more brandy than he'd ever had in his life last night in a successful effort to stop him doing any of the drugs on offer – *or Wayne*. It had been a very particular kind of torture, being so close to Wayne in the screening room during *It's A Wonderful Life*, wanting so badly to reach an arm back behind Grigor's chair and try to caress Wayne's shoulder, just to touch him; every so often, their eyes would meet, passing popcorn back and forth, and Andy was sure that Wayne had felt the same, as frustrated as he did; afterwards, they'd had a lively discussion about how creepy the story of the film was, how Mary, the Donna Reed character, had trapped poor George into marriage and symbolically castrated him, ruined his dreams of travel and seeing the world, tying him down to a small-town life where he would be the sacrifice to make everyone else happy.

Grigor had been too sloshed on Muscat by that time to object to their deconstruction of the film; they'd reached an agreement, burst out laughing in pleasure at having met a kindred spirit – and then Wayne had said that he should really get going, Andy had snapped tipsily in disappointment, 'See you around, then,' and Wayne had gone without saying another word.

What did I expect? Andy thought, walking through the kitchen, dumping the costume into the laundry room for the maids, and pouring himself a cup of coffee from the huge percolator that was always on the go for the staff. He helped himself to a sandwich from a big stack the cooks had put out on the table: ham and cheese, just what you needed after hitting the brandy heavily the night before. *That Wayne'd whisk me back with him in his Lamborghini, with all his team-mates watching us walk out together? Or that we'd cuddle up in my single bed? It was just a quick shag, Andy. Face facts.*

I just liked him, that's all. I really liked him.

Miserably, he reached for another sandwich, nodding a thanks at the cook on duty, who was whisking eggs in a huge stainless steel bowl. Even hungover and love-sick, Andy could always eat. He'd stuff himself on sarnies, finish this mug of coffee and have another one for good measure, then head back home to his houseshare and regale his housemates with the story of what he'd been up to last night—

I won't, though. For some reason, he felt hugely protective of Wayne, so deep in the closet that he'd barely had the chance to do anything with another man, but who'd been so eager, so appreciative, so sweet and tender with Andy; *I don't agree with his not being out, but I'll keep his secret for him,* he thought, and then jumped with shock as a furious howl of rage exploded from somewhere in the penthouse.

'Jesus, what's that?' he exclaimed.

Even the stolid cook paled as he said:

'Is Mr Khalovsky – angry, very angry—'

Sergei came shooting through the kitchen, moving like a sprinter, head-up, elbows working frantically, his legs whirring, propelling him through the double serving doors at the far end that led to the great room. Andy topped up his coffee and followed, curious, but careful to keep a safe distance just in case. The last thing anyone needed was to be caught in the crossfire between a furious oligarch and the target of his wrath.

But, as it turned out, there were two targets of Grigor's wrath, and neither of them was anywhere to be seen. Which was precisely the reason for his anger. He was standing in the middle of the room, a red and gold brocade dressing gown hanging open over a large, extraordinarily hirsute paunch, which in its turn was hanging over the silk boxers that Andy could only be glad Grigor was wearing. *Though honestly, Mr K's so hairy that even if he were naked, we might be spared the sight of his bits – he's probably got enough pubes to make it look like he's wearing a merkin.*

'*Chto za khernya!*' Grigor was waving a piece of paper round as furiously as if he were trying to kill a fly with it. 'What the fuck!'

Babbling in Russian, Sergei dashed over and jumped up like a dog reaching for a bone, grabbing the paper from his master's hand. His expression, as he read what was written on it, was utterly gobsmacked.

'Get Fyodorov!' Grigor yelled at one of his fiancée's father's bodyguards, who was stationed in the great room. 'Get him *now*!'

A couple of minutes later, Fyodorov emerged from the corridor that led to the guest bedrooms, yawning heavily, wrapped in a cashmere dressing gown. He was followed by none other than Diane, the madam who had provided the girls from the night before, her hair brushed and immaculate. Morning light was not Diane's friend, but her eyeliner was carefully, subtly tattooed on, her skin illuminated by her regime of serums and lotions, and her eyelashes were tinted and thickened by the application of individual, long-lasting false ones; she stood up pretty well to the test. Fyodorov, naturally, didn't give a damn what he looked like; his sparse hair stuck out at all angles, his eyes were bleary with sleep, his breath reeking. But then, it was a man's world in this penthouse. The footballers who were passed out on the sofas, or emerging from other bedrooms, escorts in tow, all looked equally scruffy, while the girls had nipped away in the middle of the night to reapply their make-up and perfume, and were as dewy and groomed now as they had been the night before.

'*Kakogo khera?* What the fuck's going on?' Fyodorov slurred at Grigor, who barked an angry response, snatching the paper from Sergei and slapping it dramatically at his guest.

As Fyodorov read it, Andy gawked at him. Grigor was hairy, but in all Andy's experience of saunas and backrooms at clubs, he had never seen a man as hirsute as Fyodorov. It looked as if he were wearing a black angora bodysuit. *My God, he could go as a gorilla to a costume party – all he needs is the head!*

Diane, who was smart enough to have learned Russian for her business, gasped as she, too, read what was written on the paper. Fyodorov swore viciously, threw it to the ground and smushed it contemptuously under his bare heel. The oligarchs engaged in a vicious, high-volume screaming match, with plenty of arm-waving, heels of hands smacked against their own foreheads, and stamping up and down the room to express fury.

'What's going on?' Andy hissed to Arkady, one of Grigor's bodyguards, who spoke very good English. Arkady's bearing was rigidly professional, but on a couple of occasions Andy thought he had spotted the bodyguard checking out the arse of one of the waiters, a French boy called Michel who had a bum like two ripe peaches.

'Zhivana Fyodorova has run away with Dmitri, Mr Khalovsky's son,' Arkady muttered out of the corner of his mouth. 'After the party last night. They left a note.'

'Oh my *God*!' Andy gasped, nearly dropping his cup of coffee. 'What a *mess*!'

'I *know*, right?' Arkady hissed back, confirming Andy's opinion of his sexual orientation.

Fyodorov stormed over to the dining table, picked up a Lalique glass vase and threw it across the room in fury.

'My bear! My bear!' Grigor shrieked, as the vase flew perilously close to his gigantic, glittering sculptured bear, still decked out with Christmas lights.

Pat de Luca, a midfielder who was stretched out on the sofa, a pillow pulled over his face to block out light and noise, yelped and jumped up as the vase whistled over his head and crashed to the floor just behind the sofa.

'The *fuck*!' he groaned, blinking in the daylight. 'The *fuck* is going on?'

'You nearly killed him!' Grigor yelled, pointing at Pat. 'He cost me a fortune!'

'My *daughter* cost *me* a fortune!' Fyodorov yelled back.

'You should have taught her how to behave while you were spending all that money on her!' Grigor yelled. 'I was the perfect gentleman, I never laid a finger on her! I'd have treated her like a queen!'

'Maybe you should have fucked her instead!' Fyodorov yelled back. 'Kept her on her back so she couldn't walk out the door!'

Diane tutted in disapproval; Grigor said indignantly:

'*Gospodi!* You talk like that about your own *daughter*, Mikhail?'

'My daughter,' Fyodorov bellowed, 'will do what the fuck I tell her to do!' He looked around him furiously for his men. 'We'll find those two brats, drag them back here by their hair, teach them a lesson about respect and doing what the fuck their fathers tell them, and then I'll march that little bitch up the aisle to marry you so fast that—'

'Mikhail, love,' Diane interrupted, pitching her voice low, so that it cut through the enraged tycoon's roar much more effectively than if she'd raised it. 'Hang on just a mo.'

Gliding forward, she put one hand on Fyodorov's arm. It was brave of her; he could easily have reacted by knocking her across the room as forcefully as he'd thrown the vase. But Diane had decades of experience with men in every state of overstimulation, and her touch was clearly soothing, because Fyodorov took a deep breath and turned to look at her, patting her hand.

'If your boys beat up Grigor's son, he's going to be well miffed,' she pointed out, tall enough so that her face was on a level with the stocky Russian's. 'And the whole plan here is for you two to join forces, not start a sodding war. Why don't we all have a cup of that lovely black Russian tea, nice and strong, and talk this over?'

She turned to smile at Grigor.

'Honestly, gentlemen,' she said soothingly, 'if you all step back and look at this from another perspective, you might realise it's the best solution all round . . .'

December 28th

Aniela

Someone was ringing the doorbell of the Canary Clinic.
More leaning on it than ringing it; as Aniela bustled down
the hallway to answer, the sound did not abate for a second.

Some real emergency, she thought, worried. *Some patient with
a crisis. Dr Nassri is on holiday in Sharm-el-Sheik and won't be
back till the New Year – I have the list of backup doctors, but none
of them are as good as him—*

So when she unfastened the locks and pulled the door open
to see her sort-of-boyfriend Lubo standing there, glaring at her,
she didn't know whether to be relieved or furious.

Fury won out. She put her hands on her hips and said angrily:

'What the hell, Lubo? You can't just turn up here like this!
I'm working!'

'Working!' Lubo snorted, pushing past her into the Clinic.
'You're doing bugger all! They're paying you a fortune just to
sit here and watch the telly!'

'You should know about doing bugger all!' Aniela snapped
back. 'I'm amazed you got off your bum long enough to come
over here!' She narrowed her eyes. 'What *are* you doing here,
anyway?'

'Went out with some of the guys,' Lubo said, shrugging. 'In
the East End. Anyway, it got late, then it got early, and I

thought, well, my girl's nearby, and she didn't even bother to give me a ring to say Happy Christmas, the miserable cow, so I might as well swing by and see what she's up to . . .'

'You're drunk,' Aniela said curtly. 'I can smell it on your breath. Beer and cheap whisky. And you've been smoking spliff.' She leaned in and sniffed him. 'Lots of it.'

Lubo was unshaven, with a stubble growth that had taken days to mature. His big, bullet-head was wobbling as if loose on his thick neck, which Aniela recognised as one of the indications that he was drunk; his eyes were bloodshot, and his clothes – a knockoff D&G shirt and baggy jeans that he'd bought at the local market, a sheepskin jacket – stank of smoke and weed.

'So what?' he said aggressively. 'It's Christmas – a man has a right to have a drink or two! Come on, Ani, give me a kiss—'

He lunged for her; Aniela evaded him. Looking him up and down, she thought: *I can't believe I lived with him, had sex with him. I must have been so lonely, so desperate.*

No more. Never again. From now on, I'm putting a much higher value on myself.

'Lubo, it's over,' she said simply.

'You what?' He was standing in the reception area, swaying on his feet, blinking.

'It's over. *We're* over. Go back to ours – *my* place – and sort out somewhere to move to. I'll be back on the 3rd, and I want you gone by then.'

Lubo's bleary eyes widened as her words sank in.

'You don't mean that!' he objected. 'You're just cross 'cause I'm a li'l bit tipsy! Come on, Ani, I'll sleep it off and then we can have a bit of fun – where's your room? I'll crash on your bed and then you can come in and play with my big salami . . .'

Aniela cringed. *I actually let this man put his hands all over me – what was I thinking!*

'No!' she said, louder than she'd meant to. 'I'm breaking up with you! It's over, Lubo.'

Lubo shook his head angrily.

'Don't be stupid, Ani,' he said. 'Your mum and dad'll be furious. They're so happy we're together – they're best friends with my mum and dad – they were hoping we'd get married and settle down – we *should* get married, I was meaning to get around to asking you—'

'Lubo! Fuck off!' she said furiously. 'I've been supporting you for years! I'm the laughing-stock of London, the only Polish girl who's stupid enough to have a lazy Polish boyfriend, when everyone else's works two jobs! You can't just say "Let's get married" and expect me to fall into your arms!'

Aniela was so angry now she was actually seeing red, blood pulsing in her eyes.

'But your parents—'

'I don't give a shit what my parents think,' she said even more furiously, 'because I'm never going to see them again! Or my brothers either! They spent all the money I sent them on drink, you've been living off me for free for years – I've been the biggest idiot going! Well, not any more.' She confronted him, hands on her hips again. 'I don't care where you go. Crash on a friend's floor, like you did with me before I was stupid enough to let you into my bedroom. If you're not gone by the 3rd, I'll get the police to kick you out. It's my name on the lease, not yours. It's over, okay? Get that into your thick skull!'

'You bitch! You're throwing me out? You can't do that!'

It had finally dawned through Lubo's drink and drug haze that Aniela was completely serious. His head thrust forward like an angry bull's, his shoulders hunching.

'Oh yeah? *Watch* me!' she yelled back, her own head coming forward, her shoulders crunching up just as aggressively.

Jon hadn't paged her yesterday; she'd thought of nothing else since she left his apartment, had checked the bloody thing's batteries multiple times, to make sure they were charged, had propped it on the back of the loo while she took her evening shower, with the door open enough so that she could hear it if it beeped, had stayed up till midnight, way past her usual bedtime, just in case he got a late-night urge to summon her. But he hadn't got in touch. He seemed to have decided that 'unique' and 'confusing' weren't attributes that interested him enough in a woman, even in the short-term.

All the frustration and misery of Jon's rejection flamed up in her now. As Lubo lunged for her, she didn't know if he meant to kiss her or to hit her, and she didn't care. Any duty nurse was accustomed, unfortunately, to dealing with patients who were drunk, or on drugs, or off their meds, and while there were usually orderlies to help, it was not the first time an angry man had charged at Aniela. She wasn't at all fazed by it.

In fact, it's a real pleasure to be able to handle this how I always want to – the way you can't in a hospital—

Taking a step back, Aniela snatched up one of the chairs that was tucked under the central table in the reception area, braced her legs wide, and as Lubo came charging towards her, arms outstretched, she sidestepped him, swung the chair back, and cracked it into his side. He went down like a cartoon character hit with an anvil.

'*Aniela!* Oh my *God!*'

The front door had swung open: Melody was standing there, silhouetted in the frame, a takeout coffee cup in each hand, staring in horror at the scene before her.

'Did he break in?' Melody rushed forward, putting the cups down on the table, bravely standing by Aniela's side. 'Was he trying to steal the drugs? Should I call the police, or did you do that already?'

Lubo hadn't been completely knocked out by the smashing blow across his torso; he was groaning, scrabbling around on the floor. His jacket was stained, his trainers dirty. With great embarrassment, Aniela realised how plausible this scenario seemed to Melody, that Lubo was an opportunistic burglar or drug addict, taking advantage of the holidays to rob a clinic.

For a moment, she was tempted to lie, out of pure shame. But that would mean Lubo being arrested, and that wouldn't be fair . . .

'He's my ex-boyfriend,' she admitted, her head hanging. 'I just broke up with him and kicked him out of my flat, and he didn't take it very well.'

'You broke my arm!' Lubo moaned. 'You bitch!'

'Hey, don't talk to her like that!' Melody snapped. 'Aniela doesn't just go round whacking people – I bet you deserved it!' She looked at Aniela. 'You're kicking him out of your place, right?'

Aniela nodded.

'Has he got your keys?'

'Yes—'

'Well, you can't let him go back there on his own – he could change the locks and squat it! Look, let's get a cab over there now, pack his stuff up and put it outside for him.' She bent down next to Lubo and pulled his keys out of his jacket pocket, holding them up triumphantly. 'Then he can just pick it up whenever. Okay?'

Aniela was dumbstruck.

'*Did* you break his arm?' Melody asked.

'Of course not,' Aniela said contemptuously. 'With the amount of padding he's got? All I did was knock him over. He's faking for sympathy.'

'All right then. You!' Melody prodded Lubo with her foot. 'Get up, go on—'

She stood over him menacingly till, complaining, he hauled himself to his feet.

'Out you go,' she commanded, stalking over to the door, dragging it open and gesturing at the street outside with all the authority of an actress who had recently played a superheroine in a Hollywood film. It worked with amazing success: still cursing, Lubo shuffled out.

Melody slammed and locked the door behind him triumphantly, then turned to Aniela.

'Right,' she said martially. 'We'll go out through the lobby, and get Kevin to put us in a cab, just in case he's hanging around. And then we can get to your place before him and put all his stuff out. Any probs, we'll call the police.'

Aniela shook her head in disbelief.

'Melody,' she said softly, 'you're a really good friend.'

'I bloody am, aren't I?' Melody said, laughing. 'Look what a top friend I am!' She picked up the Tetra Pak paper cups from the table and handed one to Aniela. 'I even brought you coffee!'

Dasha

'You don't want a divorce after all?' Dasha stared blankly at her husband. 'What the fuck, Grigor?'

They were in Grigor's private sitting room, off his bedroom. The penthouse had been designed with a master suite of rooms which comprised two bathrooms, the huge bedroom, and a sitting room, all running along the river side of the building and giving directly onto a huge private terrace. As jolly and sociable as Grigor was, there were times when he wanted to shut the world out, and he was extremely protective of his personal space: on the rare occasions he did call in one of Diane's girls for some fun and games, he always entertained her in a guest bedroom, never his own.

For anyone else but his wife, this meeting would have taken place in one of the many other public areas of the huge penthouse. And Dasha knew her husband as well as she knew herself: as soon as she had been ushered in here, she had known, not only that the conversation would be serious, but that Grigor had forgiven her for the scene she'd made on Christmas Day. A samovar was set up, ready to go: Grigor had poured her a cup of Russian tea, served himself, and then sat down cosily in the wingback Poltrona Frau armchair that was paired with the one Dasha was occupying.

'Ahh,' he had observed, settling in it contentedly. 'German design, Italian leather.' He patted the armrest. 'Best in the world.'

Dasha, though longing to ask him why she was here, had managed to keep her mouth shut and wait: it had only taken a few more minutes before Grigor dropped the bombshell about the divorce being off.

'Tell me, Dasha,' he said eventually, stirring his tea. 'Have you heard from Dmitri at all in the last few days?'

Dasha frowned, trying to work out why Grigor was asking her this. Her brows drew together; though her hair was bleached to within an inch of its life, she didn't have the same procedure performed on her brows, which were naturally dark, and heavily pencilled for extra emphasis. The contrast was, to put it politely, striking.

'He rang me yesterday,' she said carefully, wary of giving away any unnecessary information until she knew where Grigor was going with this. 'What does this have to do with you not wanting a divorce, Grigor? Are you fucking with me? Because if you're fucking with me, or trying to play our sons against me, I swear, I'll cut your heart out and feed it to the animals in the zoo—'

But Grigor was holding up his hand and shaking his head in a way that she recognised as a genuine denial.

'Dasha, Dasha. Listen,' he said, sipping his sweetened dark tea. 'Did Dmitri tell you anything about what he was up to?'

'Why?' Dasha was immediately suspicious; she drew her back up straight in the chair, shaking out her mane of hair, a lioness in defence of her cub. 'What's going on? Tell me, Grigor!'

Grigor exhaled deeply.

'Dmitri's run away with Zhivana Fyodorova,' he admitted.

'*Run away!* With—' Dasha nearly choked on her tea; she managed to put the cup down on the gold-leaf-topped table beside her without spilling it, but it was a close-run thing.

'*Gospodi!*' She sat back in the chair, the full deliciousness of this news flooding through her, a smile spreading across her face as she absorbed it. '*Well!*' she said eventually with relish. '*Well!* So Zhivana Fyodorova decided that she'd rather fuck a nice plump young dick than a wrinkled old one that needs Viagra to get it up! I can't say I blame her. I feel exactly the same way myself.'

'Dasha!' Grigor said disapprovingly. 'Those are your son's and husband's penises that you're talking about!'

'I'll say anything I want to about them,' Dasha snapped. 'I've washed Dima's dick when he was little more times than you've had hot dinners. And I've sucked yours more times than—'

'Please! Enough!' Grigor held up his hand again. 'The point is that the alliance has been made. That's what Mikhail Fyodorov and I wanted, and now we have it.'

'Alliance? So Dima and the little Fyodorova noodle are getting married?' Dasha asked incredulously.

'They bloody well will be,' Grigor said grimly, 'if Mikhail Fyodorov and I have to march them down the aisle ourselves at gunpoint. Dmitri's made his bed, and he's going to have to damn well lie in it now.'

Dasha pulled a face.

'I'd rather have you than Dima marrying that little wet noodle,' she observed disingenuously. 'What kind of grandchildren is she going to breed? They'll have less personality than a potato dumpling!'

'Maybe they'll get it from their grandfathers,' Grigor said complacently. 'Sometimes the fire in the belly skips a generation.'

Dasha shrugged.

'Well, what's done is done.' She raised her eyebrows at her husband. 'And at least we know for sure now that he's straight. I don't mind telling you, I had my doubts.'

As Grigor spluttered into his tea at his wife's bluntness, she picked up her own cup again, the strong sweet brew an extra fillip to her suddenly excellent mood. Her husband had been humiliated, rejected by the drippy little girl with whom he'd tried to replace her; her beloved son had made an excellent alliance; all in all, this news was the best Christmas present she could possibly have received. She stared out of the glass windows to the view beyond, the surrounding skyscrapers and office towers on the far side of the river basin which were almost all lower than Limehouse Reach. She could see their helipads, their gardens, their terraces, look down on them from this elevated position. It was hugely satisfying.

'So, naturally, this means that there's no need for a divorce,' her husband was saying. 'I'll call off the lawyers. No sense in wasting money, is there? I don't mind saying, Dasha, I'm not unhappy with how this has all worked out. At my age, a new young wife—' He blew out a long breath. 'I'd probably have had a heart attack trying to keep up with her. It was Fyodorov's idea, you know. He was set on me marrying her. Said boys of her age weren't interested in her, and he thought she'd suit an older man.'

'Most Russian boys wouldn't be,' Dasha agreed. 'They want a girl with a bit of flash and sparkle. Someone with confidence and sex appeal.' She looked down complacently at her leather miniskirt, her sheer dotted burgundy tights and stretch knee-length boots. 'A woman who knows how to dress so a man will notice her. Dima has more American tastes.' She sighed. 'That's what happens when you educate them abroad, I suppose.'

'Dasha.' Her husband leant over to pat her knee. 'It was just business, you know, this whole remarriage idea. Nothing personal. It was never personal. And you must admit I was going to be very generous to you.'

'Just business,' Dasha echoed.

'Yes! Of course! Nothing more! I know things were said in anger, but you know me – I don't hold grudges. And you shouldn't either. It's over.' He smiled. 'Soon we'll be seeing our son walk down the aisle, and I want us to be sitting there, holding hands, happy that he's happy. And then there'll be grandchildren! Let's face it, Alek is a real playboy – he isn't going to settle down any time soon. Little Dmitri's the one making us proud right now.'

And Dasha smiled back at him.

No divorce! I keep my status as Grigor's wife, I'm not humiliated by being set aside for a younger woman – if anything, it's Grigor who's humiliated, because his fiancée ran off with his son, for God's sake!

Finishing her tea, staring again with great smugness at the modern urban landscape outside, at all the apartments and penthouses with smaller terraces, fewer balconies, less expensive real estate than the one in which she was ensconced, Dasha could not have felt happier or more satisfied with her life.

My clever son! My clever son has solved my problem, taken care of his mother! I'll make sure to give him a really wonderful wedding present—

But then a thought struck her with horrifying force.

The hitman! I'm going to have to call him off – I only hope to God it isn't too late . . . there's more than enough money for both me and Grigor and the boys, and as a widow, I'll have much less status than I do as Grigor's wife. Damn it! Now I want the bastard to stay alive!

'Dasha? What is it?' Grigor said, staring at her. 'You've gone white – you look like you've seen a ghost!'

I hope I'm not looking at one! his wife thought, staring back at him. *I hope that man hasn't set in motion some plan that can't be undone* . . . She put down her empty cup and rose swiftly to her feet.

'I must rush,' she said. 'I've just remembered some very urgent business I need to take care of . . .'

Jon

What the hell's happened to her?

W hat the hell's happened to her?
He looked up at the clock. He'd never minded it before, the fact that it was a projection from a little box across the room; now, for some reason, it annoyed him intensely. *Stupid fucking pretentious yuppie crap – just put a fucking clock on the wall and be done with it.* Striding across the room, he located the box, switched it off and then, for good measure, pulled the damn thing's plug out of the socket.

I don't need a damn clock anyway. I know what time it is, I always do. And the only appointment I have here is Aniela, coming round at twelve noon to check up on me – and I sure as hell don't need a clock for that, because every day she's been precise to the minute . . .

It was nearly one. If she'd been planning on coming today, but some emergency had delayed her, she would have called to let him know. No doubt about that: Aniela was as punctual as she was professional.

So there was only one explanation: she wasn't coming at all.

And why should she? he asked himself. *Why the hell should she? A woman has her pride. What did you expect her to do? She told you she wanted to hook up with you, no strings attached. She was even ballsy enough to make a joke about you paying her. And all you did was tell her you were confused. Why should she show up here again? She's probably sitting down in the Clinic, licking her wounds and feeling like a fool.*

He really hated the thought that he might have made Aniela unhappy. That she might be feeling stupid, or unwanted.

Because I do want her. Real bad. I kept waking up last night and wishing she was there next to me. I was this close to paging her at three in the morning.

Ah, fuck it. Fuck it all to hell.

It was either punch a hole in the wall, or pick up the phone. And Jon was much too careful of his hands to start slamming them into concrete. So he picked Option B, taking the handset, checking the printed info sheet on which all the contact details for the Canary Clinic were listed, and dialling the number of Aniela's pager. A recorded voice told him that his call had been logged, that the owner of the pager would know he had rung, and that he could hang up now.

The relief with which he did so was huge. He felt as if he'd been lugging a seventy-pound kitbag on a ten-mile training run, and had finally been able to haul it off his shoulders and drop it to the ground. *She'll ring back. She has to – I'm her patient. Or she might just come straight up.* His heart leaped. *Either way, I'll be seeing her real soon . . .*

Shit, I should jump in the shower! Why didn't I think of that before I paged her? What an idiot!

Frustration had spurred him to work out even more than usual that day, and he looked down ruefully at his T-shirt, which was sticking to his chest with sweat. Grabbing the phone – so he'd hear her if she called – he dashed to the bathroom, pulling off his clothes as he went, hopping with one foot still caught in the sweatpants he'd dropped to the floor. He figured that he'd have just about time to rinse himself off and get some fresh gear on before Aniela could possibly check her pager, see it was him who called, and make it up from the Clinic. Not even waiting for the water to warm up, he was in and out of the shower with lightning speed, towelling off, dumping his sweaty clothes into the laundry basket and dashing into the bedroom to pull on some fresh ones.

And then, after that crazy rush, for over three hours he did sweet fuck all. He just sat there waiting for a woman, something he had never done in his life before, the tension building, feeling more like shit than he could ever remember feeling as a grown man. Wondering if she'd ever call or show up, or if he'd blown things with her, irretrievably and for ever, by not jumping all over her offer the day before.

What was I thinking? he asked himself despondently. *A woman I find insanely attractive not only accepts that I used to kill people for a living, but tells me she'll have sex with me while I'm here, no pressure to commit, no strings attached – and I just gawp at her like a goldfish and talk about how I'm really more used to dealing with hookers? I should get my head examined!*

He huffed out a bitter laugh as he caught a glimpse of his bashed-up face in the floor-to-ceiling window. *If she never shows up again, I deserve it.*

His internal clock told him that it was past four in the afternoon. *Okay, maybe she's taking a day off to calm down – maybe she's planning to come by tomorrow at noon, as per normal—*

Well, she may be able to wait that long. But I can't. If she doesn't come to me, I'll go to her.

It was already nearly night-time, the shadows of the Canary Wharf skyscrapers stretching across to trace lines on the floor of his living room; just a week after the shortest day of the year it would be dark in another hour.

Okay, that's my deadline. Five o'clock, full dark. If she's not here by five, I'll bandage up my face again and head down to the Clinic. If the mountain won't come to Mohammed, then Mohammed will go find the damn mountain and tell her that he's real sorry and that he'd love to take her up on her offer—

The doorbell rang. Jon was on his feet and sprinting across the room before the peal had even finished: he ripped the door open so fast he nearly tore it off its hinges. In that split-second, he realised that he hadn't taken any security precautions at all, hadn't asked who it was or looked through the peephole; with Dasha Khalovksy's threat hanging over his head, that was a slip in self-protection that could have cost him his life.

The crazy thing was, he didn't care. He didn't care about a damn thing but seeing if it was Aniela at the door, getting to her as quickly as possible. She was standing there, a coat over her uniform, outdoor shoes on her feet, her finger only just leaving the bell, looking taken aback at how fast he'd answered it.

'Are you all right?' she asked. 'I'm sorry, I was out – I had an emergency at home, I had to go back there and my pager was out of range. I only just got back and saw that you had rung—'

And then she squealed in shock, because he had picked her up, kicked the door shut behind her, and was carrying her into the apartment, down the hall, into his bedroom, his mouth on hers, or at least at first: he tried to kiss her as he walked, but that didn't work, because their bodies were moving so quickly, and his priority was to get her to that damn bed as soon as he possibly could. So he just kept going, reached the bedroom, and pretty much threw her onto the mattress, landing beside her, unbuttoning her coat, some of the buttons flying off in his haste, tearing the cheap felt fabric off her shoulders, ripping at her uniform, pulling it up, pulling her dress up to her waist.

He knew his haste was okay, because she was helping him, lifting her bottom to help him hook his fingers in the waist-band of her tights and panties and pull them down to her knees; behind him, he heard her kick off her shoes, and as he bared the join of her legs he pressed his mouth against her, kissing her, hoping to God it was how she liked it, what she wanted; she was wet, and getting wetter, so that had to be a good sign, didn't it? He had no idea what he was doing, but figured that it had to be the same kind of rules for a woman going down on a man: no teeth, lots of tongue and lips, careful with the pressure, and the louder her moans get, the more you're on target . . .

He glanced up, along the length of her body, his mouth still working away, and saw that her head was tilted back, her arms stretched out on either side of her body, hands grabbing handfuls of the duvet, spreadeagled, crucified. *And I'm doing this*, he thought with great pride. *It's all me. I'm making her feel this good, making her moan and scream and arch her hips even harder against me—*

She let out a long wail of pleasure; the arms outstretched along the duvet spasmed, hands clenching into fists, and then releasing as her hips collapsed onto the bed, her legs around him going limp. He was hugely smug, absolutely satisfied with his own achievement. *Like hitting a home run your first ever time at bat*, he thought complacently, sliding up her, kissing his way as he went. He was so pleased with himself that he had temporarily forgotten his own needs; his cock, which had been wedged against the duvet, sandwiched between his own weight and the mattress, had been highly stimulated by the pressure and was now, as he lay on top of Aniela, nudging its way hopefully between her legs.

He was kissing her, deep and delicious, their mouths wet and lubricious, feeling her arms wrap around him, pull him even closer. His cock slid further; she was so damp now and he was so hard that he began to enter her, with no help from either of them, no hands reaching down to guide him. He knew he shouldn't, that he needed a condom, but it felt so wonderful, and he was already half inside her, and she was gasping under him and clutching his shoulders and tilting her pelvis to make it even easier, so he could slide fully into her, his entire length enveloped in her hot clinging warmth.

I mustn't move, he thought. *I mustn't risk coming. But it feels so wonderful* – he lay there, propping some of his weight on his elbows, managing at least not to smother her, just feeling his cock inside her with utter and complete satisfaction as he kissed her, kept on kissing her, kissed her till he had no idea how long he'd been kissing her, till he couldn't even tell the difference between his tongue and hers, his lips and hers; he was in a trance of delight.

It was Aniela, below him, who eventually turned her mouth away from his enough to gasp: 'I have condoms – I brought condoms, let me get them—'

Jon was in a state of perfect suspension; he wanted both to get the condom but also to stay inside her for ever, and it was Aniela, wriggling sideways to reach the pocket of her coat, which was caught under their bodies, who dislodged him; he couldn't have done it of his own volition. It was almost painful to come out of her, to feel his cock once more bobbing in the colder air outside her warm body. He wanted to whimper like a dog, felt ridiculously sad, and the moment she ripped open the packet and stroked the condom onto him he was inside her again so fast she gasped again, all in one stroke, his balls pressed up against her snugly, firmly. It felt amazing. He didn't want to pull back, not at all. He wanted to stay like this, and so he started to rock back and forth, tilting on his elbows and his knees, his extreme fitness allowing him complete control of both his body and hers. He'd never done it like this before, never seen it done in porn either. It felt insanely intimate, so close that he could kiss her, keep kissing her as he rocked back and forth, feeling his cock grasped tightly inside her, her breasts and stomach soft beneath him, her wide hips cradling him perfectly.

He was beginning to wonder if, much as he was loving this, it was doing anything for her; he pulled back to look down at her, the angle at which their bodies were linked changing as he did so, and instantly her arms, which were wrapped around his shoulders, tightened, dragging him back down again.

'Don't stop,' she panted against his mouth. 'Don't stop, *please* . . .'

Well, okay! I guess it's working for her too. He sank on top of her again, and she pulled him even tighter, taking almost all of his weight on her pelvis now as they found the same rhythm again. She was breathing heavily, her head thrown back now against the pillows, and he propped himself just above her so he could watch what was happening to her face; her pupils were dilated, her lips parted, bright red dots glowing on her pale cheeks. She was starting to pant in time with every sway of his hips into hers and her hands dug into his shoulders with surprising strength as her eyes shut, the blonde lashes fluttering above her cheekbones, and, deep in her throat, a long slow hum started to vibrate. It rose and fell, and he listened to it, completely enchanted, extra careful not to change the rhythm in the slightest; he didn't know exactly what was going on, but clearly it was a good thing, and he'd hold out as long as he could to keep watching her, listening to the sound she was making, be sure that, whatever was happening, she was enjoying herself.

He had no idea how long it lasted. It was only when her eyes opened again, their expression dazed, staring straight into his without even seeming to see him, when she went limp under him, her hands finally loosening their death-grip on his shoulders, that the pressure in his groin burst and diffused without his even consciously choosing to let go. It poured out of him like a dyke bursting open, very different from the orgasms he'd had before; just as intense, but wider somehow. Even with the condom on, it felt as if his sperm were flooding through her entire body, to every fingertip and toe, suffusing her with its heat. And it seemed to last for minutes, holding him in suspended animation, his body rigid as his balls and cock throbbed in ecstasy, coming and coming until, when he could no longer hold himself up at all, and collapsed helplessly on top of her, he felt as drained as if he'd lost pints of vital fluids.

It was all he could do to somehow reach down and ease off the condom before he fell back against her, his head on her breasts, feeling her stroking his hair, kissing his scalp, her other arm tight around him. They were damp with sweat, their scents mingled. He licked salt from a little pool in the hollow between her breasts and didn't know if it were his or hers.

'Rubens,' he muttered drowsily, knowing there was something he'd meant to tell her.

Her hand on his head stilled.

'I don't know that word,' she said. 'What does it mean?'

'It's a name,' he said. 'The name of a painter. You look like the women in his pictures. White skin, fair hair. Pretty little – uh, bosoms and lovely big hips.'

He stroked one of her breasts. 'Soft,' he said sleepily. 'Soft like velvet.' He yawned deeply.

Sleep, he thought happily, every muscle in his body pleasantly slack; only now did he realise how tense he must have been before she appeared on his doorstep. *We can crash for a while, then have something to eat. I'm going to be starving after this. Then we can do it all over again – fuck, sleep, eat.*

Sounds perfect.

The doorbell wasn't actually that loud, but Jon and Aniela were so relaxed that it sounded like a klaxon to both of them. They jumped; Jon, with a soldier's ability to fall asleep almost instantly, had already been five fathoms deep, and he jerked awake with a start, his arms flexing, pushing himself off the bed and onto his feet in one swift swing. He was still in his T-shirt; he grabbed his sweatpants, dragged them on, and turned to look at her. She was struggling out of their post-sex haze, frowning, her eyes wide, not understanding why he had snapped into action so fast.

'What—' she began, but already he was holding a finger to his lips, signalling her to be quiet.

As she obeyed, he flattened his palm and pushed it towards her, telling her to stay in the bedroom. Keeping the door shut would look suspicious; he left it ajar as he slipped soundlessly towards the front door, tying the cord at the waist of his pants.

An unexpected visitor – or visitors – could mean only one thing. It was Dasha Khalovsky, with or without accompanying goons, and the last thing he wanted was for that woman to have any idea that Aniela even existed, let alone was involved with him.

'Yeah?' he called out, doing his best to sound as if he'd been woken from a nap by the bell; it wasn't much of a stretch. 'Who is it?'

'Let me in,' she hissed, not wanting to say her name, out there in the corridor where anyone could hear. 'I am alone.'

He went through the same routine as before, jerking open the door, pulling her in front of him, frisking her thoroughly once he had her inside and between him and any guy with a gun she might have brought along with her. She kept trying to talk, but he paid no attention till he was sure she wasn't carrying: then, leaning against the living-room wall, strategically positioned so that she couldn't get past him to the bedroom, he said:

'Okay, start again from the beginning.'

Dasha Khalovsky drew in a deep breath of frustration, her lips, big with filler, pursing crossly.

'Are you deaf? It's off! The hit is off!' she said. 'I came to tell you. That's okay, right?'

His eyebrows shot up, which would have hurt if he'd let himself register it.

'Sure,' he said slowly. 'No skin off my nose.'

'You've got enough problems there already,' she said, with more wit than he'd have given her credit for. She pulled out a packet of cigarettes from her bag and a big, shiny gold lighter; Jon shook his head as she offered him the pack. Without asking if it was okay to smoke, she lit up, the lighter snapping like a trap as it opened and closed.

'So,' she said, exhaling smoke from both nostrils, 'that's it. As you were, okay? Whatever plan you had, you can call it off. I want my husband live and kicking.'

'Hey.' Jon spread his hands wide. 'He's your husband. But this is it, Mrs Khalovsky. You had your chance, and you've changed your mind. Once you walk out this door, you have no hold on me. You got it?'

She nodded, a brief downward jerk of her head.

'Not good enough. You better make me believe it,' he said tersely. 'You don't want me taking you out to make damn sure you don't come back for another freebie, do you?'

'Fine!' she snapped, flicking ash on the carpet. 'I swear it on my sons' lives, okay? Once I walk out, we're done. I forget you existed. And I tell my investigators to do the same.'

It was Jon's turn to nod.

'We're done here,' he said, gesturing to the door. 'After you.'

Dasha Khalovksy didn't want to linger in the apartment of an ex-hitman whom she had blackmailed into killing her husband any more than Jon wanted her to hang around; in a swish of fur and bouncing yellow ringlets, she stepped quickly to the door and exited without another word or a look back. Jon closed and locked it behind her, coughing at the fug of smoke and Giorgio she had left in her wake. Then he dashed back into the bedroom. Aniela was sitting up, the duvet pulled to her chest, her eyes full of questions.

'You need to get out of here,' he said intently. 'It's not safe here any more. Get up and get dressed, *now.*'

'But she said—'

'She was lying through her teeth.' He pulled out his suitcase from the built-in cupboard and started throwing his clothes in it.

'You mean she still wants you to kill her husband?' Aniela was utterly confused.

'No, that bit was true. She lied about forgetting I existed. Now *she* has to kill *me*, just in case I go to her husband and tell him about the contract she put out on him. I recorded her just now, and she's got to assume I might have done something like that. If she could have pulled off walking in here and shooting me in the head, she'd have done it.'

Aniela's mouth was open.

'Why didn't she?'

'Who the hell knows? The important thing is she has no idea about you and me. I want you to go back to the Clinic, stay there, lock yourself in. Tomorrow, you come by here as usual – there'll be a note on the door to say I checked myself out. That covers you. You go tell Nassri straight away, just like you would if another patient took off without warning. *Don't come inside this apartment.* That's the most important thing, okay? If they come back while you're inside, you'll be in deep shit. Promise me you'll do exactly what I say.'

She was pulling her bra back on, buttoning up her uniform, her eyes on him.

'I promise. But what about you?' she asked, her voice trembling just a little. 'What will you—'

He was shaking his head.

'I'm not going to tell you. You know nothing, and that's how you got to act if anyone asks you. Get out of here now, fast. Take the stairs to that actress's floor and call the elevator from there, so no one sees it coming from this floor.'

She was slipping on her shoes; he grabbed her coat off the bed and threw it at her, taking her arm, marching her to the door. Amazingly, she didn't say another word. *This is the kind of woman you want around in a crisis,* he thought. *Calm, no panic, no fuss.* At the front door, he kissed her, hard and fast, not a goodbye, a marker for the future; he felt his cock stir the instant his mouth touched hers. She kissed him back just as hard, her hands gripping the back of his neck for a moment, pulling his head down, her tongue in his mouth just as much of a marker as his was in hers.

'I'll find you,' he said, looking down at her. 'When it's safe. I promise, I'll come find you.'

There were tears in her eyes, but she didn't say a word, just looked back at him fiercely and nodded, which made the tears brim over, falling down her cheeks. Then she was through the door and out. He watched for a moment, to make sure there was no one waiting outside, and was impressed to see that she was heading for the far staircase, the one on the other side of the building from his apartment.

And then, as a heavy fire door clanged shut in the distance, he knew she'd entered the stairwell, and made a huge effort to dismiss her from his mind.

I need to focus on fixing this problem. Disappearing for good, so Dasha Khalovsky and whatever crew she's putting together right now have no idea where the hell to find me . . .

Jon's instincts were absolutely correct. As he shot into the kitchen, scooping energy bars in boxes from the shelves into a plastic bag, fast and furious, making sure he had enough provisions to hole up for a few days, Dasha Khalovsky was downstairs in the parking garage, talking intently to two of Grigor's bodyguards.

'It's the bandage guy?' Nestor asked, spitting on the floor. 'The one who made us look like an idiot? Fuck him! I'd do that for free.'

'And I'll help you,' Ilya said intently. 'Stupid fucking stuntman cunt, showing off jumping over tables like that. Cunt. Shall we do it now?' He tapped the Glock in his shoulder holster. 'I'm ready.'

'Me too! Let's go,' Nestor said eagerly, only to find Dasha's hand, with its frighteningly long and sharp dark red talons, planted squarely against his bulky chest.

'Not *now*!' she said impatiently. 'Jesus, how stupid *are* you two! I just went to see him – he'll be on his guard. And you saw how fast he moves. He's better than both of you put together. What were you thinking – just walk up to his door, ring his bell and shoot him when he sticks his head out to make it easy for you? Do you really think he'd be stupid enough to let that happen? We don't even know if he's armed!'

Nestor and Ilya hung their huge heads. Dressed all in black, their bodies thick with muscle, they looked like two bears being reproved by a brightly coloured parakeet.

'He's not going anywhere,' Dasha said confidently. 'The state of his face, he needs to be near the doctor still. No, you have to wait a little. Be patient. Just a couple of days, and then I have the perfect plan to make sure he's off his guard . . .'

December 29th

Aniela

' *I* got the audition! Aniela, I got it!' Melody burst into the Clinic, beaming from ear to ear. 'Ow!' She giggled, putting her hands gingerly to her face. 'I have to be careful – I keep smiling, and it hurts. But I'm so happy! They've actually agreed to see me!'

Aniela was playing patience on the table in reception. The history books on which she usually relied for entertainment had failed her in this crisis; she had desperately needed something to do with her hands, some physical distraction from the terrifying speculations that were running through her mind, and had been ever since she had run from Jon's apartment the day before. She had no way of contacting him, no way of knowing that he was still alive, and it was absolute torture not to know how he was or where he was. For the first time ever, she had taken a sleeping pill the night before, and even that hadn't been entirely successful at knocking her out; she had slept only fitfully and had had terrifying dreams. She was brewing herself camomile tea every half-hour, but that wasn't helping either; only digging out a pack of cards and laying out the appropriately named patience seemed to calm her restless mind a little.

She glanced up at the clock. Just after ten. In under two hours she could go to Jon's apartment, see if the note was there. *Or if Dasha Khalovksy and whoever she brings got there first, before he could leave.*

He must have got out first, he must. He knows what he's doing. Look how fast he jumped over that table at Christmas, how he dropped that drug in Mr Khalovsky's drink. And he was sure she was coming for him – no way would he have waited around to be killed by Dasha Khalovsky.

She'd kept telling herself that all yesterday, all this morning, knowing that she couldn't go up to the apartment before noon, couldn't deviate from the instructions Jon had given her to keep her safe. Visiting at her standard time was what the Clinic nurse would do: it gave her protection. Anything else would look as if she had some personal relationship to him, especially considering that they had arrived at and left Grigor's Christmas dinner together. And Jon was obviously concerned that no one suspect that they were connected in any way that wasn't strictly professional, in case Dasha Khalovsky used Aniela to get to him.

I understand, Aniela thought. *I do. He's trying to keep me safe. But I don't want to be safe! I want to help him any way I can—*

'Will you help me?' Melody was asking, waving a dog-eared copy of *Much Ado About Nothing*. 'Will you run lines with me? I want to make totally sure I'm off the book by tomorrow – it's tomorrow, the audition! Oh my God, Aniela, *tomorrow* – can you believe it?'

At least it'll be a distraction, Aniela thought, putting down the cards she was holding.

'Okay,' she said. 'What do I have to do?'

'You read Benedick – that's the part James is playing,' Melody said eagerly. 'And I read Beatrice – those are the highlighted lines – and you correct me if I get anything wrong. I can't believe I actually get to audition! My agent said he had to beg and plead and cry and call in tons of favours, but he pulled it off! I'm *beyond* excited!'

She clasped the paperback to her chest theatrically.

You see that she's an actress when she gets like this, Aniela thought; *it's not that her emotions aren't real, but she's magnifying them. Like a normal person, but with the volume turned all the way up, as if she has extra points on the dial . . .*

'No, wait!' Melody threw the book on the table, scattering some of the cards. 'I'm too wound up to read right now – let's go for a walk by the river first! It's a lovely day out there. I'll grab a coat and meet you in the lobby. Okay?'

She barely waited for an answer, tossing a smile back over her shoulder as she ran out again.

It's a good idea, Aniela thought, getting up and reaching for her own coat. *I could do with some fresh air. I'm going mad cooped up in here like an animal in a pen.*

The events of yesterday had been ridiculously dramatic. First Lubo bursting into the Clinic, and then evicting him from the flat; *ugh, so humiliating, having Melody see where I live, and Lubo behaving like a pig while I was away*. Melody had been a trouper: she hadn't batted an eye at the filthy flat, the empty beer cans and half-eaten containers of takeaway food, pizza cartons with crusts rattling in them – *as if Lubo was too bloody refined to eat crusts*, Aniela thought savagely. His smelly shoes, his dirty underwear: they'd picked it all up, squirming and squealing, shoved it into black binliners, and dropped it out of the window to the narrow patio outside. Lubo, mercifully, hadn't shown up: *probably drowning his sorrows in a Polish drinking den*, Aniela assumed. She'd told her neighbours – none of whom liked noisy, obnoxious Lubo – that he was no longer living there, and to ring the police if they saw him trying to get in. They hadn't even tried to mask their relief at the news.

And then, coming back to find that Jon had got in touch, running up to his place, having him greet me like that . . . Her whole body flushed with the memory of how they had made love yesterday, so slowly, so surely, building to the most phenomenal series of orgasms she had ever had. *He's amazing. The most amazing lover I could imagine.*

And it's more than likely that I might never see him again . . . Ugh! Stop it! You're torturing yourself!

Pulling on her coat, Aniela dashed out to the lobby of Limehouse Reach. A walk was just what she needed; Melody had come at exactly the right time. The security guards, slumped in their office behind the reception desk, drinking tea and watching TV, with only the most occasional glance at the huge panel of flickering CCTV monitors, all visibly perked up as Melody ran out of the lift, her black hair streaming behind her. Andy, sitting, bored, at the concierge's station, flashed her a huge smile and waved at her as she grabbed Aniela's arm and whisked her out of the back doors. Melody's bruising was still visible, her cheeks and lips puffier than they should be, but you could no longer tell unless you were close to her; from a distance, she was the classic beauty she had been before the first round of plastic surgery.

'You look really good,' Aniela told her as they speedwalked, arms linked, fast along the riverfront. 'For tomorrow, on stage, they will not even see that you have had surgery, if you put on make-up to hide the bruising.'

'Oh, don't worry!' Melody said blithely. 'I have *tons* of cover-up! And I'm in good shape – I measured myself yesterday, and I've actually lost a little around my waist and hips.' She grimaced. 'I've barely eaten a thing in the last few days. Seeing James, knowing about the Felicity thing, worrying about whether I'd get the audition – *anyway*, I'm not going to think about that right now! All I'm focusing on is Beatrice. *Becoming* Beatrice. I'm going to take all that worry and insecurity and shove it right into creating her in my mind. You know, she's a little older than some of the other girls in the play, she's got this crush on Benedick but she protects herself by being witty and bitchy to hide her true feelings – there's *so* much I can use about what I'm going through myself to really dig deep and get to Beatrice's core self—'

On another occasion, it might have been torture to be forced to hear Melody rattle on like this. But it suited Aniela perfectly. She couldn't really have made conversation, she was too on edge, too worried about Jon. Melody's stream of words flowed over her comfortingly, reassuring her that a response wasn't expected.

And besides, she helped me out so much yesterday. If all she wants in return is for me to listen to her, it isn't much to ask . . .

They turned back after twenty minutes, Aniela reminding Melody that she had a patient to visit at noon.

'Okay, you see him and then come to mine to run lines?' Melody asked. 'I'll order in some lunch, my treat, and then we can run lines in the afternoon.' She glanced sideways at Aniela. 'And maybe, if you're not busy, you could hang out afterwards, keep me company? We could watch some films, I can order in dinner – I'm so buzzed, I don't want to be alone. I worked out already! Aren't I being good! I got up at eight, went straight to the gym, and then I got back and there was a message from my agent – oh God, I'm *so excited* about this audition I can hardly *breathe*— '

She was off again, the flow of words unabating, all the way back to Limehouse Reach again: they had almost reached the back doors, Melody was already reaching in her coat pocket for her key card, when all of a sudden, a man jumped out from the side of the building, levelling a long black barrel directly at them.

Melody screamed. Aniela, in a flash, assumed that this was one of Dasha Khalovsky's henchmen, and that she was the target. Her heart leaped into her mouth, and she stared at him helplessly, knowing there was nothing she could do. He was too far away for her to try to grab the gun, and too close for her to run for cover. If he wanted to shoot her right now, she could do nothing, nothing at all—

The barrel clicked and whirred. And flashed. Several flashes, one after the other. It wasn't a gun. It was a camera.

I don't understand. Aniela looked at Melody, who had

thrown up her hands to cover her face, was ducking away, running for the doors.

'Melody!' the man yelled. 'Why did you have more surgery? What've you had done? Have you still got the boobs? Any regrets about going to Hollywood? Are you—'

Aniela finally understood what was going on. She glared at the photographer, a scruffy little weasel; she would have loved to slap him, but she knew that would make the story even better. Melody had got the door open, and Aniela went swiftly over to follow her inside, slamming it behind her to make sure the paparazzo couldn't get in.

'Bastard!' Melody said savagely, shaking all over. 'Ugh, I hate them!'

He was still out there, taking shots of them through the glass doors; the bodyguard stationed inside by Grigor, whose job it was to keep that entrance under surveillance, backed away, making sure he was not in camera range. It was most definitely not part of his job to get caught up in a story which had nothing to do with his employer.

Aniela steered Melody over to the bank of lifts, out of range of the photographer's lens.

'How did he know you were here?' she asked, frowning. 'We are very discreet at the Clinic. And here, too, the staff must never gossip. The managers have given Dr Nassri many assurances of confidentiality. He will be furious when I tell him—'

Melody took a deep breath, her body still quivering with rage.

'No, don't,' she said. 'I have a very good idea who tipped off that pap I was here. And it wasn't anyone from the Clinic or Limehouse Reach.' She stamped her foot furiously. 'It was that bitch Felicity – she's trying to mess with me before my audition tomorrow. That *cow*!'

She stamped again, an expression of glorious fury on her face.

'Well, I'm not going to let her win!' she said with utter determination. 'I'm *not*!'

Jon

Jon had found an excellent strategic vantage point. He was cautiously pleased with it, which was as much as Jon ever allowed himself to be. *Except where Aniela's concerned*, he corrected himself immediately.

And that was the problem; that was the entire problem in a nutshell. Everything was starting to be about Aniela. If it hadn't been for Aniela, he wouldn't be where he was right now, on the same damn floor as his own room, so he could keep it under surveillance. He had managed to locate an empty apartment at the far end of the hallway, the corner one, which had the advantage of not only a service door from the kitchen to the waste disposal area, but another door off a secondary living room which also led out to the communal hallway, presumably left over from two apartments having been knocked together. It had been painted over, but Jon had worked it back and forth until one good wrench would pull it open; he had, of course, picked the locks in that and the kitchen doors, to allow him multiple exit points in case of emergency.

The apartment itself was huge, lavish, and echoingly empty. Everything that could be covered in dust sheets had been; it was draped within an inch of its life. Even the staircase that led down from the mezzanine level had had its elaborate, carved wooden banister shrouded in white sheets, fixed there with masking tape. *It would make the perfect place for an ambush,* Jon thought. He wasn't planning an ambush, but you never knew, and he could take out a dozen of Dasha Khalovsky's heavies if they came after him here. He had already secured the perimeter; every access door had a neatly fixed tripwire that would set off a tiny alarm in his pocket if someone was trying to get in. With another little gizmo, he had put the security cameras in the corridor outside on the fritz for the duration of his exploration of the floor, while he'd been working out which apartment to squat in, first ringing doorbells, then picking the locks and calling 'Housekeeping!', making damn sure that there was no one inside before he committed to entering.

He'd been his normal methodical self, working his way down the hall, but this apartment was clearly the best choice. From the peephole on its front door, he could observe his old apartment, see whether Dasha Khalovsky would indeed send some guys to take him out. *And I can make sure that Aniela's followed instructions. That she doesn't poke around, try to find clues to where I've gone, do anything that might call attention to her.*

If it weren't for her, I'd have holed up on a whole different floor for a week or so, waiting till Dasha Khalovsky assumed I'd already gone. Then I'd've slipped out of the building and figured out somewhere to go. But I can't leave now, not while there's the slightest risk that Dasha might try to get to me through Aniela. She's anchoring me here.

He ought to mind that, he supposed. It was like being tied down, dependent on someone else's existence to feel good about your own. *But actually, it feels pretty good having someone to take care of. Sort of like there's a meaning to my life.* His frustration was not that he had to hang around Limehouse Reach for Aniela's sake, but that he couldn't be physically closer to her, couldn't protect her as well as he would like.

But then, if I were closer to her, I'd be trying to get in her pants the whole time, he thought ironically. *Which is the best reason why I should be up here and she should be downstairs in the Clinic. No way could I protect her with a perpetual hard-on – I'd be way too distracted.*

And, if he'd needed extra proof of the way she affected him, by a quarter to twelve his heart was already beating faster, just with the anticipation of seeing her. Jon heard the lift ping as she arrived on the dot of noon, a coat thrown over her uniform; she walked towards his door, stopped on noticing the note he'd left on the door, took it down and read it; then, shrugging, she folded it up, put it in her pocket and went back to the lift bank again. The entire visit took barely two minutes. He hated to see her vanish again, but was proud of her; *that was perfect. Anyone else watching wouldn't think she was anything but an agency nurse happy to have one fewer patient on her list.*

He was quite aware that someone might be watching the video feed of that little visit, or bribe the security guards downstairs to pass over the footage. How Aniela behaved had been very important, and she'd known that too.

Smart girl, he thought, very pleased.

And then he settled down to watch the video feeds himself, having rigged a system to tap into all the cameras on that floor. He'd alternate between them and the peephole, sleeping for twenty minutes every three hours, for the next week. Pretty standard for him; and here, he had a huge sofa to crash on, which was the height of luxury for a sniper used to bivouacking in a forest. He'd once slept in a tree for three days.

So, with a clear and conscious effort, he wiped any immediate thoughts of Aniela from his mind, anything but the task before him, and set his body clock to sniper time.

Andy

*A*ndy was bored out of his mind, but that was nothing new. Well paid as this job was, he was seriously thinking about calling his contacts at a range of five-star London hotels to ask them whether there was a concierge slot opening up any time soon. The pay would be a little lower, the perks less generous, but he'd be busy the whole time, and honestly, it would be worth it; yes, it was great to come into work early, use the gym, swim against the wave machine, steam in the sauna, jump into the hydrotherapy pool, and there was no way a concierge in a luxury hotel would ever be allowed to use its facilities.

But the boredom – this is so not worth it, even for the extra dosh. Andy was bursting at the seams to do his job, sort clients out with anything they might need, and his talents were going almost completely to waste. The fun he'd had helping Grigor Khalovksy organise the Christmas festivities, fantastic though it had been, had merely reminded him, when it was all over, of how much he loved to be busy.

I should go into event planning, he thought suddenly. *Wow! Well, that's an idea—*

Pulling his iPad towards him, he started to make a list of people he knew who worked in the field, his brain racing with excitement. *This is brilliant – finally, I actually have some sort of plan to get me out of here! I'm so sick of sitting in this chair all day!*

And focusing on his career would also distract him from thinking about Wayne Burns, which he was doing pretty much all day and all night. Andy wasn't an idiot; he knew that all that had happened between them was that he and a closeted footballer had given each other blowjobs, the kind of quick, strings-free sexual encounter that was par for the course for a lot of gay men. *It'd be crazy to think it meant any more than that.* The trouble was that Andy had had that kind of swift, mean-ingless fun plenty of times in the past – *but this felt different. It felt like there was something between us. A real connection. I felt so easy with him – like we could chat for hours, hang out. It wasn't just sex. It was something more.*

Oh, shut up, you starfucker, he told himself crossly. *Just cos he's famous, you've started to obsess about him. That's all it is, a celebrity crush. Been there, done that, now move on and stop imagining that he'll come back here in his silly yellow car that cost more than someone's house, and sweep you off your feet like Prince Charming and Cinderella—*

'Heya,' said a familiar voice, and Andy, who had been absorbed in thought, his head ducked over his iPad, looked up to see Wayne Burns standing in front of him, a shy smile on his face.

For a split-second, Andy actually thought he was hallucinat-ing, that somehow he had managed to call up an image of Wayne, incredibly lifelike, wearing a leather jacket and jeans, his hands shoved in his pockets, head ducked forward, showing a faint thinning of his hair on his scalp which, for some reason, made Andy feel oddly tender and protective. *But I couldn't make that up. I wouldn't imagine that he was going bald . . .*

Darting his head sideways, he saw the yellow Lamborghini, its driver's door open and hovering over the body of the car like a wing as the parking valet climbed inside. Dazed, he looked back at Wayne, knowing that his mouth was hanging open in shock, trying to come up with something to say, but utterly failing.

'Uh, I remembered that when I was here for Mr Khalovsky's party, you said that there were quite a few apartments here for sale,' Wayne said loudly, for the benefit of Kevin on reception and the security guards who were gawping at him. 'And that you might show me round a couple. I was thinking they'd be a good investment. Well, I was in the area and thought this might be a good time . . . are you busy?'

It was the most carefully prepared, fake-casual speech Andy had ever heard. *Lucky Wayne's a footballer,* he found himself thinking. *He'd never have made it as an actor.*

'No, it's fine,' Andy said, his mind racing as he stood up. 'Happy to show you round, Mr Burns. I'll just grab my master key.'

'Oh, call me Wayne, please,' Wayne said quickly, as Andy went over to the reception desk to sign the master key out.

'Jammy bastard!' Kevin hissed at him as he handed over the key card. '"Call me Wayne"!'

God, if you knew, Andy thought frantically. *Calling him by his first name's the least of it . . .*

'Right, follow me,' he said to Wayne, his voice as loud and falsely casual as Wayne's. 'We'll go up to the high floors – those apartments are the ones with the really nice terraces and balconies. The security here is excellent,' he added pointedly as he pressed the lift button and the doors of one car pinged open immediately. 'Cameras everywhere. *Everywhere,*' he added, nodding up to the corner of the car, as they stepped in and the doors closed behind them.

Wayne, who had been leaning towards Andy, his hands coming out of his jeans pockets, promptly shoved them back again, as if he couldn't trust them merely to hang by his side.

'Is there sound recording as well?' he asked.

Andy didn't dare to look at him.

'No,' he said, and it came out as a gasp.

'I can't stop thinking about you,' Wayne said. 'What we did. It was brilliant. I want to do it again.'

Andy heard himself giggle like a madman at Wayne's bluntness.

'Ooh, you sweet talker!' he said.

'I'm not good with words,' Wayne admitted, ducking his head in embarrassment. 'I just mean what I say, that's all.'

'I didn't mean to take the piss,' Andy said quickly, turning to glance at him. 'I was just teasing you. I feel the same, honestly I do.'

Wayne swallowed hard as the lift doors opened and Andy stepped out, the key card so sweaty in his hand that it almost slipped out of his grasp. The corridor seemed endlessly long, and Andy walked faster and faster in his eagerness to reach the apartment he'd chosen, until his pace became a trot, and then almost a canter; Wayne, behind him, was moving just as fast, and almost tumbled into him when Andy came to a halt in front of the door and slid the key into the slot. It whirred, a light flashed green.

Drawing in a deep breath, Andy pushed the door open, holding it for Wayne, standing back as professionally as he could as Wayne passed through. He smelt of soap and aftershave, his cheeks showed signs that a razor had been applied to them very recently: *for me*, Andy thought with a burst of pride. *He's scrubbed himself up all nice to come and see me—*

The door swung shut. Wayne promptly turned and flung himself on Andy, kissing him with such enthusiasm that Andy staggered back under Wayne's solid weight, his back slamming into the door. Their mouths locked, they pulled at each other's clothing, Wayne tearing at the buttons of Andy's uniform jacket, dragging it open, fumbling with the buttons of Andy's shirt, pulling that out of the waistband of his trousers, sliding his big hands over Andy's smooth chest and stomach. Andy groaned deep in his throat, kissing Wayne so hard he actually couldn't breathe for a long moment; then, as

Wayne practically ripped his trousers open, tugging them
down, lifting Andy's silky Hom briefs up and over the prong
of his cock, Andy almost wailed in anticipation. Because
Wayne had dropped to his knees, taken Andy's balls in one
hand, the base of his cock in the other, and was engulfing
Andy's cock in his mouth.

Andy braced himself against the door, grateful for its
support; his head was spinning, his cock was bobbing between
Wayne's lips, and the door was all that was keeping him
upright. Remembering how Wayne had responded to dirty
talk last time, Andy gave vent to the words that were on the tip
of his tongue.

'Yeah,' he said, 'that's right, suck that dick like you're starving. Take it all, suck it right down – I want to feel it shoving the
back of your throat, come on, take it all—'

Reaching down, he took Wayne's head in his hands, cupping
his ears, jerking his hips, sending his cock in and out of Wayne's
mouth; despite his words, Andy was careful not to push it too
far, to force Wayne to go faster than he knew how. *Last thing I
want's him gagging on my cock – let him get used to it, learn how
to work his reflex back there in his own time—*

Wayne had started moaning in pleasure at Andy's dirty talk,
the vibration in his throat an extra stimulus against Andy's
eager dick head. It was amazing. But it still wasn't quite
enough. Andy had been fantasising about this ever since
Boxing Day, had knocked himself off again and again to one
specific image, and he wanted to recreate that now.

*Who knows if I'll get another chance? Who knows if he'll ever
come back? If this is the last time, I don't want to let him go without
fucking him properly* . . .

Gently, he pulled back from Wayne's mouth, holding
Wayne's head still, looking down at his face; Andy couldn't
resist taking his cock and whipping it back and forth over
Wayne's lips, watching Wayne dart his tongue to lick it, his
eyes wide and bright with pleasure.

'Can I fuck you?' Andy said, his voice so guttural he hardly recognised it. 'I'm dying to fuck you . . .'

His cock had actually swelled at the words, and Wayne licked off the drops of pre-come.

'I want to be inside you so badly,' Andy said, his voice heartfelt.

The apartment had been closed up for months, all its furniture covered in dust sheets; but looking around him, Andy saw a huge L-shaped sofa across the room below the central staircase. Bending down, he grabbed Wayne's arm, pulling him up.

'Come on,' he said, guiding him over to the sofa, pushing him down. Weirdly, it was the only piece of furniture not shrouded by a dust sheet, and despite that it was shiny, as free of dust as if it had only just been cleaned.

Wayne was unzipping his jeans, pulling them and his plaid boxers down.

'Jesus,' Andy said devoutly, 'we need to get you some better underwear. Those are granddad pants.'

'They're from M&S!' Wayne said, embarrassed.

Andy grimaced.

'*Exactly.*'

Wayne, shrugging off his jacket, took a packet of condoms out of his pocket.

'I brought them,' he said. 'In case.' He was very red now. 'But I haven't – I haven't ever—' He swallowed. 'This is my first time,' he admitted.

'Fuck!' Andy, who had snatched the condoms from him and ripped one of the packets open, stopped dead, his cock throbbing impatiently. He remembered speculating that this might be the case, from what Wayne had said on Boxing Day, but had completely forgotten in the heat of the moment. 'Really?'

Wayne nodded sheepishly.

'Did you bring any lube?'

Wayne bit his lip. 'I didn't think of it,' he mumbled. 'But I want you to fuck me!' he said quickly, seeing Andy's face fall.

'I've been thinking about this so much – I really want you to—'

Andy dropped to the sofa next to him, taking his face in his hands, kissing him.

'I want to as well! *So* much! I just don't want to hurt you on your first time— '

'No, please! I want you to,' Wayne said, his voice impassioned. 'I don't care if it hurts a bit.'

He took the condom from Andy and started rolling it over Andy's cock. Behind the sofa, the sheet hanging over the balustrade of the staircase rustled slightly, as if in a breeze.

'Ah, shit,' Andy sighed. 'That feels so good . . . ' He looked at Wayne's imploring face. 'OK. I'll go really slowly, I promise.' He kissed Wayne's mouth, hard. 'Get on your knees,' he said, enjoying the way Wayne's eyes glazed with passion when Andy talked dirty to him. 'Hold onto the back of the sofa.'

Wayne scrambled to obey; he was kneeling on the L of the sofa, with plenty of room behind him. His arse was firm and round, deliciously hairy, and Andy licked his fingers, running it down Wayne's crack, around his bum, wetting him again and again with his spit, running his thumb around in a circle, teasing him, sliding in and out of him first with his thumb, then with two fingers, then three, opening him up, getting him to relax, until Wayne, braced against the back of the sofa, was bucking like a bronco and yelling for Andy to do it, do it now, that he was going fucking mad—

Positioning himself against Wayne's bum, his whole body arching with the need to do it, to fill him up, Andy rubbed the head of his cock against Wayne, pushed it in just a fraction, gave Wayne a chance to pull back, to change his mind, decide that he wasn't ready . . .

But with the full force of his stocky, muscly body, Wayne tightened his hold on the back of the sofa, arched his back, and jammed his buttocks so strongly back towards Andy that he drove himself almost fully onto Andy's cock.

'Fuck!' he shouted. 'Fucking *'ell!*'

Andy thought he would explode then and there.

'Fuck!' he yelled too, his hands digging into Wayne's round, hard glutes for dear life; he might be on top, but Wayne, one of the top athletes in the British Isles, was using everything he had to prove to Andy how much he wanted this, how eager he was that Andy shouldn't hold back. It was like being on top of a bucking bronco, riding a mechanical bull: Wayne reared up against the sofa, his arse pumping back and forth, his huge thighs bulging with the effort. All Andy could do was hold on for dear life, and look down to marvel at the sight of his cock sliding in and out of Wayne, his hands splayed, gripping Wayne's arse, the wonderful deep dimples at the top of his bum. He'd fucked a lot of muscly boys – that was his type, hard-muscled white boys, Celtic for preference, freckled, ginger, and stocky – and many of the gym rats were in amazing shape. But there was a real difference between muscles for show and ones developed for work. The sheer power of Wayne's body, even on his knees, was extraordinary.

He's as strong as a horse! Andy thought, imagining the positions being reversed – him on his back on the sofa, legs in the air, Wayne on top of him, pumping away, those thick arms bracing on either side of Andy's body. The image was too much, too powerful for him to stand. *God, that's it, that's too much. I can't hold out any longer—*

Yelling with the force of his release, he felt his body give it up, his cock blissfully, ecstatically, flooding the condom. Desperately, he collapsed on Wayne's broad, sweaty back, as big and solid as a table, reaching round Wayne's hips to find his cock; the moment Andy wrapped his hand around it, he felt Wayne let go too, pushing back to look down at Andy's fingers clasped around his dick, groaning in sheer pleasure at the sight, spurting hot come over his lover's hand and onto the sofa below.

Thank God it's leather! Andy thought, his head spinning, as, with extreme reluctance, he eased his cock out of Wayne, pulling off the condom, curling up around Wayne's wide back, wrapping his arms around him.

'Mate,' he said contentedly, 'I've had power bottoms before, but you're something else, you know that?'

Wayne wriggled to face him, kissing Andy on the lips.

'What's that then?' he asked. 'A power bottom?'

Andy kissed him back on the tip of his blunt little nose.

'You've got so much to learn,' he said. 'A power bottom sort of leads the way from below, if you know what I mean.'

'I don't just want to do that, though,' Wayne said quickly. 'I want to fuck you too. Is that okay? Do you—'

'You bloody bet I do!' Andy said, kissing his nose again. 'Show me no mercy.'

Wayne shivered from head to toe.

'I've been thinking about this so much,' he confessed. 'Being with another man, doing everything. All of this and more.'

'I can't believe you never did anything like this,' Andy said, shaking his head in wonderment.

Wayne settled back, his arm resting on Andy's thigh. 'I was spotted by a scout at eight,' he explained. 'I was playing in the Premier League at sixteen. You know? Everyone knew who I was, everyone knew my name. I couldn't've got away with anything. I didn't know who to trust. I was scared of even ordering magazines, let alone—' he blushed – 'a rent boy or anything. I didn't even fancy that anyway. I wanted to meet someone I liked, not pay for it. I'd go out with the lads to the clubs and just sit in the corner, trying not to stare at the waiters.'

Andy stroked his cheek. 'It sounds horrible,' he said gently, wondering at the irony of the situation. 'Poor little rich gay boy.'

Wayne made a funny snuffling noise.

'Chantelle got 'old of me at one of those nights out,' he said. 'Being that way herself. Takes one to know one, I suppose. She wanted to 'ang round Corinne without anyone thinking it was a bit odd.'

'So you were perfect cover,' Andy said. 'I get it.'

'Yeah. She said if everyone thought I was shagging her, they'd never think I was . . .'

'Gay,' Andy prompted, seeing that Wayne was having problems with the word.

'Yeah.'

'Wayne, you're gay!' Andy said firmly. 'If you can take a big black cock up your arse, you can say the word "gay".'

Something rustled briefly in the sheets hanging down from the staircase.

'Sounds like they've got a mouse,' Wayne said, looking round. 'Here, mousey-mousey.'

'*Wayne.* Don't change the subject. *Say it,*' Andy insisted.

'Okay. I'm gay!' Wayne blurted out.

'There. Doesn't that feel better?' Andy giggled. 'It even rhymed! We'll have you singing show tunes next.'

Wayne heaved out a long breath, sitting up, pulling Andy with him to curl up against the back of the sofa.

'It feels a bit better,' he admitted. 'But it's fucking scary.'

'I know,' Andy agreed. 'But it'll get easier.'

Wayne rubbed his palm over the top of Andy's head.

'I really like how your hair feels,' he said. 'It's sort of tickly.'

'I love your freckles,' Andy said, not to be outdone, running his index finger over Wayne's wide chest. 'I want to get a marker pen and join them up, do drawings on you. Like join the dots.'

Wayne giggled happily.

'You know,' Andy went on, 'I always fancied you. From afar, you might say. I'd be sitting round with my mates, and we'd be talking about celebrities we wanted to shag, and I'd say you. Honestly.'

Wayne actually stiffened in disbelief.

'No *way*,' he said. 'Wouldn't you pick, I dunno, some film

star or singer or someone? They used to call me Potato 'ead at school!'

Andy traced a line between Wayne's solid pectoral muscles. 'What can I say?' he asked. 'You're my type. I've always liked working-class white boys – Irish-looking gingers. I love Welsh boys, too. That lovely accent they've got.'

Wayne was shaking his head.

'I dunno what's weirder,' he said. 'That I'm your fantasy shag—'

'*Honestly*,' Andy said, bending to kiss Wayne's neck.

' – or that you can sit around with your mates and just talk about men you fancy. I've never done that in my life.'

He took a deep breath.

'Andy,' he started, and there was something in his voice that alerted Andy to sit up more, so that he could see Wayne's expression.

'Yeah?' he prompted.

'I was thinking . . .' Wayne began. 'What with you doing, you know, the job you do 'ere, and what you did for Mr K – well, it's organising, really, isn't it? Like, at a really 'igh level,' he hastened to clarify, in case Andy was offended.

Andy nodded. 'Pretty much.'

'So I was thinking – I sort of 'ave a PA, but she ain't very good, and even if she was – well, what I mean is, you could come and work for me instead. Would you fancy that? I've got a 'uge place. You could live there if you wanted. Chantelle's got 'er own wing and I don't even know when she's there, to be 'onest. You could travel with me – you'd 'ave anything you could want, I've got more money than I know what to do with—'

Excitement raced through Andy's veins, as hard and fast as a sniff of poppers, at the idea of being with Wayne, having a job to do that would be genuinely busy, fun, exciting; travelling the world with him, finding them amazing hotels to stay in, building a life together . . .

But there was a catch, and Andy already knew what it was.

'On the down-low, right?' he asked. 'That's what you mean. Chantelle out on stage with you wiggling her tits around, me in the wings sucking you off when you get home.'

Wayne winced in distress.

'That sounds *'orrible*,' he said. 'I didn't mean—'

'Yeah, you did,' Andy said sadly. 'You really did.'

Wayne hung his head.

'I *can't* come out,' he said haltingly. 'My family – my mates – the things they say about gay guys—'

'Those aren't your mates,' Andy corrected him. 'Not if they don't even know who you are.'

'It's really 'ard in footie,' Wayne said miserably. 'The racist shit people still say when the cameras aren't on them, you wouldn't believe. And you should 'ear what they say about gays, too.'

'There's more and more sports figures coming out now,' Andy said encouragingly.

'Not in football,' Wayne said grimly.

Andy sighed.

'You'd have so much support from the gay community,' he said. 'And you're so famous, it would be the most amazing thing! You know – you're so bloody good at your job, Wayne. You're a total star. What could they do to you?'

Wayne looked away.

'The gay community won't be there when fans are yelling "poof" at me, will they?' he said.

Andy stroked Wayne's shoulder; it felt as hard as stone now, every muscle in Wayne's body tensed.

'You *are* a poof,' he said. 'Me too. It's only an insult if you let it be one. Like my best girlfriend, she doesn't get offended if someone calls her a bitch – she goes, "Yeah, I am one, so what?" She's brilliant, you'd love her.'

'Oh, Andy—' Wayne's face crumpled in complete distress;

tears squeezed from his eyes, dampening his short red lashes. 'You make it sound so easy . . .'

Andy pulled him into his arms, cuddling up next to him.

'I don't think I'm brave enough,' Wayne sobbed. 'I don't think I'll ever be brave enough. And you won't be with me if I'm not, will you?'

Andy, his mouth pressed against Wayne's forehead, realised that he was crying too.

'I can't,' he said. 'I really want to, but I can't. It would be so great, I'd love to be with you and run things and travel and everything, I think you're amazing – but I can't go back in the closet for anyone. I can't hide who I am, not even for you.'

'I'm sorry I asked,' Wayne said, crying all out now. 'I shouldn't 'ave asked—'

'No – no, it was lovely – I wish I could, but I can't, I just *can't*—'

Andy was sobbing just as hard as Wayne. The best, most magical sex of his life had transmuted into something even better, a real chance at love, and as soon as it had been dangled in front of him, he had had to turn it down. *But I can't do anything else*, he knew. *I don't have a choice, I really don't.*

There wasn't anything left to say. It was a stalemate that neither of them could resolve. So they held onto each other, and cried their hearts out instead.

Jon

Man, that was really sad, Jon thought as he crawled out from underneath the sheet hanging over the staircase. *That was* Brokeback Mountain. *Jesus, it was like watching a film that knows how to grab you by the balls and hold on tight. First it was really hot, and then it broke your heart.*

Jon stood up, stretching, looking at the sofa; they'd wiped it clean before they left, but the dents they'd made in the leather were still visible. He had to admit that the sounds of them doing it had been more than a little arousing; he'd got a hard-on listening to them fucking. *That's why guys are homophobic,* he realised. *They're scared of getting turned on watching gay guys doing it.*

He shrugged, grinning at the idea. *Who cares?* he thought cheerfully. *You'd have to be made of stone not to get an erection listening to that.*

Andy and Wayne had torn into the apartment at such speed that it was all Jon could do to roll under the staircase, hide under the sheltering sheets. And then they'd dressed and gone out slowly, sadly, in almost complete silence, the opposite of their happy, passionate entrance.

Seems a real shame, Jon thought. He remembered Andy and Wayne from Grigor Khalovsky's Christmas dinner, two nice, healthy, cheerful young men. *They like each other, they turn each other on, they want to be together, or at least give it a shot; who the hell are they hurting?*

Sport was tough, though. He could see that. Try to come out in the NFL, it wouldn't be pretty. It'd take a brave man to stand up and say he was gay in that kind of macho environment. But he understood Andy, too, saying that he didn't want to hide who he was. He was funny, too. That line of his – 'If you can take a big black cock up your arse, you can say the word "gay"' – had actually made Jon snort with laughter; he'd clapped his hand over his nose to stifle it and made the sheets rustle for a moment.

Poor guys. It's hard enough to find love. When you do, you should be able to grab it with both hands and not look back—

He was rolling back his shoulders, linking his hands behind his back, as he walked to the door to take up position at the peephole once more. But as the word 'love' ran through his mind, he stilled for a moment, staring straight ahead, as he saw Aniela's face in front of him as clearly as if it were being projected on a gigantic screen.

Dammit to hell and back, he thought. *I love her, don't I?*

This is real trouble. I'm in deep enough already. If I want to play this smart, I should get out now. Before I go even deeper and get stuck.

I should get the hell out of here and never look back.

December 30th

Melody

'Melody? They'll see you now,' the director's assistant said, sticking her head around the door.

Standing up, Melody looked down at the polystyrene cup of tea in her hand. She hadn't really wanted it, had just got it from the battered old drinks machine as an excuse to stand up and walk across the room, and it had been so disgusting that she couldn't take more than a few sips: now she didn't know what to do with it. If she threw it in the bin, the nasty brown liquid would run through the liner and make a horrible mess for the cleaners. But if she left it out, it would just stand there all day, and the cleaners would have to deal with it anyway . . .

Going over to the machine, she tilted the cup, pouring the tea into the drip tray, throwing the empty cup into the bin before following the assistant, who was looking visibly impatient. But as their careers started to take off, James and Melody had made a pact with themselves that they'd try not to act like the entitled stars they'd seen behave like imperious spoiled children, making ridiculous demands of everyone around them. And it was even more important not to act like a diva now that she was trying to convince everyone in the London theatre world that she was back from LA and more serious than ever about her stage career.

It hadn't worked on the assistant, though, who sneered at Melody as she nodded at the door to the rehearsal room. And it didn't work on Cate Bennett, the National Theatre producer, either. Women tended to be not very friendly to Melody, or at least not until she'd won them round by proving that she wouldn't flirt with their boyfriends, or rattle on complacently about how fat she felt in the expectation of being contradicted. Also, the trouble with having had the plastic surgery was that it had made a lot of other women bitterly resentful of Melody's taking what they considered an unfair advantage. Melody could understand that. Buying bigger lips and bigger breasts, turning yourself into a male fantasy version of yourself, wasn't exactly feminist.

And as she saw that Cate, sitting behind a trestle table in the rehearsal room, was barely acknowledging her entrance, let alone getting up to greet her, Melody's heart sank.

She's already taken against me. I can tell.

Martin Cavendish, the director, jumped up, exclaiming:

'Melody, darling! *Lovely* to see you!'

He was coming round to take Melody's hands, smile down at her; swiftly, Melody reached up to peck him on each cheek, so that he wouldn't try to kiss her and smear the layers and layers of light foundation and cover-up that she had spent a full hour patting on delicately with her fingertips. She had added mascara, the faintest trace of black eye pencil, and a quick gloss of Lancôme Juicy Tube, nothing else: this was for Cate's benefit, to demonstrate that Melody wasn't some vain, make-up-plastered starlet.

'Hi, Cate, it's lovely to see you again,' she said sincerely, leaning across the table to proffer her hand to the producer.

Show respect and deference to the older women. The men don't care about it as long as you flirt with them – gay and straight, they're just the same in that. But the few women in power have worked much harder than the men to get where they are, and if you forget that, they'll slap you down so hard and fast you'll be reeling for days.

'Thank you both so much for agreeing to see me,' she said, sitting down on the straight-backed chair in front of the table as Martin resumed his own seat. 'I'm really grateful.'

'Thank your agent,' Cate said curtly. 'He called in a lot of favours.'

'I'm sure he had to,' Melody agreed. 'I get that you wouldn't have been keen on me auditioning. I'd have felt just the same in your position.'

'Well, that's refreshingly honest!' Martin said, picking up a pencil from the table and beginning to gnaw on it. Melody had worked with him before, and knew that he always fiddled with a pencil while he was working, so she didn't take Martin's absent-minded munching, nor the strange faces he pulled while doing it, as negative signs.

There was no way, however, that she could interpret Cate Bennett's next words as anything but negative.

'So, Anthony said you'd had your face put back to normal,' she commented. 'Tits too? I can't see under that baggy cardi you're wearing, and Anthony was too much of a gentleman to mention your boobs.'

Melody had dressed down, the classic actress-going-on-a-serious-audition outfit of jeans over suede ankle boots, a striped T-shirt and one of her light cashmere flowing wraps, which she had caught in around her hips with a wide leather belt. She stood up, undid the belt and shrugged the wrap from her shoulders; Martin spat the pencil out of his mouth with a mumble of inarticulate protest. The T-shirt wasn't clinging, but it showed that Melody's breasts, in a wire-free sports bra that didn't irritate the scars where the implants had been removed, were demonstrably back to where they had been pre-*Wonder Woman* and the ballooning D cups.

'Had to ask,' Cate said brusquely, as Melody folded the long draped wrap around her and rebuckled her belt. 'I mean, you couldn't be bouncing round the stage like a Page Three Girl.' She sniffed with laughter. 'You couldn't have played Juliet with those tits you had done! What's she supposed to be, thirteen!'

Melody winced at the reference to Juliet, as Cate must have intended.

'I made an awful mistake,' she said firmly, biting the bullet. 'I was an idiot and I let down everyone on that production. I would never, ever do that again.'

'Well, that's—' Martin began, picking up the pencil and starting to puncture it with teeth marks again. But Cate interrupted:

'Bloody right you won't,' she said. 'Anyone who wanted to cast you again would be an idiot not to get you to sign a document agreeing to pay damages if you pull out at any stage.'

'I'd sign anything you wanted me to,' Melody said, looking her straight in the eyes. 'I want this part so badly. I'm desperate to play Beatrice. I need this much more than you need me, and this is my dream role. I'm word-perfect already. I've been doing nothing but learning lines for the last week.'

'And what about you and James?' Cate pressed on. 'We don't want any offstage drama. This production will be down in Stratford for two months before we bring it to London. That's a *small* town.'

'Village, really,' Martin chimed in through his mouthful of pencil. He removed it, picked a little bit of wood from his teeth with great delicacy and put the pencil behind his ear. 'Just five streets and a river. Any fuss or muss gets magnified in Stratford.' He looked directly at Melody. 'You know that, don't you?'

She nodded emphatically. Stratford-upon-Avon, Shakespeare's birthplace and home of the newly rebuilt Royal Shakespeare Theatre, was as small as Martin described it, at least for the actors; they lived and worked in the same tiny little geographical area, hung out in the same pub opposite the theatre – the Black Swan, known by the actors as the Dirty Duck. Martin was quite right: feuds, love affairs, romantic tangles, all became intensified in the time actors spent there.

But she had prepared for this question too.

'This happens all the time in our job,' she said, looking from Martin to Cate. 'We have to work with people who cheated on us, or we're divorced from, or who upstaged us in the last show, or walk around naked in front of our boyfriends when they drop into the dressing room to see us. It's the nature of the business. I can work with James without any problem at all, and he's a professional too. I know he can work with me. We have brilliant chemistry,' Melody added, segueing into a point she had been really keen to emphasise. 'That won't change. We're really strong on stage together.'

'Since I didn't see your Juliet to his Romeo,' Cate observed unpleasantly, 'I'll have to take your word for that.'

That was hard to take. *I've already apologised to everyone*, Melody thought savagely. *I've told them I was an idiot, and that I'll sign anything they want me to, and I've shown her that my boobs aren't ridiculously big any more – that was an unfair dig—*

But it was an audition, and Melody was an actress, and her expression of enthusiasm and sincerity didn't change one iota; she nodded seriously at Cate's comment. She didn't try to respond to it, though, which meant that it was left hanging in the air, sounding increasingly unpleasant. Martin shifted uncomfortably and put the pencil back in his mouth again.

'I see you're wearing make-up,' Cate said, looking narrowly at Melody. 'I assume that you're covering up bruising from your plastic surgery.'

Despite herself, Melody couldn't help tightening her lips a little at this. It wasn't just make-up; she'd rung a make-up artist friend of hers for advice, and he had suggested his strategy of last resort – using haemorrhoid cream to temporarily shrink the swelling on her face. Aniela, though grimacing at the idea, hadn't thought that it would interfere with the healing of Melody's surgery, and it had been surprisingly effective, bringing down the remaining puffiness, even on her lips. The foundation had been layered over the Preparation H once it had taken effect; she certainly wasn't going to admit to the existence of the latter.

'Just some cover-up,' she said, managing not to drop her eyes. 'The surgery's been a total success. I wanted to put myself back exactly the way I was—'

'Can you take off the make-up?' Cate interrupted. 'Let's have a look at exactly what we're dealing with here.'

This Melody had not expected. She had prepared for a great deal that this audition could throw at her, but not the demand to wipe her face clean. She pressed back against the chair, desperate not to humiliate herself this way, to bare her fading bruises to Cate and Martin. Her brain raced, trying to think of a good excuse to say no.

Just then, Martin chomped down on the pencil so vigorously that he broke off the rubber at the end. An expression of total surprise widened his eyes as he spat the rubber onto the table.

'Ugh!' he exclaimed. 'That tasted *vile*!'

'It's a rubber, Martin,' Cate said impatiently. 'They always taste nasty.'

'I need some water . . .' Martin got up and ambled across the room to the water fountain. 'Rinse my mouth out . . . ugh, so *rubbery* . . .'

He poured himself some water, sipped a little, and then nodded towards the door.

'Melody, come and read, won't you?' he said. 'Or not even read, if you're sure you're off the book. I think we might as well have you run a scene or two. Cate? Coming to watch?'

'But I wanted her to—'

'Oh, this isn't a film,' Martin said vaguely. He was always most vague when he was making a very definite point, Melody remembered. 'Is it? She looks fine now, doesn't she? I mean, if she suddenly looks appalling in the stage lights, we'll have a concern. So let's go and see. Shall we?'

He was holding the door open now, nodding at Melody;

with huge gratitude at his rescue of her, she jumped up, grabbed her bag and coat, and crossed the room to where Martin was standing. Behind her, she heard Cate push her chair back. *What have I done to her?* Melody wondered as Cate followed. *Why is she picking on me like this? Everything up to wiping off my make-up was fair enough: that was just nasty.*

But, determinedly, so that it didn't interfere with the performance she was about to give, she dismissed it from her mind as they made their way along the narrow corridors of the theatre, down a rickety staircase, round a flat and onto the boards of the stage. It was lit up already; Melody dumped her stuff in the wings as Martin and Cate went down the side steps and into the stalls, taking up seats next to each other halfway down the centre aisle.

'Right, Act Four, Scene One,' Martin said, pulling out a very dog-eared paperback copy of *Much Ado* from his jacket pocket. 'Hero's collapsed, exeunt everyone but Beatrice and Benedick – can someone get James? I think he went to Costa—'

'No, I'm back,' called a voice from the back of the stalls, and the next second Melody saw her ex-boyfriend appear, walking down the aisle with his characteristic loose-limbed cricketer's lope.

'We're lucky enough to have our Benedick reading in today,' Martin said airily, as Melody, momentarily paralysed with shock, stared at James. 'James, Melody says she's off the book, and you are too, aren't you? Fantastic! Look, I'm not going to say a word. Why don't you two just go for it and I'll give notes afterwards if I want you to run anything again . . .'

Melody barely heard him. There was a drumming of blood in her ears, a wild excitement rushing through her that went above and beyond the normal butterflies of the audition process. It would have been overwhelming if Melody, young as she was, didn't already have a great deal of stage experience. It helped, of course, that she'd trained at a British stage school. American actors didn't train much at drama school for stage work; the ones who wanted to work in film, which meant almost all of them, focused intently on that, and when they were cast in Broadway plays very few of the most famous names had any idea how to dominate a stage, to project their voices in a shout or a whisper, to use their bodies in proportion to the proscenium. Melody did.

And she'd already been through a ton of auditions. For *Wuthering Heights*, there had been a gruelling three rounds of call-backs; her nerves had been in pieces by the last set of them, but not a flicker of nerves had shown on her face. She'd taken every single little last bit of fear and panic, used her desperation to get the part, her knowledge that this was the big break that could catapult her out of being a complete unknown onto the cover of Sunday magazines; she'd wrapped that all up in a big ball and dived into it and come out as Cathy Earnshaw.

Watching James put one hand on the stage, vault up easily without even using the stairs, jump to his feet next to her and smile shyly, she thought, with a rush of exhilaration:

I can do that again. Thank God this is a big emotional scene. I can take everything I'm feeling and use it and be Beatrice—

This scene started just after Beatrice's beloved cousin had collapsed on what was supposed to be the happiest day of her life, her wedding to the man she loved; she had been humiliated, falsely accused of cheating on her fiancé in a cruel plot. And Beatrice was about to tell Benedick, who loved her, that he would have to take her side, take revenge on her cousin's accusers, if he ever wanted to be with Beatrice.

Tears were already forming in her eyes. She dropped to her knees, her head falling into her hands. James took a couple of steps back, turned away, gathering himself, turned back and caught sight of her for the first time as Benedick: coming quickly over, he stopped next to her and said, his voice full of concern:

'Lady Beatrice, have you wept all this while?

'Yea,' Melody said into her hands, but her voice carried clearly right up to the gallery. 'And I will weep a while longer.'

'I will not desire that,' James said, kneeling beside her.

Melody lifted her head, letting her face be seen both by him and by Cate and Martin. Tears were pouring down it. She had always been able to cry easily; it was an incredibly useful knack for an actor. 'You have no reason,' she said bitterly. 'I do it freely.'

'Surely I do believe your fair cousin is wronged,' James said.

With a fluid, shocking gesture, Melody jumped to her feet, her fists clenched by her sides. 'Ah, how much might the man deserve of me that would right her!' she spat out.

James took one of her hands, looking down at it: she wouldn't clasp his, leaving hers squeezed into a fist.

'Is there any way to show such friendship?' he asked tentatively, still on his knees.

She looked down at him, meeting his eyes. It was like a stab, as if he had driven his hand right into her chest and taken hold of her heart – which was his, had always been his. His hair fell over his face, and he shook it back, staring up at her, waiting for her answer. He was James, and he was Benedick, and she loved them both.

'A very even way, but no such friend,' she said more gently, and she opened her fist, letting her fingers wrap around his.

'May a man do it?' James came to his feet, still holding her hand; she threw it back at him as she turned away, and said, wrapping her arms around her chest:

'It is a man's office, but not yours.'

It was Melody, not Beatrice, who waited for the next words, because Melody knew what they would be, and she thought it would break her heart to hear him say them. He didn't move. He stood there, looking at her back, and said with great tenderness:

'I do love nothing in the world so well as you: is not that strange?'

Beatrice threw his words back at him, because Beatrice too was broken-hearted, but for her cousin. Melody tapped into that, used the dialogue to follow to reject him until he stormed up to her, grabbed her, turned her round, shook her till her hair fell over her shoulders, and made her admit:

'I love you with so much of my heart that none is left to protest . . .'

They were on a roll. You always knew when it was really good, when the energy was flowing between you perfectly, like a ball you were tossing back and forth in one of those drama-school warm-up exercises; but even though you were almost completely absorbed with the scene, with each other, the awareness of that audience watching you avidly was always like a great light shining on you, warming you, that you ignored at your peril. If you were tapping into it, you knew, because you felt the warmth and the illumination feeding you, growing your performance like a flower in a greenhouse.

And Melody did: she realised in a rush how much she had missed the stage, how happy she was to be back here. By the time she reached the famous lines, she was hot with conflicting emotions, love and hate wrestling inside her for dominance, hate winning as she spat out:

'Oh that I were a man! What, bear her in hand until they come to take hands; and then, with public accusation, uncov-ered slander, unmitigated rancour. Oh *God*, that I were a man! I would eat his heart in the marketplace!'

It was good. It was very good indeed. She could tell by the quality of silence as she delivered the lines, as they hung in the air of the auditorium, as Benedick's eyes widened in horror as he realised that Beatrice was utterly serious. She convinced him; he agreed to challenge her cousin's fiancé to a duel.

'I will kiss your hand,' he said, 'and so I leave you.' He suited the action to the word, and as their eyes met over their linked hands, the tension between them was palpable. James's voice dropped, deep and sensual, sending a shiver down Melody's back: she stared at him, unable to let him go; she was clinging to him, in love with him, as she had always been, as Beatrice had always been.

James raised their hands, pulling her close to him.

'By this hand,' he said softly, 'Claudio shall render me a dear account. As you hear of me, so think of me. Go, comfort your cousin: I must say she is dead: and so, farewell.'

It was the last line, the end of the scene, but they couldn't let go. Slowly, James lowered his head, and Melody stayed very still as he kissed her, a sweet promise Benedick made to Beatrice, their hands still clasped between them. Her eyes fluttered closed. He stepped back, extending his arm to its full length, their fingers stretching out, pulling apart, the tips touching till the very last moment; then he turned and ran offstage, leaving her standing there, looking after him. Crying again.

No one applauded. You never did at auditions; that only happened in films, cheesy ones where the director and producers would jump to their feet, clapping madly, and then there'd be a cut and she'd be in front of an audience, a huge bouquet in her arms, flowers raining down on her.

But the silence, intense and profound, was as good as applause. Melody stood in the centre of the stage, the lights on her, knowing how good she had been.

I should get this part. I should be Beatrice.

And there's no way Cate can deny that James and I really do have great chemistry.

'Well! That was very nice,' Martin said, standing up. 'Um. Very nice. Great work too, James.'

'Thanks.' James came back onstage, his hands now in the pockets of his jeans, his gaze on Melody. He nodded at her. 'You were brilliant.'

'Well, I think we've seen all we need to see!' Martin went on, and Melody's heart leapt; *but of course he's not going to tell me I have the part! That only happens in films too. He's going to say he'll let my agent know in due course—*

'We'll let your agent know in due course,' he continued. 'Thanks so much for coming in.'

She gathered up her bag, slung on her coat, and went down the side steps, walking down the aisle, smiling a goodbye at Martin and Cate; you got out quickly after an audition, that was protocol. You gave the people you'd read for time to digest your performance, and, ideally, leave them wanting more.

And to prepare themselves for the next actress – though you hope you don't bump into her as you go out—

Melody had wanted to exit through the auditorium, not just to give her the chance to say goodbye to the director and producer, but also to avoid precisely that, the chance of bumping into the next candidate. She wanted so badly to get this part, to play Beatrice to James's Benedick – *to rehearse with him, to kiss him every night onstage, to get him to fall in love with me again – because I really think he would fall in love with me again if we were together – I saw the way he just looked at me* – that the thought of another woman taking her place on that stage was unbearable. So she didn't look back, in case another actress was stepping on stage at this moment, smiling at James: but as she pushed open one of the swing doors at the back of the stalls and stepped into the lobby, she was horrified to see Felicity sitting there, wrapped in her tweed coat with the ruffled collar, a coffee in her hand, curled up on one of the velvet benches reading a magazine, looking as cosy as if this were her living room.

'Oh, Melody!' she said casually, uncurling and stretching out her legs. 'Are you finished? That was quick.'

It can't have gone well, the subtext ran. *Since they didn't really want you to read for any length of time.*

'It was *so* nice of them to see you!' she added, tossing back her long blonde hair. 'Cate told me she did it as a favour to Anthony. Sweet of her, wasn't it?'

Felicity stood up, threw her magazine to the bench, and

held out her coffee to Melody, who was so dumbfounded that she took it.

'Mind getting rid of that for me?' she said, walking towards the theatre doors. 'Or you could finish it if you want. I have to read now. It's a formality, really, of course. Cate's pretty much promised me Beatrice already. Oh!' She turned to deliver the *coup de grâce*. 'I saw you in the paper! Some paparazzo shot outside your building. God, those bruises! They looked *awful*. *Not* exactly the publicity you want, is it?'

She pushed open the door and went through. Melody caught the door with her foot, watching Felicity dance lithely down the aisle, bend to kiss Cate, who actually stood up to hug Felicity in return. *No wonder Cate was so hard on me*, Melody thought bitterly. *She's on Felicity's side. That audition was just a sham, a favour to Anthony. Felicity's acting as if she has this already all sewn up.*

Felicity was standing at the bottom of the stage now, in the aisle. She shrugged off her coat and tossed it onto the front row, holding both her hands up to James, saying winsomely:

'Pull me up, darling!'

James bent over, taking her hands, lifting her up; she swung her legs up under her and landed on the stage.

'Right!' she said, throwing her hair over one shoulder and flashing a big smile at Martin and Cate. 'I'm ready! What do you want me to do?'

Melody turned away, letting the door swing shut. She went slowly up the foyer stairs, her footsteps resounding on the tiled floor, feeling as if all the breath had been knocked out of her with one huge punch to her gut. A woman doing paperwork in the box office looked up as Melody passed, said something friendly, but Melody didn't notice; she was immersed in a deep dark cloud of misery.

If I hadn't done so well just now – because I know I did really well, I know no one could be better than me, I know Felicity can't be as good as I just was—

I was so close – I should have had that part! I should!

Because Felicity had taken it from her, as she had taken James. He, and Beatrice, were already gone.

The cold December air outside felt heavy and wet; snow had been predicted, and she looked up at the sky, which was dark already, at barely four in the afternoon. It was clear, another indication of snow. She went down the short flight of steps to the pavement, and as she did so a man jumped out of nowhere and a series of flashes went off in her face.

'Melody!' he said. 'Just been auditioning with Dr Who? How was it seeing your ex-boyfriend? How do you feel about his shagging Felicity Bell? And any comments on your surgery? We've all seen the photos by now!'

Felicity tipped him off, Melody knew. *Just as she tipped off that pap outside Limehouse Reach yesterday.*

She flashed her best and most brilliant smile for the camera as she walked across the pavement and held out her arm for a passing cab: she knew better than to say a word. She kept the smile on her face as she stepped in, pulled the door shut and sank into the seat, kept it plastered on as the cab drove away.

And she kept smiling, her face reflected back at her in the Plexiglas of the partition, all the way back to Limehouse Reach. Because she was damned if she was going to cry one more tear this year.

December 31st –
New Year's Eve

Andy

'*O*oh, look, it's the pretty boy!'
    Diane swept into the Limehouse Reach foyer, her girls trailing behind her in two wings: they looked like beautiful, migrating birds in arrow formation. She waved at Kevin on reception, but didn't stop there, gliding over to Andy's desk.

'Hello, darling,' she said, holding out her hand to him. 'Remind me of your name, won't you? If you're not a paying client, I've got a *very* bad memory for names.'

'It's Andy,' he said, taking Diane's hand and kissing it. She cooed at him in pleasure.

'What a lovely boy you are,' she said, patting his cheek. 'Are you coming up to party with us later?'

'We're putting on a show!' said the tallest girl excitedly. 'We didn't really do it on Boxing Day, so I thought I'd see if Mr K wanted us to do it on New Year's Eve, and he's well up for it!'

Diane shot her a frigid look.

'Um, *very keen* on it,' the girl corrected herself.

'Sounds great,' Andy said, trying his best to sound enthusiastic.

'I've got tons of cossies,' the girl went on, waggling the handle of the small wheeled suitcase she was pulling. 'And wings!' She nodded at the big flat bag which another of the girls was carrying. 'We're going to be naughty angels! Like in the Victoria's Secret fashion show!'

'God, give it a rest, Kesha,' another girl sighed. 'You're banging on about it so much I'm bored with it already.'

'Wait till you get your wings on,' Kesha said, tossing back her long fake ponytail. 'Everyone gets excited when they've got wings on.'

'That *is* actually true,' a third girl agreed.

Diane winked at Andy as she turned away.

'Come on, girls,' she said. 'You're wasting your time with this one. But we'll see you for the party, eh?'

'Yes, ma'am,' Andy said. 'I'll be seeing the guests up and then popping up later. Mr Khalovsky was kind enough to ask me.'

'Toodle-pip, then!'

Waving her fingers at him rather like the Queen bidding a subject farewell, Diane stalked elegantly across to the recessed penthouse floor lift. One of Grigor's bodyguards had already summoned it and was waiting there, holding the doors open for Diane and her girls.

Andy watched them all tuck into the generous lift car, the doors sliding shut.

'You lucky cunt,' Kevin said enviously. 'Getting to see all those gorgeous birds in the altogether.'

'Kevin, I'm *gay*,' Andy said, sighing.

'Oh yeah!' Kevin grinned. 'I always forget. It's a—'

'Compliment,' Andy finished, in tandem with Kevin, rolling his eyes. 'Look, Kev, it isn't a bloody compliment, all right? You keep saying that! It's like you think that, just because I'm gay, I have to hold myself back from jumping your big fat lardarse. And I really don't, okay? I don't fancy you.'

'Andy—' Kevin started nervously, but Andy kept going.

'It's not a compliment to be straight-acting, you know!' Andy snapped. 'I'm just being professional at work, that's all. I really don't appreciate all the "I forget you're gay" nonsense, and I'd be grateful if you cut it out in future.'

Kevin was looking mortified, but Andy didn't care. He stood up and walked swiftly to the doors, activating the automatic release, standing outside in the cold winter air. It had snowed the night before, but hadn't been quite cold enough to settle; tonight, though, all the forecasts were saying that it would. There hadn't been a white Christmas this year, but there certainly would be a white New Year's Eve.

Andy tilted his head and looked up at the sky, clear and whitish-grey. The air was sharp, and without the good-quality wool fabric of his winter uniform, he would already have been shivering. Honestly, he welcomed the cold: it was bracing, cutting through the dismal mood he was in as he faced New Year's Eve, a time for parties and celebrations and kissing the person you loved at the stroke of midnight: *well, I can't say I love Wayne, not yet. I barely know him. But I'd love to be kissing him at midnight.*

He sighed again.

And instead I'll be watching a few really rich guys fuck a bunch of escorts. Yay! I must be the luckiest gay boy on earth . . .

Aniela

She was exactly where she wasn't supposed to be. Inside Jon's old apartment. And she had a sense that he knew it, too. She didn't know how or why, where he might be. Maybe he had rigged invisible spy cameras in here or something. But she had a very strong feeling that Jon was nearby, keeping an eye on her, as she supervised the patient being wheeled into the apartment, a nose splint and surgical dressings over his heavily bruised face.

Apart from her worry about Jon's interdiction, the patient was a thoroughly welcome distraction. He was a rich business-man who had had a nasty accident on a skiing holiday in Zermatt – skied straight into a tree and smashed up his face – and had insisted on being flown back to London to have his face operated on by the plastic surgeon who had done such a good job on his nose a few years ago.

Poor man, Aniela thought sympathetically, hearing him breathing stertorously though the nose that Dr Nassri, flown in from his own holiday in Sharm el-Sheikh, had painstakingly reset yesterday. *This is not how he wanted to be spending New Year's Eve.*

Mind you, he'll be so out of it for the next couple of days on painkillers that he won't even know the date.

Aniela had been alerted at lunchtime yesterday of the patient's arrival, and had busied herself calling in another theatre nurse and an orderly from the emergency service they used; by the time Dr Nassri and the patient, Jeremy Bingham-Smythe, arrived, she had everything set up with her customary efficiency. Dr Nassri had operated, resetting not only Mr Bingham-Smythe's nose but his broken cheekbones and one orbital socket, declared the procedure a success, and left Mr Bingham-Smythe to rest overnight, with Aniela and the agency nurse taking turns to check in on him; this morning the surgeon had returned, and pronounced Mr Bingham-Smythe doing well enough to be moved to Limehouse Reach to convalesce. Aniela had tried to suggest that the patient go to the third apartment the Canary Clinic owned in the building, but what she hadn't realised was that the third one was having rewiring work done and was not in a fit state for a patient to occupy.

Dr Nassri was really odd about Jon, she remembered. *I honestly don't know whether he was relieved that Jon had taken off unexpectedly, or freaked out. Probably a mixture of both.*

So there had been nothing Aniela could do to prevent Mr Bingham-Smythe being settled into Jon's apartment. *It's been a couple of days,* she told herself. *If Dasha Khalovsky sent anyone to kill Jon, they'll have come and gone by now. Found that he's not there, and left.*

There was nothing else she could do: she had no way to get in touch with Jon. But she was planning to spend most of her time in the apartment. That way, if Dasha Khalovsky's goons did turn up, she could open the door and tell them that they had the wrong apartment, that Jon had left two days ago, and that the Clinic had installed a new patient.

And pray to God that'll work, she thought grimly, as she followed the orderly into the bedroom, and helped him move a happily sedated Mr Bingham-Smythe, his pupils dilated with Co-codamol, into the bed that she had once shared with Jon. The cleaning service had come, of course: the sheets had been changed, everything fluffed up for the new arrival. But the pillows she was stacking to keep Jeremy Bingham-Smythe's upper body propped up, so he could breathe through his splinted nose, the mattress he was resting on, even the duvet she was pulling up and smoothing over his chest, had not been changed, might, conceivably, smell of Jon still under the fresh new sheets . . .

'All right, you can go now,' she said more curtly to the orderly than she had meant.

He folded up the wheelchair and picked it up. She snapped:

'No, leave that. I might need it for taking him to the bath-room.'

'Okay. Sorry, lady,' he mumbled; he was African, she didn't know where from, his English not great; but he'd picked up the harsh tone, and looked really hurt.

'It's fine,' she said, walking him to the door, feeling guilty that she had upset him. 'Thanks for your help.'

'I just do job,' he said, shrugging as he left.

I'm getting everything wrong, she thought miserably as she closed the door and went into the kitchen to make a cup of tea. *At least Mr Bingham-Smythe's relatives won't be visiting till the New Year – that'll give me a few days to calm myself down and get into a better mood.*

English people are really odd. If I'd been on holiday with my husband and kids and I'd skied into a tree and needed plastic surgery, they'd all have come home with me. Jeremy Bingham-Smythe's family, however, had decided to continue their ski trip and come back to London on the 3rd of January, as planned.

'No point in ruining the whole holiday because Jeremy's been stupid enough to get himself all crocked up,' Samantha Bingham-Smythe had said airily to Aniela on the phone yester-day when Aniela rang her to confirm that all the arrangements for her husband's care had been duly made, and to give her the phone number of the Limehouse Reach apartment he would be staying in. 'And anyway, he'll be too drugged up to notice if we're there or not, lucky thing!'

Aniela pulled out her own mobile and rang Melody's: a few floors above, Melody responded almost immediately.

'He's all settled in,' Aniela reported. 'But I should really sleep here tonight. His breathing's still a bit shaky.'

'Oh!' Melody said, disappointed. 'I was hoping we could have a girlie sleepover . . .'

'I could come up around eleven, if he looks in good shape, so we can have company for the New Year,' Aniela suggested.

'Great! At least we can have midnight together! I'll order some champagne and we can have a toast on the balcony. There'll be fireworks somewhere along the river—'

'I like fireworks,' Aniela said, cheering up a little bit. 'Did you hear from your agent?'

'No,' Melody said. 'But,' she added bravely, 'I'm really hoping that no news is good news. They haven't just turned me down straight away, which means that at least they're considering me . . .'

'I cross my fingers for you,' Aniela said seriously.

'Thank you, sweetie! I'm really trying to stay positive. Okay, I'll see you later. Come up earlier if you think he's okay.'

Aniela clicked off the phone and put it back in her pocket. It was lovely having Melody here, another woman to hang out with – *and to be honest, also because she's another woman whose life is very far from perfect at the moment.* Misery loves company, Melody had said to her yesterday when she got back from the audition, an English phrase Aniela had never heard before, but which seemed to sum up perfectly how Aniela felt. She didn't want Melody to be unhappy, to have lost the part she wanted so badly – *but if she has, at least we can be miserable together for a few more days, before she finds herself a rental flat and leaves Limehouse Reach.*

It was a particular kind of torture for Aniela to be here, in Jon's apartment, having to sleep in the second bedroom, make it her home for a couple of days. Not knowing where he was, or what he was doing.

He said he would come back, when it was all over. He said he would come back and find me. But who knew what he meant? Maybe just that he would check up on her, make sure she was all right, before he headed off to the ranch he had mentioned and left her behind for ever. Words that he had never said, that she wanted so badly to hear from him, ran through her head:

I'll take you with me to America, to my ranch. We'll be together. I want to be with you.

I love you, Aniela.

She shook her head furiously: there was no point making up things that Jon might have said, but hadn't. Other women might be happy living in fantasy, but Aniela wasn't one of them. She had deluded herself already that her parents, her brothers were trustworthy; she'd wasted too much time with the useless Lubo.

No more. No more fooling myself. From now on I'm going to make sure I tell myself nothing but the truth.

The kettle had boiled. She made herself a pot of tea and carried it over to the dining table, setting it down and pulling out her pack of cards. She'd found a really complicated patience on the internet; she was going to play that for a while, see if it might even be distracting enough to stop her thinking about Jon.

Even if I manage not to think of him, worry about him, for a few minutes at a time, she thought, *that would be such a relief.*

She heaved a deep breath.

Honestly, it would be like a gift from God.

Grigor

*T*he party was already a huge success. Beaming paternally, Grigor watched his small group of carefully selected male guests whoop and yell like little boys, their eyes lit up with excitement, as the show began. His bodyguards had spent a large part of the afternoon rearranging the furniture in the great room, organising sofas and recliners into a wide semicircle facing the gigantic dining table, which was serving as an impromptu stage: huge, wrought-iron candelabras had been set up on either side, their oversized white candles flickering, and the elaborate lighting installed in the apartment, which Grigor had paid an Italian professional over twenty thousand pounds just to design, had been programmed to send a wash of golden shimmer over the stage area, leaving the men in a comfortably cosy, shadowy haze. The occasional backlit spot gave them just enough light to see their brandy snifters and the Carrara marble ashtrays, the round orange tips of their cigars glowing in the comparative darkness as the men drew on them; the rich woody scent of expensive tobacco blended with the smoke from the open fireplace recessed into the wall.

This was a deliberately intimate gathering, with Mikhail Fyodorov as the guest of honour. He was flanked by mutual

Russian friends, other international businessmen, as he and
Grigor liked to call themselves – 'oligarch' had such negative
connotations nowadays. There was a sprinkling of footballers,
a Formula One tycoon, the dealer who had sold Grigor the
gigantic crystal bear, all like-minded spirits ready to celebrate
the New Year in style, more than ready for the show Diane's
girls were about to perform. As befitted this smaller gathering, the cocaine was laid out on Venetian glass trays which
were being brought around at regular intervals by the waiters:
each guest had been given their own silver straw, a personal
touch with which Grigor was particularly pleased. Ecstasy
and Viagra were set out discreetly on a side table: as Grigor
looked around, he couldn't think of anything that the party
lacked.

What is it they say in English? he thought. *The host with the
most. I am most definitely the host with the most tonight.*

The lights all dipped. The men stirred excitedly, knowing
what was coming; muffled giggling, high heels clicking on the
floor, and whispers were heard, frenzied hisses and instructions
as the table creaked, girls clambering onto it with rustling and
swishing of fabric and net. Music rose in the background,
Madonna's 'Angel', and as the lights came up again, a series of
spots directed onto the table, the men's whoops grew even
louder.

Because the four girls posed on top of the table were all not
only beautiful, but dressed in the most revealing white lingerie
imaginable, as tiny as the white, marabou-trimmed wings they
wore were enormous. On their heads they all wore silver
haloes on little metal headbands, which trembled as they
moved, much as their fake bosoms did.

'Fuck,' said Patrice, the footballer, devoutly. 'It's like the
porn version of Victoria's Secret.'

In her sugar-sweet, little-girl voice, Madonna told her
boyfriend that he was an angel as the men feasted their eyes
on the girls: Kesha, as befitted the deviser of the show, had

placed herself in the centre of the tableau, her tiny white basque and thong showing off her dark skin wonderfully. She had rigged some sort of invisible string to her wings, so that they swayed slowly back and forth as she bent and kissed Jaycie, kneeling in front of her, whose breasts were already beginning to spill out of her abbreviated white chiffon baby-doll nightie.

Valerie and Lyndsey, lying elegantly on either side of them, sat up, wriggled around, and mimed shocked 'No's at the two girls who were now kissing passionately; when that didn't work, they came to their knees – with difficulty, as it was hard to manoeuvre on a table top with six-inch Perspex platform heels strapped to your feet – and each mimed pulling at Kesha and Jaycie, separating them.

'Spoilsports!' Patrice yelled. 'Let 'em snog!'

'*Vot imenno! Poslushay ego!*' shouted Fyodorov eagerly. 'That's right! Listen to him!'

Kesha, breaking the fourth wall, looked over at the audience and flashed them a huge wink before she and Jaycie piously folded their hands between their breasts: the music segued into Madonna's 'Like A Prayer', and all four girls shuffled into a kneeling line on the table, turned sideways to give the watching men a good view of their bottoms, which they were, perhaps, sticking out more than was strictly necessary to say their prayers.

'Spank 'em!' Patrice yelled. 'Spank their bums!'

Grigor stiffened at these continual interruptions.

'Patrice!' he snapped crossly. 'Show some respect and let the ladies tell their story! They worked very hard to put this show on.'

'Sorry, Mr K,' Patrice said contritely, as the girls turned back to face their audience, still kneeling, took each other's hands, and bowed their heads: the music dipped, a slow, deep, sexy pounding beat replacing the bright shiny pop songs, over which voices rose and fell: it was Massive Attack's 'Angel', like a deconstructed version of 'Enigma'. The men sat up, the music a signal that the mood was darkening, becoming erotically charged, and sure enough, a group of girls emerged from the shadows.

They were dressed in black, bad angels, perfect counterparts to the good angels on stage; their wings, their lingerie, their heels, their haloes all inky dark. In their hands they held black sex toys – whips, collars, moulded rubber anal beads. They moved close together, a tight predatory group, and as they passed the men they gestured at them menacingly with what they held in their hands: Helen, the beautiful Gong Li looka-like, slapped the string of beads against her palm in a way that made the Formula One owner sigh loudly in pure happiness and anticipation.

Kesha had worked very hard on the staging, and it showed. In a carefully choreographed sequence, the good angels feigned horror at the arrival of the bad ones, splitting up to crawl away along the length of the table. Helen climbed onto the table, pushed Kesha down to straddle her, and started kissing her passionately; Rosie, a pretty, dimpled Irish girl, and Teresa, a redhead, flanked Valerie, Rosie holding her while Teresa started to whip her bottom; Jaycie had been pulled from the table and a Japanese girl called Mia began to strip her gleefully as she struggled with big theatrical wiggles in the arms of a brunette called Lori with cascading dark curls, and a six-foot blonde called Beth.

'Oh, *yeah*,' Patrice moaned, shifting in his recliner to lean forward, his eyes gleaming. 'Give it to her good, the dirty little slut . . .'

He was fixed on the sight of Helen, who had turned Kesha over and had ripped open the back of her basque. Apart from her wings and halo, Kesha was now only wearing a tiny white lace thong, and Helen very deliberately pulled this aside with one hand while, with the other, she flourished the moulded beads, running them up and down Kesha's back, over her round buttocks, lashing her between the legs with them, gradually targeting them where every man in the audience was now dying to see them put.

Some of the men were now openly touching themselves through their trousers. Their drinks, their cigars, were totally forgotten, but the waiter, moving discreetly between the seats with the tray of cocaine, was being eagerly summoned over by Grigor's guests, who were alternately sniffing and groaning. *Like dogs,* Grigor thought affectionately, looking around the group. *Well, men are dogs. Dasha always used to say that, and she was absolutely right.*

Dasha was almost always right, to be honest, he admitted to himself. *We made a great team, back in the old days. I'm very glad I don't have to divorce her. A man should stay married to the mother of his children. She gave me two handsome sons, and I honour her for that.*

Usually it was Alek, his older son, the heir to Grigor's empire, who brought an instant smile to his father's face; but tonight, for the first time ever, the smile was for Dmitri. *He may be a wimp, but he saved his old father from a catastrophe. What the hell would I have done with a young wife? Particularly Zhivana Fyodorova. Dasha was right yet again: she's as wet as a boiled noodle just like Dasha said. The thought of having to have sex with her – spend time with her –* Grigor shuddered.

Dmitri saved me from that bullet. I had to make the damn deal – my influence in Russia is slipping perilously, now I can't go back for fear of being clapped in prison like so many of my friends. I needed Fyodorov – he had me over a barrel. Dmitri took that girl off my hands just in time. Honestly, I always thought that boy was homosexual! Who knew he even liked women?

Mind you, the little Fyodorova's so thin she'd be like a fourteen-year-old boy if you turned her over . . .

This thought amused the proud father so much that he picked up his brandy snifter, leant over to Fyodorov, and clinked his glass against his guest's.

'A great end to the year, eh, Mikhail?' he said happily.

Fyodorov was too busy shoving his straw up his nose and doing a big fat line to be able to raise his glass and toast back, but he grinned back at Grigor.

'Excellent, my old friend,' he said, when he had thrown back his head to make sure all the coke had been properly ingested. 'Truly excellent. You throw the best parties.'

A deep groan of agreement rose from all around the semicircle of spectators: Lori was eating Jaycie out eagerly as Beth licked her nipples; Valerie, completely naked and spreadeagled on the table, was being fucked by Teresa, who had a black strap-on fastened around her hips on a very smart black and silver-studded harness; and Helen had gradually inserted the full length of the anal bead string into Kesha, who was on all fours, her pretty little pointed breasts wobbling with each push of the next bead into her bottom.

The show was in full swing, and Grigor judged that it was time for the audience to become participants.

'Gentlemen!' he said, standing up and clinking his straw against his glass. 'I think it's time to join the ladies!'

He had seen that line on a BBC TV drama, and had been longing to use it ever since.

'Yeah!' Patrice was already off his chair, dashing towards the table. Other men followed; others preferred to summon the girls of their choice towards them. As usual, Grigor did not participate. The girls were lovely, sexy and willing; individually, he might have been interested in one of them. Possibly Lyndsey, a plump-cheeked little blonde.

But not with other people around. And not on New Year's Eve. Grigor adored big occasions, excuses to have parties and entertain with his legendary hospitality, but what he really enjoyed was to celebrate those occasions by drinking expensive brandy and watching films appropriate to the moment. He was impressed by the new trend in Hollywood of making films for precisely this kind of situation. Christmas, of course, was an *embarras de richesses*, with so many films to choose from, but some clever American had seen an opportunity, and made first *Valentine's Day* and now *New Year's Eve*. Grigor was just about to sneak off to his screening room and have the latter put on; he calculated that he could watch it and have twenty minutes or so at the end before the stroke of midnight.

So many good actors in this film! he thought happily as he snorted a line. *Halle Berry, Robert De Niro – Michelle Pfeiffer, so beautiful, so elegant – and Jon Bon Jovi! Very exciting!* Grigor was very much looking forward to Jon Bon Jovi's cameo. He was a great fan of his music.

The Formula One man had grabbed Teresa and was pulling her off to a bedroom, the strap-on waggling in front of her. Patrice was already getting sucked off by Lori as Jaycie rubbed her breasts in his face. From the darker corners of the room, the moans, groans, porn-movie squeals of pleasure and sounds of condom wrappers being torn open were growing louder and louder.

I can slip off now to watch my film, Grigor decided with complete contentment. *No one will miss me.*

He was just picking up his glass when Sergei, vibrating like an overstimulated tuning fork, shot up to him, panting heavily.

'We have an emergency!' he hissed. 'Mr Khalovksy, it is a disaster!'

'*What?*' This was the positively last word that Grigor wanted to hear tonight. 'What's going on?'

Squinting in the darkness, he realised that Sergei had been followed by Andy.

'Mr K, I'm so sorry – I didn't know what to do!' Andy was stammering. 'You've got unexpected visitors!'

Dire imaginings ran through Grigor's mind: *the KGB, MI6, the* Spetsnaz? *Visitors in the plural, making Sergei and Andy panic like this – which secret services could it be?*

'It's Dmitri and Zhivana Fyodorova!' Sergei wrung his hands as if they were sopping towels. 'Downstairs in the lobby! Come by to say Happy New Year to their fathers!'

'Ah, *fuck*! This is *worse* than the bloody KGB!' Grigor bellowed in frustration.

He looked around him at the orgy in progress: the girls, the drugs, Zhivana's father lying back on the sofa, being ridden cowgirl-style by Beth as he squeezed her buttocks appreciatively. *My God,* he thought in parenthesis. *Mikhail is so hairy that poor girl must feel like she's fucking a carpet. He probably even has hairs on his dick.*

'*Fuck,*' he repeated, feeling as if the breath had been knocked out of him, as he saw his successful evening shatter to pieces before his eyes. 'Andy, go downstairs and stall them. Think of something to say. Sergei will let you know when it's okay to bring them up.'

'Say Patrice threw up on the carpet and it's being cleaned,' Sergei said maliciously. 'He's always throwing up. That man is a pig.'

Grigor nodded. 'And get me Diane—'

But Diane was already gliding up to their group. Diane was the most successful madam in Europe, a title she had maintained for fifteen years by keeping an eagle eye on every aspect of her business; her entire stable of available girls had been mustered for this party, were being paid triple time in consideration of the fact that they were not only working on a holiday but putting on a show to boot, and she would not have dreamed of letting such an important occasion take place without being there to supervise discreetly but thoroughly.

'What's going on?' she asked, and even her heavily made-up mask of a face cracked into a grimace when she heard the news.

'Well, fuck *me* with a drainpipe, that's put the cat among the pigeons!' she exclaimed. 'Right. I'll get a few of the better-spoken girls dressed and back in here to be girlfriends – if it's all men in here it'll look like a sausage fest. Rest of 'em can go back downstairs and entertain any of the gents who want to pop down to get their tubes cleaned. Sound like a plan?'

The men nodded gratefully, Andy dashing off to the lift to go back downstairs to explain to Dmitri and Zhivana. Diane marched over to the bank of lights, which she had been operating for the show, and flicked them all on in one brutal flash. Yells of protest burst out, as men in flagrante delicto around the room howled complaints.

'Sorry, gents!' Hoicking up her skirt, Diane climbed onto the table and stood there, dominating the room. 'Bad news! Mr K's son's just turned up with Mr F's daughter – they want to say Happy New Year to their dads. That's put a spanner in our works and there's no mistake! Finish up what you're doing if you can manage that quickly, and you can keep the party going downstairs if you fancy, which I bet you do. Kesha, Valerie, Lyndsey, Lori, Mia, you clean up best. Go get your kit on and come back up here, with your best posh voices on. Rest of you girls, I don't want to see you up here. Got it?'

'Oh *no*! Do we have to take our wings off?' Kesha wailed, jumping off the footballer she'd been straddling, the beads half out of her bottom now, where they dangled like a comedy tail.

Fyodorov, sprawled, hairy legs wide, under Beth's long lanky body, jerked up his head at that news.

'*What?*' he shouted. '*Zhivana* is here?'

Beth, a consummate professional, reached down, cupped his balls with one hand, slid a finger of the other hand up his bottom, and pressed hard on his prostate.

'Ugh! Aah! *Ty blyadina* – you dirty whore!' Fyodorov yelled, his head flopping back onto the sofa cushions, his whole body juddering with orgasm.

'Thought I'd just finish him off, Diane,' Beth said to her boss. 'Poor sod, he won't get to cop off now otherwise, will he? Not with his daughter turning up and all.'

'Quick thinking.' Diane nodded approvingly as Fyodorov's grunts died down. 'Nice work, Beth. I like a girl who takes a bit of initiative.'

Andy

Oh my God, what a night! Andy thought, as the lift carried him down to the lobby again. *Talk about drama!* His job was absolutely the opposite: to make everything run smoothly and seamlessly for his clients, to avoid drama wherever possible. But no one could have helped, even fractionally, being entertained by the sight of all those stunning girls in their big wings and haloes, the various sexual permutations which he had glimpsed around the great room – *that one with the thing up her bum in particular*, he thought, sniggering. *Big white wings and a bobbly tail, that was hilarious!*

I wish Wayne had been there – it would've been fun to have someone to giggle with at how the girls were all tarted up.

Before we sneaked away to have our own fun, of course.

Andy caught sight of himself in the mirror panel in the lift: his expression was ludicrously sad, like a clown miming misery, mouth and eyes pulled down at the corners. He couldn't stop thinking about Wayne, and all it did was make him want to cry.

Stop it! Pull yourself together! he told himself crossly as the lift doors opened. *Get out there and make up some story about Patrice – Sergei's quite right, he's always in the tabs for getting pissed and falling out of clubs, they'll believe that one. Or at least be polite enough to pretend to believe it . . .*

Pasting a professional smile onto his face, he walked briskly from the lift, rounded the enormous Christmas tree, stepped into the lobby, and stopped dead. Zhivana and Dmitri were sitting on the edge of the pond, looking down at the huge golden carp floating over the glittering red and green stones, Zhivana trailing her fingers to try to entice a fish to come close as Dmitri murmured something in her ear that made her laugh. In the short time she'd spent with Dmitri, Zhivana's style had changed markedly. The furs she had left Grigor's apartment wearing had vanished, replaced by a fitted, padded silver-grey coat with a fashionably oversized scarf wrapped round her slender throat; above it, her braided hairstyle now looked like the height of Shoreditch fashion.

She whispered something to Dmitri in response; they were too absorbed in each other even to notice his arrival, and it wasn't them he was looking at in any case.

It was Wayne. Who was standing awkwardly by Andy's desk, his hands shoved in his jeans pockets, head thrust forward, his eyes fixed on Andy. He managed a smile, mouthing 'Hi'. His leather jacket was buttoned up tightly, a stripy scarf looped around his neck dusted lightly with snow: on his hands were red woollen gloves, which matched his cheeks. He was stocky, his legs so solid and wide that his body seemed almost rectangular in shape. His features were small, his eyes piggy, the set of his round ears on his round skull making him look like a child's toy.

But to Andy, he looked like Prince Charming, love incarnate—

Oh no! Andy thought in horror at the words which were spooling through his head at the sight of Wayne. *I just used the 'love' word – which is mental. I barely know him – he doesn't want to be with me, not properly – oh no, he's going to break my bloody heart, the bastard—*

What's he even doing *here?*

'Mr K mentioned his New Year's Eve party,' Wayne said, clearly, so that everyone else in the lobby could hear as well. 'And I thought I'd just drop by.'

'Nothing else going on?' Andy said curtly, walking towards him; the shock of seeing Wayne so unexpectedly had loosened his tongue. He found himself caring much less about professional decorum than he ever had in his life. 'No other fun dos to go to? Or did you find yourself fancying the sight of Mr K's special guests all dressed up and dancing?'

He had lowered his voice by this time, so that Zhivana and Dmitri wouldn't hear.

'Oh!' Wayne looked a little taken aback. He turned away from the pond, their backs now to the young lovers, for extra discretion. 'That kind of party, is it?'

'Like you wouldn't believe.'

Andy couldn't stay angry at Wayne, not when there was such juicy gossip to share. *And besides,* he thought, trying not to let his heart leap too much with anticipation, *he's here for me, isn't he? He's turned up to see me on New Year's Eve, and though it's shredding my nerves, I couldn't be happier to see him—*

'The girls put on this whole show,' Andy said under his breath. 'It was mental up there. Good angels, bad angels, sex toys, the whole works – hilarious. I thought everyone was here, so I popped up to have a look – and when those two walked in—' he nodded at Dmitri and Zhivana – 'one of them was up on the table getting stuff stuck up her bum, another girl was getting spanked, all of 'em with these enormous great wings on – it was all I could do not to crack up, they were really going for it! And then we got the word to clean up, and this poor girl only had a flipping string of black rubber beads sticking out of her arse – she didn't know what to do, she was running around with it waggling like a tail out of her bum—'

'Pin the tail on the donkey!' Wayne said, in full giggle flight. 'Shit, I wish I'd seen that, it sounds brilliant!'

'Yeah, it was top entertainment,' Andy agreed, laughing at the memory. 'Oh, and her dad—'

He hissed into Wayne's ear the story of Beth's finger going up Mr Fyodorov's bottom. Wayne howled with laughter.

'Blimey,' he said, 'it sounds like it's bum central up there!'

Andy managed, through a heroic effort, not to throw in any reference to himself and Wayne in the fortieth-floor apartment just a couple of days ago.

'Your mate Patrice was going at it,' he said. 'Two girls and him, just like you said.'

''im.' Wayne sniffed. 'Any opportunity, 'e gets 'is knob out. And it ain't even that much to see.'

Andy giggled again. He realised that, as before, he and Wayne had fallen instantly into easy, happy, laughing, companionable conversation, a back and forth with no awkward pauses or stares at the floor; *that's what makes it so hard to say no to him.*

'Andy,' Wayne said very softly, glancing around them to make sure there was no one to overhear. 'I came to see you. You know that, right?'

Andy nodded.

'But what I said before,' he muttered, 'I haven't changed my mind.'

'Is there anywhere we can be alone?'

Firmly, determinedly, Andy shook his head.

'No way,' he said. 'Cos I know what would happen.' He wanted so badly to kiss Wayne that he actually had to take a step back to avoid the temptation to reach out and touch him; his brain had made the decision to put more distance between them, but his body was yearning for Wayne, so much so that it was actually beginning to tilt towards his.

'Do you not want to—' Wayne started, looking so cast down and miserable that Andy had to interrupt.

'Of course I do!' he hissed furiously. 'I want to snog your face off right here! But I'm not going to, and I'm not going somewhere alone with you, cos we'd just – you know – and that would make me feel even worse after, cos I meant what I said before! It was hard enough to come out without you trying to cram me back into the closet again, even if you do suck my dick when we're both in there!'

It was a magnificent speech, but the trouble was that saying the words 'suck my dick' in this close proximity to Wayne just made Andy's own cock stiffen, pressing uncomfortably against the heavy wool fabric of his uniform trousers. It was all he could do not to reach down and adjust it to a slightly more comfortable angle. Wayne had unwrapped his scarf, and above the welted-knit collar of his leather jacket, Andy could see his pronounced Adam's apple bob as Wayne swallowed with nerves. For some reason, the sight sent a wash of tenderness flooding through him. Tears pricked at his eyes, and he turned away to hide them.

'I'm supposed to be delaying down here till they get all tidied away upstairs,' he muttered. 'Make it look all respectable.'

'They going to let you know when it's okay to take 'em up?' Wayne asked gruffly, nodding at the two young lovers, still sitting happily on the rim of the pond, whispering sweet nothings to each other.

Andy shrugged. 'Yeah, they'll give me the all-clear.'

'Cos 'e's waving at you,' Wayne said, nodding at the burly bodyguard stationed by the lift, who was beckoning to Andy with a cupping gesture of his fingers. The bodyguard met Andy's eyes, looked over at Zhivana and Dmitri, and nodded, an unmistakable signal that the coast up in the penthouse was clear.

'All right, then,' Andy said. He looked at Wayne. 'You coming up, then?'

Wayne looked ridiculously hangdog, and very young indeed.

'D'you want me to stay?' he said softly.

Andy was suddenly unable to speak. He nodded abruptly. There was a huge lump in his throat.

'Of course. Yeah. But I can't be alone with you,' he finally managed to get out. 'It's not fair. Not when you can't—' The lump felt the size of the Boulder Dam by now. 'I *can't*, okay?' he managed.

Swivelling on the heel of his polished dress shoes, he walked over to the carp pond.

'Miss Fyodorova? Mr Khalovsky?' he said, in his best professional-concierge voice. 'Can I show you up to the penthouse? I'm *so* sorry to have kept you waiting. Mr Burns is coming up with us – Mr Khalovsky is *so* happy you're all joining his New Year's Eve party!'

And then the phone on his desk rang; he stepped over to answer it, his head tilted as he listened to Sergei babble a string of instructions.

'Okay,' he said. 'No problem.'

He put down the phone.

'Miss Fyodorova, gentlemen,' he said to the three assembled guests, 'could I ask you to go up to the penthouse? I have just a couple of errands to run for Mr Khalovsky before I join you . . .'

Jon

*H*e was on high alert, had been ever since the new patient had been wheeled into his old apartment, slumped back in his wheelchair, obviously comatose on sedatives and pain-killers, with Aniela walking behind the orderly. *Fuck, fuck, fuck! How unlucky is this!* Clearly some emergency had taken place, something unforeseeable, because no one would choose to be operated upon by a plastic surgeon between Christmas and the New Year. *And because it was an emergency, it'll be worse than a planned operation. Aniela will need to stay with him more closely, be around that damned apartment much more – which is the last place I want to see her—*

He'd taken a lightning-fast decision; as soon as the coast was clear, the orderly gone, and Aniela, presumably, installed for a while with the patient, he had activated the device that scrambled the CCTV video feed once more and cleared out of the corner apartment, moving into the one next door to the Canary Clinic one. It was unoccupied, he knew, from his long hours of observation; there was no wreath on the door, too, which meant that no one had been in when Andy had come by with the wreaths and mistletoe from Khalovsky upstairs. Naturally, there was always the risk that its owners might be planning to stay there for a London-based New Year's Eve, and this apartment was infinitely less suitable for a trained assassin who would never, normally, have dreamed of taking a position this weak: with only one door, and no possibility of exiting out the windows, the apartment was literally a deathtrap.

But I'm right on her doorstep. I'll be able to jump in to save her, if and when Dasha Khalovsky or any goons she sends shows up to try to take me out.

It was possible, of course, that Dasha had already been informed by Dr Nassri that Jon had upped sticks and disappeared; that was his hope, and why he had insisted that Aniela tell her boss as soon as she officially became aware that he had cleared out of Limehouse Reach. If that was the case, he had nothing to worry about. But Aniela's presence in the apartment worried him tremendously. Even the slightest possibility that she might be at risk was immensely distressing to him, made his palms sweat as if he were about to go into physical combat.

He didn't have any weapons with him, but Jon was more than used to improvising. The occupants of this new apartment had a very nice collection of kitchen knives, stored in a designer knife block made of tiny rubber filaments which held the knives suspended, without any wooden slots that might blunt their blades; but Jon had also found a knife sharpener, and used that to bring the two smallest Sabatiers to a state in which they could have sliced through tissue paper in one swift hiss. He would have loved the knife holster he had in storage, with leather sheaths for throwing knives, but had improvised with a webbing strap meant to fasten round a suitcase, which he had found in the closet. Two sweatshirts, worn one over the other, protected his chest from the blades stuck through the strap, which was fastened crosswise over his chest.

And the kitchen had proved a fertile weapons-locating ground even beyond the knives. As so often with the ultra-rich, they had stocked it with every conceivable luxury item, and then never used a single one, from what Jon could tell. There was a pastry-making set, composed of a huge marble board that was way too big to be used as a weapon, and a matching marble rolling pin that was almost perfect for his needs. He had spent quite a lot of time improving that rolling pin, using the wire that came with a cheese-cutting machine – *who the hell needs a cheese-cutting machine?* – to groove indentations into one end, making the slippery pin much easier to grip, to wield, and he was very pleased with the results. It would be perfect for close-quarters combat, which was precisely the arena in which he would find himself if Dasha Khalovsky turned up with a gun, or goons, or both.

Prepare for the worst, hope for the best. Jon had nothing to prove; he would be delighted if all his careful preparations were for nothing. He was staking out next door, and would do so for as long as it took until he was sure that the situation with Dasha Khalovsky was resolved; but the ideal scenario would be that all his waiting proved for nothing, did not explode into action. He had sworn never to kill again, and he meant to keep that vow.

And then what? When it's done, one way or the other? Do I just head off to the States? Or do I try to see Aniela again?

He writhed in confusion. *What the hell do I do?*

Damned if I know, came the answer. The thought of never seeing her again was like a physical pain; not a stab, but his entire body ached, as if he'd been worked over by a whole group of guys with hammers, and was bruised through to the bone.

But what's the alternative? I guess it's that she comes with me. Jesus, I never thought I'd live with a woman! I don't know how! I need a hell of a lot of time on my own, that's for sure. Could she deal with that? What if she expected me to be with her every minute? I couldn't take that, I know I couldn't—

The lift doors pinged, and Jon, sitting by the door on one of the high kitchen stools, with a rigged-up tube pressed against the peephole to allow him to watch the corridor outside without actually pressing his eyeball against it, sprang to attention. Because no one came to this floor – no one but Aniela, who was already inside the apartment, and Andy and Wayne, two days ago.

Maybe it's the boys, he thought. *Kissed and made up, figured it all out, coming back for Round Two.* The idea cheered him up: *at least two people're having a good time on New Year's Eve, instead of stuck like this with a wall between them like some corny old film.* The irony that he was so close to Aniela, but unable to be with her, had not escaped him.

Swift footsteps came down the corridor, and Jon saw a flash of burgundy uniform, a smooth black head: Andy, dapper as ever. Alone, and coming this way, not towards the corner apartment. He rang the doorbell of the Clinic apartment, and after a minute or so – *Aniela checking to see who was there through the spyhole* – the door swung open and Jon felt a rush of pleasure as he caught a sideways, blurred image of Aniela standing there in her white uniform. He couldn't catch everything Andy said, but it sounded as if Andy were inviting her and Jon to Mr Khalovsky's once again.

'He's not here any more,' he heard Aniela say loudly, as loudly as she could without making Andy wonder why she was shouting at him. 'He checked himself out a few days ago. I have a new patient here now.'

For the benefit of anyone who might be lurking around, he thought, more proud of her than ever. *Smart, thinking on her feet. Doesn't miss a trick.*

Andy said something else, and Jon saw Aniela shake her head, the blonde hair gleaming in the corridor light.

'Thank you, but I should stay with my patient. Please say thank you to Mr Khalovsky for me.'

'You're sure?' Andy said.

Aniela nodded.

'Thank you,' she said again, closing the door, and Andy retreated back down the corridor; as far as Jon could see, Andy wasn't stopping at any other doors on the floor. The building really was nearly empty.

Huh, Jon reflected. *Khalovsky's throwing another come-one, come-all party? At* – he glanced at his watch – *ten-thirty, just an hour and a half to go before midnight? Something's definitely up.*

And I wonder if this'll shake things up at all . . . is his wife in the penthouse too? Now that she doesn't want him taken out, are they all celebrating together?

He didn't have long to wait for his answer: fifteen minutes later, the lift pinged again. And this time there were two sets of footsteps coming out of the lift car: *Andy and Wayne?* But then Jon saw the men emerging round the corner of the corridor: a matched pair of Grigor Khalovsky's bodyguards. Jon had been trained to develop as close to a photographic memory as possible, and he recognised the blunt Slavic features instantly. Silently, he picked up the kitchen stool, moved it back from the door, cleared the decks: *this could be showtime. Or it could be Grigor extending another of his party invitations. Wait and see.*

He unlatched the door in complete silence as the body-guards passed, stopping ten feet further down, in front of the door behind which was the woman Jon loved. And although Jon knew that his position, tactically, had been chosen to give him maximum advantage, that if he had been next door he and Aniela would have been sitting ducks, while from here he could fall on the unsuspecting bodyguards from behind, ambushing them, if they turned out to have any nefarious intentions, every fibre of his body was resisting this impeccable logic. It was telling him that he should be with her, keeping her safe, taking a bullet for her if necessary—

Something clicked in his head, like a switch turning on a light, clear and white and burning illumination into every corner of a room. He eased open his door, just fractionally, as the bodyguards rang the doorbell of the next-door apartment; he could hear the ring, faintly, from where he was positioned.

There was no answer. Aniela must have looked through the peephole and decided not to respond: *sensible girl*.

'Hello!' one of the bodyguards called, in heavily accented English. 'Hello! We come from Grigor Khalovsky. He invite you to his party. Are you there to come to the party?'

He jabbed on the bell again. Beside him, his companion muttered something, his hand rising to the holstered automatic under his arm.

And then Jon heard something in the apartment. He slid out, silently, in the shoes he had borrowed from the owner of the flat in which he was squatting; leather shoes, way better than sneakers in a flight, with harder toes in case you needed to kick someone, and heels that would hurt like hell if you ground them into a soft part of the body.

The locks were disengaging, the door was opening, and, to his utter disbelief, he saw a man in pyjamas and a bandaged face emerge in the opening. The man was propping himself on the doorjamb, clearly unsteady, but he said gamely, his voice slurred from whatever combination of drugs he had been given:

'I say, chaps, I think you have the wrong place. Awfully nice of you, but I'm in no condition to make it to a party, as you can see. What number do you have again?'

'*Chto on skazal?*' said one bodyguard to the other.

Jon spoke Russian okay, and understood it better. And now the door was open, he could hear them fine. *What did he say?* the first guy had asked. And the second guy was answering:

'*Kher ego znaet! Zasun' ego vovnutr', zavalim ego i vsyo dela.*'

Which meant: *Fucked if I know! Shove him inside so we can shoot him and get this done.*

Jon's body tilted forward, rising onto the tips of his toes. *Here we go. Definitely showtime.*

'I'm feeling awfully dizzy,' the man said politely, 'so if you don't mind, I think I should probably be getting back to bed. I do hope you find the bloke you're looking for.'

He started to close the door. The closer bodyguard thrust out an arm and blocked it.

And that was when all hell broke loose. The patient, suddenly realising the danger he was in, reeled back, the bodyguard lunging for him, grabbing him by the throat of his pyjamas. The second bodyguard was already pulling his gun, which made him Jon's first target: with the marble rolling pin in a backhanded grip, he took two swift steps forward and smashed the guy across the back of the skull. As the bodyguard staggered, reeling forward, Jon raised his leg and kicked him squarely into the wall; his face hit the flat surface first, and even as he started to slide down it, Jon was over him, ripping the jacket open, dragging the Glock out of his shoulder holster, flipping the rolling pin into his left hand to hold the semi-automatic in his right.

The first bodyguard, still with his hand twisted into the collar of the poor patient's pyjamas, was twisting round to see where the sudden flurry of blows behind him had come from. He had barely a second to register Jon's face, his jaw dropping in comical shock at the realisation that there was not one, but two men with horribly bruised faces in front of him, before Jon lunged forward, dropping briefly to one knee, coming up with the rolling pin squarely in the man's sternum, a crushing blow that drove all the breath out of his target. The bodyguard gasped, the hand on the patient's pyjamas falling away, his body arching up with the blow. He hung, suspended for a moment on the tip of the rolling pin, before falling back heavily on the body of his colleague. His eyelids fluttered up, showing only the whites of his eyes. Jon frisked him, removing his Glock and a knife strapped to his calf, then rolled him off the first guy and took his time frisking the latter, finding a Glock B26 revolver in an ankle holster.

'Jeez, these guys *love* their Glocks,' he muttered, piling up the pistols by the still-open door.

Out of the corner of his eye he saw the patient reeling back, one hand to his throat. Jon jumped to his feet, heading to catch him; but just then, another set of arms came around the man. It was Aniela, steadying her patient, grabbing him under his armpits.

'What *happened*?' she panted. 'I just went to the toilet! He must have got up and opened the door – are you all right?'

In her arms, the patient started to thrash around, his hand still clutching at his neck.

'Help!' he yelled. 'Help! They're going to kill me! Help!'

Aniela could barely hold him; one of his arms flailed back at her. With a stride, Jon was on him, grabbing one shoulder firmly while his other hand cupped round the patient's neck, found the carotid, and pressed for precisely three seconds. He was ready for the immediate reaction, and took the weight of the patient's fainting body before he could collapse on top of Aniela. Hauling the guy over his shoulder, he moved past her, heading for the bedroom.

'Grab the guns and bring them in here,' he said economically; in thirty seconds he had dumped the patient on the bed and was back, seeing the pistols lined up on the kitchen counter and Aniela standing, wide-eyed, beside them. He took her shoulders, kissed her hard, and released her swiftly, heading for the door.

'I'll clean this up and come right back,' he said. 'Lock the door and don't let anyone in but me. And give that guy something to knock him out. That way he'll just think he had a crazy codeine dream.'

She nodded, coming after him; he heard the locks turn as he hauled one, and then the other, comatose would-be killer into the next-door apartment. The first one, who had been hit on the back of the head, was fully unconscious, the second beginning to come to, wheezing: Jon dealt with that by knocking him out with a judiciously placed blow with the rolling pin, and then hogtied both men with strips cut from the apartment owners' hand-printed Provençal linen tea towels, gagging them with extra pieces of fabric just in case. He paused momentarily to appreciate the very good quality of the material.

Say what you will, he thought, slicing it up with one of the knives he had pulled from his improvised chest holster, *it pays to spend on the good stuff. These'd last a lifetime.*

Or would have, if I hadn't been cutting 'em up, of course.

He paused, looking at the label hanging off one of the tea towels, then shrugged, cut it off and shoved it into the pocket of his sweatpants.

I'll need this kind of stuff for the ranch house. Bet I can order these online. You can get anything on the internet nowadays.

He had been careful to wear gloves most of the time in the apartment, but as a basic precaution he did a full sweep anyway, wiping clean every surface that might conceivably bear his fingerprints. He put back the knives, webbing strap and rolling pin, but kept the shoes: rich as they were, these people would probably not even notice the missing items, let alone make a police report, but Jon was nothing if not careful. He did allow himself a moment of amusement imagining how on earth they would explain to themselves the grooves that he had cut into the rolling pin. But then he realised, almost with disappointment, that since it was purely for display, the likelihood of them noticing the changes was infinitesimal.

Once he was sure that he had obliterated all traces of his presence, he shut the door behind him and headed back to the apartment in which Aniela was anxiously waiting for him.

'We've got to get out of here,' he said economically. 'You got that guy pilled up?'

She nodded. 'I gave him some liquid codeine drops on his tongue. He'll be out for a while.'

'Right, let's get him into that wheelchair.'

He saw her eyes widen again in surprise that he knew there was a wheelchair in the apartment, and he grinned.

'I've been watching you for days, hon,' he said. 'I saw that chair come in, but I didn't see it leave.'

'I couldn't help being here,' she said quickly. 'I did exactly what you said. But then Mr Bingham-Smythe had a skiing accident, and the other apartment the Clinic owns is having work done, so he had to come in here—'

He bent to kiss her once again, her body soft and strong in his arms, a delicious contradiction, wide and warm and completely fulfilling; his heart melted into her as he held her fiercely.

'You're okay,' he said. 'That's all I give a damn about. But I have to keep you that way – you're my responsibility. This place isn't defensible – the Clinic is. Plus there, if we get into a siege situation, we call the cops and they'll be right over. Ground floor, easy access for them, no trouble with the security guys. Got it?'

She nodded.

'I have to keep *him* safe,' she said, nodding at the bedroom door. 'Mr Bingham-Smythe. He's my responsibility.'

'I know. That's why I love you,' he said without thinking.

And then he looked down at her in utter horror at what he had just said. She was perfectly still, her self-control extraordinary: the only change was the dilation of her pupils, dark circles at the centre of her pale blue irises. Jon was struck dumb by his own words, and Aniela herself paused for a suspended moment, time hanging in the air. Her lips parted as she worked out how to respond to this very unexpected declaration.

But clearly she decided that now was not the time to try to deal with anything but the pressing emergency facing them. Briskly, she said:

'We must get Mr Bingham-Smythe downstairs and settled in. I have to make sure his vital signs are all right. He was under general anaesthetic yesterday. This shock will not have been good for him.'

Still unable to speak, Jon nodded.

'The wheelchair's in the front hall cupboard,' she said. 'Will you set it up and bring it in?'

He nodded again; she turned and went into the bedroom where the unconscious Mr Bingham-Smythe was lying. *On the same bed we slept on and fucked on,* Jon thought. *No, dammit,* he corrected himself. *We didn't fuck. We made love.*

Jesus, Jon! How deep are you into this?

He drew in a long breath, crossed to the counter, picked up the little Glock and pushed it into his sock. One of the other Glocks went into his waistband; after a moment's thought, he pulled the wheelchair out of the cupboard, unfolded it, locked it open and dropped the second Glock into the pocket at the back of the seat, where it would be easily reachable.

One damn thing at a time. First let's get her and that guy safely out of here.

Then I can figure out what the hell I do about this whole love mess.

Melody

I said I wouldn't cry again before the end of the year, and I'm sticking to that, she told herself firmly. *And I mustn't get too pissed either.*

She'd had a bottle of champagne sent up from Four Seasons room service, and had already polished off a couple of glasses. She'd had tea with Aniela earlier in the day, and they'd planned to keep each other company at midnight: *I can't have any more,* Melody thought, looking at her watch. *Twenty to eleven. What's keeping her? I have to make sure that there's plenty for both of us at midnight.*

She was horribly lonely. Only the knowledge that she had someone with whom to count down the passing of the old year and the incoming new one was keeping her together. *I should just have packed up and got on a train and gone back home for New Year's Eve. It's my stupid pride keeping me here, and for what? Being alone here in a luxury apartment in a skyscraper at Canary Wharf isn't proving anything to anyone.*

I did my audition, and I know I nailed it. I was really good. I can't believe that anyone read better than I did. And I walked out with my head held high. That was what I needed to prove. After that I should just have taken a taxi straight to Paddington and jumped on the next train to the West Country. Mum and Dad and Ash would have been so happy to see me – I'd've gone down the pub with all of them for New Year's, it would have been lovely. And instead I'm just sitting here like a lemon.

There would be plenty of parties in London, of course. Melody would have had to make just a couple of phone calls to find out where. *Honestly, I could just turn up at Shoreditch House,* she thought. *Sign myself in, go up to the rooftop – there'd be bound to be tons of people I know there.* She and James had spent the last New Year's Eve partying on the rooftop terrace with a whole group of friends, lying together on one of the huge outdoor beds, wrapped in warm coats, flames flickering in the open fire pits, fireworks snapping and bursting open overhead, sparklers in their hands. Cold air around them, but James's arms around her, mulled wine heating her insides, his mouth on hers hot and eager – the contrast between her previous New Year's Eve and this one was so atrociously painful that Melody had to push away every single memory of last year so that she didn't whimper aloud with misery.

But I'm in no state to go out. Not yet. I'd have to field hundreds of stares at my face, hundreds of questions about James, Felicity, the Much Ado *audition.*

She still hadn't heard whether she'd got Beatrice, wouldn't until the New Year. It was normal practice for an actor, post-audition, in the waiting period, to smile brightly and deflect queries about how it had gone, if their agent had got any feedback, whether they had anything else lined up: all part of the game, and an actor had to be tough enough to deal with the downs of his or her career as well as the ups. The ones who didn't have an inner core of steel and self-confidence dropped out, and Melody was definitely not going to do that.

But I'm too vulnerable right now. I still need to hole up and lick my wounds. I said I wouldn't go out in public until my face was

*one-hundred-per-cent completely healed, and I need to stick to
that . . .*

The doorbell rang. She jumped up from the sofa with great
relief: *Aniela's come up at last! She must have decided it was
okay to leave her patient—*

But when she pulled the door open, it was Andy standing
there, the handsome concierge, smart in his uniform and
smiling at her, his teeth flashing white.

'Miss Downs?' he began.

Melody couldn't help smiling ruefully.

'Oh, you can call me Dale,' she said. 'I mean, everyone here
knows who I really am by now.'

'I'm *so* sorry about that paparazzo jumping out at you at the
riverfront doors,' Andy said: he had already apologised on
behalf of the management, but was very contrite, seeing it as
Limehouse Reach's failing that Melody had been ambushed
right by the back entrance.

She shrugged.

'Honestly, Andy, like I said before – it's not your fault,' she
assured him. 'I know who set me up, tipped off that pap, and it
wasn't anyone who works here.'

Andy pulled a face.

'They're awful, the paps,' he said sincerely. 'Anyway, on a
happier note, Mr Khalovsky is having an impromptu party in
his penthouse, and he thought you might like to join? That
nice Japanese family are coming too.'

'Oh.' Melody hesitated. 'I'd love to, but I said I'd spend
midnight with Aniela—'

'I already asked her,' Andy said, 'and she said she couldn't
leave her patient. It's a new one, some poor bastard who had a
skiing accident – that stunt guy left, apparently. Funny, isn't
it?' he added in parenthesis. 'I wouldn't have thought he'd be
okay to check out for *weeks*, would you?'

'I don't like the idea of leaving Aniela alone,' Melody began,
but already, the thought of a party upstairs was a huge

temptation: she would have company without intimacy, be surrounded by people but not ones in her world, nobody who could use the gossip about her to make her suffer.

'Look, why don't you come on up, and then we can ring her and tell her to join us just before midnight?' Andy suggested. 'That way she'll be with everyone for a nice toast to bring in the New Year. Mr K's got fireworks and everything – we're going to shoot 'em off the terrace—'

'Oh, that sounds lovely!' Melody couldn't resist. 'All right, give me five minutes to slap on some make-up and put on a dress. Ten,' she corrected herself, dashing inside. 'Come on in and have a glass of fizz while you're waiting, why don't you? I'll be as quick as possible—' She grinned. 'Actresses can put on make-up *really* fast when we need to.'

'I don't mind if I do,' Andy said gratefully, coming inside and pouring himself a glass of champagne. 'I don't mind telling you, I'm having *quite* a rollercoaster ride this New Year's!'

Melody hugged him briefly but fiercely.

'You and me both,' she said. 'And Aniela too. She and I've been through the wars in the last few days. Can't *wait* to raise a glass with you two in—' She looked up at the clock. 'Shit, barely an hour!'

Dasha

*D*asha was pacing up and down on the concrete floor by the back door to the parking garage. It should, of course, have been guarded, but Dasha was alone: Nestor, who was supposed to be on duty there, had been summoned by Ilya, who, up in the penthouse, had decided that this was the ideal time for him and Nestor to take out the stuntman. The disarray and confusion after Diane's girls had had to abort their show, the bustle of trying to clear up and make the party respectable for Dmitri and Zhivana, had provided an excellent opportunity for Ilya to slip out and meet Nestor in the lobby before heading up to the fortieth floor.

But it had been over forty minutes since Nestor had left, and still she had heard nothing.

Not good. Not good at all. Nestor should be back down here by now, or at least have sent me a text to let me know what the hell's going on.

Dasha had been holed up in this garage for two hours now, ever since Nestor had let her in the back door to wait with him for Ilya's signal to meet up. She was getting pretty damn sick of the sight of concrete walls and columns; there wasn't even a gleaming array of cars to look at, as the few here were all carefully shrouded in custom-made protective covers. The only one that was visible was a bright yellow Lamborghini, which had just been driven down in the huge elevator by the doorman on duty. He and Nestor had ooh-ed and aah-ed over the big shiny thing as Dasha concealed herself behind one of the pillars, rolling her eyes in contempt.

Boys and their toys, she thought contemptuously, lighting a Sobranie cigarette from the butt of the last one, throwing the butt to the ground and grinding it under the sole of her five-inch Louboutin. *They make me sick. If they put that money into precious stones, it would be a good investment. With those cars, they might as well just piss it away.*

She checked her watch yet again. *Jesus Christ, where the fuck are those two incompetents? What are they doing, having tea with him instead of shooting him in the head? How long does it take to kill someone?*

Dasha answered her own question. *No time at all.*

She had done it herself many times, and was planning to do it again tonight, twice over: take out Ilya and Nestor herself, after they'd dealt with Jon, covering her tracks. It was imperative that no avenue was left for Grigor to one day discover that his wife had planned to have him murdered. Nestor had disabled the CCTV in the garage before letting Dasha in, so there would be no video evidence of what she was going to do as soon as Nestor and Ilya came down here to report their success. She would shoot them both, take out their guns, put them in their hands and fire another shot; at a cursory glance it would look as if they had killed each other in a shootout. It might, or might not, be connected to Jon's murder, depending on how much Grigor allowed the local police access to investigate, but that was not Dasha's concern. Once she had taken out the two bodyguards, she would disappear out of the parking garage, go back to her car and drive back to the Dorchester, where she was staying.

No one would ever connect her to the three deaths. She was sure of that. But it all depended on Nestor and Ilya's succeeding in killing Jon Jordan . . .

Dammit! she thought furiously. Her feet were starting to hurt; she had been standing up for over two hours. *What's that English expression? If you want a job done well, do it yourself!*

She pulled her mobile from her bag and dialled both Ilya and Nestor's numbers. They rang for five rings each and went to voicemail. *Fuck it. This is not good.*

Dasha's careful plan was dissolving into smithereens before her eyes. She was going to have to go upstairs, something she had had no intention of doing; but she couldn't stay here for ever, waiting for those idiots to return. Something had clearly gone wrong, and, as usual, she was going to have to fix it . . .

Her heels tapped out a vicious, menacing tattoo as she strode across the garage to the lift that would take her up to the fortieth floor; she was so livid that she forgot she was still smoking, and had to throw the cigarette out of the lift just as the doors began to close, the smoke alarm blaring for a split-second before it cut off again.

In Dasha's YSL silver handbag, among other things, was a Glock B26, tiny but lethal, nicknamed the 'baby Glock' by gun sellers. She pulled the handbag across her chest and held it open with her left hand, her right hand hovering at the opening; as the doors slid open at the fortieth floor, and she stepped out, listening intently for anything from a scuffle to a gunfight, she moved her right hand down, feeling the familiar weight and heft of the pistol. It was just over four inches high, fitting neatly in her palm; she worked the long nail of her index finger as she manoeuvred it around the trigger. She had a full magazine: ten rounds.

More than enough for all three of them, if necessary, she thought grimly as she moved down the corridor.

On full alert, she paused at the corner around which Jon's apartment door was located. All she could hear was a faint thumping noise, which could have been anything, even a dishwasher being run. *Though who runs a dishwasher this late on New Year's Eve?* Edging around the turn in the corridor, she found it empty. Closed doors, a wreath hanging on Jon's apartment door, none on any of the others. They were all unoccupied but his; she knew Grigor's habit of offering wreaths to any other occupant of the building when he was in residence for Christmas.

And no one turns down a gift from Grigor Khalovsksy.

But if there's no one staying in the apartment next door, why am I hearing thumping coming from inside?

She pulled out her phone and dialled Nestor's number. Twenty seconds later, she heard the unmistakable sound of a mobile phone ringing behind the door of the apartment from which the bumping noise was issuing. With great caution, Dasha tried the door handle; unsurprisingly, it was locked.

The phone was still ringing inside. Making a snap decision, trusting her instinct as she had so often before, Dasha picked up the hem of her coat with her left hand, doubled up the heavy fur into a fold, hoicked it up over the lock of the apartment door, nestled the barrel of the Glock against the coat and fired a shot. The sound was muffled very successfully by the fur, a dull metallic plop; letting the coat fall, Dasha saw with satisfaction that the small, 9 mm bullet had blown a neat little hole through the lock, disabling it. The coat had not only muted the gunshot, but prevented any tell-tale scorching on the metal of the lock; unless you bent to look at it closely, you wouldn't even notice the bullet hole.

She was inside in a second, closing the door behind her. Nestor and Ilya were lying on the floor of the living room, and she saw them immediately, on their sides, their hands and feet tied together, limbs bent up awkwardly behind their backs, hogtied with great efficiency. Ilya was still unconscious, but Nestor was awake, his eyes meeting Dasha's frenziedly; he was trying to yell, but the gag prevented him. The thumping she had heard had clearly been him, trying to break free of his bonds, to no avail.

'Useless cunts,' she muttered, pulling the Glock out of her bag.

Picking up a pillow from the sofa, she walked over to Ilya

and shoved it over his face. Bending over him, she worked the gun into one of his eye sockets and shot him. Nestor's eyes were so wide now that the eyeballs looked as if they were about to pop out of their sockets, his heels drumming on the carpet as he attempted desperately to wriggle away from her. She couldn't even relish the moment, she was so angry about their failure.

'Fuck you,' she said, kneeling down beside him, pillow in hand. Covering his face, she repeated the process; she would have preferred to see those madly staring eyes freaking out as the barrel approached, but she needed to use a sound suppressor, and the pillow was perfect. The eye shot was her preferred method of execution. There was no risk of the victim surviving with a bullet fired straight into his skull. Also, it was particularly upsetting for anyone who saw the body, which added a nice touch of intimidation. Dasha firmly believed in ruling through fear.

Nestor's body slumped sideways, an instant death.

Too good for him, she thought, standing up. *I would have gutshot those losers and left them to die in agony, but I couldn't take the risk of their being found and spilling the beans about who hired them.*

Right.

She threw the pillow aside and strode towards the door.

Two down, one to go.

She was just about to open it when she heard movement outside. Angling as best she could to squint sideways out of the peephole at the next-door apartment, she saw Jon emerge. Even with this distorted, fish-eye vision, she knew that he was carrying; his right hand, hovering at his waist, clearly indicated that there was a gun in the small of his back. She tensed, thinking he was coming here to check on the bodyguards; *it's perfect*, she realised. *If he comes up to the door, I can shoot him right through the peephole.*

But he didn't. He was sweeping the area, backing away,

covering the door from which he had just exited, moving out of her line of sight, and then she realised why; something was sliding out, a wheelchair, pushed by a nurse, that white uniform unmistakable.

Damn. He's on the move. He knows that Nestor and Ilya came to kill him. He might even be heading up to Grigor's now to tell him everything – who knows?

There was no time to speculate on what was going on, why on earth there was another patient in that room, accompanied by a nurse. If Dasha didn't act quickly and decisively, everything might be lost. Jon would survive, and his knowledge was simply too dangerous for her to let that happen. And she couldn't leave any witnesses behind.

I have no choice. I've got to kill them all.

Aniela

*D*asha's improvised silencers had worked very effectively. Jon and Aniela had been in the bedroom, lifting Jeremy Bingham-Smythe into the wheelchair, when she had been firing the Glock, and the noise had not carried through the walls separating the apartments, especially since they were mirror-images of each other, each kitchen wall heavily tiled and lined with sound-muffling appliances. So they had no idea of Dasha's presence next door; the reason Jon chose to turn right, rather than left, coming out of the apartment was to head for the further bank of lifts.

'Anyone who knows where this apartment's located is likely to take the closer lifts,' he said swiftly, as they fastened the straps around Mr Bingham-Smythe's unconscious body to hold him into the chair. 'We'll have a better chance of avoiding anyone by going that bit further. I'll take point, you push the chair. Don't say a word and keep one eye on me the whole time, okay? Just follow my lead.'

He opened the door and slipped out, leaving it open; twenty seconds later he gestured for her to follow with the chair. Aniela was so used to pushing wheelchairs that she could manoeuvre it with comparative ease, and she swivelled it round the corner and down the corridor, fast, keeping pace with Jon, avoiding the side tables positioned along the walls every ten feet or so. Jon's head swivelled constantly from side to side, taking in every aspect of their surroundings, but he walked very swiftly, up on the balls of his feet, and Aniela felt the muscles of her back, her arms, the front of her thighs, flexing as she pushed the chair equally fast.

It was too fast for Dasha: they had practically shot out of the apartment, Aniela kicking the door shut behind them, and they were halfway down the corridor before she had even got her own front door open. Dasha was no sniper, and she had never engaged in a shootout. Her skills were close-range torture and execution. If she had had a Kalashnikov, she could have taken the entire group out from a distance, spraying them with bullets: but instead of an AK-47, she had a pocket handgun which held ten rounds, and she had fired three of those. She couldn't afford to waste any more bullets firing at random, especially against Jon, who she had to assume had all the armoury that Nestor and Ilya had been carrying, besides any of his own he might have already possessed.

Stealth was the only way. She stripped off her coat, hiked up her skirt above her knees, and kicked off her shoes, and as soon as they disappeared around a corner, she shot out down the corridor in pursuit, the Glock in her hand. They had already rounded the next turn, were getting close to the lift bank; Dasha knew she needed to act as swiftly as possible . . .

Aniela's heart was beating fast, but she was managing to stay calm and collected, despite the fact that she could see a gun shoved down the back of Jon's sweatpants – *and there's another one in the pocket on the back of the wheelchair*, she knew. The pale blue vinyl was distended with the bulk of the pistol, the gleam of steel inside unmistakable. They were at the lifts now, Jon pressing the call button then moving away, to scope out the corridor that ran along the far side of the lift bank, making sure that no one had looped around and was coming at them from that direction—

Oof! Someone grabbed Aniela from behind, an arm around her throat, dragging her off balance. The hand round her neck was sharp-nailed; the tips dug into her as she struggled to catch her breath. And then she felt something cold and hard shoved into her right temple.

'Don't move,' Dasha Khalovsky hissed in her ear, her breath stinking so strongly of cigarette smoke that Aniela couldn't help flinching back. Aniela's head was twisted to one side in Dasha's grip: beside her, Dasha said loudly to Jon:

'Drop your gun or I'll shoot her in the head!'

Jon had dragged his gun from his waistband in a blur of movement, unbelievably fast. He was aiming it two-handed at the women, his legs slightly bent, his eyes absolutely calm and focused. Aniela had never had a gun pointed at her in her life; it was the most terrifying thing she could imagine, even with Jon behind it. She trusted him completely, and still, the sight of that wicked dark barrel, so small and so lethal, was paralysingly frightening.

'It's you I want!' Dasha hissed at Jon. 'I'll let these two go if you drop the gun!'

The big Glock spun in Jon's right hand, pointing up into the air, his hands spread wide. His voice was very calm when he said:

'Okay. I'm going to put this down, slowly, so it doesn't go off. I'm going to kneel down and put it on the ground. Let me just do that, and then we can talk this over—'

But Aniela felt the pressure of the gun against her temple abate; Dasha was already pulling it away to aim at Jon.

No! I won't let her! Pulling away, shoving back with all her might, Aniela saw Dasha's arm lowering as she targeted Jon. Later she thought that she had seen Dasha's finger tightening on the trigger, the pointed red nail gleaming, but that was obviously impossible; there was no way she could have noticed that level of detail, not with the speed with which it all happened. Aniela lunged forward, grabbing Dasha's arm, pulling it down just as the gun went off. The bang seemed incredibly loud at such close quarters, but Aniela couldn't let herself be distracted by it; her entire focus was on the gun, getting it pointed into the carpet, away from Jon, away from the wheelchair.

The two women wrestled, panting, Aniela's strong hands closing around Dasha's wrist. Aniela's job was physical, and she had peasant genes that had blessed her with solid, strong muscles; she had the advantage on Dasha, and she used it mercilessly. *I want to break this bitch's wrist!* she thought viciously, bending it till Dasha screamed in fury. The gun went off again, the recoil shocking Aniela, but it was pointing down and away; that shot at least went wide of everyone.

But what about the first one? How badly is Jon hit? The worst part of all – worse than the frenzied struggle with Dasha, her foul breath so close, the nails of Dasha's left hand digging into Aniela's arm, trying to pull it off, drawing blood – was that Aniela could not afford to glance ahead, even for a moment, to see how Jon was – *because she must have hit him! If she hadn't I wouldn't be fighting her alone, he'd be over here dragging her off me—*

The thought of Jon lying on the ground, bleeding out, needing her desperately, while she was unable to run to him, gave her extra strength, rage rising in her like a red cloud of fury. She forced the Glock from Dasha's hands so violently that Dasha screamed again. *I hope I broke a finger!* Aniela thought, as the gun flew out of her grasp, across the hallway.

The doors of the closest lift slid open with a ping and, with appalling luck, the gun landed inside the car. Dasha, who was marginally closer, precipitated herself towards it, Aniela throwing herself on top of her. The breath shot out of Dasha as Aniela landed on her, flattening the thinner woman, her bosoms squeezing out on either side of her body like fat, padded balloons. Dasha's arm, reaching out for the gun, was plastered flat to the lift floor. Aniela tried to drag herself over

Dasha to grab the Glock: it was all she could see, her utter and total focus, lying there in the far corner, its metal dull against the shiny floor and marble walls, a stubby, compact black gun with a squat, wide stock. Such an ugly small thing to be able to kill, to make two women fight to the death, if necessary, to gain possession of it—

Grabbing Dasha's hair, Aniela pulled up the Russian woman's head, meaning to slam her forehead down into the lift floor. It should have been a knockout blow, but Aniela had clutched the hair so hard that half of it came away in her hand, a dry, crispy mix of tinsel extensions and real hair that Dasha had bought and had woven into her own. Aniela stared in shock for a moment at the contents of her fist, and Dasha, howling like a dog, bucked up underneath Aniela, jerking her off to the side.

The lift doors slammed shut. Panicking, Aniela reached up, frantically trying to find the button that would open them again; but she must have hit the wrong one, because the lift hummed into life, the floor falling away below the two women as it started to drop. Dasha, twisting round, punched Aniela in the face. Aniela hit her back with the hand still gripping Dasha's clump of hair. Dasha's red-lipsticked mouth gaped wide, and Aniela shoved the hair into it, Dasha coughing and choking and simultaneously trying to bite down on Aniela's hand.

What do you do when a dog bites you? In a flash, Aniela remembered what her father had done years ago when a neighbour's dog had bitten his leg: he'd grabbed the dog's head and rammed it further into his calf, choking the animal, forcing it to release its hold; then, with the grip he'd got on the back of its neck, he'd hurled the mutt away, right over the fence that separated their gardens. The dog had been very subdued ever since.

Do it! Against every physical instinct, Aniela shoved her hand into Dasha's mouth even further, forcing Dasha's jaw to yawn so wide that she couldn't bite down any more. Blood was running down Aniela's arm from where Dasha's pointed nails had dug in, and now there was blood on her knuckles from Dasha's bite. Spitting the hair out of her mouth, Dasha reached both hands out, eyes narrowed into slits of fury, and lunged for Aniela's neck.

'You stupid Polack bitch!' Dasha gasped, grabbing hold of Aniela, trying to strangle her: they were on their knees now, facing each other.

'Russian whore!' Aniela snapped back, wrapping her arms around Dasha's back, splaying her fingers, and grabbing every last strand of Dasha's hair she could, feeling an odd series of knobbly knots under her fingers where the extensions had been put in. Snagging her fingers around them, she pulled back viciously, snapping Dasha's head back on her neck with an audible click; Dasha's grip on Aniela's neck weakened as her own windpipe closed up.

Aniela shook partly free of Dasha's hands, lunging over her to try to get the gun. As she did so, the lift landed with a little bump, and Dasha's head came upright. The women smashed their foreheads into each other's with a crack of bone against bone, an unintended head-butt that sent them both reeling, seeing stars.

The lift doors slid open. Aniela tried once again to get past Dasha to the gun, but Dasha blocked her, throwing her body into Aniela's, and they fell back, towards the lobby, where the lift had come to rest, through the doors.

Get back – up to Jon – get the gun – knock her out and get back in the lift—

The trouble was that both of them had exactly the same goal, and neither of them had anything left to lose. Aniela was frantic to save the man she loved, make sure Dasha couldn't finish what she had begun; Dasha had to kill Jon, *now*, because she had shown her hand, and Jon would be heading straight to Grigor if she didn't silence him as soon as she possibly could . . .

Dasha was over Aniela, her hands raised into claws, coming for her face. Aniela, on her bottom, scrabbled away, crab-like, looking desperately around her for a weapon of any sort, a way to hit Dasha without getting her face ripped to pieces. The gun was in the lift car, with Dasha blocking her access, and might as well have been on Mars for any good it was to her.

At the end of the lift bank was one of the decorative tables with which Limehouse Reach was strewn; on it was a big transparent-glass hollow spherical vase, exactly the same shape as a goldfish bowl, but containing orchids floating in water instead of a small orange fish. The orchids were white, and Andy had made the effect Christmas-like by dropping green and red ornaments into the vase too, and twining it round with ivy. Aniela crab-crawled back even further, trying to lure Dasha towards her, away from the gun, putting the best frightened expression on her face that she could. Dasha's lips pulled back from her teeth in a snarl, her eyes lighting up in a predatory gleam of triumph, as she dived towards Aniela like a raging hyena.

And as she did so, Aniela twisted round, grabbed the vase with both hands, and brought it down on Dasha's head. Water spilled everywhere as she dragged the vase off the table, making the big vase slippery and hard to aim, the ornaments sliding out, the ivy landing round Dasha's neck. It was a glancing blow, imperfect, but enough to send Dasha staggering back, and Aniela crowed in triumph:

'That's for Katyn, you Russian bitch!'

'Fuck you!' Dasha reeled towards her, grabbing for the vase, catching hold of the rim; they wrestled for it, and it shot out of their hands in an arc, landing with a crash on the smooth floor of the lobby.

Shouts were heard from the main reception desk as the vase shattered spectacularly over the palazzo tiles. Aniela staggered to her feet, picked up the table the vase had been standing on, and smashed it across Dasha's body as the Russian lunged for her; but as she did, her heel slipped on the water that had poured from the vase, and she fell backwards, winding herself as she toppled to the ground. Dasha, knocked to all fours, crawled towards her. Aniela managed to get her elbows under her body, pushing herself up, but she had hit her head in the fall and her vision was blurry, her head woozy. Dasha, with an insane light in her eyes, grabbed her head, shoved her back and started to try to force her back into the sunken carp pond; three sides of it were surrounded by a low black slate rim, on which Dmitri and Zhivana had been sitting earlier, but the fourth was a decoratively flat, bleeding-edge drain-off, and Dasha, taking full advantage of Aniela's visibly dazed condition, proceeded to drag her shoulders up far enough so that she could get Aniela's head underwater.

'This is for fucking *Stalingrad!*' she screamed, completely beside herself with fury now.

The chilly water was actually the best temporary cure for a head blow imaginable. In the seconds before her face went under, Aniela's eyes snapped open with shock, the pain in her skull fading: Dasha shoved Aniela's head under and started to push it down, but Aniela's hands came up, grabbed Dasha's arms, and, with everything she had, twisting, turning, her strong Polish peasant body lifted Dasha's, hauling it towards her, dragging the Russian woman right into the carp pond with her.

Water splashed everywhere. Below Aniela, a long slippery body folded and pushed away from her with a slick muscular contraction, a poor hapless koi carp whose peaceful existence had just been brutally invaded. Dasha had tumbled on top of her, and Aniela started to push her off, but then she felt Dasha's weight lifting, miraculously allowing Aniela to rise to the surface. She came up, spluttering, shaking her head, to see the pond surrounded by men: the security guards, Kevin the desk guy, the doorman in his overcoat, and two of Grigor's bodyguards, leaning down to pull their employer's wife out of the water, one heaving on each arm.

'Dasha Sakharova! *Vsyo v poryadke?* Are you all right?' one asked solicitously.

'Ugh!' Dasha's hair was plastered to her face, the knobs of the remaining extensions showing now that it was wet. Her make-up was smeared, her expression livid. Kevin was bending over, helping a soaking Aniela out of the pond: Aniela was freezing, shivering, but had never felt clearer-headed in her life. Gaining her feet, she saw that Dasha was balancing herself, her left hand on one of the bodyguard's arms, her right hand snaking inside his jacket, reaching for his shoulder holster—

Fuck! Fuck! She's going for his gun!

Aniela launched herself towards Dasha just as the Russian woman dragged the gun from the holster. Their bodies collided; the gun flew from Dasha's hand; Dasha tottered backwards, Aniela on top of her, and they crashed into one of the smaller Christmas trees, a ten-footer in a pot by the side of the carp pond, knocking it over as they tumbled to the ground, locked in a wrestling hold.

Absolutely Everyone

*T*he doors of the penthouse lift opened into the lobby, and a whole group of people tumbled out. Melody was in the lead; the last one in, she was the first to leave, and she was the lithest and the fastest. Seeing a gun fly through the air and clatter to the tiles, she dashed towards it and grabbed hold of it, picking it up and holding it as carefully as if it were made of glass.

Behind her, Andy, Wayne, Dmitri, Zhivana, Grigor, and three more bodyguards piled out of the lift: they had been summoned by a frantic call from Kevin to tell Grigor that his wife and the Canary Clinic nurse were, for some reason, engaged in a major catfight in the lobby of the building.

'Dasha!' Grigor yelled. 'Where are you? What the fuck is going on? Why are you *here*?'

'*Mama?*' Dmitri called, looking around him. 'Where are you?'

But Dasha and Aniela were hidden by the bulk of the Christmas tree, lying on its side. A ping came from the main bank of lifts, a green light flashing on as car doors opened and Jon limped out. Melody looked at him and screamed: blood was clotted down one leg of his sweatpants, and he was naked to the waist, his T-shirt pulled off, twisted into a rope and tied tightly around the upper thigh of the bloodstained leg, an impromptu tourniquet. His jaw was set grimly, his bare chest beaded with sweat, and he carried a gun like the one Melody was holding, pressed to his thigh. He looked like an action hero in the last reel of the film, beaten up by the bad guys, left for dead, risen from the grave.

He looked at Melody.

'Where is she?' he said, his voice husky, limping towards her as fast as he could. 'Is she all right? For God's sake, tell me she's all right!'

'I don't know!' she wailed, feeling helpless. 'I don't know what's going on!'

'Melody!' A new arrival stood in the entrance to the lobby, the revolving doors slowing down behind him. 'My God, what's happening?'

He looked in disbelief at the scene in front of him; the bodyguards, the water spilled everywhere, the fallen Christmas tree, the expressions of panic on everyone's faces.

'*James?*'

Forgetting everything but him, Melody dashed towards him, throwing herself into his arms. His closed around her tightly, the leather of his jacket smelling deliciously familiar, his scent as enveloping as his embrace. She couldn't believe it, couldn't take in that he was here, but when she looked up, she saw his face so close, so dear and tender, and she burst into tears of hysterical happiness as he kissed her, clinging to him fiercely. This was everything she had wanted, James back in her arms, kissing her hard, and she heard herself sobbing as she twisted her fingers in his fine silky hair and kissed him back, pressing her whole body against him, crying so hard that she could barely breathe.

When he pulled back, he exclaimed:

'Oh God, darling, your face – am I hurting you?'

All she could do was shake her head, tears running down her cheeks, snot bubbling in her nose, and laugh and cry simultaneously, as James produced a handkerchief from his trouser pocket – that was James all over, he always had a linen handkerchief on him – and started, with gentle care, to blot her face.

Then he reared back, horrified.

'Melody!' he said, looking at her right hand. 'Why are you holding a *gun*?'

Grigor's bodyguards had just noticed that Jon, too, was armed, and they had taken a very proactive approach: one of them came up behind him with his own Glock pulled and aimed it at Jon's head, clicking off the safety.

'*Brosay oruzhie*!' he yelled. 'Drop it!'

'Mr Khalovsky, Aniela's in danger!' Jon said urgently to Grigor, obeying the bodyguard. 'The nurse – she saved you when you fainted – your wife's trying to kill her—'

Grigor's hands rose to his head; he looked as if he were trying to pull out the little hair he had left.

'Dasha is *mad*!' he wailed. 'Completely mad! I never know what she will do next! Why is she trying to kill a *nurse*, for fuck's sake! She is *completely* ruining New Year's Eve for me!'

'Mama!' Dmitri took a few steps towards the fallen Christmas tree. 'Mama, what's going on?'

Then almost the entire lobbyful of people gasped in shock as Dasha rose to her knees behind the wide sprawl of tree branches. Only the bodyguards and Jon, trained in combat, didn't react audibly, but even they flinched at the sight of her. She looked as if she had gone twenty rounds with a cage-fighter. Her face was a livid mask, her hair hanging down in clumps, a big patch on the side of her head bald where Aniela had pulled out more extensions. Her blouse was ripped and torn. In one hand she held a long shard of glass, one of the points of the ornamental star which had been on top of the tree and had snapped when it crashed to the ground. Dasha's other hand was twisted in Aniela's hair, and now Dasha dragged herself up to her feet, pulling Aniela with her, the broken point of the star jabbing into the nurse's neck, beginning to draw blood.

'I'll kill her!' she screamed. 'I'll do it!'

'Dasha, what the *fuck*!' Grigor spread his arms wide. 'Are you trying to kill me? Are you trying to give me another heart attack? Why the fuck are you *doing* this?'

'Papa! It's not always about you!' Dmitri said angrily to his father.

'It *is* about you,' Jon said urgently to Grigor, pitching his voice to cut low, through the high-pitched screams. 'She wanted me to kill you.'

'*What?*' Grigor exclaimed. '*Fuck*, Dasha, *why?*'

'You wanted a divorce!' she screamed, the ornament wobbling dangerously close to Aniela's jugular. 'To marry that little bitch!' Dasha jerked her head at Zhivana, who clung in fear to Dmitri's arm.

'*Mama!* You're talking about my wife!' Dmitri yelled back angrily. 'She's your daughter-in-law now – show some respect!'

'You got *married?*' Grigor stared at them. 'I thought you were just engaged!'

'We eloped,' Dmitri said, going pink. 'To Gretna Green. We were going to announce it at midnight, but—'

'I read about it in a Regency novel by Georgette Heyer, going to Gretna Green to get married,' Zhivana piped up excitedly. '*Black Sheep.* You can still do it! I was so excited!'

'Jesus,' Dasha said, looking at Zhivana contemptuously. '*That's* what's going to breed my grandchildren?'

'Dasha!' Grigor turned to yell at her again. 'Shut *up*! *Suka ty sumasshedshaya!* You are a mad, crazy bitch!'

But Dasha was on the move, pulling Aniela with her, the glass of the Christmas star still pressed deep into Aniela's neck. She was edging round the tree, heading for the cover of the second lift bank.

'I'm going out the back door,' she said loudly. 'Don't try to stop me. Or I'll kill this big Polack cow.'

She jabbed the tip of the glass shard so hard against Aniela's skin that she drew more blood: Zhivana let out a wail as she saw the blood trickling down onto the collar of Aniela's uniform. Aniela was very pale, her head tilted at a painful sideways angle as Dasha dragged her along, forcing her to walk in front of Dasha, a human shield. The two women, wedged into each other awkwardly, like a parody of an embrace, moved past the base of the tree, almost their entire bodies exposed to view now. Blood was clotted on Aniela's arm from Dasha's nails, and smeared into Dasha's hair where Aniela had hit her with the bowl. The sight of the two combat-scarred women was so grotesque that everyone stared at them in horror. Grigor's bodyguards had their guns drawn, but none of them knew what to do: this, after all, was their boss's wife.

'Tell him to take the gun off me!' Jon said urgently to Grigor. 'She'll kill her! I can stop her!'

Grigor barked the order at the bodyguard holding the Glock on Jon, who dived for his gun. But Dasha and Aniela were already out of range for Jon's Glock; they were concealed by the angle of the tree, the jut of the lift shaft.

'That's right, you dumb Polish cow,' Dasha hissed at Aniela, twisting the glass into the wound on her neck, making Aniela gasp in pain. 'Keep up with me or I'll tear your throat out . . .'

The next second, a shot rang out. Dasha toppled back, grasping her arm, from which blood was spurting. Aniela pushed her away and fled, jumping over the tree, heading straight for Jon, hitting his body like a cannonball fired at close range. He took the impact without flinching, a net in which she landed, his arms wrapping round her, her head buried against his chest. Everyone else looked around in shock, unable to understand who had fired the bullet, because no one had had a clear shot at Dasha: the lift shaft blocked them almost completely.

And then, as one, their heads slowly turned. Everyone gradually worked out the angle from which the shot must have come, and they swivelled round to stare in disbelief towards the lobby doors, where Melody stood with James. He was lowering the Glock that Melody had retrieved earlier, a modest little smile of satisfaction on his face.

'Oh my God, it's Dr Who!' Andy exclaimed. 'Did you use your sonic screwdriver?'

'*You?*' Grigor exclaimed in disbelief. 'But you are an *actor*! *You* shot my wife?'

'I'm terribly sorry,' James said apologetically. 'But she was hurting that poor girl, and I thought she really ought to be stopped. I just winged her.'

'You make an amazing shot!' Grigor said, shaking his head in disbelief, and several of the bodyguards murmured in respectful agreement.

'She's getting away!' Wayne called, as Dasha, one hand plastered to her arm, from which blood was pouring, ducked around the back of the lift shaft, going for the back door; Grigor barked an order and two guards ran to cut off her escape route, catching her shoulders, frogmarching her back.

'I've been cast in *Mission Impossible VI*,' James explained, carefully clicking on the Glock's safety. 'I'm the German villain, rather amusingly. The director's awfully keen on authenticity, so he's been having me do lots of target shooting – it turns out I'm rather good with handguns. My instructors are very pleased with me.'

Jon, raising his head from Aniela's, let out a long slow whistle.

'Jeez,' he said. 'That was quite a risk you took, buddy. You could have shot my girl.'

'Oh, I'm used to moving targets too,' James reassured him, smiling. 'I've been clay pigeon shooting since I was ten. Not to worry.'

'Clearly,' Jon said dryly.

'Don't listen to him!' Dasha screamed from the far side of the lobby; she was being bundled away by the bodyguards.

'He's from the CIA! He's an assassin for them! He's a CIA assassin, Grigor – he was trying to kill you, not me—'

In Jon's arms, Aniela stiffened with fear. But he remained perfectly calm, shaking his head, smiling, as if he couldn't help being amused by this blatant lie.

'She's just angry because I wouldn't do what she wanted,' Jon said to Grigor. 'I don't even know why she asked me in the first place. I'm just a stuntman – I don't go round killing people.'

'Liar!' Dasha shrieked. 'You are a liar!'

'And *you*,' Aniela yelled back at her, 'don't even know your *history*! The Poles didn't do anything to the Russians at Stalingrad, you stupid bitch! It was the *Germans*!'

But then the bodyguards shoved Dasha into one of the lifts, and the insults she screamed back at Aniela were blurred by the closing doors. They could still hear her for a few seconds more, ululating in fury as the lift descended.

'She is a mad, crazy woman!' Grigor said furiously. 'You saved me from her on Christmas Day,' he added to Jon. 'I know you are not trying to kill me, my friend. Not to worry.'

He slapped Jon on the shoulder; Jon staggered a little, and Aniela, remembering that he had been shot, pulled back, shocked.

'Oh my God,' she moaned, her usual professional calm completely deserting her, 'your *leg* . . .'

Everyone looked down at Jon's thigh and winced.

'It went straight through,' he reassured her. 'I've had—' He was about to say *worse*, but remembered, just in time, that he was a stuntman, not a hitman. 'I've taken plenty of knocks in my job,' he corrected himself. 'But we should get this cleaned up, make sure there isn't any fabric in the wound.'

Grigor snapped orders at the bodyguard who had been holding the Glock on Jon; the big, burly man strode over to Jon, took him firmly under one arm, and half-carried him over to the door that led to the Clinic, Aniela bustling after them.

'Everyone!' Andy, the party organiser, called. 'It's nearly midnight!'

'Quick! We must go up to the party!' Grigor said excitedly.

'No, there isn't time!' Andy raced over to his desk, turned on his little TV and cranked up the volume to maximum. 'There's only a couple of minutes to go!'

' – a really amazing atmosphere in Trafalgar Square, despite the falling snow,' the reporter said, her voice raised over the din of the happy crowd behind her. 'You can hear them now – "God Save The Queen"'s being sung by a big group behind me, very patriotic – and the countdown is about to start, it's almost just a minute to midnight—'

The noise of cheers, singing and revellers yelling poured from the TV's speakers. Dmitri took hold of Zhivana's hands, the two newlyweds smiling with enchantment into each other's faces. By the Clinic door, Jon paused, and the bodyguard stepped back as Jon reached for Aniela.

'I've never been so scared in my life as when I saw those lift doors closing on the two of you,' he said solemnly. 'I felt so shitty not being able to protect you.'

'But I am all right!' Aniela reassured him. 'I was so scared for *you* – I didn't know if she had killed you—'

She shivered at the thought.

'Aniela, I want you to come with me,' he said, pulling her into his arms. 'To the States. I want you with me the whole time, so I can do my damndest to make sure nothing bad happens to you.'

'I can't be with you the *whole* time,' Aniela said, happiness flooding through her like bubbles, making her feel as light as air.

'I'll keep you as close as possible,' he vowed.

'And when you're not there, I can be saved by Dr Who!' she said, dizzy with disbelief that this was actually happening, that her dream was coming true.

Jon laughed. 'So you'll come?' he said, his arms tightening

round her. 'You'll come to Montana with me and live on a huge ranch with just me and a whole bunch of animals?'

'I would *love* to!' Aniela said joyously, her eyes sparkling at the prospect. 'I love animals! I am a farm girl. Can we have dogs?'

'Sure! Maybe Rotties?' he said. 'You OK with them? They have a bad rep, but—'

'Oh no, they are very good dogs,' she agreed. 'And if you have cows, they are very good indeed. You know, they were bred for—'

'Herding cattle,' he finished, grinning. 'You really are a farm girl. You won't be lonely?' he added. 'Out in the middle of nowhere with me and the dogs?'

She reached up and pulled his head down for a kiss.

'No. Only you and some dogs, that is fine,' she said contentedly. 'I told you before I didn't like people.'

'Yeah, I never got that,' Jon said. 'How come you went into nursing if you don't like people?'

Aniela, whose name in Polish meant 'angel', smiled at him.

'I wasn't a nurse because I liked people,' she said simply, 'but because I like to fix things. Make people whole.' She reached up and patted Jon's cheek. 'And now I'm fixing you.'

He stared down at her, swallowing hard, because he was unable to speak.

Slowly, he shook his head, not in denial, but in shock at how his life had utterly changed since he had met Aniela just nine days ago.

'Oh!' He reared back. 'I have to tell you something – before you decide to come to the States with me – *This is the hardest thing I've ever done*, he thought. *The bravest I'll ever have to be*.

'I killed my father when I was seventeen,' he blurted out in a rush. Looking anxiously down at her, waiting for her reaction, he had never felt so nervous in his life. Not even on his first mission.

To his amazement, Aniela reached up and stroked his cheek again. 'I'm sure you had a good reason,' she said.

Over at the doors, James was handing the Glock back to the bodyguard it belonged to, who received it with a ceremonial nod of his head.

'You shoot good, Doctor Who,' he said, backing away as James turned eagerly to Melody.

'Darling, you got the part!' he blurted out. 'You got Beatrice! Isn't that wonderful?'

Melody actually thought she was going to faint; the blood rushed from her head.

'That's why I shot over here, to tell you! I was at a party with Martin, and he'd had quite a few – he told me he'd talked Cate round, convinced her to cast you – and of course, I've been telling both of them that you were the only one I wanted for Beatrice,' James went on eagerly.

'Not Felicity?' Melody asked in disbelief. 'You didn't want her? She said—'

'Felicity said a lot of things,' James said grimly. 'She told me you and Brad were having an affair from the moment you went to LA, that you pulled the casting-couch thing to get the part. And that you were only trying to get back with me because LA didn't work out.'

'Oh *no*! I—'

'I should never have believed her,' James said softly. 'She made a big push to seduce me at my Christmas Eve party, and I was so lonely, I fell for it. I was a total idiot. Kathy tried to warn me, but I was pretty much on a bender for a couple of days, and Felicity sort of clamped on and wouldn't let go. God, I'm so sorry.'

'No, *I'm* sorry!' Melody said quickly. 'It was my fault, I left you in the lurch—'

'Stop, darling!' He kissed her again. 'I've forgiven you. I saw those photos of you in the press, and I felt so awful about what you'd been through – all the pain you put yourself through. Kathy told me a couple of days ago that she was sure it was Felicity who set the paparazzi onto you.' He shook his head. 'I was such an idiot to get involved with Felicity at all. I promise it didn't mean anything. I was just so lonely without you – in our house, with all the memories of you everywhere . . . I was so hoping you'd get Beatrice. I thought it would be a perfect way for us to get back together – and when I saw Martin, and he told me, I couldn't wait, I wanted to come and see you right away, and so I rang Kathy and badgered her until she told me where you were staying, and I found a cab and rushed straight over—'

'Oh, James, I'm so happy!' Melody said, clinging to him. 'I'm just so happy!'

'Wey-hey! Happy New Year!' yelled a loud voice. 'We brought you the party!'

It was Patrice, who, with a couple of other footballers, tumbled out of the lift, a few of Diane's girls in their wake. Patrice was carrying a magnum of champagne, its wire and foil already pulled off: his thumbs were cupped under the cork, and he started to ease it out, yelling, with the others, 'Four! Three! Two! One!'

Wayne, standing beside Grigor, suddenly sprang to life, running across the lobby. His stocky body moved with a sprinter's speed, and as he reached Andy's desk, he put one hand on top and vaulted up and over it. Gymnasts, male and female, can't grow too much: when coaches cherrypick children for training, they ask how tall the parents are, to make sure that they're not wasting their time coaching kids whose bodies will be too long to be effective. The push of Wayne's big thighs sent him flying through the air, and his compact body made it easy to control his direction. He landed exactly where he had planned to, squarely next to Andy, who goggled at him, amazed.

He was even more amazed when Wayne pulled him into his arms, announced loudly:

'I'm gay, everyone! I'm totally gay!'

And slammed his mouth into Andy's just as bells rang out and fireworks exploded on the TV screen.

'Happy New Year!' Patrice shouted obliviously, spraying everyone with champagne. The girls squealed, the bodyguards backed off, Grigor waved his arms in delight.

'Happy New Year!' he yelled, beaming wide. 'Happy bloody New Year!'

Patrice, swivelling the huge bottle like a machine gun, turned to direct it on Wayne and gawped at the sight of him embracing Andy, not having heard Wayne's coming-out battle cry.

'*Mate!*' he exclaimed. 'What the *fuck*! Is that a *man*?'

Sergei, by Grigor's side, sneered in triumph at the sight of his rival kissing a man so passionately. He looked as if, several days late, he had been given the best Christmas present he could conceivably have wanted.

'I'm gay, Patrice!' Wayne dragged his mouth from Andy's. 'Get used to it!'

Patrice's eyes bugged wide in shock. He turned to Grigor.

'Mr K?' he said weakly. 'You know about this?'

Grigor glanced over at Wayne and Andy. Beside him, Sergei was so eagerly awaiting his boss's reaction that he had completely stopped breathing; his cheeks were blowing up like a chipmunk's, and he was red as a turkeycock.

'Wayne can fuck sheep if he wants, as long as he keeps scoring goals for me,' Grigor said, shrugging. 'What do I care where he puts his dick?'

All the breath shot out of Sergei as if he had been punched in the stomach. His lower lip trembled visibly with his disappointment at Grigor's indifference to Andy and Wayne having coupled up.

'It's where he puts his balls that matters!' Andy said irrepressibly. 'Right, Mr K?'

Grigor roared with laughter. 'Right! Andy, you are a good boy! You keep him happy!'

'But – Chantelle—' Patrice managed, still having a hard time processing this revelation.

'Patrice, she's a lezzer!' Wayne said. 'She fucks your Corinne every chance she gets! They're probably at it right now!'

'*Really?*' Patrice's eyes widened.

'Everyone!' Grigor shouted, waving both arms in the air. 'We go upstairs now, to set off fireworks! Everyone is invited!'

Andy wrapped his hand into Wayne's as the guests began to head towards the lift.

'You all right?' he said in an undertone.

'Never better,' Wayne said decisively.

'It wasn't the drink talking? You're not going to regret this when we sober up?'

Wayne shook his head, squeezing Andy's hand.

'I feel like I've got the weight of the world off my shoulders for the first time ever,' he said, grinning like a madman. 'It's brilliant! I wish I'd done this years ago!'

'Oh my *God*, Mr Bingham-Smythe! I completely forgot about him!' Aniela pressed her hands to her cheeks in horror and turned to the bodyguard helping Jon. 'I can take Jon – please, can you go up to the fortieth floor, there's a man in a wheelchair there, can you bring him back down and into the Clinic—'

But just then, a ping came from the closer bank of lifts, and out of one of the cars came stumbling a very confused-looking man in stripy pyjamas and with a heavily bruised face.

'I just woke up in a wheelchair,' he said, 'and there was no one around – so I thought I'd better come down here and see what was going on – oh, I say, *this* is the party those chaps were talking about!'

Holding onto a marble pillar for support, he took in the scene around him: water and champagne puddled over the tiled floor, a whole cluster of people turning to stare back at him. Jeremy Bingham-Smythe looked from the famous face of Patrice, still clutching the magnum, to the even more famous face of Wayne Burns, hand in hand with a burgundy-uniformed concierge, to a gaggle of impossibly beautiful girls in tight dresses and high heels, to black-clad looming bodyguards with Grigor at their centre, to Zhivana and Dmitri still in their coats, thin and pale – and over by the lobby door, to a couple who were the most recognisable of all—

'Oh my God, I'm hallucinating!' he exclaimed, clapping one hand to his forehead, and looking at the contents of his other hand with bemusement. A bodyguard rushed over to relieve him of the Glock he was carrying.

'Thank you so much! Is it yours?' Jeremy Bingham-Smythe said. 'It was in the lift for some reason – I thought I'd better retrieve it. Not particularly safe to leave it lying around, eh?'

He grabbed onto the bodyguard's arm and looked up at him with a confidential smile.

'Tell me,' he asked, pointing to James and Melody. 'Is it just me? I'm on a *lot* of drugs. Can *you* see Wonder Woman over there, kissing Dr Who?'

Grigor herded everyone but Jon, Aniela and poor bemused Jeremy Bingham-Smythe up to the penthouse to drink champagne and celebrate the New Year, with many cheerful waves and gestures and assurances that he would follow immediately. He was flanked by two bodyguards, who were staying with him; as Dmitri filed in, and Grigor met his son's worried eyes, Grigor gave him a short sharp nod.

'Okay,' he said brusquely, the hail-fellow-well-met bonhomie wiped from his face the second the doors slid shut. He held his hand out, palm up, as he strode off to the other set of lifts: the closer bodyguard instantly removed his Beretta from his shoulder holster and placed it in his boss's clasp.

They descended to the parking garage in silence. It was eerily bereft of cars, and the shadows cast by the wide supporting concrete pillars lay in thick dark diagonals stripes over the empty parking spaces, white-painted, numbered according to the apartments to which they belonged. Grigor's bodyguards had Dasha pinned in the far corner; she hung between them, head tipped forward, what was left of the ratty blonde extensions drying now, hanging over her face in elf-locks. A few strands of the tinsel showed against the artificial yellow colour, and her red silk blouse and zebra-print ponyskin skirt stood out vividly against the grey concrete wall and the black uniform of the bodyguards. She was barefoot, and her tights were ripped, red-painted toes poking through, blood on one calf, more blood clotted on the side of her temple; as she heard Grigor's footsteps approaching, she raised her head, glaring at him furiously.

'You're a bastard,' she spat, taking in his blank expression, the gun in his hand. 'You deserved to die for the way you treated me.'

Without saying a word, Grigor walked right up to her, raised the Beretta, and ground the barrel of the gun into her right eye as if he were screwing in a monocle.

'This is how you like to do it,' he said. 'Isn't it?'

And without waiting for an answer, he pulled the trigger.

Dasha jerked back against the hands holding her. Her body sagged. Grigor stared at her, waiting.

Until, finally, she raised her head again. Now her eyes were dull, defeated; all the fight had gone out of her.

'You're going to do it slowly, aren't you,' she said. It wasn't a question.

'This was your warning,' Grigor said.

He took the magazine out of his pocket, which he had removed as the lift sank to the lower floor, and jammed it back into the stock of the semi-automatic. Raising the Beretta again, he worked the barrel against the other eyeball.

'Our son is upstairs. He just got married. He pleaded with me for your life. What could I say?' His finger hovered on the trigger. 'Next time you try anything, Dasha, you are dead. You know that I will do it.'

She couldn't nod. She could only mutter a 'Yes' as he continued:

'You are the mother of my children. That will not protect you next time. I said I would not get a divorce, and I meant it. But now I have changed my mind. You must be punished for this, Dasha. I will get a divorce. And you will agree to whatever settlement I give you, or be turned over to the police for assaulting that nurse. You will pay her a hundred thousand pounds from your settlement. Oh! And the stuntman! Two hundred thousand for him, for being shot.' He stared at her grimly. 'Your allowance will be cut to the bare minimum. You will have to leave Monaco. You'll have to settle for a much lower class of gigolo.'

Dasha whimpered. She would never be able to afford Marcos now; he demanded a steep weekly allowance, plus a stream of gifts, and he insisted on being put up in five-star-plus luxury. The Uruguayan oil millionairess from whom Dasha had poached him had been circling him again, she knew, and though he definitely preferred Dasha's full-blooded brand of sexual sadism, as soon as he heard that her income had decreased so dramatically, he wouldn't stick around for longer than it took to pack his matching Vuitton trunks and shoot off to Punta del Este.

Tears started to form in her eyes as she thought of Marcos's slender tanned body, his thick penis, his tight hairless buttocks. He was waiting for her right now back in the Dorchester suite, tied up on his knees, well-oiled, Putin's Surprise lying on the table in front of him so that he could contemplate, trembling deliciously, the dimensions of what Dasha had promised to brutally pound into him at the stroke of midnight.

It was all ruined now. She wouldn't have the heart even to fuck Marcos one last time. She was a broken woman, utterly defeated.

'And don't try complaining to the boys about it,' Grigor added. 'Dmitri saw what you did. He will tell Alek. They will both be grateful to me for sparing your life. Believe me, they will not take your side. If you complain, I will hear about it. And it will not be good for you.'

He pulled the Beretta away from her face and handed it back to the bodyguard to holster. Turning away, he nodded at all the guards to follow him. The two men holding Dasha let her go, and she fell to the floor. As they walked back to the lift, Grigor did not once look over his shoulder at his soon-to-be-ex wife.

He didn't need to. He could hear her desolate sobbing echoing round the cold concrete walls of the garage, the sobbing of a woman who had played for the highest of stakes, and lost everything.

Up in the penthouse, the party had resumed with zest and gusto; magnums of champagne were being popped open, the footballers shouldering aside the waiters to take on the task themselves, spraying each other with great white foamy cascades of bubbles.

'That's *so* gay,' Wayne commented, delirious with his own bravery, looking back inside at the showers of champagne foam; he and Andy were on the terrace, watching the firework display up and down the river, arms wrapped round each other. 'Look at them covering each other in spunk.'

Andy giggled. 'You're going to fit right in with my friends,' he said happily. 'I can't *wait* for your first foam party!'

Wayne cuddled him close. 'Will you be with me?' he asked. 'Take me around to bars and clubs, so I don't 'ave to do it all on my own?'

'As long as you want me,' Andy said very seriously. 'I don't want to hold you back if you fancy going out and sowing a lot of wild oats.'

'I don't think I will,' Wayne said, hugging him. 'I think I'm going to be an old-fashioned gay man. Traditional. Are there any of those?'

Andy smiled. 'You mean monogamous? Of course! Takes all sorts.'

Wayne nodded. 'Yeah, monogamous, that's the word. Like my mum and dad. I'm not one for playing around.'

Andy kissed him. 'Honestly, Wayne, you don't know that yet,' he said. 'It's really early days for you. We'll take it slow, okay?'

'Can we fuck a lot while we're taking it slow?' Wayne said, grinning.

'*Oh* yes,' Andy said devoutly. 'Don't you worry about that. Talking of which, did you hear about Hari? The Japanese kid?'

Wayne shook his head. 'What's that?'

Andy told him the story: Mr and Mrs Takahashi, who had been invited to the party along with their son, had gone into the screening room, along with Grigor, to watch *New Year's Eve*, and had stayed in there when Grigor had been summoned out in a tearing hurry. Only when the film finished had they emerged, to realise that Hari was nowhere to be found. A hue and cry had gone up, as the Takahashis panicked that Hari had been abducted or had fallen off one of the balconies; eventually, Sergei had been drafted into the search and had produced Hari, who had ambled up from the lower-floor apartment with an expression of utter, transcendental bliss on his face.

He had been taken down there by Kesha as soon as she laid eyes on him. The girls who had been banished downstairs to entertain overweight, ungrateful, hairy old oligarchs had fallen on a slim, beautiful, smooth and virginal youth nearly their own age with unrestrained enthusiasm; in a couple of hours, Hari had been turned from a boy into a man. He had the look in his eyes of someone who had seen paradise. As his parents fussed over him, and Lori, who had shepherded him upstairs, explained with smooth conviction that he and she had been playing video games, he smiled at his mother and father with such genuine affection that they both burst into tears, hugged him, and swore that they would all spend more time together as a family in future.

'Nice!' Wayne said appreciatively. 'Here, let's go congratulate him.'

They went back inside, spotting a dazed-looking Hari; Wayne wove through the crowd and clinked glasses with him.

'Hear you had the time of your life just now, mate,' he said. 'Congrats.'

Hari puffed up his chest. 'I did it *five* times!' he said proudly, after checking that his family weren't within earshot.

'Jesus, five times!' Wayne toasted him again.

'Girls,' Hari said, in the tones of a very recent religious convert describing his moment of revelation, 'are *amazing.*'

'Oh well,' Andy said, grinning at Wayne. 'Each to their own.'

Sergei, slipping past, spotted Andy – now not only a guest, but the blissfully happy consort of Grigor Khalovsky's star player, his arm wrapped happily around Wayne's sturdy waist. The bile Sergei usually managed to suppress in public rose up with disastrous results, primed by the glass of champagne he had allowed himself to celebrate the end of the year. Glaring up at Andy and Wayne, he hissed vindictively:

'*Homosexuals!*'

Andy tensed, looking nervously at Wayne. Wayne had literally only just come out; this was exactly what he had feared, his sexual preference turned into a spitting insult. Andy opened his mouth to tell Sergei to piss off, but, magnificently, Wayne was there first.

'That's right!' he said, turning to smile at Andy, to clink glasses with him. 'We *are* 'omosexuals! And look! 'eterosexuals!'

He pointed at Melody, who, swimming on a happy sea of champagne, her arm wound through James's, was floating up to Andy and Wayne with a beautiful smile. Sergei, thwarted in his attempt to upset Andy, slithered away in fury.

'He looks like that snake in the cartoon,' Andy said. 'Prince John, in *Robin Hood*. After someone *stepped on his head*,' he added loudly to Sergei's retreating back.

'Ah, ignore the little fucker,' Wayne said, planting a big smacking kiss on his lover's mouth. ''e ain't worth it, mate.'

'Congratulations on coming out!' Melody sang out sweetly, kissing Wayne on each cheek. 'If the footballers are mean to you, just come and hang out with the actors, won't you? Half of them are gay anyway, you'll fit right in!'

'It's great that you two're back together,' Andy said, looking at her and James's big smiles. 'That's lovely. I was sad when you broke up – you always looked like such a lovely couple in the papers.'

Melody and James beamed at each other.

'We're *completely* back together,' James said, unable to take his eyes off Melody, 'and we're acting in *Much Ado About Nothing* with the RSC this summer. You two must come. Let us know when you want to see it and we'll comp you tickets.'

'Ooh!' Andy grabbed Wayne's arm excitedly. 'I *love* Much Ado!'

'You what?' Wayne said nervously.

'It's Shakespeare,' Andy said. 'You wanted me to make arrangements for you, didn't you? Book tickets to things? Well, we're going to see Melody and James in Shakespeare!'

James laughed as he finally tore his eyes away from Melody's face and took in Wayne's terrified expression.

'Don't worry, it's a comedy,' he said.

'I s'pose I could give it a try . . .' Wayne stammered.

'There you go!' Andy said happily.

'Ladies and gentlemen!' Grigor bustled in, making an entrance, bodyguards trailing after him. Sergei dashed towards him with a glass of champagne, which Grigor took and held high in the air. 'It is New Year, and we must make a toast! Happy New Year, everyone!'

'Happy New Year!' everyone chorused.

And then Wayne, looking around him, and nodding fiercely at all the guests to join in, started to sing:

'For 'e's a jolly good fellow, for 'e's a jolly good fellow . . .'

The only people not singing were Hari and Lori, who were making out in a dark corner: everyone else, guests and staff, bodyguards and waiters, Mr and Mrs Takahashi, Fyodorov, Sergei – worship shining in his eyes as he stared at Grigor – Patrice and the rest of the footballers all joined in, carolling out the words:

'Which nobody can deny – which nobody can deny–'

'Mate!' Patrice hissed to Wayne under cover of the noise. 'D'you think your Chantelle'd like to move in with us? Keep Corinne company?'

'They've been wanting to for years!' Wayne muttered back.

'*Man*,' Patrice sighed in ecstasy at the thought of having his wife's girlfriend under his roof.

'For he's a jolly good fe-eh-*low*—' the singers' voices rose – 'which nobody – *can* – *DENY*!'

Grigor looked around his assembled guests with an expression of utter contentment on his face. He took a deep pull of champagne and beckoned Dmitri and Zhivana to his side, hugging them both, an arm around each of them.

'Happy New Year!' he bellowed, raising his glass in a final toast. 'To my son and his wife!' He looked at his son.

'You are happy?' he asked fondly. 'After all this fuss you cause? You are happy, Dima?'

'Oh, *happy*,' Dmitri began dismissively, pulling on one of his sideburns. 'That's such a bourgeois concept, isn't it, Dad? Sartre said that—'

But Zhivana, her cheeks actually flushed with a little colour, raised one thin arm and shot out a finger at her new husband, ramming it sharply into his ribcage.

'Shut up!' she said firmly. 'It is a party! No one wants to hear what Sartre said!'

Grigor gawked at this show of firmness, the first ever from Zhivana.

'Very good!' he said approvingly, turning to his ex-fiancée. 'Very good! It's true, no one wants to hear about Sartre at parties! Or, in fact, at all.'

Zhivana nodded firmly. 'Kierkegaard is *much* more profound,' she said seriously.

Dmitri raised her hand to his lips and kissed it fondly. 'My dark little soul,' he said adoringly. 'My gloomy little girl.'

Grigor balked, looking from his son to his new daughter-in-law. 'Well, you are a good match,' he said, shrugging. Determined to find something positive to say, he finally managed it. 'You are in love. They are in love, Mikhail!' he yelled, his voice rising. 'To love!' He raised his glass.

'To love!' echoed his guests.

Dmitri and Zhivana held hands across Grigor's bulk, while the other two pairs of lovers turned to their partners and repeated the words once more, softly, to each other.

'To love,' Wayne and Andy said, hugging.

'To love,' Melody and James whispered before they kissed.

Across the room, Lori surreptitiously pulled Hari Takahashi into one of the back bedrooms, his total score that evening about to rise to six; it might not be love, but it was certainly yet another happy ending. Downstairs, Jon and Aniela, having settled Mr Bingham-Smythe into bed, were curled up on Aniela's narrow single mattress, arms wrapped round each other, identical happy, incredulous, dizzy smiles on both of their faces. Even Sergei, dashing over to refill Grigor's glass, was beaming with happiness as Grigor tossed back more champagne while genially patting his adoring secretary's head in thanks. And outside, on the terrace, Grigor's remaining bodyguards were letting off fireworks that blazed bright in the snowy sky, opening with fizzing hisses into sapphire and emerald and diamond-white chrysanthemums, the sparks falling with the tumbling snow onto the black waters of the Thames below.

Turn the page to discover

REBECCA CHANCE'S **NAUGHTY BITS**

Deleted scenes previously considered too hot for print!

In which Carin takes Rico's sexual education to a new level

Carin Fitzgerald, having put her rich old husband into a coma, is enjoying herself very thoroughly after a workout in her private gym . . .

As the door closed behind her new personal trainer, Carin was already stripping off her exercise gear and admiring her toned, naked body in the mirror. She was incredibly horny, despite the disappointment she'd felt on realising that the trainer was gay; she'd thought that not only was she going to get thoroughly laid, but that she would be enjoying the particular and specific pleasure of putting a new man through his paces, seeing how extensive his experience was. Could he teach her anything at all? That was rarer and rarer, a man who could show Carin something she didn't already know. But even the excitement of a new body, a new cock, was enough to give an extra fizz to her sex life.

Well, she'd have to make do with Rico. He might not give her the excitement of fresh meat, but at least he was hung like a horse.

The door of the gym swung open, and there he was, bulked up with muscle, wearing a black t-shirt tucked into black flat-fronted trousers, his uniform. She'd bought this outfit in bulk for him when she first took him on. Thank God for American stores, they were used to large sizes: Banana Republic made trousers big enough to fit over Rico's pumped-up thighs and shoulders. And she wasn't spending more than Banana Republic money on a jumped-up bouncer.

Because that was what Rico had been when she found him, a bouncer. Now, ostensibly her bodyguard, he was really her dark shadow behind the scenes. Rico did any heavy lifting that Carin needed done. Buying her drugs when she wanted to get high. Leaning on people she needed leaned on. Finding a nurse who was prepared to kill her husband for a lot of money – and perjure himself about it for even more money.

'I thought the new guy was here?' Rico said, looking confused at being called down here, at the sight of Carin's nakedness. 'Or was he no good?'

'He's gay,' she said curtly.

A nasty smile curved Rico's lips. His many spells in prison hadn't exactly done anything to curb the homophobia that was rampant in his native Cuban community.

'You want me to teach him a lesson?' he asked hopefully.

'Jesus, no!' Carin said curtly. 'Are you nuts? What's that going to do, stop him liking men?' She rolled her eyes. 'Leave him alone, OK. He's a great trainer. I don't want you pulling any stupid shit on him.'

She walked towards Rico, watching their reflections in the huge mirror panels on the walls, enjoying the contrast between them – she was so pale, and Rico, with his Latino colouring and his black clothes, so dark. When she reached him, she grabbed a handful of t-shirt, pulling it out of his waistband, and shoved one hand down his trousers, feeling for his dick. It was hardening even as she reached for it.

'That's more like it,' she said with satisfaction.

Holding his dick firmly, feeling it grow and grow in her grasp, she led him across the room to the pull-up machine, enjoying his awkward shuffle as he tried to move fast enough to avoid her pulling uncomfortably on his penis. The kneeling pad on the machine was down, and she climbed onto it, releasing him as she did so, reaching up to grab the pull-up bars above her.

She spread her long legs, hooking her feet around either side of the metal frame. The leather beneath her bare buttocks, the cold metal at her ankles, were extra stimulation, extra sensation. She was raring to go, wet and more than ready for the big, slightly curved dick that Rico was pulling out of his trousers. He dived into his pocket for a condom and ripped off the wrapper, working it hurriedly onto the swollen head of his penis.

'Fuck me,' she commanded, looking down at her white-blonde bush, widening her eyes as Rico shoved down his trousers, kicked them away, and approached her, holding his dick, angling it between her lips, mingling his thick dark mat of pubic hair with hers as she screamed with the initial pain of having something that big shove its way up her. Wet as she was, it always hurt on the first few strokes, and she always loved that part. Maybe she'd have him put it up her ass next.

And then her contorted mouth twisted into a smile as she thought of an even better idea.

The muscles in her upper arms, already sore, protested as she clung on to the bars above her. Her inner thighs were screaming with the extra work of holding herself in position, tilting her pelvis up, so that Rico had full access to her pussy, so he could get as far into it as his big dick could go, pumping her with everything he had. He loved to fuck. He wasn't a sophisticated lover; his idea of fucking was pumping away, ramming her hard and fast, just like this, no variation. But he could go forever, and Carin had enough imagination for the both of them.

Rico knew what his job was: to be a fucking machine. Carin was the one at the wheel.

And she loved to drive.

Letting go of the bars, she slid herself forward, tilting her pelvis impossibly higher, groaning as Rico's dick smashed repeatedly against her cervix. She reached her arms around him, feeling the sweat gathering in the small of his back, running her fingers in it, sliding them down to cup his buttocks. Rico was too engrossed in his work to notice her demonic smile as she clamped together the second and third fingers of her right hand, worked them down his hairy cleft, paused for a moment, toying with his ass, drawing moans of pleasure from him as she flicked her fingers around it.

Then she shoved both fingers, lubricated with his own salty sweat, up his asshole in one swift, unstoppable, practised movement.

'Fuck!' he yelled. 'Fuck! You fucking bitch!'

'You fucking *love* it.' Carin worked her fingers against his prostate, pressing too hard for it to be purely pleasurable. 'You love it, don't you?'

'No, I fucking don't, you *bitch*—'

He writhed and bucked, but Carin held on tight. She'd trained him up with a thumb first, knowing how much it would humiliate a tight-ass Cuban macho man like him to enjoy a woman shoving something up his ass: now, for the first time, she'd made him take two fingers. And it wouldn't end there.

'You're almost ready for a strap-on,' she taunted him, watching the fury in his face, his corded neck straining, a vein popping out on his temple as he kept fucking her, harder than ever now, his black eyes hard and hot with fury. 'Come on, give it up, show me how much you love it—'

She hooked her fingers inside him, laughing at him as he gasped at the extreme sensation.

'You fucking *whore bitch*—' he moaned, as his body jerked in great spasms, his semen flooding out of him, coming despite himself, filling the condom.

Her other hand between her legs, Carin brought herself off, coming almost immediately. The sight of Rico's humiliation was the most potent aphrodisiac she could imagine.

'How you love it—' she grunted as her orgasm hit her hard, 'getting fucked in the ass by me – ugh—'

His dick was still enormous inside her. She spasmed around it, one orgasm hitting her after the next, grinding herself down on him to prolong the sensation, her eyes squeezed closed to savour the intensity even more.

'I'm going to buy a strap-on for you,' she groaned. 'Just a small one at first. God, you're going to come so hard – it'll take you to a whole different place, you'll see—'

Her eyes opened, and she caught Rico staring down at her, still braced in position. He caught himself and ducked his head, reaching down between their legs to pull himself out, careful to keep the condom on.

But in that stare, she had read everything. Satisfied lust; resentment, for the way she dictated how and when he could fuck her; hate, because she did things to him that violated his entire concept of what it meant to be a man.

And furious, dark, burning desire. Because somewhere inside him, that humiliation was what he craved. Carin would buy that strap-on, and fuck him with it, and she'd make him come so hard he'd shatter into little pieces.

God, it'll be so much fun, she thought lazily, in the aftermath of her own orgasms. *A whole new game to play with him. I can hardly wait.*

In which Niels and Lola celebrate her acquittal

*L*o la Fitzgerald has been acquitted of the charge of murdering *her father, and is ready to celebrate with Niels Van der Veer, who has carried her into a limo and is whisking her away to a Thai island to recuperate from her ordeal.*

The glass of the windows was smoky-dark, the panel between the seating section and the chauffeur in front was shut tight. Niels and Lola found themselves once again sealed together in a dimly-lit, leather-upholstered limo, with the world shut out. Gruffly, he said:

'Champagne?' and leant forward to reach for a bottle of Veuve Cliquot propped in a gleaming ice-bucket.

'Afterwards,' Lola said, putting one small hand out to push him back in his seat as she kneeled up and climbed on top of him, swinging one leg over to straddle his thighs, hearing the slit in the back of her skirt rip as her legs stretched wide.

She didn't even bother to read Niels's expression. She just grabbed his face with both hands and pulled it towards her as she kissed him deeply, her tongue sliding past his lips, grinding herself into him with all the pent-up frustration and excitement and relief of the past few weeks, the stress of her trial, the misery of Niels's apparent disappearance. As soon as she had chosen him, Lola had felt as light as a feather, and not just because he had swept her up in his arms as easily as if she weighed nothing at all.

This is how it feels when you make a decision that's a hundred per-cent right for you, Lola realised. *Absolutely, totally, completely right for you. I feel as if I drank a whole bottle of champagne already. I feel like I'm floating on Cloud Nine. I feel like—*

And then Niels grabbed her round the waist and shifted her so that his erection was wedged firmly between her legs, just where he wanted it, pressing up insistently, so big and hard that she moaned into his mouth, suddenly desperate for him, not wanting to wait another moment, writhing down on his cock, rubbing herself against it, working herself so lithely that she could feel its tip pressing into her through the layers of fabric that separated them, trying to enter her despite the obstacles, feeling so good that she heard herself moaning in pleasure as it made contact with her most sensitive parts.

Niels lifted her up and pushed her back, and she cried out in frustration even as she reached forward, wrestling with his belt buckle and zip, pulling out his cock, but she barely managed to touch it before he picked her up, put one hand between her legs and ripped at the crotch of her tights so hard that she heard the nylon rending apart, the slit of her skirt ripping still further, and Niels shoved aside her thong, the sensation of his fingers on her naked damp skin so intense that she screamed in delight, raised her still further and, one hand guiding his cock, the other on her waist, slid himself into her and right up inside her in one deep thrust.

Lola's eyes rolled back in her head so far that she could barely see. But she didn't need to. All she needed to do was feel. Niels's hands were both on her waist now, lifting her up, pulling her down as he thrust up inside her in long jerking strokes. But Lola was doing most of the work, her slim legs and core so toned from Pilates and yogacise that she had excellent control over her movements, splayed out as she was to accommodate Niels's wide, sprawled thighs. She rode him, grinding herself against him, utterly concentrated on the purely selfish goal of bringing herself to the hardest, fastest orgasm she could achieve; there was no time for subtleties, for teasing, for slowing down for some soft delicate strokes where they kissed and moaned into each other's mouths. All Lola wanted was to get off like an out-of-control train slamming into buffers. She was mad for him, mad for his cock, mad to explode in a release that would wipe her brain clean of all the tension and misery of the previous weeks, and she bit her lip and forced herself down on him, her hands on his shoulders for extra leverage, whimpering every time her clitoris ground against the hair at the base of his cock, single-mindedly taking herself towards fulfilment.

Niels reached his hands between her legs and ripped her tights still further, the sound of the fabric splitting so erotic that Lola moaned even louder and pounded at him even faster, his hands raising to pull open her jacket, rip at the buttons of her demure blouse, tear at it so he could cover her breasts with his hands, rolling her small pink nipples between his fingers, pinching at them lightly. He pulled her forward, sinking his head into the soft skin, biting at her neck, her breasts, his whole chest pressed against hers, and she grabbed at his hair, so unexpectedly soft and silky, trying to find a lock long enough to wrap through her fingers and pull so she could drag him even closer to her, wind herself even tighter against him.

And then she heard him groaning against her neck, felt the wide thigh muscles below her begin to thrust up uncontrollably, and she knew he was very close. His hands began to slide down her, to her waist, getting ready to lift her off him just before he started to come.

Oh no you don't! Lola thought furiously. *Not this time!*

Her brain racing, her body on the verge of orgasm, she pulled one hand off Niels's shoulder, sliding her fingers into her mouth, licking them to get them damp, simultaneously tilting her pelvis forward just enough so that she could reach her hand between her legs and caress herself, leaning back a fraction to watch Niels's face as she did so. His pupils dilated till his eyes were near-black, his hips pumping up inside her frantically. It took her a bare few seconds to reach orgasm, and Niels was right there with her, the sight of her touching herself sending him completely over the edge.

Any effort to pull her off him collapsed as the shudders raced through him, his hands convulsing on her waist, digging in tightly as the hot come flooded up inside her, his cock throbbing convulsively. Lola held on for dear life, thrusting herself against him, coming again and again as she felt him twitch and spasm, the exquisite sensation of him losing control inside her so powerful that she felt like she could have come forever just riding that wave.

It was the best high she had ever had.

And then there was no sound but their panting breath as she collapsed against him, her head buried in the crook of his neck, and felt his arms close around her back, holding her tightly, his lips against the crown of her head.

There's nowhere else in the world I want to be, she thought.

'I hope you got what you wanted,' Niels said gruffly into her hair.

'Always,' Lola mumbled into his skin, breathing in the heady mixture of his dark apple-wood aftershave and the intoxicating scent of his sweat.

'Watch it, Princess,' Niels said. 'Don't get cocky.'

'No, that's your job,' Lola said smugly.

And she wrapped her arms around his neck and clung on to him tightly as the limo powered up the West Side Highway and turned onto the massive span of the George Washington Bridge, heading for Teterboro airport, the waiting LearJet, and the private Thai island.

In which Evie begins her new burlesque career and meets a contortionist called Jerome

Kicked out of the Tribeca penthouse where she was being main-tained by a sugar daddy, Evie has returned reluctantly to her old job – stripping at a Manhattan club called the Midnight Lounge. But she has ambitions to become a burlesque performer, and is visiting Maud's, a burlesque club where she's due to audition the next day, to check out its acts . . .

When the darkness slowly began to lift, a single rosy spotlight, growing gradually stronger, illuminated the centre of the stage. On it was a coil of rope, six feet high, wider than a barrel at its base, narrowing in a cone shape to barely a foot in diameter at the top. The audience hushed, chatter dying away, the curiosity of the spectators piqued by their inability to imagine what this act could possibly be.

And then the rope began to unwind, from the top of the cone. Evie couldn't see how it was being done, and that impressed her. A cord from above, probably, but the motion was very smooth and even, which couldn't be easy to manage. Gold flashed behind the rope as it unwound. The gold of a woman's hair, piled up high on her head, resembling the shape of the coiled rope. More rope uncoiled, beginning to fall now down the cone as it unwrapped itself, and more and more of the woman's very curvaceous shape was revealed. She was naked, her skin very pale, her nipples gilded, and as the cone of rope slowly undid its shape, exposing more and more skin, a man whooped at the back of the room.

The loud, raucous noise fell into silence, and was absorbed almost immediately by the dark. This striptease had nothing titil-lating about it, in the sense that the performer needed to be egged on with yells and salacious cheers. The woman, gazing straight ahead, seemed not to be aware even of her audience: she kept her position, arms gently curved at her sides, feet together, until the rope was almost completely undone. When she did eventually move, it was a shock: more than one person gasped. She raised her arms, and started to undo her hair. Evie couldn't tell what had been fastening it up, but it must have been something very simple, because with one motion, curls of golden hair – it had to be a wig – cascaded over her shoulders, partially concealing the slope of her breasts.

And something was revealed, something resting on the crown of her head, which had been concealed by the hair. Unbelievably, it was a vase of water, narrow, fluted at the top. The audience gasped as they realised what it was.

She took it in both hands, raising it and holding it high above her head, like a goddess on a Grecian vase holding an amphora. And then she tilted her head back and poured the water over herself, opening her mouth as it flowed down over her body. There was a moment's pause, everyone staring at her, amazed, as the water poured down her breasts and her rounded stomach, the empty vase still held over her head.

Then, completely unexpectedly, her head still angled back, a miniature cascade of water arched out of her mouth, as if she were a statue at the centre of a fountain. It was a bright curve of liquid that splashed through the air, sparkling in the rose-coloured light, tiny beads of water spinning off and dancing to the ground, a spectacle that was both beautiful and strangely erotic; people at the front of the cabaret stage pushed forward, eager to be splashed by the stream of water that was issuing from between her full red lips. Squeals and groans of excitement rose as the drops of water landed on the willing victims.

The jet of water ended; the woman straightened up. Immediately, the lights went out, plunging the room into darkness; only the little candles burning on each table provided the tiniest gleams of illumination. The act was over.

The audience broke out into cheers, applause that was long and prolonged. The house lights went up, and Evie spotted a man at the front dabbing his head with a napkin, red-faced and smirking with pleasure at having caught most of the fountain of water.

'You don't sit down at the front if you don't wanna get up close and personal, right?' the bartender said, leaning on the bar and grinning at Evie. 'Another mineral water?'

'Please.'

'I can't talk you into a cocktail? I make a damn good Cosmo. Not that sugary shit they call a Cosmo now – mine's the real deal.'

She shook her head, explaining:

'I got to be at work in an hour.'

'No prob,' he said, pouring her another glass of water.

New York wasn't quite the city that never slept, but you wouldn't even raise an eyebrow at someone being due in forwork at one in the morning. Evie's heavy makeup – she'd done part of a shift at the Lounge already, talked Paulie into giving her a couple of hours off – indicated that she wasn't heading to proof-read at a law office, or pull a late shift at an open-all-hours pharmacy. It was probably pretty obvious that she was an exotic dancer. But, like Natalie and Jeremy's circus troupe, the burlesque crowd were nothing if not open-minded.

She liked all of them. A lot.

'Staying for Carrie On?' he asked, momentarily ignoring a hipster down the bar holding out a folded twenty.

Evie nodded.

'Great! You don't want to miss her, she's always a blast. Jeez, I'm coming, okay? Hold your horses.'

The hipster got his designer beers just as the lights dipped again. A trapeze descended from the ceiling, a double trapeze hung from ropes on each side and one at the centre. A brief round of clapping greeted Natalie and Laura, each hanging from it in a single knee lock, something that Evie, from brief experimental trials over the last few days, had found incredibly painful to hold. Wearing shimmering leotards and white leather boots, Natalie and Laura performed a routine that consisted of them mirroring each other perfectly: even when they dropped to an ankle hang, swung in two huge beats and pulled themselves, amazingly, up to sitting and then to standing so fast it took your breath away, they moved in absolute unison.

It wasn't at all sexy, though. And because it wasn't sexy, it wasn't burlesque. Evie sensed the audience growing restless, and the applause at the end was more polite than appreciative. This wasn't the kind of place that Natalie and Laura usually performed: they'd been asked to fill in because a filthy comic had dropped out at the last minute, and had simply done one of their regular routines, sexed up a little by Natalie's last-minute suggestion of wearing the white boots.

This dim, low-ceilinged, cabaret venue was much more Evie's atmosphere than theirs. Evie knew how to dance sexily, always leaving something back, something to the imagination, something that teased you by remaining perpetually just out of reach, but so close you felt you almost could grasp it, could caress it, for a split-second, with the tips of your fingers. Evie knew how to make men, and sometimes women gasp, convince them that they had seen more than they had, but leave them even more desperate to see it again. It was a game, where you gave just enough but promised more, a promise you never quite filled, so that you kept your audience in an endlessly-burning state of wanting, longing, flushed and swollen with desire for you that they could never completely satisfy.

In the Lounge, Evie showed a lot less skin than some girls. She'd never needed to do the gynaecological stuff, the writhing on the floor playing with yourself, pulling at the crotch of your g-string titillatingly, sliding it back to make it look like you were going to show everything. And, without doing any of that kind of porno crap, she made more tips than anyone else there – which the other girls always resented.

The barman was busy setting up trays of drinks for the table service waitress, everyone wanting to get their rounds in before the final act for tonight, the headliner. Evie was squinting at his watch, trying to work out the time. She'd told Paulie she'd be back by half-midnight, like a skanky, low-rent Cinderella.

Which, let's face it, was exactly what she was.

And unexpectedly, the thought of going back to the Lounge depressed Evie so much that she felt herself slump on her stool, her back sagging. She wanted to put her head down on the bar and weep.

Bam! The club was suddenly plunged into darkness. Music blared from the speakers, an old-fashioned bump-and-grind of trumpets and saxophones and the sexy pluck of a double-bass. People were applauding already, knowing what was coming, psyched up for the headline act. Evie swivelled on her stool to face the stage. And there, in a blast of white spotlights, she was: Carrie On, one of the biggest stars on the new-burlesque circuit. Literally.

Not that you could see much of her right now: her body was entirely concealed by two huge, beautiful mauvy-pink feather fans, each held in a gloved hand, her face peeking over the top. She winked, and the audience clapped some more. White-blonde hair in a fall over one eye, very Veronica Lake. Cat's-eye black eyeliner, flicked up at the corners, and fake lashes so long and luxurious they must have been mink. Red lips, glossed and glittery, pursed into a perfect bow. And a black heart-shaped beauty spot high on one cheekbone. She looked like a boudoir fantasy, a girl from a chocolate box come to life.

She started to dance, slowly, a controlled and choreographed routine of shimmies, wiggles, and the occasional dramatic leg kick. It was a game she was playing with the audience, to the sound of the pumping trumpet: see what you can spot as I undulate and bend over and spin around, always covering myself with my fan . . . is that a round white hip curving through the trembling feathers for a split second? The top of a breast? Or are you just imagining it, because the more I dance like this, the more you want to see what's behind the fans . . .

And all the time, she was laughing, winking, flirting madly and naughtily with the spectators, making each and every one feel that she was connecting directly with them, dancing just for them. She had them in the palm of her hand. Evie was fascinated. This was pure burlesque: the knowingness, the playfulness. The opposite of what Evie herself did, the opposite of stripping.

In Carrie On's dancing, everyone was in on the game, everyone was having fun. This audience was happily mixed: women, men, straight, gay, all enjoying the spectacle. Carrie On was teasing, revealing, teasing, revealing, playing with them just as a stripper did – but when you stripped, nobody laughed. God forbid. It wasn't witty, playful, like this: it was deadly serious. In the Midnight Lounge, the audience was almost entirely composed of straight men, with a few idiot girlfriends trying to prove to their boyfriends how cool they were. As if, Evie thought ironically. Dumb bitches. Strippers despised those girls even more than the male clients; they were either secretly gay – so come out already! – or they were, no matter how much they might deny it to themselves, in competitions with the strippers to be sexier. I mean, I don't go into their jobs and try to show I can do them better, do I? Idiots.

Plus, the only feedback you got from the clients of the Lounge, Evie reflected, you did your best to ignore. You fed off their attention, sure: you knew you were performing for them. But apart from that, you pretended they weren't there. Really. The more you looked at them, the more gross you felt. You blurred their faces so you couldn't see their expressions. You sang songs in your head, loudly, so you couldn't hear what they said to you. You pretended you were looking at the bulges in their crotches admiringly, but really you were glazing your eyes, trying not to see any of the gross gestures they made to their fly area.

And if you were like the majority of the girls, you were hopped up on something extra – pills, booze, powder – to help you get into a happier place and blur out the clients still further . . .

Boom! Carrie On popped a hip and a silvery garment shot off as if fired from a gun. She pantomimed surprise. The audience whooped with laughter. To the next trumpet blare, she popped the other hip. A garter magically pinged off her leg. It was with wide-eyed amazement that she let the fan she was holding over her breasts slip down so they were revealed, two enormous white globes imperfectly covered by a silver bustier. She looked down at them. Pop! The bustier flew off, revealing the silver tasselled pasties on her nipples. The audience was in ecstasy as they watched her jiggle her breasts in perfect synch, spinning them in circles, the tassels flying out. As the music reached a crescendo, she swirled around, turning her back to the room, slipping away the fan covering the equally rounded and enormous white spheres of her ass, enough so that so they could see the glittering silver G-string threading between them. She bent over, thrusting her bottom at the audience, just as the trumpet wailed to a final top note and the lights dropped to black.

The audience went wild. Cheers, screams, whoops of applause. As the spotlights snapped on again and Carrie On, covered again by her lavender-pink fans, curtseyed demurely, laughing and waving one silver-gloved arm in acknowledgement of her adoring public, Evie was already slipping off her stool and heading for the door.

'Hey!' called a voice behind her. 'Hang on a minute!'

A tap on her shoulder made Evie swing round, realising that the voice had meant her; she looked down to see Sallie, the stage manager of Maud's, a small, efficient, tubby little woman in a black bandage dress that turned her figure into Ursula's from The Little Mermaid. The thought made Evie smile: her own act, which she'd been choreographing with the help of Natalie and Laura, cast her as a mermaid: maybe I can get Sallie to come on and do a witchy cackle, she thought, even as Sallie said:

'So! Want to do your audition in front of an audience?'

Evie's jaw dropped. She'd been visiting Maud's that evening as a prelude to her audition the next day, which was scheduled for the afternoon, well before both Maud's and the Midnight Lounge opened for business. There was no way that there would be an audience here tomorrow afternoon; so Sallie must mean—

'Natalie and Laura didn't go down like a house on fire,' Sallie said bluntly. 'Too much acrobatics, not enough sex. They say you're the one to bring the hoochie. You want to take their slot in the late set? It was their idea, so you won't be stepping on any toes.'

'I wasn't expecting—'Evie started.

Sallie shrugged. 'Your costume's here, right? Give it a shot. You'd be going on after Jerome.' She grinned widely. 'Trust me, he knows how to work up a crowd – he gets them all hot and bothered, it's a great act. So.' She put her hands on her hips. 'You in or out?'

I don't have a choice, Evie thought. It's now or never. And she wasn't some newbie just off the bus, fresh out of stage school in Oklahoma, suddenly getting her big break because the lead in the musical turned her ankle: she'd been stripping for ages, in front of a much more hardcore audience than this one. What the hell am I pussying around for?

'Let me just ring Paulie at the Lounge and tell him I won't be back, okay?' she said, pulling out her phone.

'You can do that from backstage,' Sallie said, bustling her out of the bar, through an anonymous black-painted door and down very scruffy corridors.

All backstage areas look the same, Evie thought as they went; she'd visited one of the girls from the Lounge who'd got a gig as a Rockette at Radio City Music Hall last Christmas season, had been so excited at the prestige, plus being in a show her kids could come to see. She was back at the Lounge now, telling all the girls there who met the height and leg length requirements not to even think about trying out for the gig: they worked you like dogs, two shows a day, and backstage at Radio City was apparently a shitheap into the bargain.

Maud's, at least, had little separate dressing rooms for its acts, partly so that they could store all of their props. Evie's mermaid tail, her pasties and body makeup, were already in the cubbyhole that Natalie and Laura were using for the night. They passed Carrie On's dressing room, which was so full of huge feather fans, glittering hula hoops, showgirl's headdresses, that Evie didn't know how Carrie managed to wriggle her ample figure inside it. The next room was the opposite, just a few day clothes hanging on pegs, no props at all. Just a giant, shaved, black man, sitting on a wooden stool, wearing only a tiny black jockstrap that barely contained his privates, a jumbo-sized bottle of baby oil in his hand, dripping its contents over his body and working them in.

Evie stopped dead. She couldn't help it. No-one could. She had broken up with Lawrence, but she had only moved one floor down, to a room in the big apartment that Natalie, Laura and the rest of the circus performers shared. So not only was there always the chance of seeing him – bumping into him on the stairs, on the sidewalk, in the subway – but the horrible idea that he had taken up with Autumn, his roommate, who was dying to get in his pants. She had been working up the sexiest act of her entire life while, simultaneously, not getting any herself; she and Lawrence had been hugely sexually compatible, had fucked like maniacs, and Evie was, frankly, burning up with the frustration of having him so close and not being able to – well, have him.

So it was naturally quite impossible for her to take her eyes off this huge, gorgeous, entirely-shaved, glistening slab of rich dark chocolate. His wide shoulders, his long muscled legs, his pumped arms seemed to fill the entire dressing room; sensing her stare, he looked up, his slanting dark eyes widening with interest as he looked her up and down as thoroughly as she was surveying him.

Oh, thank God! she thought, smiling with relief. He's straight! Gay guys outnumbered the straight ones in this branch of the performing arts; and especially with his lack of self-consciousness at displaying his body, the statistical assumption about a man this handsome – and this oiled-up – was that he was very unlikely to be heterosexual.

'Hi,' he drawled, dripping more oil into his hand.

'Hey,' Evie said, leaning on the doorjamb. 'Let me guess – you're Jerome.'

'How'd you know?' he said, still rubbing baby oil into his stomach, which was so cut his abs were as ribbed as an old-fash-ioned radiator.

'Sallie said Jerome gets the crowd hot and bothered,' she answered, hooking her thumbs into the belt of her tight jeans. 'I figured that had to be you.'

'Damn right,' he said, holding her gaze as his hand slid lower, to his groin area, where the narrow strip of black fabric slung around his hips held his fabric pouch in place. Its contents stirred, stimulated by the sight of Evie in a form-fitting t-shirt and equally snug jeans, plus Jerome's caressing hand slipping down to his inner thighs, anointing them with oil; Evie bit her lip as her eyes dipped downwards, following Jerome's huge hand as he dripped more baby oil onto his pink palm, his eyes never leaving her body as he stroked himself in slow circles, working in the oil.

In front of her, Sallie huffed out a laugh. 'Jerome, this is Evie,' she said. 'She's going on after you. Trying out for a slot.'

'Hey, good luck,' Jerome said to Evie. 'I warn you, though.' He sprawled back, spreading his legs, putting down the bottle of oil, wrapping both hands behind his head, his body six foot six of lean, dark, nearly naked, masculine perfection, his lips curving in a come-hither smile. 'I tend to get the crowd pretty worked up. You think you can handle that?'

'Oh,' Evie said, the corners of her mouth quirking in response. 'I've never met a . . .' She sketched a pause, flicking her gaze up and down the entire length of Jerome's phenomenal body – '*crowd* I couldn't handle.'

He sketched a long slow wink as she pushed herself off the doorjamb, arching her back fractionally as she did so to show off her slim figure.

'I bet you haven't, baby girl,' he purred as she walked away, a positive sashay in her step, down the corridor to where Carrie was indicating the room in which her costume was stashed.

'Oh, shit!' Evie exclaimed, remembering what the brief encounter with the insanely hot Jerome had briefly pushed from her mind: she needed to ring Paulie and tell him she wouldn't be back for the late shift.

And I'd better nail this audition, she thought grimly as she tapped the screen of her cellphone. *Cause Paulie's going to go crazy when I tell him he's one girl down on a busy night. If I don't get the job here, I'll be lucky to have one to crawl back to at the Midnight Lounge . . .*

Paulie had, predictably, thrown a fit. Yelling curses down the phone, telling her that if he even let her back to the Lounge, she'd be working the shitty daytime shifts from now to eternity, pointing out that the money she'd make doing burlesque was sweet fuck all compared to what she pulled in onstage at the Lounge – let alone what she could make giving private dances.

And Evie knew he was absolutely right.

What the hell am I doing? I want to make a ton of money. I want the big bucks, the high life, the rich men who come into the Midnight Lounge and pick out girls to set up in apartments and spoil the hell out of. I got one sugar daddy by shaking T&A on the Lounge stage – no reason I can't meet a second just the same way. Lawrence broke up with me because he wanted to be exclusive and I couldn't promise him that. I wanted to look for another rich guy and keep Lawrence as my hot piece on the side, just like before.

So I lost Lawrence, but my chances of meeting a big fat wallet on legs are way less likely if I'm doing burlesque at Maud's. I'm turning into a performer, not someone you'd expect to be selling sex. What the fuck am I thinking? I must be insane!

But standing in the wings, her face and body made up in the shimmering green, silver and aquamarine tones she had spent the last few days designing for her mermaid look, neat little silver shells covering her small breasts, a matching silver thong her only other piece of clothing, her mermaid tail held carefully in her hand – to avoid smudging her body makeup – she could not have been more excited at the thought of embarking on this new career. Her heart was pounding as she listened to the audience gasp in excitement, and pictured them, in the space of a few minutes, making the same sounds for her . . .

I'll be lucky! she thought, watching Jerome, who, amazingly, had curved his body into a perfect hoop and was rolling round the stage. This is a damn hard act to follow – he's the hottest, sexiest contortionist I ever saw in my life . . .

Jerome's body seemed to bound like a spring, popping out of the hoop into a handstand, the transition so smooth that even Evie, who had been a gymnast in high school, caught her breath, unable to see how he had done it. His legs were spreading wide in the handstand, the muscles of his arms bulging as he held his torso perfectly still, his legs now wide in a centre split; the audience whooped and cheered as the split opened further, his impossibly flexible hips allowing his legs to drop down on either side of his body, until, amazingly, his toes touched the stage.

The pose made his crotch bulge out even more. The audience whooped as he folded forward, his round buttocks now on full view, just a narrow black strip of fabric between them, his body so smooth that he must depilate on a daily basis – or maybe he's had himself lasered, Evie thought. From her position in the wings, she could see Jerome much more clearly than the audience, the bright spotlights directly on him, and his skin looked like slippery, coffee-coloured oiled silk. She imagined running her hand over those buttocks, confirming for herself how velvety the skin was, stretched over those long, lean muscles like plump upholstery; her nipples perked at the thought, her lower body jerking involuntarily, a little dampness softening the thong between her legs.

Great, she thought. Take all this and use it in your act. Get as turned on as you can watching Jerome, and then slide down that pole pretending it's his big black cock . . . the audience always knows when you're feeling the sex yourself, not just going through the motions . . .

She giggled under her breath, watching Jerome, who had now lifted his legs again into a handstand, and was raising one hand off the floor, tilting his body a little sideways to balance on one palm while he ran the other one up his torso, caressing himself, flicking his fingers under the edge of his jockstrap, teasing the now-screaming spectators with a reveal.

'Evie!' Natalie hissed. 'You need to get up to the gantry!'

Evie snapped out of the sexual trance into which she had fallen, just another member of the audience dying to see the contents of Jerome's posing pouch, and scrabbled over to climb the ladder at the back of the stage. Her act entailed her descending slowly down a pole, evoking a mermaid swimming down into the depths of the sea; it was more upper-body work than she had ever done before, because she was wearing the elaborately-painted Neoprene tail she had spent the last few weeks sewing and decorating. She couldn't hold onto the pole at all with her lower body when the tail was on; everything was done with her arms and back, and if they couldn't hold her, she'd crash to the ground and smash her face onto the stage. The sheer magnitude of the task she'd set herself was overwhelming, and as she sat down on the gantry and pulled on the tail, fastening it around her waist with the quick-snap Velcro ties she and Natalie had devised, a quick cold rush of pure fear ran through her at the prospect of what she was about to do.

Not just that – I have to make it look as easy as anything. As if I'm swimming without a care in the world . . .

Jerome had, like the character in the PG Wodehouse novel, formed himself into a hoop once more and rolled away to tumultuous applause; the stage lights dimmed as two techs ran on to fix Evie's pole to the centre of the stage, one below, one on the gantry with her, screwing it into the floor and ceiling, testing it by pulling on it with all their weight before they let go and gave her the thumbs-up that it was safe to commit herself to it. Heart pounding, she wriggled along the gantry, rubbed her palms into the tray of resin there for maximum grip, and took hold of the pole.

'Hey! Baby girl!'

With a shock she looked down, over the edge of the walkway; Jerome was standing there, so tall she didn't have that far to stare. His teeth gleamed in the darkness as he whispered:

'Break a leg, okay?'

'Thank you!' she hissed gratefully. He was sweaty from his act, his skin glistening even in the dark, and the luscious scent of his body hung around him, mixing with the sweetness of the baby oil. It was as intoxicating as the scent of rich earth after rain, fresh and ripe, and it made every nerve in Evie's body tingle.

Jerome's head ducked as he slipped away, and the first beats of 'Underwater Love', Evie's backing track, began to play.

This is it. No going back. She manoeuvred herself into position, twisting into a shoulder stand, her legs rising to curve around the pole, her hands in a death grip on the pole as she pushed herself off, her core contracting with everything it had to keep her in position as she began to work her way down, her legs undulating to move her tail in a slow swimming motion, her silvered blonde hair extensions tumbling below her. The audience gasped as the spotlight found her, high up in the air, seeming to slide effortlessly, headfirst, down the pole; she heard them catch their breath, their energy all focussed entirely on her and the moves she was making.

Excitement rushed through her, the adrenalin of performance kicking in, blood flooding to her head with the inverted position.

I've got them already, she knew. *Now all I have to do is keep them with me . . .*

Evie's head was still spinning with excitement as she walked into her dressing room high on the success of her performance, the screams of applause, the people rising to their feet at the front to whoop at her.

And then she stopped dead.

Natalie and Laura had stayed to congratulate her when she came off stage, but then shot home: they had a day-long workshop to teach the next day and were grateful to be gone. Evie had expected the dressing room to be empty of everything but her own clothes and makeup. But sitting on the one chair in front of the narrow dressing table was Jerome, all six foot six of him, his long legs stretched out and reaching nearly to the opposite wall. Beside him was a bottle of champagne, and as she entered, he reached down and picked up two brimming flutes, handing one to her. Evie took it automatically.

'To your good news,' Jerome said, smiling a long sexy smile, leaning forward to chink his glass against Evie's.

'How did you know it was good news?' Evie asked, taking a sip of the champagne.

'Oh, I heard that crowd,' Jerome said. 'No way Sallie didn't just tell you management'd be booking you in here again soon.'

Evie nodded; despite her attempts to be cool, she knew she was grinning from ear to ear.

'It went really well!' she blurted out, her entire body fizzing with happiness. 'Did you watch?'

'*Oh* yeah,' Jerome said, grinning widely. 'Up until you flicked off those shells on your boobs and threw them into the crowd. When I saw 'em all scrambling to catch 'em, I knew you'd nailed it.' He took a drink from his glass. 'And I went to get you some champagne to celebrate.'

'Thank you,' she said, overwhelmed. Evie hadn't expected to be performing tonight, and she'd have called friends if she'd known, people to watch and hopefully to toast her success afterwards; you needed that, the comedown process, after you'd knocked yourself out on stage. Especially if, like Evie and Jerome, your act wasn't just breathtaking, but potentially dangerous too.

She was actually hugely grateful to Jerome for being here to congratulate her, to share a drink with her. Otherwise, she'd just have been folding up her tail, wiping off her body makeup, and getting a very late L train home.

But, meeting Jerome's dark, slanted eyes, she had the sense that she wasn't going home for some time yet . . .

'Might as well close that door,' Jerome said. 'And why don't you go ahead and lock it too?'

Evie looked at him, fluttering her long fake silvered eyelashes.

'And why would I want to do that?' she asked him flirtatiously.

'Because I thought you and I could get it on, babe,' Jerome said frankly. 'You feel like a little celebration?'

Evie drank some more champagne, the bubbles tickling the back of her throat.

Do I? she wondered. Am I ready for it? I still miss Lawrence so bad it hurts. But fuck it, Lawrence is probably screwing Autumn's brains out. Maybe he's doing her in the shower right now, the way he did me. And Jerome's so hot he sizzles.

Evie turned round and leant against the flimsy wood dressing-room door, pushing it closed with her butt. Though Jerome was sitting and she was standing, he was so tall he was at eye level with her, and she looked at him, taking her time. He was ridiculously handsome; slanting dark eyes, high cheekbones, a straight, flaring nose that drew the eyes down to his full lips, whose colour was a deep, dark plum at the edges and blossomed into a rich tempting pink at the centre, like a fruit you couldn't wait to taste.

Jerome let Evie look him over without saying a word. He sprawled there, legs wide, drinking champagne from a glass that looked small and fragile in his huge hand, a smile on his lips, so sure of her answer that he didn't need to prompt her any further.

Fuck it, Evie thought. What am I going to do, spend the rest of my life moping after Lawrence? We don't want the same thing. And there's a hot, hot guy sitting in front of me, just waiting for me to say yes. Plus, he's right: I've got stuff to celebrate.

I'd be nuts to turn this down.

Not taking her eyes of Jerome's, she reached out with her left hand and turned the latch of the door, locking it. And then, with a swift, practiced shrug of her shoulders, she slipped the robe off her shoulders, letting it slide down to drop on the floor. Beneath it she wore only her G-string and the silver dust that still clung to her skin like body paint.

Jerome finished off his champagne in one go, putting the glass on the dressing table. His hands went to his crotch, stroking his cock through his track pants, showing Evie the full dimensions of it.

'Babe, you got me rock-hard already,' he drawled, smiling at her. 'Hard as fucking wood.'

Jerome wasn't heavily, obviously muscled: a contortionist couldn't be, because he needed to be as lean, as stretched-out, as possible. But to hold the positions he did, he had to be strong, strong as tensile steel, and the veins showed on his forearms as he worked on himself, the light gleaming on his dark skin and striking crimson and auburn lights from the sheen of sweat at his neck, on his bare shaven scalp.

Evie walked towards him till she was standing between his legs. She reached down to replace his hands with her own, but to her surprise, Jerome gently pushed her away.

'I got a way I like to do things,' he said, patting his thigh for her to sit down. 'You wanna hear about it?'

'Sure,' Evie said, taking a seat on his impossibly long leg, watching his hands come up to cup the small points of her breasts, relishing the contrast of black on white, of the fact that his hands were so large they almost covered her entire chest. She arched into them, and Jerome cupped her more firmly, stroking her nipples with his thumbs, the slow steady gesture showing the pink pads of his fingers, the paler skin on his palms.

'What I like to do to start proceedings off with a bang,' Jerome said, stroking her so she started to moan in pleasure, 'is eat pussy. I really, really like to eat pussy. You down with that?'

He was so close to her now that Evie could lean forward just a touch and kiss his plummy lips, those full soft lips that no white guy could possibly possess. She brushed her mouth against his, relishing the yielding, cushiony feel, and whispered:

'Sure, Jerome. I'm down with tha—'

Boom! The next thing she knew, she was spinning in the air. Jerome had grabbed her ass, picked her up and lifted her effortlessly, his big arms bulging as he threw her into the air, turning her round, catching her waist as she hung upside down, her legs pointing up to the ceiling.

'Hold on tight,' he said, as she wrapped her thighs around his neck, one ankle crossed over the other, her lean legs all sleek muscle, forming a lock that even Jerome would have needed to use considerable force to break. He was supporting her, his hands under her small buttocks, which were barely bigger than his palms; but though he was taking most of her weight, she still needed to keep the lock around his neck.

It was a game, and they both knew it. Jerome had to hold up Evie, Evie had to keep locked onto him, while, simultaneously, they pleasured each other; it was a glorious showing off, a celebration of the extraordinary strength, flexibility and athleticism they had both worked so hard to achieve. Jerome had swung Evie into an extreme Kama Sutra sex position that was like an extension of the gymnastic routines they performed on stage: as he shifted Evie, supporting her now on just one hand, so that the other one could hook around the g-string at her crotch, pulling it up and aside, his full, plump lips curved into a smile of complete satisfaction.

'*Oh* yeah,' he said complacently. '*This* is what I'm talking about.'

It was all Evie could do not to writhe so much her ankles loosened their twist. But she couldn't; if she did, she would fall clumsily into Jerome's lap, and worse, she would lose the amazing sensation of his mouth licking and sucking between her legs. She had never felt this much heat in her life. It was like having a hot water bottle pressed directly onto her crotch, a sex toy that somehow kindled to blood temperature. My God, she thought dizzily, the excitement instantly sparking in her belly, if someone could invent that they'd make a fortune . . .

Jerome was licking her lubriciously, long swipes of his tongue, each one ending with a flick that made her hips jerk upward, wanting it there, *there*, now, *now*, wanting him to stop teasing her with the big delicious licks of his tongue and settle his mouth down onto her, direct his attention to the very specific place where she was increasingly desperate to have him concentrate, where she *had* to have it . . .

She was moaning, her head pressed into his thigh, her shoulders resting on his big quads, the scent of his skin all around her, his sweat making his skin glisten. Her hands were wrapped around his thighs, as much as they could; they were so huge that she couldn't have enveloped one in both hands, even stretched to their maximum. She felt the big quad muscles standing out under her palms, like heavy ropes under the skin, laid on top of the bones, and she pushed down on them, lifting herself, working her body back, until it laid right against his, their chests pressed together, their sweat slickening the contact, until her head was directly between his legs.

She didn't even need her hands. Her thumbs dug into his hip flexors, her fingers curled into his groin, raising her just enough so that she could nip with her teeth at the edge of his pouch, pulling it away from his body. Just an inch or so, but that was all his cock needed to spring free; it had been fighting against the fabric already, and now it bounced out like a spring being released, fat and eager, darker even than the rest of him, sinking into Evie's mouth almost instantly, plunging to the back of her throat, filling her up.

As if synchronised, Jerome's tongue dove right inside her pussy, diving deeply into her; she groaned in pleasure, the back of her throat vibrating, sending his cock even deeper, its head titillated by the rippling sounds Evie couldn't help making as Jerome worked on her, circling her sweet spot, flicking it back and forth, bringing her inexorably to a screaming climax. She sucked at him frantically, her lips wrapped over her teeth, her mouth stretched to its maximum, wanting to give him the same sensations he was giving her, to fully return the absolute delight she was feeling.

It was pure sex; she barely knew him, he barely knew her, their bodies linked, not their minds. A simple, pure, animal attraction, their mouths pressed eagerly between each other's legs, tasting each other, smelling each other. Racing each other, now, in another game; the game to make the other one lose control and come first. Evie managed to close her mouth around the head of Jerome's cock, to wrap her tongue around the bulging vein on its base, hearing him, above her, groan into her pussy, his hot exhale of breath an extra surge of heat, which made her gasp in ecstasy. She was so close, she knew it. Her entire lower body felt as if it were melting, as if Jerome's heated mouth were a flame dissolving her like candle wax.

I can't hold on much longer! Evie thought in near-desperation, knowing that her legs were weakening. Her inner thigh muscles were trembling, more, even, than they had done onstage earlier, that tell-tale vibration that meant they were being worked to their limit. The sweat working up between them was making them slippery, making it extra-hard to hold on, Jerome's wide neck as slick now as his cock in her mouth. *I'm going to let go . . . I'm sliding off him . . .*

And then she thought: So, let go! Let go with everything! And the next second, she was coming, coming against Jerome's mouth, her crotch bucking and bouncing against his full lips, her strong slim hips sending her frantically against him, eking out every moment of the orgasms he was giving her, again and again and again, so consumed by the heat and the rush that she didn't even realise that his cock had swollen even more, that its pounds against the back of her throat had become frenzied, that he, too, was about to come.

Jerome held out as long as he could, until he felt her body going limp, her grip on him almost non-existent, the orgasms ripping through her and making her weak; when, finally, his desperation was at crisis point, he tore his mouth from her and grabbed her waist, hauling her up with one smooth easy gesture, his cock slipping from her mouth just in time, spraying its white stream up over her neck and small pointed breasts, the pale come spurting from his deep brown cock a contrast so stunning that, even with her body still throbbing from multiple orgasms, even hanging upside down, dazed and blurry-eyed, Evie watched it with dizzy pleasure.

She felt him moving her, finally, after his cock had shot its load, and flopped back, happily content, against his ripped stomach. He raised her, letting her unwrap one leg from around his neck, and then lowered her into his lap, where she curled up in post-orgasmic bliss, her entire body utterly relaxed, her back against his chest, her legs stretched out over his, feeling absolutely tiny against his enormous frame.

'Here,' he said eventually, and his hands, which had been around her waist, reached up to cover her breasts, rubbing them in long slow strokes. At first, Evie thought it was a lingering caress, or maybe even a sign that Jerome wanted to start things up all over again. Then she realised what he was really doing. Just as he had worked baby oil into his skin before, to make himself smooth and supple for his act, now he was working his semen into her breasts.

'You got a Jerome body treatment. Best thing for your skin,' he said lazily against the top of her head. 'Full of proteins. Keeps you soft. Nothing like it.'

'That right?' Evie managed, glad he couldn't see her smile.

Men, she thought. They're all the same. How they love to talk about their come. Like it was holy water or something.

'Yeah, it sure is,' Jerome was saying. 'And I don't like to boast, but all the ladies tell me mine's top quality. Even richer than normal.'

'Wow,' Evie said, not daring to say more in case he heard how big her grin was now.

'Yeah,' Jerome said complacently, working the last drops of his come into her stomach. 'Next time, if you want, I'll give you a facial. You leave it on for half an hour at least. When you rinse it off, you'll be amazed how tight and smooth your skin is.'

Evie reached out for the glass of champagne, which was on the dressing table, and upended its contents into her mouth.

'Jerome,' she said, swallowing, 'do you by any chance give yourself your own, um, "facials"?'

'Well, sure!' Jerome said, sounding surprised. 'Every time I knock one off on my own! Here!' He picked up one of her hands and raised it to his cheek. 'Feel how smooth that is, baby girl! You won't get that kind of skin from Elizabeth Arden!'

Evie bit her tongue hard.

'And hey, it's free!' Jerome finished smugly. 'I mean, what's not to like?'

'Nothing,' Evie managed to say, her body blissfully relaxed, bubbles bursting in her throat, her brain dancing with laughter. 'Nothing not to like.'

Kandee

Win one of five pairs of Kandee Shoes!

Kandee Shoes are a UK based high-end shoe brand with global success. Josh Wayman, or 'Mr Kandee' as he is better known to his fashion followers, is currently conquering the fashion world with his style philosophy of setting trends instead of merely following them. Mr Kandee continues to set the standards of design in the fashion footwear industry – he is quite literally one foot ahead of the others in the industry!

After debuting at London Fashion Week in 2011 and showcasing at Barcelona Fashion Week in 2012, the Kandee Shoes trademark 6.1 inch high heels have become a regular feature in major fashion publications across the world and appear daily on the feet of A-List Celebrities.

2012 will see Mr Kandee and his Kandee Shoes brand going from strength to strength – **all of the past Kandee collections have sold-out so make sure you keep up to date with the Kandeelicious shoe craze at:**

Website: **www.kandeeshoes.com**

Twitter: **@KandeeShoes**
       @MrKandee

Facebook: **Kandee**

To enter and for more information visit
www.simonandschuster.co.uk